W.D. Tienert climbed the steps to the porch of his house and thought of all the hard cash locked securely in the vault of the Jubilation Bank and Trust Company. It gave the banker a good warm feeling.

He stepped into his foyer, crossed to the parlor, and struck a match to the wick of a lamp. A pleasant glow illuminated the room, striking the highlights on the polished woodwork of the cupboard, the polished brass at the fireplace — and the polished Colt .45 pointed at him by the outlaw standing in the shadows.

"Sit down, Mr. Banker," Parson said quietly. "It's a mite early yet, but come full dark you and me will take us a trip to that bank of yours so you can open that safe for me!"

BEST OF THE WEST
from Zebra Books

THOMPSON'S MOUNTAIN (2042, $3.95)
by G. Clifton Wisler

Jeff Thompson was a boy of fifteen when his pa refused to sell out his mountain to the Union Pacific and got gunned down in return, along with the boy's mother. Jeff fled to Colorado, but he knew he'd even the score with the railroad man who had his parents killed . . . and either death or glory was at the end of the vengeance trail he'd blaze!

BROTHER WOLF (1728, $2.95)
by Dan Parkinson

Only two men could help Lattimer run down the sheriff's killers—a stranger named Stillwell and an Apache who was as deadly with a Colt as he was with a knife. One of them would see justice done—from the muzzle of a six-gun.

BLOOD ARROW (1549, $2.50)
by Dan Parkinson

Randall Kerry returned to his camp to find his companion slaughtered and scalped. With a war cry as wild as the savages,' the young scout raced forward with his pistol held high to meet them in battle.

THUNDERLAND (1991, $3.50)
by Dan Parkinson

Men were suddenly dying all around Jonathan, and he needed to know why—before he became the next bloody victim of the ancient sword that would shape the future of the Texas frontier.

APACHE GOLD (1899, $2.95)
by Mark K. Roberts & Patrick E. Andrews

Chief Halcon burned with a fierce hatred for the pony soldiers that rode from Fort Dawson, and vowed to take the scalp of every round-eye in the territory. Sergeant O'Callan must ride to glory or death for peace on the new frontier.

Available wherever paperbacks are sold, or order direct from the Publisher. Send cover price plus 50¢ per copy for mailing and handling to Zebra Books, Dept. 2209, 475 Park Avenue South, New York, N.Y. 10016. Residents of New York, New Jersey and Pennsylvania must include sales tax. DO NOT SEND CASH.

JUBILATION GAP

DAN PARKINSON

ZEBRA BOOKS
KENSINGTON PUBLISHING CORP.

ZEBRA BOOKS

are published by

Kensington Publishing Corp.
475 Park Avenue South
New York, NY 10016

First printing: November 1987

Printed in the United States of America

*to Jim and Peg Case
 for the borry of the Bard;
to George Cook
 for the power of the pipes;
and to Wallace Exman
 for his patience . . .*

I

For a week they holed up at an abandoned farm north of Pleasant Valley. The place was low in the hills, off the roads, and shielded by stands of cottonwood and scrub cedar all around. Some squatter had clung long enough to finish a slap-up shack and a pole barn, and there was wood and water.

Cole had found the place a year before, and noted it. It was far enough from Hays City to be beyond the range of local possemen on a winter run, yet close enough so Cole and his men could make it with one change of horses. And the fresh mounts themselves, picked up just short of their turn off the main trail toward the hideout, would fool any longhunters or bountymen. Fresh horses meant plans for a long run, and the trackers would take the roads east looking for a trail.

Maybe there were long-hunters and maybe not. Cole took no chances. They stayed to crusted streambed all the way to the hole, then dug in and waited. The days went by and there was no one on their trail. Snowfall covered any sign they might have left, and they stayed close and showed no smoke in daytime or light at night.

The four with him were hard men, hand-picked. They were not men content to follow orders, but what Cole said do they did, and there was no argument. No one argued with Cole Yeager and lived to speak of it.

Two men had died at Hays City, and maybe a third. The bank clerk was dead, and one of the tellers. A grizzled rancher in the lobby had gone for a gun and they left him on the floor with a hole in his belly. The bank's open safe and cash boxes yielded only pocket money. It was late winter and commerce was slow. But the false safe beneath the floor held $28,000 in railroad funds. The money rested now in Cole's saddlebag and the four were content to await their split. They had not choice. He was Cole Yeager.

A foot of snow lay across the hills, gentle fall that made no drift, and they were well provided. Yet before the week was out Cole became moody and restless. He watched his men and he watched the sky, and when hard gray clouds hung low and it was colder in the wind he said, "There's a bank at Pleasant Valley and storm is on the way. We'll go in with it, hard and fast, right at closing time."

There was no argument, but Parson had been watching too, watching the weather build. "Where to from there, Cole?" he asked. "Blizzard can kill a man."

Cole only glanced at him. "You'll know when I tell you. But not back here. We've been in this place too long."

They waited for the telltale wind, the wind that had the teeth in it. Then they packed and saddled and Cole looked at the sky. "Right on time," he said. "It'll hit at dark and we'll be there then. Blizzard just strikin', dark as sin an' hellish cold, the people will be indoors. Nobody out, nobody on the street. We go in right at six."

"What if that banker closes early?"

"He never does. I've watched him. Saddle up."

By the time Howard Sills topped out on the valley's north side, the sky was gray and low and a rising wind was in his face. He shivered and pulled the wool scarf higher over his nose, his hat brim almost meeting it. The little spring wagon crunched through foot-deep crusted snow and Crowbait seemed to sag for a moment, catching his breath from the long climb. Howard let him walk for a mile, then twitched the reins. The dapple's breathing had steadied, brief, regular fogs that whipped away in the freezing wind. Hard, dry flakes of snow slanted toward him and he urged the horse to an easy trot. From here to Pleasant Valley the trail was gentle and almost straight.

Leaving Bad Basin early, on a crisp morning that was a dazzle of bright sun and snowy hills, he had expected to be in Pleasant Valley by noon. But the Cimarron Basin was deep and wide, and there were drifts down there where the last snow's fall had been mounded by playful winds.

It would be dark soon, and Howard wished he had never started out. He was cold, he was hungry, and he was far beyond the point of no return. A sky like burnished lead hung morose, low overhead, and unforgiving wind carried crystal chill that rattled against his hat like thrown sand. The wool scarf crackled tinily as he moved his head, its fibers

9

sheathed with ice from his freezing breath. A faint mist seemed to flow from Crowbait as the dapple trotted on into the deepening cold. Then, to the north, he could see the vague, distant shape of the town of Pleasant Valley—the blocky outline of the courthouse, the pair of steeples above mist-naked trees, the jumble of roofs that was the commercial section—and beyond, lowering, the gloom of the approaching winter storm.

It was Howard Sills's fourth winter in Kansas, and he was learning to read the signs. Late blizzards often were the worst. They were winter's last all-out assault before surrendering to the coming of spring, and they summed up all that winter stood for. Sometimes, briefly, he missed the relative civility of Maryland weather.

But then, he told himself, it had been his choice. He could have stayed. He could have accepted the role of younger brother of the heir to the Sills estate, and chosen a life of genteel ritual in a settled and corseted land. He could have, but he had not.

Howard's place at Bad Basin was remote, effectively isolated from all except the bizarre little town of Jubilation eight miles away, and often lonely. But he liked it. Often he felt he didn't know from one day to the next what he was doing there, and the puzzled expressions of the few people he knew—people like Nat Kinley, who came by now and again to visit on his way to the watering holes at Jubilation, or the banker W. D. Tienert, who handled his trusts and his transactions for him—indicated they were just as unsure of his direction as he was. Still, it was his choice, it was his life as he had determined it, and he liked it.

Thought of Tienert reminded him of the banker's pretty niece, Penelope Becket, and his ice-tinged ears reddened with embarrassment at the thought. He wondered if he would ever be able to confront an attractive young woman as other young men did, smoothly and coolly, without making an idiot of himself. It was something he had never been able to control, and just seemed to get worse as time went on.

He was timid around women. And the more attractive they were, the more befuddled he became. He wished he could forget his first encounter with Penelope Becket.

He had met her in her uncle's bank in Jubilation. That was two years ago now. She had looked at him with her lavender eyes and he had turned bright red. Then she had smiled. He would never forget. He had tripped over a chair, grappled with a coatrack, and kicked Mr. Tienert's spittoon into the fireplace. And the words . . . his words: "Honor to miss you, meet Penellypie."

God!

And that was only the first time. Just the sight of her reduced him to a jibbering wreck, and he had absolutely no defense against it.

The cold was seeping through his coat, right into his bones. Just ahead now was the main street of Pleasant Valley and he sighed his relief. At least he could find a warm stove and a good meal and not have to worry about encountering Penelope Becket. He was certain by now that—if she recognized him at all—she must consider him a total idiot. Best just to avoid her at all cost.

But Jubilation was miles away. Pleasant Valley, with its freight line and variety of mercantile establishments, had the supplies and hardware he needed. He would rest over, wait out the storm, and then haul his goods back to Bad Basin.

He concentrated on the field he planned to break out come spring, ten acres that he would fence and plow and plant. He hadn't decided what to plant there, but he could decide that later.

The streets were deserted. Winds that rose by the minute howled among the buildings now, flinging real snow in horizontal veils along Main Street, blocking the view of the buildings. He turned Crowbait and went a block west, then north again on Osage Avenue to the big livery barn.

It was closed and locked.

Leaving the rig standing in the lee of the building he walked across Osage, leaning left against the blizzard winds, and along the little alley that led through to Main Street. He saw the bank across the street, the hotel a few doors away with lights in its windows, the narrow alley straight across from him that led between the bank and the Strother Building—which was a two-story pigeon roost full of lawyers and county offices. Past it was the courthouse. The narrow alley over there was shadow-dark now, a tunnel in the storm leading back to the old shale pit beyond. The pit would be full of snow now, he knew. It was only worked in summer.

He turned right and entered a hardware and tackle shop. A man looked up from his books at the counter. "Howdy. Gettin' fierce out, ain't it?"

Howard stamped frozen feet and beat his mittened hands together. "It sure is. I stopped at the livery but it was locked. Are they closed up for the winter?"

"Yeah," the man said. "Simon went off to Winfield to bury an uncle or somethin'. The depot barn is handlin' his trade for him till he comes back."

"I'll go there, then. Where is it?"

"Next to the depot. That's why they call it the depot barn. You got a rig?"

"Spring wagon. I need some things when it clears. I left it by the livery."

"Oh. Well, just drive right up the alley out here, into the street, and turn right. You'll see the depot across that little patch up from the hotel. The barn's right next to it. Needin' some tack, huh?"

"Yeah, quite a bit."

"Well, fine. Come in when you're ready to load up. I carry the best line of goods in Pleasant Valley. When you get to the barn tell 'em Foley sent you. They'll treat you right."

Outside again Howard turned toward the alley. The storm was hitting its full force now. Gale winds whipped streamers of dark snow in the gloom, howling around the structures of the town. Visibility was only a few yards at best and growing less, blotted by the coming dark and the curtains of driven snow. For an instant he had an impression of a rider in the street, going north into the teeth of the storm. But he could not be sure he saw anything. In the alley he was sheltered from the wind, but not from the intense cold and the sifting snow falling dark between rooftops where the gale winds raged and sang.

Out of the alley he was blind and buffeted, fighting his way across Osage to the livery barn, which he couldn't see until he was within feet of it. Winds whipping him, he scuffed and skidded around the corner. Crowbait snorted cold mist and looked at him accusingly. He climbed aboard the spring wagon, took his reins, and persuaded the horse out into howling blindness, across the street, and into the frigid shelter of the little alley. At its far end Crowbait hesitated, not wanting to enter the punishing wind again. But Howard slapped reins and the horse pulled out, straight into the blind fury raging

13

along Main Street.

"This is hell out here, Cole," the man said, shouting above the wind. "We need to find shelter, quick!"

"What did you see?" Cole demanded. "Is it clear?"

"Street's deserted. Not a soul in sight. Lights in the bank windows. People in the hotel and a couple of stores, but nobody out. Be crazy to be out in this."

"Then let's go," Cole barked. "With the wind, hard and fast. Right down the street to the bank, three of us inside, clean it out, mount, and head south. We'll shelter when we're done."

No one argued with Cole Yeager. At a dead run he led them, past sheds and scattered houses, angling into a Main Street they could barely see. Idiot winds pressed them from behind, and blind snow-shadow ran with them and ahead of them. They drew their guns as they rode, and tiny glows ahead told them of lighted windows.

Then there was something before them, blocking the street. Cole hauled his reins and his horse pawed air as it ran, swerving sharply to the left. Hooves skidded and danced, throwing clouds of dark-white powder. The rider behind bumped him, and two others collided abruptly. He clung to his horse as it almost went down, then found its balance again, now pounding at right angles from their first course, straight toward darkness. In the instant he recognized the dim shape. A horse and wagon, outline of a man on the seat, pale shape of a face turned toward him. His horse sheared past the draft animal so close that its hitch-buckle burned his knee. Then he was in darkness, trying to slow his frenzied

14

mount. Beyond the darkness was dim open space, a broken gate, and then nothing. He caught his breath, saw the gate whip past beneath, then he was falling. . . .

One by one but all in the passing of an instant, five dim riders hurtled through the alley, over the broken gate and into the blind, snow-filled gloom of the old shale pit.

"Damn him!" the thought flashed through Cole Yeager's mind. "Whoever he is, damn him!" But there was no time to form it into words.

Howard Sills hauled hard on his reins, bringing Crowbait and the spring wagon around in a smart turn onto Main Street. He peered over his shoulder into the rising, driving storm and his eyes were wide. What had he seen? In that instant there, the sudden explosion of many hooves against frozen ground, the jumble of abrupt, shattering sound . . . the vivid impression of men on horseback, looming and racing. But he could see nothing now. Whoever had been there was gone. The snow-blind street howled lonely and was full of rising storm.

Something dark swung from the hitch-buckle on Crowbait's off side. Howard reined up, climbed down, and went to see. It was a frozen leather saddlebag, stiff and crusted. Howard looked for someone to claim it, but there was no one around. Returning to his seat he opened the keeper-box, tossed the frozen bag inside, and took up his reins. With the blizzard at his back he headed for the depot barn. He would see Crowbait tended and fed, then walk back to the hotel.

Howard was stiff and half-frozen by the time he hung his coat and hat in the bright lobby, stamped the snow off his boots, and paused to thaw his hands before a hearth. A waiter came and led him to a table, and he sank into the chair gratefully. A warm supper and a warm bed . . . he wanted nothing more. It had been a long, bleak day. But now he was secure. Nothing more could go wrong.

He ordered soup and a beefsteak, then closed his eyes and rubbed them languidly. There were a lot of people in the dining room, guests and townspeople gathered in warm haven against the raging storm outside. A man and woman were at the next table, their backs to him, and he was vaguely aware when someone joined them. He was tired. Then a subtle scent of lilac water touched his nostrils and he glanced up, directly into the lavender eyes of Penelope Becket, large, curious eyes that looked at him past the people with her, W. D. Tienert and Mrs. Becket. He hadn't noticed who they were.

He blinked, reddened, and felt his tongue grow large and unwieldly. Dread settled upon him and he hunched over his table, eyes fixed on its cloth cover. He wondered what disaster would befall this time.

II

Of all people . . .

Panic hung like spider shroud quaking in the wind, and he felt the trembles start. Dire memories crowded in on him, overlapping: "Honor to miss you, meet Penellypie" (God!) . . . "Why, Biss Mecket, I just left your buncle at the ank" (worse than God!) . . . a store, a basket of fresh eggs there, a twenty-five-pound bag of lead shot in his hand, and she walked in (God, what a mess!) . . . tipping his hat on the street, walking headlong into a porch pillar . . . sweet cider flowing an inch deep across the floor at Stapleton's Market, she gazing at him quizzically (mortification—as if he hadn't done enough, he tripped over the spilled cider barrel) . . . they went on and on.

Eyes down, nerves under tight control he raised a glass of water . . . and raised his head to drink. Lavender eyes were on him. Half the water went down his shirt front and some entered his nostrils when he gasped. He gagged, coughed desperately, and fumbled for a napkin, trying to breathe. A vase of paper daisies fell, rolled to the edge of his table,

17

and clattered to the floor.

The noise brought Mr. Tienert around in his chair to gape at the strangling young man behind him. He stared, then nodded. "Good evening, Mr. Sills. I didn't know you were in town."

Beyond the puzzled faces of Mr. Tienert and Mrs. Becket, Penelope caught his eye again. She smiled a puzzled smile.

Visions of angels danced in Howard's head. He managed to gargle something at Mr. Tienert and Mrs. Becket, then became absorbed with the juggling of a spoon and a water glass. He caught and lost each of them several times before managing to get them to lie quietly on the table.

"Poor fellow has a problem," he heard Tienert say softly to his sister. "Seizures of some sort, I think."

"Pity," she whispered back. "Such a nice-looking young man too."

By the time Howard regained any composure they had turned away, and Penelope was gazing into distance as though she had never seen him. His soup arrived and he devoted himself to it, head down, trying to concentrate on other things.

The building seemed to shake as howling blizzard winds battered it outside. Chandeliers rattled at the gusts. All around were conversations—people at their ease, having dinner, waiting out the storm.

". . . flagrant disregard for the law," a man was saying. "Not just a bit of illicit trafficking, you understand. These are open saloons . . ."

"Direct violation of the Prohibition Amendment . . ."

". . . no corresponding local ordinances . . . unthinkable . . ."

That would be Jubilation they were talking about, Howard knew. The little town across the Cimarron was widely known for its taverns. Twenty-seven of them, he had heard. Yet he had heard no indication that Mr. Tienert or any of the other Jubilation business leaders had any strong objection. The ladies did, of course, but then . . .

". . . no sign of them . . ." drifted over from another table. "I heard they got nearly thirty thousand at that bank in Hays City. . . ."

". . . just disappeared. Gone into the territory, most likely . . ."

"Good thing. That Yeager, now. Bad 'un, that . . ."

". . . a killer, yes . . ."

". . . settlement southwest . . ." from another direction. "Since Crook captured Geronimo, land out there is . . ."

And from elsewhere, "Cleveland's still the man. You mark my words. . . ."

". . . they say Benjamin Harrison, though . . ."

". . . never happen. He'd close down the big ranches in the strip."

He tried to lose himself in the babble, and felt a little better. He thought pleasant thoughts: his cozy house in Bad Basin, secure on a cold night . . . tending his fire, making tea, sitting in his rocking chair to play his pipes for an hour . . . Pericles the cat trying to find somewhere to hide from the music . . .

The thought brought a wave of homesickness. He wished he were back in Bad Basin right now, instead of here, in this crowd, in dire peril of making a fool of himself again because of Penelope Becket. His ears reddened and he turned his thoughts away. I don't have a rocking chair, he reminded himself. That's what I need. A rocking chair.

He kept his head down, finishing his soup. Then,

unmistakably, he felt the presence of eyes looking at him, devastating lavender eyes, and the delicate scent of lilac water. He blushed and could barely control his clattering spoon. Why did she keep looking at him that way? Why did she effect him so? What was he going to do? Despite his resolution, he looked up.

She was gazing at him, her eyes wide and curious. She seemed to be wondering about something. Her eyes . . . he felt as though he were drowning. Then, with idle curiosity akin to the poking of a frog to see if it will jump, she winked.

It was purely reflex that brought him up out of his chair, directly under the extended arm of the waiter bringing his steak. Steak, platter, waiter, and chair went in separate directions and Howard stood for a moment alone, his face blazing and all eyes on him. He turned and beat a hasty retreat from the hotel.

The blizzard raged and pounded the little town, and Howard took refuge in the depot. He shared a glowing stove there with several other men. There were three cowpunchers on the drift between seasons, riding grubline. There was the depot agent, sound asleep. There was a scruffy, stoop-shouldered man with dark stains on his hands and his coat, and there was a brightly dressed drummer waiting for a stage.

Defeated and miserable, Howard joined them to share their glowing stove. Anecdotes in progress resumed as he pulled up a chair.

"She's only got one horn," a cowboy was telling the others, "but they say she can open gates with it."

"I don't believe it," another snorted. "I've punched critters for fifteen years, thereabout, and I never seen a smart one yet."

"Well, this one is. Her name's Mary. Ol' Wentworth has put her up the trail to Dodge six-seven times an' she always comes back, an' every time she comes she brings part of the herd back with her . . . an' other brands too. Ol' Wentworth has a real prize in that cow. I heard there's been lawsuits an' a couple of shootin's up at Dodge, all because of her. Course, no man worth his salt would ever tell the buyers about her, so she keeps on gettin' loose an' goin' home. Six-seven years now."

"A homing cow!" the stained man said. "That's something you don't hear about just every day."

"You from around here, friend?" the salesman asked.

Howard nodded. "Bad Basin, over across the river. I'm just in to buy supplies."

"Bad Basin," one of the cowboys said. "I heard there's some squatter down there that's got hisself a freeze-proof windmill an' a storm-proof outhouse an' . . . what else was it? Oh, yeah! An above-ground storm cellar! Did you ever hear the like?"

"Yes." Howard nodded gloomily. "That's me. I got tired of rebuilding every time the weather changes."

"I guess you're not from Kansas originally, then."

"No. Maryland."

They looked at him with deep sympathy. "Well," one allowed finally, "man can't help where he's from."

"No need to feel bad about it at all," another agreed. "Why, I knew a fella one time that was from California."

"What sort of supplies are you here for?" the drummer asked.

"Hardware and tack. Nails, roll wire . . ." He shrugged. "When the weather breaks I'm going to

21

fence ten acres by my barn, maybe put in some vegetables or something."

The drummer brightened. "I travel in seed," he said. "I might suggest a garden variety for you. How would fresh peas sound next spring? And lettuce? Good soil for lettuce around here, they say. My, yes. And potatoes and maybe some squash? I happen to have one remaining selection of garden vegetables in my trunk, sir. Marvelous variety, our entire line. Could make a good price on those seeds, save me carrying them back to St. Louis."

Howard's stomach growled at the mention of food. He wished he had had an opportunity to eat that steak.

The man cocked his head. "Just think. Think of sweet corn and asparagus. Leaf spinach. Tomatoes, radishes, two kinds of beans. Carrots, of course. Red beets, onions, big, succulent squash . . ." He talked on and on.

"Is Bad Basin near Jubilation?" the scruffy man asked.

"Not very far. Just a few miles."

"That's where I wish I was right now," a cowboy said. "Jubilation! Best little town there is these days for a drinkin' man. I've heard they got more than twenty saloons down there."

"Twenty-seven," Howard said. "That's what I heard."

The scruffy man licked his lips and drew a stained sleeve across unshaven cheeks. "You know a man named Clarence Hanks?"

"Slightly," Howard said. "He runs the newspaper there. The Tribune."

The man nodded. "That's where I'm going. Hanks needs a printer. I'm one." He extended a hand. "Thompson's my name. Bert Thompson. Be glad to help you load supplies if I could get a ride down there."

"Twenty-seven saloons!" a cowboy breathed, enthralled. "I might just ride along too. I haven't got anyplace better to go."

"Far as I know," another said, "I haven't either."

"Me too," the third one chimed in. "Then maybe I might drift on down to the Wentworth place an' see that homin' cow."

The drummer shook his head. "Wish I could go too. But I have to catch a stage if one ever comes through." He glanced at Howard. "Shame if I had to take all that seed back with me, though. Probably could shave the price a bit, if a man was interested."

"I guess you know the trail across the Cimarron?" a cowboy asked Howard. "I mean, where to cross even if there's a lot of snow?"

"I'll have to wait. I have a spring wagon. I'd bog in deep drifts."

"Not if you had three wranglers on horseback to throw a line an' drag you through. I mean, I don't know why I'm settin' here in this tea-party town when I could be in Jubilation."

"Me too," another agreed.

Bert Thompson raised his head, listening to the wind. "This might let up by morning."

"Fresh, tender peas melted in butter," the drummer murmured suggestively. "Sweet corn. Carrot stew."

Howard's stomach growled and he hunkered in the chair by the stove, wishing he had never heard of Penelope Becket. Outside the winds of winter storm whined in the eaves.

"I heard Cole Yeager might be in these parts," a cowboy said sleepily.

"Doubt it," another responded. "What would the

23

likes of Cole Yeager be doin' in a place like this?"

"Twenty-seven saloons," the third one muttered, then began to snore.

Two men managed to escape the old shale pit that night, and three horses. The rest remained there, and sifting snow soon buried them. They would be found in the spring, and there would be wonder at who they were. The two still living searched among them for a lost saddlebag. They searched carefully. It contained all the loot from Hays City. But it was not found.

Cole Yeager scrambled upslope finally, frozen and battered, leading two horses. Parson came behind him with one. Blizzard winds whipped at them, and they were blind in snow and darkness. Yet Cole Yeager burned with a hatred so violent it warmed him. Somewhere, some day he meant to find a man he had barely seen — a man with a spring wagon. He meant to find him and kill him.

On a morning that was gray and still, when nothing could be seen but muted spent clouds and muted, drifted snow, a spring wagon and three bundled horsemen crept southward out of Pleasant Valley and across the blanketed miles, dark dots on a cold and featureless landscape where nothing moved but them.

The spring wagon was piled high with various goods that Howard Sills would need in the spring. High atop the load sat a rocking chair, its rockers lashed down. And deep under the wagon seat rested fourteen large tins of guaranteed first-quality garden vegetable seed.

24

"It seems like I've heard that name before," Howard said. "Bert Thompson. It's familiar. Are you the Bert Thompson that—?"

The man beside him hunched his shoulders in his coat and shook his head.

"Not me," he said. "Different Bert Thompson. That other one died. Fell under a train or something. That was years ago."

III

Spring breezes touched the greening pastures and fresh fields of Bad Basin, and Howard Sills had ten acres of ground plowed, tilled, and fenced before he discovered that all fourteen of his tins contained identical seed. And then it was only by planting and tending it, rigging a flue and ditches to irrigate it, and watching it through the growing season that he finally learned what sort of seed he had planted.

For a number of evenings thereafter, when sunset deepened to purple dusk over the range country and the first stars showed in the sky, Pericles the cat sought refuge and old Ambrose—who had given up a peaceful twilight in Maryland to come to these far hills to look after Mister Howard—took to the barn and shut himself in. For in that hour of those sad evenings Howard sat in his rocking chair on the porch, and the penetrating disharmonies of fine pipe music grew in Bad Basin and drifted with the winds. Many a wanderer on those evenings turned up later on the high side of Jubilation to drown the torment of one who has heard the laments of souls in hell.

Nat Kinley happened by on one of his regular pilgrimages into Jubilation the morning Howard ascertained that his crop was coming ripe. Nat had a place upstream and across the river, a long, toenail-clipping-shaped spread just south of the Kansas line but defended by the river from the big spreads across from it. Nobody else much wanted the place, and Nat and his brothers made do there with a few rangy cattle and a Mexican bull named Conquistador that they let to stud now and again.

Nat sat his horse alongside Howard's corner posts and gazed in awe at his neighbor's flourishing field. Nothing in his experience had ever prepared him for the sight of 440,000 square feet of fence-to-fence turnips. It was a monumental crop, and Nat removed his hat in awe as he gazed at it. Although it was only a small part of Howard's spread, ten acres of solid turnips was a sight beyond comprehension.

"What did you have in mind to do with that many turnips, Howard?" he asked.

Howard shook his head sadly. He leaned on his fence and his shoulders seemed to sag as he thought about it.

"I was thinking of a truck garden," he said.

Kinley put his hat back on his head. "If it was me I guess I'd have shot for a little more variety. You got enough turnips here to bloat everybody in Kansas and the territory and maybe half of Texas. Had you thought about maybe puttin' in a few onions and squash and like that?"

Howard sighed and turned away. He didn't want to talk about it.

"I got to go on in to Jubilation and get drunk," Nat explained. "But maybe when I get through I could swing on up to Pleasant Valley and send you out some boys to help harvest those. Looks to me like they're comin' on ripe."

Howard looked up at him, squinting against

morning brilliance. "Do you know any place where they might buy turnips?"

Nat puzzled over it, tugging at his bristly chin. "No," he admitted, "I can't say I ever heard of anybody that bought turnips. But I'll ask around when I sober up. How many turnips do you guess you have there?"

Howard had already estimated it. "About two hundred thousand, if they all make."

"That's countin' them by the head." The number was beyond Nat's capacity to conceive. "What would that be in bushels?"

"Sixteen thousand and some," Howard said thinly. He turned away again, looking bleakly around at his holdings. The barn and the windmill had been here when he bought the place, but there was almost as much of his time and labor invested in them as in the tidy house he had built, the pens and fences, the spreading acres broken out and planted to crops. He had known before he came to Bad Basin that there would be trials and burdens. Life was like that. The problem was, he felt now that he had missed the point somewhere in all that he had read, all the advice he had listened to, all the planning he had done. He had come expecting hot summers and cold winters, storm and drought and flood and pestilence and a lot of hard work. He felt somehow he should also have expected turnips.

"Don't take it too hard," Nat Kinley said with deep sympathy. "We'll think of somethin'. Give me a few to take along."

Unlike the Kinley place, which was on the north side of the Cimarron but south of the Kansas state line, Howard Sills's claim in Bad Basin was south of the river but in Kansas, north of the line. This was made possible by the fact that the south boundary

28

of Kansas was a straight line drawn on a map by someone in Washington, D.C., and had nothing whatever to do with either logic or terrain. So while the laws of men solemnly recognized a line of demarcation totally invisible except on paper and ignored the existence of things like a river valley several miles wide and a thousand feet deep some places, the river wound on oblivious to all this, crossing that line three times in a distance of thirty miles.

The upstream result was the long, skinny strip where the Kinleys had their place, happily protected from Kansas law by a state line north of them and from the big outfits in the Outlet by the river valley south of them. At the downstream point of the Lazy K the river crossed back into Kansas again. The next twenty miles east was a longer and wider island of isolation anchored by Bad Basin at its west end and by the town of Jubilation to the east. The widest place in this crescent of rolling prairie was the point where the Cimarron took a slow bend, meandering now southeast toward its third and final crossing of the Kansas state line. The bend was four miles north of the line, and it was here, among stair-step hills south of the valley, that Jubilation had grown.

As Nat Kinley trotted his horse across the wide, packed swath of the Higgins-Wentworth Trail where it angled downward through a lazy cut between bluffs that was called Jubilation Gap, he was thinking about Howard Sills's turnip problem. A few miles ahead he could see the buildings of Jubilation—the roofs of those at the foot of the bluff where propriety and sobriety were enforced, and the cluster atop the bluff where they were ignored. The sight of the place increased his thirst. Although the elevation of Jubilation's bluff was a modest 2,000

29

feet, it was considered in many circles to be the highest point in Kansas. More distilled spirits were dispensed annually in the little town's twenty-seven saloons, it was said, than had been consumed in all of Kansas before the state went constitutionally dry.

There was just nothing like Prohibition to give men a thirst.

For a while, watering holes had sprung up all along the Oklahoma side of the line, places where thirsty Kansans could ride across and wet their whistles. But howls of outrage from the forces of Prohibition had brought floods of marshals into the Strip to close down, burn out, and otherwise lay to rest these little oases.

As it stood now, so far as Nat Kinley knew, the top of Jubilation Bluff was the only place anywhere around where a man could get himself a drink. There were bootleggers, of course, but Nat did not consider a jug cooling in the well house as a proper answer to a man's needs. If the Almighty had meant for whiskey to be consumed out behind the barn, he reasoned, He would never had condoned the invention of playing cards.

Consideration of whiskey and playing cards gave a feeling of urgency to Nat's mission and he put his horse into a lope. Howard's problem of what to do with ten acres of turnips nagged at him, but after eight miles of hard thinking he still didn't have any ideas. It was the sort of problem that needed to be addressed by a committee. A man could almost always find a committee on Jubilation Bluff. One of the reasons Nat went there on regular occasion was the amount of truly original thinking that took place around the tables at Patman's Pleasure Palace, Richardson's Refreshment Emporium, and other such establishments. The discussions that took place there often were stimulating and intellectual, and the subjects were unrestricted. Nat had heard discourse on such widely varied matters as the distance to Alaska, the ability of Nubian goats to see in the dark, and what to do about that wart Benjamin Harrison.

"Somebody ought to go up to Washington and shoot the scutter," Elmer Wallace declared. "All that talk about closin' the leases in the Outlet, I can't tolerate that kind of talk from anybody even if he does get to be president."

Clarence Hanks had been at the table that night, cheerful and fuzz-tongued from good rye. "But Elmer," he said, "he wants to do that so they can open the Outlet to homesteaders."

"Squatters!" Wallace spat. He glared across at Nat. "We already got squatters. Don't require any more."

"The Kinleys don't bother anybody," Nat said bristling. "Besides, you couldn't graze both sides of that river even if we was to let you. Which, with all due respect, we won't."

The rancher was still thinking about Benjamin Harrison, and the thought made him bitter. "Never could tolerate squatters," he declared. "A man that would squat would graze sheep."

"I don't hold with that sort of talk," Nat told him. "Finish your drink and let's step outside."

Clarence Hanks had raised his hands. "Gentlemen, please! Jubilation has already had two shootings this week. We are beyond our quota. Let us assimilate peaceably, if we may."

Nat particularly enjoyed those conversations that included Clarence Hanks. Hanks was editor and publisher of the *Jubilation Tribune*, and his head contained a vast store of words which he tossed about lavishly. His presence always added spice to

31

intellectual discourse on Jubilation Bluff.

The evening had progressed peacefully. Nat Kinley and Elmer Wallace had refrained from shooting each other, and nobody had left for Washington to shoot Benjamin Harrison. More often than not, good conversation was enough to satisfy a man.

By the time he was halfway across the trammeled expanse of the Higgins-Wentworth Trail Nat was convinced that Howard Sills's turnip problem could be resolved in Jubilation. He would seek out the finest minds still functioning there and buy the first round, then they would reason together.

Nat's concern for Howard Sills's problems stemmed from a feeling of protectiveness that was shared by many south of the Cimarron. Almost from the day Howard had arrived in the valley, he had been a puzzle to everyone who encountered him. Though he had been farming in Bad Basin for four years now, Howard somehow just didn't seem like a farmer. He worked as hard as anybody Nat had ever known, and had made some remarkable improvements on his place, yet he never seemed from one day to the next to know exactly what he was doing or why. He was a fine-looking young man, tall and well filled out, with a ready smile and honest eyes, and was always hospitable and friendly. Yet he kept to himself over in Bad Basin and rarely went to town except for supplies. Nat suspected he was shy, and sensed that he was lonely. He had wondered at first if maybe Howard was stupid, but had decided against that. Howard wasn't stupid at all. He read books a lot, and could talk about things Nat had never even heard of, like trigonometry and the Roman Empire. Yet when he farmed in Bad Basin it was hardly ever the way anybody else farmed anywhere else.

Nat considered himself Howard's best friend, and concerned himself with Howard's problems. And right now the problem was 16,000 bushels of turnips ripening in the ground.

It would be a good topic for a serious discussion. Lately the talk had mostly been about how much money Iron Jack Fuller was making on his gambling operations, and what evils must surely befall now that women were allowed not only to vote but also to run for public office, and speculation on the whereabouts of the outlaw Cole Yeager. And, very recently, there had been much talk about Marshal Gault's threat to cordon off the boundary below Jubilation and dry up the town's supply of spirits. Some speculated that the Coleman County Attorney, Justin Case, was in cahoots with the Oklahoma lawman on this scheme, and there was considerable learned comment about Case himself.

"Somebody ought to run up to Pleasant Valley and shoot the scutter," Elmer Wallace declared. "Can't tolerate that kind of meddlin' down here."

Nat was just climbing the rise beyond the Higgins-Wentworth Trail when he heard a halloo from his right. A rider had appeared on the crest above, where the wide trail began its slope toward the Cimarron. The rider waved, then spurred his horse. Nat waved back, pulled up, and waited.

The approaching horse kicked up spurts of gray-white dust which streamed off across the sage and buffalo grass, little clouds disappearing in the wind. The rider came on and finally hauled up beside Nat. It was Pistol Pete Olive, top hand for the HW Connected. Hiram Wentworth's spread was more than a hundred miles south, down in the Outlet, and Nat only saw Pistol Pete and others from there about twice a year.

"Howdy, Nat." Pistol Pete grinned. "Looks to me like you're makin' a trip in to Jubilation."

"That's right, Pistol Pete. I got to go in and get drunk. What you doin' up this way? You got cows?"

"Four hundred head an' a few. We're takin' 'em up to Dodge for Mr. Wentworth. Drive's late this year. Mr. Wentworth shot himself in the foot a month ago and couldn't make up his mind whether to lead this drive or just send me." He gazed toward the bluff a few miles east, the little town sprawled at its base and the cluster of roistering establishments crowning its peak. "Wish I could lope over to Jubilation with you, Nat, but Mr. Wentworth said if any of us was to stop off before we get these cows to the pens at Dodge he'd not take it kindly."

"Hiram Wentworth is a hard man," Nat said sympathetically.

Pistol Pete had been riding short point, and cattle were visible now on the crest, a widening herd coming along at a good pace, sensing water a few miles ahead. Nat Kinley squinted, shading his eyes with his hat brim. "Is that old Mary out front there, Pistol Pete? How many times has she led drives for you fellows now?"

"Seven," Pistol Pete said. "This is her eighth. Last drive, she came back with forty-one prime steers. Six of 'em was our own brand."

"Hiram Wentworth has got himself a real prize in that cow," Nat admitted. "What Mr. Wentworth ought to do is to rent Conquistador from us and breed her before he loses her. Maybe homing breeds true in cows. That way he could have a reserve critter."

"Mr. Wentworth has his own bulls if he wants to do that," Pistol Pete pointed out.

"He don't have Conquistador," Nat said. "But we

34

do rent him out from time to time. How did Mr. Wentworth come to shoot himself in the foot?"

"Rattlesnake," Pistol Pete said, gazing hungrily at Jubilation in the distance. He did wish he could stop off and visit the place. It was a long ride from the HW Connected to Jubilation. "It was under his horse and he decided to shoot it, so he pulled out his gun and shot himself in the foot. Took his third toe clean off."

"Did he hit the snake?"

"Missed it by a foot." Pistol Pete turned sadly from the view of Jubilation in the distance. "You could do me a turn, Nat, if you don't mind, and I'd stand you a round for it on the way back."

"Glad to oblige," Nat nodded. "What is it?"

"Trail wagon will be here directly. We got a fellow in it that needs to be dropped off someplace. Maybe you could run him on in to Jubilation and hand him over to somebody. He's not normal. Calls himself Bloody Mare or some such, and that's about all we know. He showed up at HW Connected walkin', come from east someplace. Mr. Wentworth fed him and tried to put him to work but he's about useless. Mr. Wentworth told us to take him off and get rid of him."

"Guess I can drop him at Jubilation," Nat said. "What kind of name is that, *Bloody Mare?*"

"It's what he says. He can't rightly talk at all except to jabber a lot of words that don't make any sense."

The cattle came on, a few riders from HW Connected chousing them to tighten the herd as they arrowed toward Jubilation Gap below. Nat and Pistol Pete reined their mounts aside and climbed a rise to be out of the dust. The trail wagon was close behind the drag, not bothered by dust in the brisk southwest wind. Pistol Pete rode out and stopped the wagon, then came back to where Nat waited. A small man with a straight beard and a wool cap walked behind him. The man was thin and squint-eyed. He carried a parcel on a stick and a bulky case.

"Nat," Pistol Pete said, "this here is Mr. Bloody Mare. He ain't normal but he seems harmless enough. I expect he could get work at Jubilation. I'm obliged to you for takin' him off our hands." He tipped his hat. "Remember, I owe you a round when we come back through." With that he touched heels to his mount and hurried to catch up with his herd. He needed to be at point when they reached the gap.

Nat looked down at the bearded little man standing on the prairie. The man looked up at him, curiously. Nat leaned down to extend a hand. "Name's Kinley. Nat Kinley."

The man took his hand, thunked his heels together, and did a quick, stiff bow. "Bloody mare nickle eye a bitch melon cough," he said.

Nat blinked. "If you say so." He shrugged. "Climb up here behind me now. I'll tote you on in to town."

He had to gesture and point a few times before Bloody Mare got his meaning, but then the little man swung up behind him and they set off, Nat's big sorrel easily carrying double.

Although Pistol Pete was far beyond earshot the little man behind Nat waved at him in the distance. "Doe sweat on ya," he called.

"Pistol Pete was right," Nat said. "You say words but they don't make any more sense than tits on a rake handle."

Bloody Mare squirmed, trying to seat himself more comfortably. Nat's saddle was the short-seated roper variety, and the high, bulging saddlebags made

36

it hard to ride passenger without being violated by the cantle. Bloody Mare shifted and squirmed. He said something that sounded to Nat like, "Cover your stool."

Nat swiveled to squint at him. "I've run across some funny-talkin' folks, but you sure pull the plumb."

The little man fidgeted again, clinging to his luggage as the sorrel loped along. He wound his knees around the saddlebags and their pressure pushed a turnip above a flopping flap. He stared at it curiously, then pulled it out. "Raw bear," he told Nat. *"Ya khochu!"*

"Bless you," Nat said. "That there is a turnip. Howard Sills has sixteen thousand bushels of those and I figured I'd see if anybody in Jubilation might use a few."

Behind him the man said something like, "Sparse Eva," and there was a crunching sound. Nat turned. The little man had taken a huge bite out of the turnip and was munching on it happily. "Sparse Eva," he said again, "ya looble, you."

Startled, Nat swiveled again, nearly spraining his spine. "What did you say?"

"Horse piss on ya," the little man said, taking another bite of turnip. "Robber," he added.

"Now you look here," Nat snapped. "You're goin' to have to learn to mind your mouth. I don't hold with that kind of talk. You might be addled, but if you're goin' to ride on my horse you're goin' to have to quit cussin' at me."

"Men use a boot Bloody Mare," the passenger said. He spoke slowly and distinctly, tapping himself on the chest with a grimy thumb. "Bloody Mare Nickle Eye A Bitch Melon Cough." He tipped his head, waiting for some sign of understanding on

Nat's part. Nat only blinked. *"Ya Russkiy,"* the little man insisted.

Nat decided he was out of his depth. He turned forward again, pulled his hat low over his eyes, and flicked the sorrel's reins. Jubilation lay ahead. Behind him the little man leaned around to peer into the open saddlebag, then helped himself to another turnip.

IV

Vladimir Nikolayevich Malenkov clung grimly to the bouncing back of the tall horse and pondered his fate. He was not sure why he was here. For that matter he had only the vaguest concept of where "here" was. He had been lost for months.

He munched on a turnip and watched the little town ahead take on form as they approached it.

Life had been a confusion for Vladimir Nikolayevich virtually from the moment he had stepped off the boat at Tver eight years earlier, innocently hoping to sell to the *zemstvo* directorate an idea he had for improving the efficiency of distillation coils. He had never arrived at the directorate.

It was the misfortune of Vladimir Nikolayevich to have arrived on the same boat that carried Aleksei K. Soloviev, and to have followed that notable, who was a stranger to Vladimir, up the gangway to the docks. Vladimir had no more than stepped on the dock, bedazzled at the display of mounted Cossacks and resplendent carriages filing past on the facing street, when the man ahead of him drew a revolver from his long overcoat and fired five shots in the direction of a brilliantly uniformed man in an open carriage.

The man fired at, Vladimir learned later, was Tsar Alexander II, Emperor of Russia. At the time, though, all Vladimir knew was that all hell broke loose. Screams and thunders erupted. Bullets tore at the tails of his coat as he tumbled over the rail and fell into the dark water between the boat and the dock.

By the time Vladimir was able to creep from hiding beneath the dock he was half-frozen, disoriented, and alone on the dark street except for a hunched man nailing up a notice on a *raspisanya* board facing the public square. When the man had gone Vladimir looked at the poster. It contained his own name, Vladimir Nikolayevich Malenkov, and an accurate description of him. Further, it accused him of complicity in the attempted assassination of the Tsar, and identified him as a leader of the terrorist group known as *Narodnaya Volya*.

The fact that Vladimir Nikolayevich had never had a political thought in his life did nothing to alleviate the situation.

His four frightening attempts to escape from Tver, and those long nights of hiding before Ivan Petrunkevich found him and indoctrinated him into the very *Narodnaya Volya* he was famous for leading, were times he preferred not to remember.

They had been interesting years, though, those that followed. He had learned to shoot guns and to fuse bombs, and he had traveled widely — from the Volga to the Dnieper, from Kiev to Novgorod, and even to Moskva. Eleven times he had fired weapons at gentry of the *Rossiiskaya Imperiya*. He had even had the honor of taking a shot at Prince Kropotkin himself. Unfortunately shooting was not Vladimir's highest skill. He had missed all eleven times. He was better, his comrades found, with bombs.

His crowning achievement as a revolutionary terrorist would have been the destruction of the great house of General Trepov, Grand Master of Police. Unfortunately, the man who was to place the bomb after Vladimir fused it, a Black Slav named Gregor Mikhailevich Puchik, had weak kidneys. Instead of the great house of General Trepov, it was the bathhouse across the square that was reduced to rubble that day. It was an embarrassment to the *Narodnaya Volya,* but Ivan Petrunkevich absolved Vladimir of any blame. He even complimented him on a fine bomb. Pieces of Gregor Mihailevich Puchik, they said, were found as far away as Gorst.

Even love had come to Vladimir in those breathless terrorist years. He always thought he might have married Vera Ivanova. Unfortunately, she was caught and executed the third time she shot at General Trepov.

And, through it all, Vladimir had pondered the inadequacies of distillation coils and developed his ideas for perfecting them.

Garrets in St. Petersburg and Minsk and a cellar in Novgorod had known the reek of his mashes— stenches of fermenting peach, apple, grain, sugared soy. He had even made cabbage rot in such a manner that it could be distilled.

"Vladimir Nikolayevich," his comrades often said, "could make vodka from a boot. His tubs may stink to heaven but his coils spurt spirits faster than a horse makes water,"

In Russian it rhymed, and the decadent intellectual Oleg Narodnik made a song of it to a tune so sweet it always made Vladimir cry to hear it.

Fine days, those had been. Unfortunately the Tsar's police still knew his name and had his description. The day after they blew up the dining room of the Winter Palace, Ivan Petrunkevich came to him. "Valdimir Nikolayevich," the gentle old terrorist said, "it is time for you to leave."

"Leave St. Petersburg?" Vladimir asked, surprised.

"Leave Russia," Ivan said. "In fact, leave this hemisphere. It is my best advice."

"But why?" Vladimir quivered. "Why now?"

Ivan Petrunkevich put a hand on his scrawny shoulder and regarded him with great, sad eyes. "The Tsar," he said, "is pissed."

Thus Vladimir Nikolayevich Malenkov had come to America. He had found his way to friendly shores. He had even found his way to St. Louis, always looking for a place called Kansas, where—he had once been told—a cousin of his father's second wife had emigrated to raise wheat.

Kansas, he had gathered from a Pole with an atrocious accent in St. Louis, was west. Vladimir Nikolayevich had gone west.

That was months ago. He had been lost since that day.

The man on whose horse he was riding seemed friendly enough, and didn't seem to mind sharing his lunch.

It was noteworthy to Vladimir that most people he had met since coming to America had been friendly. There had been a few exceptions, such as the Cossacks outside St. Louis who had thrown him into the river and tried to steal his box, and the *politsiya* in that little town in Arkansaya—where the people were as furtive as Balkan Serbs yet as audacious as boyar land-raiders—who made him spend three days in jail over some misunderstanding. Then west of Arkansaya he had run afoul of a band of Tatars who called themselves Cherakeem and threw sticks at him. But then, even in Russia one often ran afoul of Tatars. They were as dark and surly in that land as in this. But for the most part, people had been hospitable to him. The man in the saddle to which Vladimir now clung, with his heavy box lashed to his back and his parcel and stick balanced across his lap, certainly seemed friendly enough. Vladimir's efforts at conversation had failed, but that was only because the man knew no more Russian than Vladimir knew of *Angliyski*. The man was providing him with transportation and all the *repas* he could eat, and had not asked him for a ruble.

The trail became a road, and the road became a street lined with leaning elm trees and whitewashed houses. As the dark horse trotted along, a group of ladies emerged from one of the houses and glanced at him. The man in the saddle raised his hat and Vladimir raised his cap. The ladies muttered and glared and raised their noses as they turned away. Nyetkin Lee — Vladimir had sorted out that that was his friend's name, though it seemed a negative sort of name — crammed his hat back on his head and ignored them, but Vladimir felt the occasion demanded some courtesy. "Good morning, ladies," he called. "How are you?" An instant later he was almost thrown from the horse as Nyetkin Lee swiveled full around in his saddle, his eyes bulging, and clamped a hand over Vladimir's mouth.

A short distance away the horse stopped walking and Nyetkin Lee make it clear to Vladimir Nikolayevich that he was no longer welcome aboard. He was unceremoniously unloaded, bag and baggage, and left standing in the street as the man rode away.

Vladimir shook his head sadly. Up the street, he saw another horseman swing in beside his lost friend, and saw them talking together as they rode away. Both of them turned to look back at him, but kept going. Vladimir raised his cap. *"Do svidanya, Nyetkin Lee,"* he said. *"Spasibo."* Goodbye and thank you. Vladimir wondered, as he picked up his belongings and began to walk, whether he was anywhere near Kansas yet. Things were very confusing.

"A drinkin' man's got enough trouble ridin' through Downtown Jubilation," Nat Kinley told Twist McGuffin, "without some little jaybird insultin' the mayor's wife and the whole Wednesday Ladies' Reading Circle. Lordy, I guess we'll all be hearin' about that."

McGuffin glanced back at the forlorn little figure standing in the street, wrestling with a large box and a parcel on a stick. "What did he say to 'em?"

"Called 'em damn skinny cock dealers, that's what he said. "I couldn't hardly believe my ears, even though I been listenin' to his chatter for miles. That isn't the half of what he's been callin' me ever since I took him off Pistol Pete's hands out on the trail, but I let most of that pass because he ain't normal, like Pistol Pete said. But I don't hold with that kind of talk around women — not even those damned old biddies in the Wednesday Ladies' Reading Circle."

"Good thing you put him off your horse," Twist allowed. "A man gets known by the company he keeps." He glanced at Nat's bulging saddlebags. "You're packin' a load today, 'pears to me."

"Them is turnips," Nat said. "Howard Sills was tryin' to grow himself a few vegetables and he wound up with sixteen thousand bushels of turnips. He's not just real happy about it. You know anybody could use some turnips?"

Twist shook his head. "I don't know anybody that holds with turnips. And I don't know anybody except Howard Sills that could set out to grow truck and wind up with turnips. How many did you say?"

"Sixteen thousand bushels, he figures. That whole ten acres past his barn, it's solid packed with 'em."

Twist was impressed. "I guess I ought to go out and see that. Somehow I just can't imagine ten acres of turnips. He have any notion what to do with them?"

"Not a one. That's why I brought some along. I figured we might get a committee together and think on it for him. You know something, Twist? This isn't Wednesday. It's Tuesday. What are them biddies doin' out paradin' around on a Tuesday?"

"Way I hear it, they're goin' door to door downtown, circulatin' We See To You petitions." The street turned to the left and angled upward, climbing toward the top of Jubilation Bluff. A wide trail from the south joined it, and ahead of them they could see a line of whiskey wagons from the Outlet, laboring upward toward the high side of town.

"Last time they had a petition they were the only ones that signed it," Nat said.

"Well, I hear they're doin' better this time. Dutch Henry Vargas said his wife told him they had more than three hundred signatures on this one. Even the mayor signed it. Course, he was drunk at the time. But they got a head of steam up, that's for sure. We all need to step a little careful."

It was Nat's turn to be impressed. "Three hundred names?" He whistled. "What's been goin' on here, Twist?"

McGuffin leaned downwind to spit, then wiped his chin. "Well, they ran advertisements in Clarence

45

Hanks's newspaper, for one thing. Clarence doesn't care what goes in that paper as long as it pays. Then some of the boys from H-Four came in and got likkered up and went downtown and roped a bunch of Martha Haggard's chickens. They even branded her best layin' hen. Been better if they hadn't done that. She got pretty upset about it."

"I can see how she might. Why didn't somebody keep them boys up on the bluff till they sobered up?"

Twist glanced at him, amused. "You know anybody offhand that can keep the H-Four crowd anywhere they don't want to be?"

"I don't know. Leonard ought to be able to. Where was he?"

Twist laughed and shook his head. "Leonard was busy elsewhere. A bunch of the boys over at Patman's saw him comin' on street patrol so they pried the top off a barrel of Patman's best whiskey and lifted it up against the ceiling. Then they poked a broom handle under it and when Leonard came in they hollered, 'Leonard, come over here,' and when he came they said, 'Hold this,' and gave him the broom handle. Then they all left. He was there until after midnight, holdin' that barrel up with that broom handle and hollerin' about the law."

"I wouldn't want Leonard mad at me," Nat said.

"Oh, them boys don't have to worry. They left town that night, and Leonard can't remember anything very long."

"That's a fact," Nat agreed. "Probably one reason he's a good deputy."

"On the other hand," Twist added, "there aren't many men that can hold up a whole barrel of whiskey with a broom handle. I sure wouldn't want to have Leonard mad at me."

Ahead of them the road spread on a packed shale bench, and switched back for the last leg of its climb to uptown Jubilation. The wagons had completed their turns and were above the two riders now, and thirty feet away.

"Yo, Nat!" the lead teamster called as they came abreast. "Yo, Twist! New load comin' in, top-grade spirits straight up from the Strip."

"Right behind you, Finn," Twist called back. "My throat's so dry I'm breathin' dust devils."

"Well, drink up while you can," Finn shouted. "Talk over east is that Marshal Gault's had his boys scoutin' the whiskey routes. Don't know why, but if he goes to messin' with deliveries this juice could get real scarce."

"Don't tell Patman that or he'll double his prices," Nat called. Then he and Twist looked at each other, worried.

"You don't suppose they'd really do that?" Twist frowned. "I Mean, this Prohibition thing, it's just a Kansas law. What do the federals care what goes through the Outlet?"

"I don't know." Nat studied on it. "It's more than a law. Them Jayhawks up an' amended their state constitution. But you're right, it's still state. The Kansas constitution don't mean diddly-squat south of the State Line. Naw," he decided, "that's just talk. They won't cut off the whoopy juice. After all, Jubilation is the last respectable waterin' hole within three hundred miles. Nobody would mess that up. That'd be like . . . like dessicatin' a shrine."

Some distance behind them, just where the road made its first bend to climb the bluff, a tall, stoop-shouldered man paused, shook his head and rubbed his eyes, then scowled blearily at the little bearded man standing before him. Bert Thompson was nursing a hangover and was in no mood for puzzles. Yet the little man stood there, wool cap in hand, a large box strapped to his back and carrying a parcel on a stick, and looked up at him with wide, innocent eyes. Bert squinted and shook his head. "Sorry," he said. "I didn't understand a word of that. You better say it again, I guess."

The little man stared at him as though trying to sort out what he had said.

"Look," Bert said, "I didn't hear you, all right? Try it one more time." He extended his hands in confusion and the little man grinned, grasped one of them, and pumped it enthusiastically.

"Bloody Mare," he said. "Bloody Mare Nickle Eye A Bitch Melon Cough."

"Bloody Mare—?" Bert started, and the little man grinned and nodded, tapping himself on the chest. "Bloody Mare! *Kak dela!*"

It dawned on Bert that he was making an introduction. "Bert Thompson," he said, pointing to himself. Then he withdrew his hand. The furious pumping of it was giving him a headache. "What was the rest of that?"

"Ya khochu—"

"Bless you."

"Ya khochu kopit' pivo. Pivo." He put a hand to his mouth and belched. He grinned again, dug into his voluminous coat, and pulled out part of a turnip, displaying it. *"Ya yem repa. Pazhalusta, mne nuzhno pivo."*

It was only chatter, but there was something vaguely familiar in the sound of it and Bert searched his aching memory. Someone, somewhere . . ." "Polack?" He pointed at the man. "Are you . . . Polish?"

The man seemed mortified. *"Nyet!"* he snapped.

"Nyet, nyet! Ya nye Polyak. Ya Ruskiy!"

"Rooski? You're a Russian? Well, what in God's name are you doin' here?"

"Da. Russkiy. Spasibo." He pointed at his mouth, breathed drily and pantomimed a man lifting a mug. *"Ya pl'yu pivo."*

"Pivo?" Bert scratched his head with ink-stained fingers. "Beer? You want a beer?"

"Da! Beer. *Pivo. U menya est' dengi."* He pulled a few coins from a pocket and showed them to Bert.

"You want a beer and you have money. And you're a real honest-to-Pete Russian?"

"Da. Ya Russkiy."

"Well," Bert allowed, "I guess if I was full of turnips — what did you call them? Rahpers? I guess if I was full of rahpers I'd need a peevah too." He pointed toward the top of the bluff. "There's all the peevah you'll ever want, right up there. Da, peevah. There. You can kopeet plenty of peevah up there. Just look for Patman's Peevah Parlor. If you miss it there's twenty-six others just like it."

The little man grinned at him like a long-lost friend. *"Spasibo,"* he said. *"Spasibo.* Bert Tomsahn." He gave his hand another enthusiastic shake and started up the hill.

Bert watched him go, then turned to walk along a rutted street where shops and offices faced each other across a two-wagon span lined with narrow boardwalks. It was near midday and deep shadow stood beneath the intermittent awnings, but Bert shuffled along in mid-street. His shoulders hunched in a perennial stoop, big hands swinging at the end of uncoordinated arms clad in dirty sleeves. He walked at a shuffling pace and sweat beaded on his brow. Maybe the sun would cook some of last night's whiskey out of his brain, he thought. His mouth tasted sour and his mind was soggy. He wondered what a Russian was doing in Jubilation, and he wondered whether he should tell Clarence Hanks about it. The little wart might want to put something in the newspaper. Bert couldn't remember any Russians coming to Jubilation before.

No, he decided, let the little wart find his own news. It was his paper. He could find the garbage to fill it. Bert's job was just to set type and run the press.

Ahead in awning shadow loomed the front door of the office of the Jubilation Tribune. Bert frowned, turning toward it. He glanced beyond and up, toward the crest of Jubilation Bluff. Up there was comfort in the form of repeated shots of rye whiskey. Up there was solace. Yet the sun was high and only by setting type for Clarence Hanks could Bert assure himself an income. He scowled, wiped his brow with inky fingers, and shuffled toward the Tribune's door. Later, when the town's little bullsheet was locked up for printing, he could climb the hill. Right now there was work to do.

At the boardwalk he stopped to let Jubilation's deputy marshal pass.

Even unencumbered, Leonard was wide enough to occupy a boardwalk by himself, but now his width was doubled by the two cowboys he carried, one under each arm. One was struggling feebly against the massive arm wrapped around his ribs. The other was unconscious.

Bert wondered vaguely why Leonard hadn't deposited the sodden pair in the town jail, which was uptown, instead of carrying them all the way down here. But then there was no mystery why Leonard did the things he did. It was because he wasn't smart enough to do things any other way. These two had committed some infraction on the high side of town — something serious enough to attract Leonard's attention. Therefore he was taking them down to Marshal Ben Cutter's office to find out what he should do with them. The fact that the marshal would tell him — as he always did — to take them back up the hill and put them in the jail was not something Leonard would anticipate in advance. Thinking ahead was not Leonard's style.

In a way, Bert Thompson liked Leonard. The man was simple. Like a buffalo he was simple. As a matter of fact, Bert realized, Leonard had much in common with a buffalo.

"Stand aside!" Leonard thundered as he came abreast. Bert was already aside. "Business of the Law!" Leonard roared. "Stand aside!"

"Mornin', Leonard," Bert said. "What did they do?"

Leonard paused to stare at him, scowling hugely. "What did who do?"

"Those two there that you're toting. What did they do?"

Leonard glanced at his two burdens as though recalling again that he had them. Then he scowled again at Bert. "Broke the Law!" he roared. As far as Bert knew, Leonard had only one tone of voice, and windows rattled up and down the street as he spoke. Bert wished he hadn't asked. He had a headache from the hangover and the sun.

"These men broke the Law!" Leonard thundered. "Stand aside!"

Bert shrugged. He had all the information he was likely to get. He made a show of standing aside and Leonard thudded onward with his prisoners, shaking the boardwalk and adjacent structures with each step.

Shoulders sagging with the burdens of defeat, heat, and whiskey neat, Bert entered the office of the Tribune. Clarence Hanks, Ed. & Pub., was at his desk scribbling furiously, his stub of pencil making barely decipherable scrawls on a sheet of yellowed paper. He glanced up. "You're late again."

"So what else is new?" Bert shuffled past him and gazed sourly at the pile of scrawled prose waiting beside the type fonts. He sighed heavily, then went to work, pondering distantly on destiny and wondering vaguely what sort of fate would be required to bring any improvement to his life as it was at this moment. He coughed, spat, and tried to concentrate on the dingy type forms. He didn't like to think about fate. Bert Thompson had seen fate in action too many times to feel comfortable at the thought of it.

But at that precise moment, several miles away, fate—in its typical way—was beginning a new knit. Its first two stitches were a fugitive turnip and a one-horned cow named Mary.

V

Pessimism, to Howard Sills, was an uncomfortably alien attitude. The discovery that his cherished crop was in fact ten acres of turnips—a fruit for which he knew no civilized use and no established market—had cast a bleak pall over his reflections. But such dark shadows were tenuous in a mind accustomed to seeing the bright side of things.

Since coming to Kansas four years ago, Howard had faced adversity many times. In his first spring a tornado had knocked down his hay shed, demolished the beginnings of his house, and turned over his outhouse. Later heavy rains had washed impassable gullies across his road, collapsed his storm cellar, and carried away his outhouse. That same winter heavy snows had collapsed his new roof, driven his cattle away, and buried his outhouse. A late blizzard the following spring had frozen his windmill, scattered his chickens, and reduced his outhouse to kindling. But Howard had persevered and rebuilt, each time adding innovations that left his neighbors wide-eyed with wonder.

Howard was an optimist. Each cataclysm was an opportunity to innovate and improve, and he met each hardship as a challenge. People from miles around had stopped by to see his insulated windmill, his above-ground storm cellar, his reinforced barn, and the high-pitched roof on his house—and stories of Howard Sills's element-proof outhouse drifted as far as Missouri and Texas.

Thus, even in the face of a plethora of turnips, Howard Sills did not long remain defeated.

Nat Kinley's visit revived him. Nat had given him hope. Nat felt a market for turnips might be found at Jubilation. Before Nat was out of sight, riding eastward across the flats out of Bad Basin, Howard was in his field with a hand trowel and a wheelbarrow, harvesting ripe turnips, barrowing them out to load aboard his spring wagon. By the time Nat Kinley reached the Higgins-Wentworth Trail Howard Sills had more than 900 turnips loaded into his wagon's little bed, greens and all, and was hitching Crowbait into the traces. If Nat found a market for turnips in Jubilation, Howard Sills decided he would be there with the goods, ready to begin selling.

At the very least, he reasoned, he should be able to sell the greens at Stapleton's Market for enough to pay for the trip.

Armed once again with optimism, Howard Sills headed for town.

Crowbait was in good spirits and the spring wagon sailed along Howard's fresnoed roadway to the rolling grassland above Bad Basin, then wound along the curved trace that spanned the miles to the Higgins-Wentworth Trail. It was only at the trail that the driving became rough. The wide, barren trail was pitted and rutted from years of cattle drives and leaching rains, and Howard was busy enough at the reins not to notice that he was leaving a trail of turnips behind him, one or two every hundred yards or so. If he had noticed, it wouldn't have mattered. He had enough turnips in his wagon to feed half of Coleman County, and an inexhaustible supply where they had come from.

From the notched crest of Jubilation Gap to the lush and wooded bottoms flanking the Cimarron River was a drop of less than a thousand feet and a span of nearly two miles—a little over an hour's march for a fresh herd moving downhill with water ahead. Mary set a crisp, jogging pace and the herd followed. Pistol Pete Olive, riding point, found he had nothing more demanding to do once they passed the gap than to stay out of their way. Mary, it seemed, knew exactly where she was going.

Riding back along the upwind flank of the rippling ribbon of beef, Pistol Pete pulled in alongside Wednesday Warren and draped his reins across the saddle horn to roll a cigarette, letting his horse pace itself to Wednesday's buckskin.

"Not much to this job of point when you got a critter like that cow to mark trail," he said. "She purely knows the way."

"Ought to," Wednesday allowed. "She's been up this trail seven times each way. Probably knows ever' foot of it, right into the loadin' pens at Dodge. I don't suppose you'd entertain a reasonable suggestion, would you, Pistol Pete?"

"What would that be?"

"We'll be at the river in a bit. Why don't we put 'em to the water for an hour or so, then pull back an' bed them down?"

Pistol Pete licked and sealed his Spanish roll, then glanced at Wednesday. "It ain't even noon yet. How come we'd bed the herd this early?"

"Jubilation town is back there."

"You know as well as I do what Mr. Wentworth said about that." He struck a light and puffed smoke. "He wouldn't take kindly to it."

"Don't see what difference it could make. I got the need to play a hand of poker or two."

"We all do, Wednesday. And to have six or eight good drinks while we're about it. But I can't allow it. I been workin' six years to get to be top hand and I sure don't aim to take any chances with the job now that I have it."

"You're not top hand because you worked six years. You're top hand because Mr. Wentworth shot himself in the foot. Seems to me like that would shed a different light on the subject."

"Trail bossin' is trail bossin' however it comes about," Pistol Pete said coolly. "And a man that wants to get ahead in this world don't take trail bossin' lightly."

"Well, all I can say is, you're a hard man, Pistol Pete." Wednesday stood in his stirrups, squinting into the declining distance. He shaded his eyes. "Doesn't bein' trail boss mean you're supposed to make these cows go where they're supposed to?"

"Sure it does. That's easy when you got a smart lead critter."

"Well, Pistol Pete," Wednesday said, "Maybe you better talk to that cow because it looks like she ain't takin' us to the deep hole crossin'. We're way off to the right, and that's the bogs we're headin' for."

Pistol Pete's mouth dropped open, the smoldering shuck dangling from his lip. "Lord a'mercy!" he declared. An instant later all Wednesday Warren could see of him was coattails flapping above the running rump of his horse.

It was too late. Unerringly, Mary had channeled

the lead animals between cleft banks, through a growth of cottonwoods, and down to a broad expanse of bright sand and clear pools a hundred yards from the river's flowing verge. It was a flood backwater on an outer bend. Rabbit trails laced its smooth sand tops, skirting around the water-pooled depressions. Mary, in the lead, broke out of brush at the edge of it and stopped. Her nose was down, one-horned head weaving from side to side. Dimly she understood that this was not something she had encountered before, and she didn't like it. With a snort she backed up, cattle milling behind and around her, then veered sharply left and headed out again, staying to the grassed areas, skirting the bogs.

Most of the cattle followed her. A few did not. By the time Pistol Pete Olive arrived, followed by other riders from the flanks and drag, a dozen bellowing beasts were mired in quicksand. White-faced, Pistol Pete drew his Colt and fired three shots into the air, bringing the entire crew down to help. By the time the first cow was dragged back up on dry ground, the horses were lathered, the men sweating, and the main herd out of sight, angling back toward the trail and the crossing at deep hole. Mary had recovered her bearings.

For an hour the cattle drank, grazed, and milled quietly on good grass at the main crossing, before Mary felt the urge to again be on the move. She shook herself, snorted, and ambled into the clear, shallow water, her eyes on the far bank. But when the water was at her hams she stopped, and those behind her stopped too. She stood for a while, vaguely aware that something was supposed to happen now. She was supposed to be urged onward by raucous young men on horseback. to be driven across to the far side of the river. That was how it was done.

Still, no young men came. No shouts, no splashing horses, no swats with coiled ropes. There was just the rippling cool water, the drone of lazy insects, the gentle breeze of the valley. After a while Mary turned and waded past the steers standing in the river. She went up the bank, past those ranked animals waiting there, and headed up the trail toward home. Slowly, the herd began to peel back, some following her, others following them. Mary set her stride and the others fell in behind her. Four hundred HW Connected beeves, a mix of rangy longhorns and brush-tough crossbreeds, headed toward Jubilation Gap, southbound on the Higgins-Wentworth Trail. Their pace was slower going up toward the Gap than it had been coming down. By the time they topped the crest and flowed into the main trail, the sun was low in the west. It was a mile beyond that point that Mary discovered her first turnip.

She sniffed at it and nuzzled it, rolling it over with her nose. She chewed at the leafy crown of it, then bit into the turnip itself. It was crisp and cool. A short distance to her left was another one, and she wandered over to it to repeat the snack. Some distance away she saw another.

Gradually, the herd realigned itself, moving again. But this time its direction was neither toward Dodge nor toward home range. This time it was headed for the town of Jubilation.

Opal Twiddie—Mrs. Mayor Twiddie as she preferred—paused a few steps from the front door of the wide, false-front building whose jutting sign proclaimed *Jubilation City Hall. Mayor A. P. Twiddie,*

Ding Cox City Clerk, and, on an appended slat, *Office of the Town Marshal.* The spring-closing outer door had just crashed open, slamming itself against the wall, and a thrashing mass of humanity was emerging. It was Leonard, still carrying his brace of cowhands. Both of them were conscious now, complaining bitterly. The door was narrow for the deputy and his burdens, but Leonard was not one to negotiate carefully in narrow confines. Door-frames creaked and scraped as he forced his way through, and one of the dangling cowboys howled as the bruising wood added further indignities to his battered self. The spring door, rebounding, hit him on the head and he howled again.

"Stand aside!" Leonard roared. "Stand aside in the Name of the Law!"

Opal Twiddie and her following stood aside, looking pained. Behind her Martha Haggard hissed, "Horrible. Just horrible."

Leonard glanced at them, little eyes dull in a huge, unshaven face. He nodded and raised an arm to lift his hat. The cowboy on that side sprawled on the boardwalk, then tried to scuttle away. Leonard put a foot on him to hold him in place. "Afternoon, ladies," he thundered. Then, having completed his civilities, he replaced his hat, scooped up his dropped miscreant, and plodded away up the walk. "Stand aside! Law comin' through! Make way!"

Little Agatha Sturgis, frail and tiny in her layers of severe gray linen, moved close to Opal and tugged at her sleeve. "You mark my word, Opal," she said. "They're all in league."

"In league with the devil," Polly Cox agreed. "Every one of them."

"I suppose he is taking those men up to the jail," Emma Spalding said doubtfully. "I suppose the law

59

is being enforced . . . after a fashion."

The others glanced at her, their eyes disapproving. Emma blushed and subsided.

Agatha Sturgis drew her tiny frame to its full height and her mouth was compressed in revulsion. Emma held her breath, remembering the time Agatha had slimmed herself that way, in a moment of righteous indignation, and had lost her corset in the process. It had dropped right out from under her dress. Emma could still hear the sound of its rigid stays hitting the schoolhouse floor, and she could still see the fierce little woman standing there, riveted to that spot, trapped and pale, until some of the women realized her predicament and managed to bustle her into a cloakroom to reassemble herself.

"Really, Emma," Opal told her now, "if we expect to succeed in our crusade we must be resolved in our purpose. Absolutely resolved."

"But I only pointed out," Emma shook her head, "there may be some—"

"Emma!" Opal scolded. "We must remember what Mrs. Mayhew said in her excellent treatise on the maintenance of zeal!"

"I'm sorry," Emma whispered. She couldn't for the life of her recall what Mrs. Mayhew had said.

Across the street Morris Stapleton appeared at the door of his produce and sundries market, blinking in the sunlight as he looked upstreet to where Leonard, still bellowing inanely, plodded onward with his captures. When Stapleton turned and saw the cadre of severe gray-clad women across from him, he ducked back into the shadows of his store.

"All in league," Agatha Sturgis repeated.

Opal Twiddie squared her shoulders and assumed her regimental stance. "Forward, ladies," she commanded. The spring door ahead of them opened a few inches and then closed abruptly. Beyond were confused sounds: a babble of male voices, the thudding of hurried footsteps, the closing of interior doors. As Martha Haggard scurried ahead to open the door for Mrs. Mayor, they could distinctly hear a back door closing.

Only one man was visible inside when they entered. Marshal Ben Cutter was already standing, and had removed his hat. Now he came around his desk, a practiced smile on his lean, handsome face. "Come in, ladies," he beamed. "Come right in. What can I do for you?"

Beyond the polished railing to the right, all three of the official offices had closed doors, but a furtive shadow moved behind the frosted glass of the first one. Gilt letters arced across it proclaiming *Ding Cox, City Clerk*. Polly Cox glanced that way, then ignored it, but her eyes glittered. Emma Spalding shivered. Ding Cox was going to catch it when he got home.

Ben Cutter looked exactly the way a town marshal should look. Fairly tall, trim, and craggy, he wore a flowing mustache. It emphasized a face that would have graced any political poster and lent credibility to any medicine label. The sun-lines beside his wide-set eyes bespoke wisdom, the seams in his cheeks radiated patience, his cleft chin and solid jaw promised strength and courage. Everything about him, from his carefully brushed hair to the slim gold watch-chain crossing his dark vest to the ivory-handled Colt low on his hip, proclaimed him as town marshal and ultimate authority in Jubilation. Opal Twiddie knew better.

"Where is Alfred?" she demanded. "Is he in his office?"

"Why, no, I'm sorry," Cutter said. "Mayor Twiddie

had some unexpected business to attend to. I'm the only one here at the moment. Can I be of assistance?"

"All in league," Agatha Sturgis chirped with such indignation that Emma edged toward her, concerned for her corset.

"Very well, Marshal," Opal said. "I'm sure you can serve as well." From her voluminous purse she drew a sheaf of papers and handed it to him. "We have here a legal petition calling for — demanding, in fact — that every den of iniquity bespoiling our fair city be closed immediately, never again to be reopened. As you can see, we have referred to legal counsel in the drafting of this document — "

"I wonder who," Cutter said under his breath, his eyes narrowing. It was common knowledge that the county attorney, Justin Case, had made several trips down from Pleasant Valley to meet with the Wednesday Ladies' Reading Circle.

" — and there are three hundred and nine legal signatures on it. You may count them if you wish."

"I'm sure that won't be necessary, ma'am. But just what is it you want me to do?"

"Well, enforce it, of course. That *is* your job, is it not?"

"My job is to enforce the law in Jubilation. This is a petition."

Emma Spalding sighed. Somehow she had known this wasn't going to go smoothly and pleasantly. Glancing at Opal, she saw the dark flush that crept from her collar, the tight-lipped, slit-eyed expression that meant she was going to war.

Opal dug into her purse again. The paper she brought forward was yellowed and dog-eared. She waved it before the marshal's impassive face. "This is the law! This is an exact copy of the Prohibition

Amendment approved by the voters of Kansas in 1880 — seven years ago! It distinctly prohibits the dispensing of distilled spirits, fermented beverages, and alcoholic substances anywhere in the State of Kansas. It's the law. It's part of the constitution!"

Cutter sighed. "Yes, ma'am. I've read it."

"Then enforce it!"

"I'm only the town marshal, Mrs. Twiddie. I enforce ordinances of the City of Jubilation. The City of Jubilation doesn't have an ordinance against selling liquor."

"But the constitution says we must!"

"But we don't," Cutter explained. "We have been through all this before, I believe."

"But not with a petition," Opal said, pouncing in triumph. "This is a legal petition. The citizens have spoken."

Cutter thumbed through the sheets in his hand, his mustache twitching in mild humor. "Most of these signatures are . . . ah . . . the signatures of ladies, ma'am."

Opal's eyes smoldered. "In case you haven't heard, Marshal, Kansas Civil Statute number 441 — enacted this very year! — gives women the right to vote in city and bond elections, to *sign petitions,* even to run for public office if they see fit! These are all legal signatures. You must accept them!"

"Wouldn't that be something." Cutter grinned.

"What?"

"Women in public office. Can you imagine?"

"Marshal Cutter!" Opal's voice took on a thin, steely quality. "I shall remind you that my husband is the mayor of this town!"

Cutter grinned at her. Emma looked away. Oh, for heaven's sake, Opal, she thought.

"What do you propose to do about this then?"

63

Martha Haggard tried to come to Mrs. Mayor's rescue.

Cutter shrugged, still thumbing pages. "Why, nothing. The only thing a petition does is direct a matter to the attention of the City Council. And then only after it has been signed by the mayor and attested by the city clerk. I don't see those here."

"My husband signed it!" Opal shouted. "I made him sign it!"

"Ah?" Cutter peered at the pages. "Oh, yes. Here's his signature. A little shaky, I'd have to say, but legible. But you see, ma'am, he signed as a citizen, not as mayor. The mayor has to sign at the bottom of the last page. And the city clerk has to attest."

Polly Cox marched through the railing gate and pounded on the door to her husband's office. "Ding Cox, you come out of there this minute and attest this petition!"

Silence followed.

"I know you're in there!" Polly rasped. "You just wait 'til you get home!"

Ben Cutter shrugged and handed the papers back to the fuming Opal. "I'm afraid there's nothing I can do, Mrs. Twiddie. Maybe if you ladies would come back some time when the mayor is in . . ."

Opal sputtered, flushed and furious. Martha Haggard looked as though she were contemplating murder. Polly Cox stamped her foot, glaring at the silent, closed door of the city clerk's office. Tiny Agatha Sturgis drew herself to her full height of four feet eight and there was a thud—the sound of corset stays against a wood floor.

From the street outside came the sounds of a spring wagon being halted, and the sound of men's voices, distantly. The silence in City Hall was complete enough that Morris Stapleton's words carried clearly from across the street.

"Gosh, Howard, I don't know. I don't remember anybody ever asking for turnips."

VI

"I shall leave it to you to put this one to bed, Bert." Clarence Hanks closed his rolltop desk, hung up his eyeshade, and peeled off his sleeve covers. He straightened his tie, put on his coat, and tapped a rakish derby onto his head. "The muse calls and I must make my rounds. I'm certain you can manage."

Without a backward glance the editor and publisher of the Jubilation Tribune strode to the door, opened it, and departed. Through paned windows Bert Thompson saw him turn purposely to the left and proceed up the street, heading for uptown Jubilation. "The muse calls," he muttered. He wondered which of Jubilation's refreshment stands the muse frequented on Tuesdays these days. He rubbed an inkstained hand across the stubble on his chin and resented Hanks. There were still two galleys to set before he could lock up the fourth and final page of this week's bullsheet and it had to be done today. Wednesday was press day . . . followed by delivery day, followed by payday.

Clarence Hanks would be home in bed—or passed out in a doorway somewhere—by the time Bert got a fair start on his evening's libations.

Bert Thompson was a large man, slow and stoop-shouldered, with an unkempt mane of hair graying at the temples and the beginnings of a bulge swelling over his belt. Large, aching feet spread wide below his long apron, he turned again to the chest of type fonts and selected one for the next headline, his eyes sullen as they followed the handwritten copy Hanks had left. Fingers too large for the task darted from bin to bin as he set characters in the stick, mouthing the words as they grew.

"Mayoral Candidates Undecided," he set, then pursed his lips sourly. It seemed to Bert that the editor and publisher of a newspaper — even a fodder-wad like the Tribune — should have learned to count. The line was too long by two letters in the twenty-four point.

"What's a shorter word for 'undecided'?" he growled to himself. He was tempted to substitute "confused," but that wouldn't solve the length problem. With a sigh he removed "al" from "Mayoral," making the line fit.

"Undecided, nothing," he muttered. "Twiddie'll run again like always and Hester'll run against him like always and lose like always. Why can't that little wart ever stay around and help with this garbage?"

Outside, the shadows of sunset engulfed downtown Jubilation, blue shadows with momentary glows from the sunlight still reflected by uptown Jubilation sitting on its bluff. Horsemen, wagons, and buggies passed the multi-paned windows, men coming into town on their way uptown, to relieve their burdens with an evening's relaxation atop the bluff. All the joys of a wide-open little town awaited them there, and all for a price.

Bert caught a glimpse of Howard Sills's spring

wagon passing on the street. Crowbait plodded tiredly along oblivious to the skittering cowponies, enthusiastic teamsters, and jaunty buggies hurrying by. Howard sat dejectedly on the seat, and the wagon bed was piled high with . . . what? It looked like turnips. Puzzled, Bert looked over the ranked galley trays and ran a smudged thumb down rows of inverted typeface. Yes, there it was, a tiny item in the flowery, sardonic prose of Clarence Hanks. Under "Items of Note," it stated that Howard Sills of Bad Basin, famed for his impervious outhouse, had once again produced the unusual. Bad Basin, Hanks implied, had been converted to a gigantic turnip farm. "One wonders," Hanks sniped, "what new wonders one might next behold."

Why in heaven's name had Howard Sills planted turnips? Bert glanced out the window again, in time to see Howard jerk upright in the wagon seat, then haul his reins. Crowbait veered hard to the right, cutting across noisy traffic, and the spring wagon disappeared into the shadows of the chute bay at Bunker's Mill. A moment later Howard reappeared, half-hidden, peering furtively along the street.

Bert went to the window to look. A few doors away Penelope Becket was strolling along the walk followed by several young townsmen carrying her parcels and sacks, glaring at one another as they vied for her attention.

Across the way the load-bell rang at Bunker's Mill. Even in the shadowed bay, Bert could see what had happened. Howard Sills, ducking back out of sight, had tripped over the bell cord.

"I never saw the like," Bert muttered, returning to his work. He picked up his tray, selected a galley stick.

"Mr. and Mrs. Homer Rambo are the proud parents of a bouncing baby boy," Bert set in tight ten-point, a sneer curling his lip. How did they know it bounced? Had they dropped it?

His feet hurt from hours at the galley table. His shoulders and neck ached. His eyes burned from reading dirty type in poor light. He finished the cherub section and crumpled Clarence Hanks's words of prose into a ball, which he tossed toward the overflowing trash bin. Then he slid the type from the galley-stick into the page form and inserted hardwood spacers to make it fill the column. Penelope Becket passed the paned window and waved at him, then went on, with her retinue trailing after her. Across the way Howard Sills was nowhere in sight, though his laden spring wagon still stood in the mill's chute bay. Bert saw Puff McVey, Bunker's on-duty millhand, staggering across the street in bleary fashion, responding to the recent clatter of the load bell.

Bert shrugged and began setting obituaries. Somewhere atop Jubilation Bluff a piano was tinkling and there were the rich sounds of beginning revelry.

At one time in a checkered career that Bert tried hard not to remember, he had stopped in Topeka long enough to learn typesetting and composition. These modest skills were what kept him on the payroll of Clarence Hanks. Aside from Hanks himself and a couple of freckled printer's devils who showed up now and again, Bert *was* Hanks's payroll.

At any rate, though he detested the job, being Hanks's typesetter and printer provided Bert with the wherewithal to maintain a meal or two each day, a cornhusk bed in a shack at the edge of town, and enough rotgut whiskey each evening to drive away the haunts and let him sleep. There was also enough, barely, to allow him to pay five dollars each week to Iron Jack Fuller so that Iron Jack Fuller would not send men to break his legs. Fuller was serious about gambling debts.

Bert's fingers fumbled at the type fonts. ". . . faithful husband and father," he set. "Mr. Chesterton will be sorely missed by his loving wife and his eleven children."

"They'll miss him, all right," Bert muttered. "Probably won't know he's gone till they have to go out and steal their own chickens."

He squinted at the pencil scrawls of Clarence Hanks's deathless prose, then paused to light a lamp, bringing it from the editor's desk. Hanks insisted the lamp be kept on his desk. It gave the impression he might work late sometimes.

Beyond the panes an evening glow settled over Jubilation and there were cattle in the street. Bert glanced at them, then looked again. He went to the window. Everywhere he could see, there were cattle—rangy, half-wild brush cattle and scrub longhorns. People ran here and there, trying to get out of their way. A bucking horse danced past, its stirrups flying, while its rider clung to the awning of a store up the street. A stray pig, no more than a shoat, wandered by.

Doors slammed, wagons rattled past, and there were shouts and screams up and down the street. Bert stared out the window and a placid brute ambling along the boardwalk paused to look in at him, then went on its way. The cattle seemed focused on Bunker's Mill across the street. Bert saw Puff McVey run to close the wagon gate there, then climb a rainspout as a one-horned cow flipped the gate open and went through, others following. Howard Sills's wagon still stood in the chute bay, but Crowbait looked back at the approaching cattle and trotted away, through the bay and into the alley beyond. The cattle followed. It was hard to tell in the fading light, but Howard's wagon seemed empty now.

"Never saw the like," Bert muttered. He returned to his work. Completing the obituaries, he began setting the final page of written copy. It was a muddy little account about Cole Yeager. The outlaw, it seemed, had been seen in the vicinity of Medicine Lodge a week or so ago. "Wouldn't that be somethin'," Bert told himself. "Imagine if Cole Yeager was to come to Jubilation. That sure might liven this place up a little. It could use it."

Completing the galley, he transferred type to the page form and laid in furniture to tighten it. He set a border around the advertisement below—an impassioned plea by the Wednesday Ladies' Reading Circle for a return to law and order and an end to the "rule of John Barleycorn in our fair city."

Before clamping the page he scanned it, reading the typeface upside-down. He arched an eyebrow and a smile tugged at his cheeks as he silently counted lines high in the second column and at a place lower down in the fourth.

"Ah," he said. Easing the lockups he lifted sections of type from the two columns—an equal number of lines from each—and reversed their positions. With a smile of satisfaction then he completed the lockup and slid the page into place for tomorrow's printing.

Among its items of interest, this week's edition now would advise its readers that the culls from Joe

Hargis's cattle auction would "lie in state Monday at Moore's Funeral Parlor" prior to their burial at Blessed Peace Cemetery and, in another column, that the remains of the beloved Mr. Chesterton would be sold by the pound at the cutters and packers auction at Sterling.

"That ought to give the little wart something to think about," Bert assured himself. He tugged on his tattered coat, slapped a shapeless hat on his head, blew out the lamp, and locked the door behind him. Down the street shouting riders were trying to get ropes on a steer that was ducking and bolting in the street outside City Hall. Across the way two others had laid siege to the door of Stapleton's Market. Beyond, a few more cattle were making their way along a line of backyards. One had a clothesline full of wash dragging from its horns. But most of the cattle were gone.

From atop the bluff drifted evening sounds of roistering hitting its stride. Laughter, piano music, breaking glass, and the rise and fall of hundreds of voices, punctuated by an occasional gunshot, indicated the evening was well under way on the high side of town. Dimly, he heard what seemed to be a spring wagon making its way up the bluff trail, and he thought it might be Howard Sills. But then he saw Howard Sills across the street, wandering through the chute bay at Bunker's Mill, deep in thought.

Counting the coins in his pocket, Bert Thompson turned left and headed for the footpath that led up the bluff toward uptown Jubilation.

By dimming light Howard Sills explored the alley

behind the mill and the streets beyond in both directions, then returned to the mill, pausing now and then to scrape cow droppings from his boots.

In the mill, lamps were lit, an old mule trudged at its turnbar, and a bleary-eyed Puff McVey was just completing a run. But the place this time did not have the fresh scent of ground grist normal to its dim interior. The smell now was a pervading sweet-sour vegetable odor, and a huge vat below the grindstones was filled to overflowing with whitish mush.

"Will you look at this!" McVey complained. "Look at this mess! Bunker'll have my hide if I don't get them stones scoured by mornin'. What was them things anyway?"

"Are you talking to me?" Howard asked, peering around the dim interior, hoping against all reason that maybe he might find his horse and wagon there. "I don't suppose you've seen my rig, have you? I thought I left it right outside there."

"If that was yours, then so is this," McVey blustered. He pointed at the vat of mush and Howard walked over to look at it.

"What is it?"

"It's whatever that was in your wagon . . . ground up. Lord, just look at this mess. Don't you know this mill is for grain? Not squash and cucumbers an' like that!"

"Is that my turnips?" Howard was stunned. "Why did you grind my turnips?"

"Why did I . . . look, when a wagon pulls in to that bay out there an' a man rings that bell, I come an' load the chute, then I run the mill. That's what Bunker pays me to do. If you didn't want this mess ground, what was you doin' there? You have to pay

73

for this, you know. Not just th' run, but there'll be a scourin' charge too, like as not. You'll have to talk to Bunker about that. What are you goin' to do with that slop?"

"Well." Howard scratched his head. "I really don't know. I hadn't though about grinding those turnips. I sort of figured I might sell them whole."

"To who?" McVey inquired.

"I don't know. Nat Kinley said he might find someone. Have you seen him?"

"He's yonder." McVey pointed toward the bluff. "Right where I'd be if I didn't have to scour these stones. Him and Twist McGuffin was buyin' rounds for the house when I come down to answer the bell. Hadn't been for that, I'd be right up there with 'em. But no. Now I got to clean up this mess. An' you got to decide what to do with that stuff. All we have is flour sacks, an' I don't think sacks will hold that mess. Be like tryin' to sack oatmeal mush."

Howard gazed at the vat, the befouled stones and dripping spout, the bleary man before him, and his shoulders sagged at the enormity of it all. "I guess this was pretty much my fault," he admitted. "I guess I better help you clean it up, but you'll have to show me what to do."

"Well, that's decent of you," McVey said, somewhat mollified. "Look, there's a stack of barrels out back. Bunker goes out an' gathers them up when the boys up there gets out of hand an' rolls 'em down the hill. Then he sells 'em back to the whiskey-runners. I guess we might pour off the vat into some of them for th' time bein'. All they've had in 'em is whiskey. I reckon they won't hurt your mush."

"I can't see how that would matter."

"Prob'ly not," McVey said. "Besides, it ain't pure

74

mush anyhow. There's tailin's from the last corn grind in the bottom of that vat. I didn't think to scrape it out. Hell, I didn't know when I started grindin' that I was goin' to get anything like that."

"Let's get started," Howard said. "I still have to find my horse and wagon."

"I'll help," McVey said. "It's my recommendation that we begin our search up there on the bluff. I'll stand the first round."

VII

Patman's was crowded to the walls. It looked as though every puncher in the Outlet had got loose and come to Kansas, and they were all packed into Patman's Pleasure Palace. The place next door, Grange Recreation Center, was nearly as packed, with farmers from across the river. Bert Thompson shrugged and crossed the street. A high-smelling honey wagon stood a few doors away, but Richardson's Refreshment Emporium was upwind of it and Bert went in. Richardson's was a little genteel for his taste, but he was tired and a drink is a drink.

Most of those inside were townspeople. Bert had noted before that the higher-class inebriates of Jubilation tended to all flock to the same few places, preferring the company of their peers to the constant mass of tourists that was uptown's major clientele. The gentry of Jubilation sometimes were choosy about their visiting riffraff.

Several disapproving glares were directed at Bert when he entered. Richardson's tended to be the turf of bankers, politicians, and leading businessmen, a crowd Bert avoided as a matter of course. He knew from long experience that association with the peerage — in any town — led to nothing but trouble. The feeling, as far as he could tell, was mutual. Clarence Hanks tolerated him because he could set type. But in most circles Bert was considered an important bad example. "If you don't behave yourselves," mothers would tell their children, "you'll grow up to be like Bert Thompson."

He found no fault with that. He had no wish to see any of Jubilation's younger generation follow in his footsteps. If anyone ever did that, he hoped it would be a better class of people.

This evening, though, he was tired and surly and didn't care who glared. He found a secluded corner and sat, and Jiggs came with the bottle.

Scattered about the large room among the revelers were two poker games in progress, four or five conversation groups that might progress to the point of brawls as the evening developed, and at least one table of serious discussion. The liquor was flowing freely at that table, only a few feet from Bert's corner, as its occupants discussed affairs of state.

"Somebody ought to ride out there an' shoot the scutter," Elmer Wallace pronounced sagely, refilling his glass from one of three fresh bottles on the table.

"What scutter is that?" Clarence Hanks asked vaguely. He sat with his back to Bert and had not seen him enter. For his part, Bert wished he had placed himself somewhere else. It was bad enough to listen to the little wart all day without hearing him in the evening as well. But Jiggs was there, filling a glass for him, taking his dime, and Bert was tired. He stayed.

"Whoever we was just talkin' about," Elmer Wallace explained. "Who was it?"

"It was Howard Sills," Nat Kinley reminded him. "I was pointin' out that he's got a corner on the

77

world's supply of turnips out there an' as I see it, it's up to us to advise him in the matter."

Prosper O'Neil and Ike Ferguson sat side by side facing Hanks and Twist McGuffin. Now O'Neil raised his head to survey Kinley with bleary eyes. "Why?"

"Why what?"

"Why do we want to talk about some come-lately's turnips? We don't even know him."

"We do too. He's been in these parts four years, for heaven's sake! You haven't been here much more than that, yourself, Prosper."

"Yeah, but I didn't come from back East an' go to growin' turnips. This is cattle land. Turnips eat all the grass, there'll be . . . no, that's sheep."

"But turnips is worse," he added.

Ferguson shook his head sadly and poured his friend another round.

"Imbibery progresseth," Bert Thompson muttered to himself.

"Don't talk sheep," Elmer Wallace rasped. "Can't tolerate talk about sheep. Let's go shoot the scutter."

Twist McGuffin grinned crookedly at Nat Kinley. "You don't seem to be gettin' very far with this."

"It's hard to keep a committee's attention," Nat agreed. He glanced around the packed room, then squinted and pushed back his hat. "Lookit there!"

Most of them turned to look. "Where?" a few asked.

"Right there, at the bar. Between Bubba and Hoss. It's that feller I was tellin' you about. Mr. Bloody Mare."

"Where?" Elmer Wallace peered. "All I see between Bubba an' Hoss is a box."

"You can't see him because he's between Bubba and Hoss," Nat explained. "But he's attached to that box. That's why it's hangin' there like that."

"He the one that cussed the ladies?"

"He's the one."

"Ought to step over there an' shake the scutter's hand," Wallace allowed. "Can't tolerate them ladies."

"Best mind your step," Clarence Hanks said. "I heard they got three hundred signatures on the We See To You petition. You can mark my words, they mean trouble this time."

"You might stop takin' their advertisements for your newspaper." Wallace hiccupped. "Ever think of that?"

"Not for a minute," Bert Thompson muttered, downing his second neat rye. Clarence Hanks glanced around, recognized his printer, and frowned. Bert grinned at him and signaled for Jiggs. Hanks turned away.

"A great newpsass . . . pardon . . . newspaper must be the clarion of the community!" Hanks said.

"It must be," Bert muttered. " 'Cause it sure isn't the Tribune of Jubilation."

The box at the bar moved and a small, bearded face peered out from between the broad backs of Bubba and Hoss. Bloody Mare caught sight of Nat and his beard split in a cheerful grin. "Nyetkin Lee!" he called. *"Kak dela!"*

Bubba and Hoss both turned and looked down, as though noticing the little man for the first time. "What did he say?" Hoss asked.

"Called Nat Kinley a cock dealer, I believe," Bubba said.

They both peered across the hazy saloon, squinting. "Can you tell whether Nat's wearin' his gun?" Hoss inquired.

"I believe he is," Bubba said.

79

With a nod both of the big men took their beers and moved to another part of the long bar, leaving Bloody Mare standing alone, still grinning happily.

The little man sipped at his beer, then noticed Bert sitting beyond the group at Kinley's table. *"Khorosho sevodnya,* Bert Tomsahn." He raised his mug. *"Ya pl'yu pivo!"*

Hanks swiveled around, squinting at his printer. "Do you know him?"

"I told him where to kopeet some peevah," Bert shrugged. "Looks like he found the place."

"Well, what's all that he's saying?"

"I don't know. I don't speak Russian."

"Spasibo!" Bloody Mare called.

"Pazhalusta," Bert said.

Hanks tried to focus bleary eyes on his printer. His gaze kept wandering off to one side or the other. He was well into his evening. "Wash shat . . . pardon . . . what was that you said?"

"It means 'you're welcome.' I guess. Heard it someplace."

"Somebody ought to invite that scutter over here an' buy him a real drink," Elmer Wallace said, chuckling as previous words began to soak in. "Never heard it put better in my life. 'Cock dealer!' Never could tolerate squatters that rented out bad bulls."

Kinley bristled. "I don't hold with that kind of talk, Elmer. Maybe we better step outside."

Twist McGuffin sighed and pushed Nat back down in his chair. "I thought you was tryin' to get a committee discussion started here," he said. He waved his arm and Bloody Mare grinned again and crossed to join them.

"Howdy do, there, Mr. Bloody Mare." Elmer Wallace stood to extend a hand across the table. "I'd admire to buy you a drink."

Bloody Mare took the hand and shook it briskly. "Horse piss on ya," he beamed.

Wallace's face turned bright red, and he withdrew so quickly his elbow collided with the back of Clarence Hanks's head, sending his derby flying.

"Here, now!" Hanks slurred. Without a glance back he got to his feet and went after his hat.

Bert shook his head. The little wart never could hold his liquor. He supposed somebody eventually would guide Hanks home and pour him into his bed. But he had no intention of doing so himself. Sudden commotion had erupted at the committee table. Elmer Wallace, unsteady on his feet, was blustering and trying to get his Colt out of his holster. Nat Kinley and Twist McGuffin were restraining him and everybody was yelling except Bloody Mare, who had backed off a few steps and was watching the scene in wide-eyed amazement.

"Unhand me!" Wallace roared. "I got to shoot the scutter!"

"Calm down, Elmer," Nat shouted at his ear. "He didn't mean that. He isn't normal."

Prosper O'Neil had sprawled back in his chair, laughing so hard he seemed to be strangling, and now the chair teetered uncertainly and then crashed backward. Jiggs, on his way to replenish Bert Thompson's rye, stepped over the gagging O'Neil with the patience of one who has tended saloon for many years.

The fracas at the rear table had diverted attention elsewhere in the saloon, as the first brawl of evening usually did. For a moment, the place was silent except for the whining of Clarence Hanks looking for his hat.

In the silence, distinctly, there was a sound of

cattle beyond the doors of Richardson's . . . the unmistakable lowing, clatter of horns, and thudding footfalls of a herd on the move. Men looked at the door, looked at one another, and the batwing doors slammed open. Leonard stood there, crouching as his bulk filled the doorway.

"Make way!" he bellowed. "Business of the Law! Stand aside!" He glared around him, satisfying himself that everyone in the place was appropriately standing aside. Then he wagged a large finger in front of his face. "The Law says no cows can go uptown! Somebody's breakin' the Law!"

Silence reigned throughout the place, men staring at one another, wondering what Leonard was talking about, and why there were cows passing by in the street beyond him. The sounds were unmistakable, the distinctive blend and chorus of a herd on the move.

Of all of them there, only Clarence Hanks was far enough gone not to be puzzled. He crawled out from under a table, brushing off his derby. "Enforcement of the law, by all means," he proclaimed. "Judicious enforcement of our municipupple . . . minicipipple . . . munu . . . city ordinances. Most important. Keep our fair city . . . ah . . . fair. Judicissious enforcement at all times. Maintain the highest moral standards. Pride in our comm . . . commu . . . town. Place where women can walk the street . . . sounds like cows out there. Boys are really gettin' out of hand tonight. Ah." He had managed to get to his feet and tapped the derby onto his head at a precarious angle. He turned. "Ah, Leonard. Come in, come in. Have a li'l drink."

"Cows are against the Law!" Leonard thundered. "Somebody's under arrest!"

Clarence Hanks wandered toward the blocked

door, still talking, pleased that he seemed to have the crowd's full attention. "Wholesome atmosphere for the nur . . . nurturing of our young. Wonderful town, this. Indeed. Fine new school, two churches . . ."

"And twenty-seven saloons," Bert Thompson muttered. He wondered whether Hanks was going to bump into Leonard. Having noticed him once, the editor and publisher seemed no longer aware of the deputy.

"Must go about my rounds," Hanks declared. "It seems to me I hear cattle. Salubrious climate. Sounds carry for miles."

There was a general movement then toward the windows, men crowding forward to see what was outside, and Leonard stepped in, shaking his finger at them. "Stand aside! Business of the Law!"

In the instant he moved, Clarence Hanks was past him and gone, into the darkness, weaving and blithering.

Bert Thompson shook his head and counted his coins. He extracted a dime from his diminishing supply and signaled for Jiggs. "One more," he told himself. "One for the bedbugs." It was obvious he would be working the press alone tomorrow. Clarence Hanks would be in no condition to help.

The sounds outside had grown in volume, added to by shouts and the commotion of men flooding into the dark street. Bert was curious, but he didn't want to spoil the final minutes of his relaxation. He sipped his rye. Someone would say what was going on outside. At the moment it was just a babble of voices, but he would hear the straight of it soon. He glanced up. Bloody Mare stood beside him, still holding a mug half-filled with *peevah*. The little man was looking toward the front of the saloon.

"Chto eto?" he asked, pointing.

"I sure don't know." Bert shrugged. "Sounds like cattle."

"Govyadena," Bloody Mare corrected him.

"If you say so." He raised his glass. "Here's to govadeenya, and the price of beef. Cheers."

"Za vashe-to zdorovya," Bloody Mare said, touching glasses.

The building seemed to rumble from the noise outside, which now sounded like a combination stampede and Louisiana wedding. Glass rattled behind the bar, and the saloon echoed to the thud of boots as men hurried outside to join the fun.

"If they're fightin' out there," Bert told Bloody Mare, "I hope they don't kill anybody important. The front page is already locked up."

Gradually the thunders diminished, though shouts and gunshots still rang out in the street. Voices now were distinguishable above the general uproar. "Where'd they go?" "Dunno, some of the boys followed 'em to the bend." "Whose were they?" "Too dark. Couldn't tell. Good herd, though." "What the hell were they doin' up here?" Then: "Man down! Man down! Somebody bring a lantern over here!"

Bert Thompson sighed, his chin dropping to his chest. "Oh, Lord. What do you bet it's somebody important."

"Make way!" Leonard was shouting in the darkness. "Make way for the Law!"

"You better go get the marshal," somebody else said. "I never saw nobody deader than that."

Reluctantly, Bert finished his drink and got to his feet. He shuffled toward the door on aching feet, Bloody Mare trailing along after him. Outside there were pools of jogging lantern light. The street was a mess, rutted and ripe with fresh manure, and directly beyond the door of the saloon was a bright red mess. The only thing immediately recognizable about Clarence Hanks was his derby hat. Men stood around in a growing circle, staring at the trampled body.

"Thing you'd better do," Elmer Wallace said at Bert's elbow, "is put something in the paper about this."

"I already locked up the forms," Bert sighed. "Now who's gonna pay me Friday?"

Marshal Ben Cutter had arrived, squatted briefly beside the remains, then had strolled through the crowd in time to hear the question.

"You better talk to Dub about that." He pointed toward the banker, W. D. Tienert, who stood nearby in lantern light looking very pale. "But I agree with Mr. Wallace. I think there ought to be something in the paper about this. You can say the matter is being investigated by Marshal Benjamin Cutter. Use Benjamin, not Ben. It sounds better. Say the marshal's department was on the scene within minutes and we can expect a breakthrough in the case very soon. You might want to mention that the cow herd that trampled the deceased was an illegal cow herd and was promptly removed from the top of Jubilation Bluff. By Marshal Benjamin Cutter, of course."

"You weren't even here!" Wallace protested.

Cutter ignored him. "You can say the citizens of Jubilation have nothing to concern themselves about. Local law enforcement continues . . . ah . . . strongly. With Marshal Benjamin Cutter in charge."

"S'pose it'd be all right if he was to mention the deceased in this article?" Nat Kinley suggested.

"Say something nice about the deceased," Cutter said.

"I can't think of anything nice to say about him,"

Bert muttered. "I knew he wasn't going to help me run the press."

A little way down the street Howard Sills approached the crowd. His boots squished occasionally in shadowy mounds, and his nostrils twitched at the warm, rich scent of fresh-passed cattle.

At the first group he came to, he paused to ask, "Has anyone here seen a horse pulling a spring wagon? I can't imagine where he's gotten off to."

He asked the same question several times before a frowning man carrying a lantern confronted him. "Is that your rig? Dapple horse and a green spring wagon?"

"Yes. Oh, good. I didn't know where he'd gone. Where is he?"

"Well." The man scowled. "Your horse is standing in the alley behind my saloon over there. Patman's. I'm Patman. Your wagon is inside. It's too wide to go out the back door."

Howard stared at him. "Then how did it get in?"

"Came in through the front," Patman said. "Tried to go out the back. If you'll come with me we'll talk about the damages."

Midnight had passed and uptown Jubilation had returned to normal by the time Howard Sills led Crowbait, unhitched, down the alley and around two corners, carefully avoiding a fistfight at the first corner and a free-for-all just past the second. The fistfight seemed to have been in progress for some time. The participants, a strapping young cowhand and a hard-fisted farmer, seemed to be moving in slow motion as they took turns knocking each other sprawling, back and forth across the street. As Howard passed, a waiter came from one of the saloons with a bottle and a pair of glasses and the combatants took time out for a few drinks before resuming hostilities. The brawl was of more recent origin, just spilling into the street through the open batwings of a place called the Loving Arms Saloon. It flowed into the street, a wave of combative humanity punching, grunting, cursing, and mauling one another at random, and Howard led Crowbait far around to avoid it. He was tired and ready to go home. The day had been long, frustrating, and costly.

His spring wagon waited in front of Patman's, and through the windows he could see people rearranging tables and chairs inside. He rehitched Crowbait, then walked around his wagon, trying to see the extent of its damages. He knew from his inspection indoors, by lamplight amid a chaos of scattered and broken furniture, that it was going to need repair.

Several people lay in the wagonbed, more than one of them snoring loudly. Howard scratched his head, wondering what to do with them. He looked them over, poking and prodding. They all seemed to be alive. One of them, near the bottom of the heap, was Nat Kinley. Two or three others were men he had seen now and then but did not know. Howard sighed, dropped the tailgate, and began unloading unconscious men. The boardwalk under Patman's window was commodious and he ranked them there, side by side, sound asleep. The task was made more difficult by the fact that two of them kept getting up and returning to his wagon. One of these he had to unload three times, and the other twice, before they stayed where he put them.

He was tempted to leave Kinley aboard, find his horse, and take him along as far as Bad Basin, which was on his way home to Lazy K. But he didn't know whether Nat wanted to go home, and Nat was in no condition to comment. He decided not to presume, and dragged his friend out of the wagon to lay him out on the boardwalk alongside the others.

The brawl was still going on down the street, and some other altercation had developed a block or so away in the other direction. Several gunshots rang out in the night, followed by shouts and laughter. Three staggering cowhands approached from up-street and paused to gape at the neat row of bodies Howard had arranged in front of Patman's. All three removed their hats. "May they rest in eternal peace," one said.

Downstreet a pair of riders eased skittish mounts past the general skirmish there and then came on. "I wouldn't want to be in your boots, Pistol Pete," one was saying to the other. "I've heard of trail bosses losin' their herds, like to Indians or stampede or hoof and mouth disease . . . but I never heard of anybody just *losin'* a herd. I mean, just plain *losin'* it."

"Goin' downtown?" someone asked.

Howard turned. A tall, seedy-looking man and a little bearded man with a box on his back stood by the wagon. After a moment, Howard recognized his winter passenger, Bert. The little one grinned and thrust out a hand. "Bloody Mare," he said.

"I'm going to Bunker's Mill," Howard said tiredly. "Get on if you want to."

He climbed aboard the wagon seat and took the reins. His two passengers got into the bed. Bert Thompson—sagging and more than a little bit drunk—sat with his legs dangling over the open tailgate. The little one squinted into the darkness, then crawled forward to peer under the seat. He reached into the space there and drew out a turnip. "Raw bear," he told Howard. *"Ya khochu!"*

"Bless you," Howard said. He flipped the reins. "Get up, Crowbait."

The horse ambled into the street and turned left at Howard's tug of the rein. The wagon shuddered, groaned, and collapsed as its right front wheel parted from its hub and rolled away into darkness.

VIII

Dawn's enthusiastic banners danced atop Jubilation Bluff to herald the waking of the sleepy town below. What with the slow creaking of Digger Moore's hearse along dark streets in the wee hours, the passage of mounted men up and down Commerce Avenue all night, the bellowing of Leonard on various trips back and forth, several incidents of gunfire uptown, and intermittent ringing of the town's fire bell by some of the boys from H-Four, it had not been a restful night.

Will Ambler arrived early at his livery stable to find a dapple horse grazing in his back pasture and a battered green spring wagon waiting in front of his smithy shed. Its right front corner was supported by a wheelbarrow lashed beneath it. A splinted wheel rested against its side and in its bed Howard Sills, Bert Thompson, and a small, bearded individual were sound asleep.

While Will was sorting out what it all meant, Puff McVey came along and paused to stare blearily into the wagon bed. "That there is Howard Sills," he told Ambler. "That one there. Him an' me spent half the night scourin' millstones. I see he found his wagon.

He's supposed to be over at the mill, pickin' up three barrels of squish."

"Not in this wagon, he isn't." Will knelt to inspect the sheared hub above the wheelbarrow. "Not for a while, anyhow. Three barrels of what?"

Puff walked around the wagon and reached in to shake Howard's shoulder. "Wake up," he said.

The motion was enough to rouse all three of them. Howard sat up, stretched, and rubbed his eyes. "Good morning," he said, then looked around, getting his bearings—the smithy shed rosy with morning sun, the sad slant of his wagon on three wheels and a wheelbarrow. His yawn became a sigh. Behind him the little man opened his eyes, blinked and sat up.

"Allo!" he said urgently. *"Gde tualet?"*

Puff tilted his head. "What?"

Bert Thompson rolled over, groaned, and squinted at the mill hand. "He wants to know where the privvy is," he explained. "He's full of peevah." With many a groan and mutter Bert dragged himself out of the wagon. He tried to straighten the kinks out of his frame and gave up. He hurt all over. Crooking a finger he said, "Come along, Bloody Mare. The twalyet's out back."

There were more people on the street now. Morris Stapleton walked past on his way to his market, and he and several others stopped to gaze curiously at the manner in which the wheelbarrow had been lashed under the wagon's axle.

Howard Sills stood in the street, stretching and yawning, rocking on his toes. "I'm sure today will be a better day than yesterday was," he assured himself. Smells of breakfast drifted from the Golden Rule Cafe up the street, and a lot of men were converging upon the place.

"Sure is Wednesday," Will Ambler noted.

Howard glanced at him. "What?"

"It's Wednesday. Man in Jubilation wants breakfast on a Wednesday he finds it on his own. The Wednesday Ladies' Reading Circle is too busy makin' the world a better place to live in to worry about feedin' their husbands."

Puff McVey was eying the mill next door, a worried frown on his face. "We ought to get them barrels of squish out of there before Bunker shows up," he said. "I doubt he's partial to the smell of turnips. How about if we roll them out to the shed? They can stay there till Will gets your wagon fixed."

A buggy full of stern-faced women passed, heading for the schoolhouse at the end of the street. Howard noticed that townsmen scattered like quail ahead of them.

"Damn biddies is out early," Puff McVey muttered.

As Bert Thompson reappeared at the front of the smithy a covey of ladies afoot went by, then stopped, glaring at him. He was dirty, unshaven, red-eyed, and smelled of whiskey. The lady in the lead swerved aside to confront him, followed by the others. Their slit-eyed, high-nosed regard of the man reminded Howard of the time his uncle, the Reverend Burgess Sills, had ordered what he thought was veal cutlets in a French restaurant and then found snails on his plate.

"*Mis*-ter Thompson." The leading lady tipped her head far back to stare down her nose at the grimy printer. "We have, of course, heard of the unfortunate demise of dear Mr. Hanks the past evening. The poor man obviously gave his all while observing the sinful conduct of those dreadful people atop the bluff."

"Matter of fact," Bert said evenly, "the little wart was drunk as a skunk."

"The dead do not require defamation," the woman snapped. She pulled a sheet of paper from her purse and thrust it at him. "Since the poor man had no kindred locally, several of us have taken it upon ourselves to write a fitting obituary. Please see to it that this is placed in this week's newspaper."

She turned away without further comment and the entire covey proceeded down the street toward the schoolhouse.

Bert unfolded the paper and read it, disbelief growing on his furrowed face. He shook his head, sighing. "I never read such out an' out trash in my whole life. Besides, I already locked up the forms."

Puff McVey's voice carried real concern. "I sure wouldn't want to have them biddies mad at me, Bert. You prob'ly better do what they say."

"I'll probably be movin' on soon anyway," Bert said. "No Hanks, no newspaper. No newspaper, no job. Maybe I'll head over to Arkansas." He thrust the paper into a pocket, then started off in the direction of the Golden Rule Cafe. A few steps away he stopped, turned, and tipped his head at Bloody Mare. "Well, don't just stand there. Come on if you want some breakfast." He rubbed his stomach and pointed at the restaurant. "Breakfast! Understand?"

Bloody Mare stood for a moment, puzzled, then he grinned. *"Ya khochu!"* he said, and ran to retrieve his box and bundle from Howard's wagon. Then he followed along after Bert.

"Bless you," Howard said.

"You know somethin'?" Puff confided to Howard. "I don't believe that little feller is normal."

"We better move those barrels, Mr. McVey."

The sun had fully topped Jubilation Bluff now,

and there were more people on the street — men in various degrees of civility and sobriety, wandering here and there as they began their day, women of various proportions and degrees of disapproval making their way toward the schoolhouse for the weekly meeting of the Wednesday Ladies' Reading Circle. Looking back over his shoulder at McVey, Howard Sills stepped up on the boardwalk and ran headlong into Penelope Becket, walking by with two other somewhat younger girls.

He hadn't seen her coming, hadn't seen her there, yet suddenly he found himself thoroughly entangled with someone soft and supple and smelling of soap and lilac water. Totally off-balance he flailed for equilibrium. His right arm went around her waist to keep her from falling and her left arm clung to his shoulder. His left hand and her right, waving for balance, caught and clasped, and he completed his step by pivoting half-around, swinging her with him.

"Merciful heavens!" she gasped, trying to pull away, again destroying their precarious balance. Clinging to each other they whirled, their feet a flurry of counteracting steps, as passersby gaped dumbfounded at the waltzing pair.

Puff McVey squinted at them as they passed. "Mr. Sills," he pleaded, "are you gonna move barrels or are you gonna dance?"

Howard almost had the situation under control when he glanced down and saw huge lavender eyes, wide with surprise and confusion, looking up at him. His recovered balance was destroyed. The pair tilted at a precarious angle, whirled abruptly, executed a fancy dip and dive, and spun away into the street in a choreographed confusion of flashing feet and flowing skirts and petticoats. They narrowly missed collision with a passing buggy. W. D.

94

Tiernert hauled at his reins as Mrs. Becket, beside him, stood full upright, gaping. "Penelope? Penelope! What in the world are—" The horse snorted and lunged and Mrs. Becket thumped into her seat, clinging to her hat.

In mid-street Howard managed to control his spinning and regain his balance. For a moment they stood, clinging and breathless. Then he released her and took a step back. His face was as red as hers was white.

"My goodness," she gasped, staring at him.

"I . . ." he tried, and backed off another step, then another. "My . . ." He wrung his hands, back-pedaling. "We . . . oh, Lord." He turned, tripped, and sprawled full length in a watering trough. Cascading water drenched a dozen onlookers. Penelope stared, speechless, then picked up her skirts and ran.

By the time her friends caught her, a block away, she had recovered only a little of her composure. The converged on her, wide-eyed, then turned to look back at the crowd where Howard was being helped out of the trough.

Sally Spalding's dark eyes glowed with wonder. "That was Howard Sills," she declared.

"Yes, I know," Penelope whispered, still shaken. "I don't think I've ever met a stranger man in my whole life."

"He's so handsome," Betty Stapleton gushed. "Oh, my!" She turned to Penelope. "What were you and he doing just then?"

"I think he likes you," Sally said.

Betty clasped her hands with excitement. "Is he always so abrupt? Goodness, Penelope, I didn't even know you knew him. Does he come to call?"

Penelope stared at the younger girls.

"Howard Sills," Sally repeated, awestruck. "Just

imagine. Why, Penelope, he's adorable."

Penelope shook her head. "He isn't either! He's—"

"And such a wonderful dancer," Betty noted. "Of course, Momma says he's from back East someplace and he's probably been to all the best schools and everything. Momma says he's a younger son."

"A what?"

"Younger son. Like in fortunes and inheritances. You know."

"Tall and handsome and rich," Sally breathed. "Penelope, you are the sly one."

"I don't even know him!"

"Oh, you do so. I know he does business at your uncle's bank—"

"So does everybody! I don't mean I haven't met him. I just mean I don't . . . well . . . know him. I just see him sometimes."

"You *see* him?" Sally whispered.

"No! I don't . . . anyway, all I've ever seen him do is bump into things and trip over things. All a person has to do is look at him and he sort of . . . well . . . goes berserk and does the strangest things."

"You call that strange? Sweeping you off your feet like that and waltzing you across the street? Why, Penelope Becket, I believe that's the most romantic thing I ever saw. Oh, my." She sighed. "I only wish he'd do that to me."

"Maybe he'll come to your window and serenade you." Betty giggled. "Momma says he is quite musical. And I'll bet he is ever so lonely, living all by himself like he does, way out in Bad Basin. Momma says Mrs. Finch told her that some of the men have heard the saddest music coming from there sometimes at night. She says it just kind of floats on the night wind and makes all the coyotes howl for miles around. Oh."

Sally stamped her foot. "Oh, Betty, stop sniveling. After all, Mr. Sills is Penelope's beau, not yours."

"He is not!" Penelope exploded.

"I know what I saw," Sally said, smugly. "My, I wish somebody would court me that way."

It was a thoroughly embarrassed Howard Sills who made his way across the street to Ambler's livery and hid in the shadows there until the crowd had dispersed. He helped Puff McVey move his three barrels of turnip slush out of the mill and into a leaning shed behind. Even with the lids on, the barrels were beginning to reek.

"Stuff'll mortify pretty fast with them grain tailin's mixed in there," McVey confided. "Whatever you plan to do with that mess, you better do it soon."

Later Howard borrowed a creaky old saddle from Will Ambler, cinched it onto the surprised Crowbait, and headed for home, keeping to the back ways until he was well past town. He was wet and embarrassed and ashamed of himself.

He was halfway across the Higgins-Wentworth Trail when Nat Kinley caught up with him.

"Where's your wagon, Howard?" Kinley asked, reining alongside.

"I lost a wheel. The smith is fixing it."

"You're a little wet," Kinley noted. "Everything all right?"

"Fine," he said. "Just fine."

"Well, you're all that is, then. I just heard, Justin Case in on his way from Pleasant Valley with a sheriff's escort and a court order. He aims to shut down uptown Jubilation."

"I thought you said the county couldn't do that."

"Well, they can't. Not permanently. But they can order the town council to vote on a temperance ordinance and allow a week for petitions and public testimony. In the meantime there's an injunction."

"Oh." Howard had never been a participant in Jubilation's favorite sport, but Nat was his friend and he shared his concerns. "Well, you said they'd done all that before. You said all it meant was a dry week and then things got back to normal."

"Yeah, well maybe not this time. Them women have got things so stirred up with their We See To You movement that some of the boys figure Marshal Gault will close the strip to liquor wagons. Then there'll be real trouble, without any source of supply."

"I see. Well, I suppose a lot of the saloons would have to close down," Howard said.

Nat gritted his teeth. "God help us all," he said. "There isn't another waterin' hole in three hundred miles. What kind of life are they tryin' to make us live anyway? It's like dessicatin' a shrine."

"Desecrating," Howard said absently.

"That too," Nat agreed fervently. "That too."

For the price of breakfast, Bloody Mare was delighted to crank the press. He was, in fact, thoroughly capable, having printed many a revolutionary broadside in Russia in the good old days.

"Gazechik," he told Bert Thompson, tapping himself proudly with his thumb. *"Khorosho gazechik."* Then he slid the first form expertly onto the plate, applied ink, and began printing the back flat.

"Well, I'll be damned," Bert allowed.

Feeling somewhat better about the world, he

fished out the testimonial written by the Reading Circle ladies, steeled himself against the tidal wash of unrestrained superlatives lavished on the late, lamented Clarence Hanks, and began setting type. He was a little queasy when he finished. Easing the page one form, he scrapped enough of the first two columns to make room for the piece of prose. He set the galleys in place, stood frowning for a moment, then adjusted it downward far enough to place an advertisement at each end, selecting them from page two and filling the spaces with lineage scrapped from page one.

He bordered the obituary in eight-point bold black. In the finished form it stood alone, dominating two columns, with an honor guard of bold-type advertisements. The one above was a plea from the local Chautauqua Society with the sober injunction "Let Ignorance Be Trampled unto the Soil." The ad below was a medicine tout featuring wart removal.

IX

On Friday morning Bert Thompson washed his hands, put on a clean shirt, and went to the Jubilation Bank and Trust Company, where he marched straight through to the partitioned cubbyhole of W.D. Tienert, President.

"Marshal Cutter said to bring these over here, so here they are." He deposited three small ledgers on the banker's desk. "This one shows who owes what for advertising and subscriptions, and how Hanks was doin' the collections. This next one has order schedules for newsprint, ink, and spare parts . . . things like that . . . and the second part of it has payrolls. The other one is income and expense tallies by the month. Pay me."

"Do what?" Tienert adjusted his glasses and looked over them at the printer.

"Pay me. Cutter says you're the trustee for the Hanks estate. You'll see right there how much the Tribune owes me for the past week. I added a day's press wages for that Russian because he helped get it out. Today is payday. Pay me."

"Ah." Tienert nodded. "Very well. I will give you a voucher to Mr. Green for a draft on the Tribune account. He will pay you." Tienert leaned back in his chair and smiled. "Please sit down, Mr. Thompson. Ah, do you mind if I call you Bert?"

"All right with me." Bert shrugged and sat on the edge of a facing chair. "You never called me anything before. I'm . . . I was . . . just Hanks's printer."

"Sadly enough, circumstances change." Tienert steepled his fingers and smiled his best smile. "I've been meaning to talk with you, Bert. Ah, do you suppose you could manage the newspaper for a time? I mean, just until poor Clarence's estate is settled and someone comes to take it over?"

"No."

"It is important, after all, that the newspaper continue to publish. A periodical that does not publish loses its value as a . . . what did you say?"

"I said no. I don't know anything about writin' a newspaper. I set type and crank the press. That's all. When can I get paid?"

"Momentarily, Bert," Tienert said. "Momentarily. But you see, there isn't anyone else around here who knows how to run a newspaper."

"Includin' me." Bert shook his head. "I don't even know much about the part of it I do. Clarence just hired me because I work cheap. I sure don't know anything about writin' articles."

The banker fluttered a hand, dismissing the disclaimer. "Neither, frankly, did Clarence. But readership in Jubilation has never been very demanding—"

"I'm leaving anyway," Bert said.

"—so it isn't that much of a task. . . . What do you mean, 'leaving'?"

"Leaving," Bert repeated. "As in going away. I've been here long enough. The bedbugs chewin' on me every night learned about me from their grand-

101

daddys. An' it's come to where a man can't even get a decent drink—"

"That's only for a week. I'm sure our . . . ah . . . refreshment stands will be back in business very shortly. Besides, there are reasonable stockpiles available. If I can be of assistance—"

"Couple of bottles of good rye," Bert said. "Take it out of what you owe me. I better go now."

"Please sit down, Bert." Tienert fixed him with honest, concerned banker's eyes. "Very well, I'll come right to the point. My bank's fee as executor depends upon the value of the estate handled, as of the point of inheritance. You know as well as I do that the fixed assets of the Tribune—I mean the shop, the equipment, tools, and inventory—aren't worth a tenth of the paper's value as a going business. Receivables, Bert. That's what business is all about. Receivables. It may be a matter of weeks until the estate can be transferred. In the meantime, the Tribune must continue to publish newspapers. What would you say to an additional ten dollars?"

"Money talks," Bert said. "No question about that."

"Does it talk loud enough to persuade you to take care of the paper for . . . say . . . three or four weeks if necessary? You wouldn't have to do it all, of course. You'd have the Sims boys to help."

"They aren't much help," Bert pointed out. "Now maybe if Mr. Bloody Mare was to stay around . . . but then I don't know what his plans are and there's no way to find out unless you know somebody that talks Russian."

"Bloody Mare? Oh, the little man with the box? What does he keep in that box he carries around, anyway?"

"I haven't got the slightest idea. But he knows

how to set up forms and crank the press."

"Maybe you could discuss it with him. And I have an idea. I think I might be able to find someone who could take advertising and write articles for you."

"That would help."

"My sister, Mrs. Becket, has been anxious to find some constructive endeavor that my niece Penelope might undertake—something suitably genteel for a young lady—and writing articles for the Tribune might be just the ticket."

Bert shifted uncomfortably. "No offense, but your sister, Mrs. Becket—well, I don't think she has a very high opinion of me. Right along with all the other ladies downtown, I might add."

"As it happens," Tienert said, pulling an earlobe and gazing blandly at Bert, "my sister, Mrs. Becket, is leaving on tomorrow's stage from Pleasant Valley. She is going East for a visit, and shall be gone for a time. So that might not be a problem."

"No, but there's another one. No offense again, but that niece of yours—well, she's of an age, you know. And she does cut quite a figure. I mean, I've seen fights break out around here just from her walkin' down the street. What I mean is, if she was mine I'd be slappin' her into a chastity belt before some hard-britches young yayhoo gets her sap to flowin' an'—"

"Mr. Thompson!" Tienert slapped a plump hand on the desk top. "That is quite enough of that kind of talk!"

"Sorry." Bert subsided. "But what I mean is, I've knocked around enough years to learn how to stay out of trouble most of the time, Mr. Tienert. I go my own way and I don't associate with the gentry. And I don't write articles for newspapers. And most of all I don't babysit for hot little honeycakes that throw every young stud in the county into rut every time they blink their eyes. Maybe we better just forget all this. Pay me."

For a long moment Tienert stared at the scruffy, stained man. Then his kindly banker's eyes took on a hard glitter. "Bert, there's something I keep meaning to ask you. It's about your name. I mean, well, it's a name I've heard before. It seems like there was a Bert Thompson at—"

Bert clenched his teeth in aggravation. "That wasn't me. Some other Bert Thompson. Anyhow, he died. Got caught up in a baling machine or something. That was years ago."

"Names are funny things, aren't they?" Tienert smiled. "Very curious."

Bert glared. "You said ten dollars?"

"Five," Teinert suggested.

"Ten."

"Oh, all right. Agreed. Mr. Green will pay you. And, Bert, I expect you to do your best to keep the Tribune operating profitably for a time. Oh, by the way." Tienert opened a drawer and took out a stack of paper. The handwriting was that of Clarence Hanks. "You have been making sense out of Clarence's penmanship for a while." He thumbed through pages and pulled one out. "I can't make head nor tail of some of this. What is this name here?"

Bert glanced at the sheet. "What is this, a will?"

"It's a will, and it's private," Tienert said firmly. "Just tell me what that name is."

Bert squinted at it. "Looks like Cornelius. Is that one of his brothers?"

"Apparently so. I thought maybe you'd know. Did Clarence ever mention having brothers? Did he talk about a Curtis? Or a . . . ah . . . Crispin? I think that's what this says. Or — ?"

"That isn't Crispin," Bert told him. The scribbling was familiar, even upside down. "That's Crispus. And that next name looks like Conrad. But no, if he ever mentioned brothers I wasn't listenin'. I never paid much attention to the little wart. Which one of them inherits the paper?"

"I said it's private. Quit reading it." Tienert covered the pages with his hands.

"Sure didn't think much of them, did he? '. . . sorriest set of unsatisfactory siblings. . .' Sounds just like him, though. Which one gets the paper? Cornelius?"

"If you're already read it, why are you asking me?"

"Politeness," Bert shrugged. "When's he going to get here?"

"I have no idea. I'm just writing to him."

"It'll take at least a week for a letter to get to Illinois," Bert pointed out. "Why don't you send a telegram?"

"What difference does it make to you?"

"Cut a week or so off the time I have to babysit Miss Penelope," Bert explained. "Besides, when your sister, Mrs. Becket, gets back you don't want to have to explain why you turned her dumplin' over to me, do you? You see if you can't get Cornelius Hanks out here the quickest way possible."

On the street again, Bert tipped his battered hat to a covey of ladies doing their Friday marketing. He was rewarded with glares of scalding disdain as they trooped past, noses high.

"And a nice day to you too," Bert muttered.

Spotting Bloody Mare and Puff McVey over by the mill, he headed that way.

McVey was red-faced and sullen, his fists coiling and uncoiling spasmodically as he glared at the Russian, who was talking, gesturing, and waving excitedly. As Bert approached he wrinkled his nose. Something smelled awful.

Bloody Mare saw him coming. "Bert Tomsahn!" he called and waved. *"Dobroye utro!"* Then he lapsed into an excited string of fast Russian.

McVey turned, scowling furiously. "Thompson, if you can make sense to this here popinjay, you better tell him to shut up, else I'll have to beat hell out of him."

"Why?" Bert came up to them, looking around, trying to find the source of the ungodly smell that hung in the air here. It smelled like a blend of horseradish and dead mice. "What's he done?"

"He's been jumpin' around and cussin' at me. He keeps callin' me things, an' I've had about all of it I can stand. I'm gonna have to beat hell out of him."

"Just cool down," Bert told him. "He isn't cussing you. He's talking Russian."

"I know what I heard," McVey insisted. "I don't stand for anybody talkin' to me that way."

Bert pulled money from his pocket and counted out Bloody Mare's press wages.

"I ain't no robber," McVey said. "And my name ain't Pete and I ain't got toad dimples!"

Bert handed Bloody Mare his money. "For you," he said. "Rubles . . . gazyet-chick rubles."

"Sparse eva," Bloody Mare said. He pointed at three leaking barrels standing in front of the mill shed. "Raw bear. Vermin! Vermin itch!"

"There he goes again," McVey said.

"Bomba!" Bloody Mare shouted, spreading his arms and stepping back. As though to emphasize his point, one of the barrels oozed and rumbled.

"I'm gonna beat hell out of him," McVey rasped.

"What's in those barrels?" Bert asked him.

"Turnip squish. It belongs to Howard Sills an' I wish to hell he'd come and get it. It's stinkin' up this whole end of town."

"Well, what's Bloody Mare so excited about?"

"I don't know. He just keeps cussin' at me and he thinks there's a critter in there. I've had about all I can stand."

"He thinks there's what?"

"A critter," McVey said. "A hot critter."

Bloody Mare nodded enthusiastically. *"Otkryto!"* He looked at McVey and spoke slowly, his eyes imploring. "Raw bear! Vermin itch! Aht kreetah! Horse piss on ya!"

McVey's face went from red to white and he lurched forward. "Beat, hell! I'm gonna kill him!"

Bert stepped between them, holding McVey back. "Hold on! I think there's a misunder—"

The smallest of the three barrels hiccupped and bulged visibly. With a hard crack like a gunshot its seal rings parted and its lid shot high into the air. Thick, reeking sludge rose like a living thing above the barrel, then flowed turgidly down its side. The smell that came from it was almost overpowering.

"Jesus in Heaven!" McVey gasped.

"It's fermenting," Bert pointed out.

"Da. Vermin itch." Bloody Mare sighed. He said something that, except for the words, might have been "I told you so."

Will Ambler stuck his head out of his shop next door. "McVey, for heaven's sake! Will you get that mess away from here?"

As if on cue, the plug of a larger barrel shot skyward, followed by a highspeed stream of stinking

107

sludge.

"Got a real head on it," Bert allowed.

The third barrel belched and Bloody Mare ran into Ambler's smithy and came out with a hammer. He edged up to the third barrel, took a deep breath, swung the hammer against the plug in its bung hole, and scurried back as a column of gray morbidity streamed upward.

"Look at this mess!" McVey mourned. "Just look! And the smell . . . what's Bunker gonna say?"

"Turnip wine," Bert mused. "Of all things."

"Fermented squish. My God."

"Vermin itch squish," Bloody Mare agreed, his nostrils flaring as he savored the fragrance of it. *"Khorosho* squish." He returned Will Ambler's hammer and came back with a metal rod, which he thrust judiciously into the small, lidless barrel. The sludge bubbled and reeked contentedly. Bloody Mare stirred the mess a few times, then withdrew his rod and looked at it critically. He smelled it, looked at it again, then tasted it. His face lit up and he beamed at the other two men. "Tam vine squish," he said. *"Ya khochu!"*

"Bless you," McVey said.

Bloody Mare tasted the sludge again, savoring it. He licked his lips. *"Nuzho sakhara."*

McVey's brow wrinkled. "What's he saying?"

"He likes it. But it needs sugar."

Bloody Mare dug in a pocket and retrieved some of the money Bert had brought him. He handed it to McVey. *Ya kopit* squish," he said. *"Spasibo."*

McVey stared at him. "What?"

"He bought it," Bert explained. "The squish."

"I can't sell that. It belongs to Howard Sills."

"Sell it," Bert urged him. "How else you gonna get rid of it?"

McVey considered that, then nodded. "Done."

"*Spasibo*," Bloody Mare said.

McVey seemed to have forgotten about beating hell out of Bloody Mare, so Bert took the Russian aside and waded through several minutes' worth of noncommunication. Finally, though, he was assured that Bloody Mare understood that Bert wanted him to continue gazyet-chick-ing for the Tribune, and that he would be paid press wages and could sleep in the storeroom behind the shop. At least, the little man seemed to have the general idea, and to agree.

With that settled, Bert sighed, scowled, and set out for the footpath that led to uptown Jubilation. It was Friday, and Iron Jack Fuller would be waiting for his installment. Bert was aware, as were a great many people connected with the high side of town, that it was not a good idea it keep Iron Jack Fuller waiting.

Climbing the path, he turned to look back. Downtown lay below him, bustling with activity. Friday was market day, and the day was in full swing. Distantly he saw Puff McVey still standing by the mill, and Bloody Mare coming out of Ambler's with a wheelbarrow. It was the same one they had borrowed three nights before to serve as a crutch for Howard Sills's wagon.

Unlike downtown on this day, uptown Jubilation was a subdued, sad place. The injunction had gone into effect and court deputies were stationed on the streets to enforce it. It was going to be a long, dry week.

Most of the saloons were closed, but the doors were open at Patman's and Iron Jack was at his usual Friday morning stand, a table in shadows near the back. Bert paused at the bar, savoring the aroma of stale beer, but the barman shook his head and pointed at the sign pasted to the mirror. "Court Injunction. Closed until Further Notice." Bert settled for a late breakfast of pickled pigs' knuckles, hardboiled eggs, and okra. In the shadows Iron Jack sat alone at his table, fiddling with a deck of cards. One by one, men came in, walked back to that table, left money there, and departed. Bert shook his head. How many were there? It seemed like half the men in town owed Iron Jack Fuller something.

Iron Jack Fuller had a large face. Thick black hair with just a touch of gray capped a head with outset ears, bulging brows, a long, heavy nose, broad cheekbones, a cruel, fleshy mouth, and a wide, square chin. His elbows on the table, the man's large frame towered above it, dominating it. Wide shoulders and a thick chest, always dressed in the finest of clothing, seemed to radiate power. Sitting, he gave the impression of a very tall man — unless one happened to look beneath the table where short, burly legs thrust outward from the chair seat. Iron Jack rarely stood when anyone was watching, because standing he was no taller than when he sat. His proportions, Bert thought, might have seemed ludicrous. But nobody laughed. People who would laugh at Iron Jack Fuller stood the chance of being hurt. Badly hurt.

Finished with his breakfast, Bert walked back to the table. He sighed, his shoulders stooped, and he asked, "How much do I owe you now?"

Iron Jack did not look up from his cards. They whirred, fanned, spread, and slipped back into a neat deck. "Fifteen dollars, Bert." The voice was a rumble, like gravel falling into a hole.

"And after I pay you five today, how much will I owe you next week?"

"Fourteen dollars, Bert."

Bert sighed. "Takes a long time to pay off a debt with that kind of interest."

"Credit is credit, Bert. You agreed to the arrangement."

"Sure I did. I was drunk on rotgut whiskey. Just out of curiosity, how about if I was to pay off the whole debt . . . all fifteen dollars at one time?"

Iron Jack glanced up at him. "That would come to seventy-five dollars."

"Seventy-five? To pay off fifteen?"

"That includes the interest, Bert. I don't waive interest. Bad for business."

Bert placed five dollars on the table and Iron Jack's hand swallowed it up. "Thank you, Bert." Then he looked up, little eyes dark between prominent lashes. "I take it you're staying on to run the paper, Bert."

"Yeah, just till the new owner shows up. Don't worry. I won't leave town without paying you off."

"I hope you wouldn't even consider that, Bert. The boys wouldn't take kindly to that. Not at all. Would you, boys?"

In the shadows someone moved and Bert looked around. Packer and Hemp, two of Iron Jack's hired toughs, stood there only a few steps from him. Packer grinned and cracked his knuckles. Hemp looked doleful. "We sure wouldn't want that to happen, Boss. No, sir."

"However," Iron Jack suggested, "I expect your income has improved of late. Now, if you'd care for another game one of these evenings . . ."

"Once is enough," Bert assured him.

"In that case, Bert, goodbye."

Walking out of Patman's, Bert felt crawly. "Play poker with a sneak," he told himself, "like playin' footsie with a snake. Man can sure get bit." Again he paused by the bar, gazing solemnly at the sign on the mirror. The barman leaned on crossed arms and grinned at him.

"When's the last time you was sober this long, Bert?"

Bert frowned, then reached out a stained hand and cupped the man's jaw and jowls in hard fingers. "Alas! Poor Yorick! I knew him, Horatio: a fellow of infinite jest, of most excellent—"

The barman's eyes went wide and he backed away, wrenching his face from Bert's hand. "Here, now! You cut that out!"

"Where be your gibes now?" Bert extolled. "Not one now, to mock your own grinning? Quite chapfallen? Now get thee to my lady's chamber—"

Hard hands landed on his shoulders, propelling him forward. "Get out of here, Bert," Packer said as he lurched through the door. "You make too much noise."

Bert caught his balance, winked at Flossie Mulligan, one of Patman's girls, and headed down the street thinking of the two bottles of rye Tienert had promised him. He also thought about his deal with Bloody Mare. Clarence Hanks had never let Bert sleep in the back of the shop, so Bert was paying rent for a shack. But Hanks was gone. If he could let Bloody Mare sleep in the shop, he could give himself the same privilege. Tienert hadn't said *how* to manage the newspaper. He could save himself a dollar a week by moving out of the shack.

He wondered how Iron Jack had known so soon that he was staying on. He wondered how soon he could accumulate enough to pay off Iron Jack. He wondered how much Tienert was going to charge him for those two bottles of rye.

Halfway down, the path was blocked by the great

bulk of Leonard, standing off a half-dozen cowboys from the H-Four.

"Uptown is closed!" Leonard roared. "No drinkin' uptown! It's the Law!"

"Won't hurt if we just go look, will it?" one of them argued.

"It's the Law!" Leonard thundered. "Go away!"

Two more cowboys approached from downtown. One of them carried a spade. "Found this," he told the others. "Will it do?"

"The very thing," another said. He took the spade and handed it to Leonard. "Here. Hold this."

Leonard held the spade, glaring at them. They stood back and looked at him. Moments passed. Then one of the waddies stepped forward. "How come you're just standin' here like this, Leonard? Don't you have a hole to dig?"

"What hole?" Leonard roared. "Stand back in the Name of the Law!"

"Well, what are you doing with that spade, then?"

Leonard looked curiously at the spade. In his hand it seemed no more than an oversized spoon. "This is a spade!" he shouted.

"Yes, and you ought to be using it," the cowboy explained.

"For what?" Leonard puzzled.

"For digging that hole, I suppose." He pointed. "You see off there, where the bluff breaks away? There ought to be a hole there, and there isn't one."

"There ought to be a hole there!" Leonard announced. "It's the Law!" With vast determination Leonard set off across the slope, carrying his spade, his roar diminishing as he went. "Stand aside! Stand aside for the Hole!"

The cowboys watched him go, admiration touching them.

"Wisht I had him full time," one of them said. "I'd quit punchin' cows for Higgins, and I'd get me a medicine show wagon an' go from town to town showin' him off. 'World's dumbest living thing.' Might even get on th' Chautauqua circuit."

They started up the hill, howdying Bert as they came abreast.

"Leonard was right," he told them. "Uptown's shut down tight. Nothing up there but court deputies and pickled pigs' knuckles. Might last a week, they say."

"I just don't see how they could do such a thing," one of them said. "It's like evacuatin' a shrine."

Downtown, Bert turned toward the Tribune office. In the distance he saw W. D. Tienert coming out of the bank with Miss Penelope. Tienert was talking to her, pointing toward the newspaper plant. Bert frowned, wondering what the coming weeks would bring. Among the immediate futures he could imagine, none offered serenity.

He reached the Tribune and hurried inside, then stopped, wrinkling his nose.

"Oh, Lord," he breathed. He almost ran to the storeroom door and threw it open.

The air beyond was hot and heavy with a cloying stench. Fire blazed in the belly of the iron stove, and a samovar sat atop it, beginning to steam. Bloody Mare stood on his box, happily stirring sludge in a half-circle of open barrels.

"*Dobri'y den'*, Bert Tomsahn," the little man grinned. "Vermin itch squish. Raw bear squish. *Ya delayu vodku. Sevodnya* raw bear, *zavtra vodka! Khorosho!*"

Behind him, in the front shop, Bert heard the

door open and a female voice. "Mr. Thompson? I . . ." A pause, then, "Mr. Thompson, what is that awful smell?"

He turned. Penelope Becket had entered, trailed by Emma Spalding.

Emma nodded at him. "Good morning, Mr. Thompson. Since Penelope is to be working here, I thought I'd come and help her get — heavens! That smell is awful! What is it?"

They crowded past him, peering into the reeking store room.

"Ladies," Bert stammered. "this is Blood . . . ah . . . Vladimir. He'll run the press."

Bloody Mare swept off his cap and bowed. "Damn skinny hollow," he beamed.

Emma's eyes widened. "What?"

"He speaks Russian," Bert explained.

Penelope stared at the bubbling barrels. "Whatever is he doing?"

Bert shrugged. "He's . . . ah . . . he's making solvent. Newspapers use a lot of solvent."

X

Perched atop the third slat bin, Howard Sills saw a pair of riders approaching, coming up from the river valley. He shaded his eyes from the glare of high summer sun. Cowboys, sweat-stained and trail weary, riding tired horses. But they weren't coming from the direction of the Higgins-Wentworth Trail. They approached from the west, from upstream. Maybe a couple of Nat Kinley's brothers, he thought, then decided not. They were strangers.

" 'Nother load ready, Mist' Howard," Ambrose called from below. The winch on its A frame rattled, and Howard turned to take up slack. On the ground Ambrose, white hair haloing his dark face, stepped back as two muscular youths spat on their hands and began hauling the lift line. Block and tackle creaked, and Howard's improvised hoist swung free and rose toward him.

Beyond Ambrose and the youngsters, several others pushed empty barrows toward the barn and the field beyond where still more strong boys worked, glistening in the sun, harvesting turnips.

Nat Kinley had kept his word about rounding up a harvest crew. Howard wished he had been less

116

prompt about it, though. He had worked around the clock devising hoist, frame winch, and suitable bins to contain his crop, working furiously to stay ahead of the harvest. Two of the four tall slat bins now stood full to the top with fresh turnips, and the third was filling fast. A youngster on a fast horse was even now on his way to Pleasant Valley to place an order for more milled slats, roll wire, nails, and sailcloth to build more bins. It seemed incredible to Howard how many turnips were coming from his field. And he tried not to think of the bill he was running up in Pleasant Valley.

The mail had come with the last order of supplies, and the letter from Uncle Chester lay where he had left it, on the hutch in his house. He supposed Pericles was asleep on it at the moment. The letter was brief and to the point. In four years' effort to prove himself a farmer, Howard had steadily depleted his inheritance—Uncle Chester demanded and received regular reports on his nephew's funds—and if he did not begin to show a substantial profit soon there would be barely enough left to get him home to Maryland, where he might expect some modest charity from his family in return for a promise to marry—Uncle Chester strongly recommended either Flutilla Culver of the Shasta Plantation Culvers or Mimrose Finch of the Finch Shipping and Mercantile Finches—and accept his responsibilities in the area of perpetuating the fortunes of the Sills Family of Maryland. Uncle Chester made it very clear— Uncle Chester always made it very clear—that *Sills Family of Maryland* was the only appropriate way to identify any Sills. So far as Uncle Chester was concerned, any Sills independent of the *Sills Family of Maryland* was perforce nameless.

Howard didn't want to think about Uncle Chester's letter just now. It was better to be too busy to think.

The hoist reached the top of the bin and Howard shifted his perch to grab its frame with work-blistered hands and jockey it into position on the top brace. Then he signaled, the sweating youngsters below eased their line, and he guided the tilt of the hoist to tumble another 300 pounds of topped turnips into the maw of the enclosure.

A few more such loads and they would top out. He glanced across at his field. There were still acres of turnips, their leaves rich emerald in the sun.

With the hoist empty, Howard loaded his tools into it and swung it free to be lowered. He had been completing the bin while they had loaded it. He had only finished its crisscross bracing a few minutes ago.

The two riders were near now, guiding tired mounts carefully between his fields, their hats tipped up, heads swiveling as they gaped at the huge field of turnips, gawked at the tall slat silos bulging with purple and white spheres, then turned in unison to stare in awe at Howard's legendary outhouse.

He wiped his brow, rebound his sore hands, and climbed down to welcome them.

As they reined in, the lead rider pointed toward the outhouse. "I heard about that all the way down in the Outlet," he said. Then he lifted his face, letting his eyes climb the heights of the turnip silo. "Heard about them too, but I can't say I believed it."

He dismounted and thrust out a gloved hand. "Howdy. I guess you're Howard Sills. I'm Pistol Pete Olive and that there is Wednesday Warren. We're lookin' for some cows."

Howard shook his hand, then the other puncher's. "I only have two. Started with three, but one of them disappeared a couple of years ago. Nice little star-faced Jersey. You can see the ones I have left if you want to."

"Don't mean cows like milk cows," Pistol Pete corrected. "The cows we're lookin' for is cows like in beef. Range critters. Four hundred and a few. I don't suppose you've noticed four hundred cows lately, have you?"

Howard looked at them, wide-eyed. "Can't say I have, and I'm sure I'd have noticed if they had come around. Were they stolen or something?"

Wednesday Warren dusted his hat against his leg. "Mislaid, more like. Pistol Pete here is trail boss for Mr. Hiram Wentworth and was supposed to push that beef to Dodge. But now he can't find 'em."

"Shut up, Wednesday," Pistol Pete snapped. "They're around here somewhere. We'll find 'em."

"Never in my life heard of anybody losin' a trail herd," Wednesday rasped. "I mean, just *losin'* 'em. Indians, maybe. Or even a flash flood or Act of God. But to just *lose* a—"

"Wednesday, just shut up."

Howard had the impression Pistol Pete had heard all he wanted to hear on that subject. "I heard there were a lot of cattle over in Jubilation the other evening. At least, they say that newspaper editor that died was killed by a stampede. But that was uptown. On top of the bluff. Nobody seems to know how—"

"That was them, all right." Pistol Pete scuffed his toe in the dust and looked totally unhappy. "But nobody knows where they went. I got men out combin' the country for 'em, but—"

"We know where some of 'em are," Wednesday explained, casting a mean glance at his trail boss. "Some woman over there in the town has two of 'em penned up. Says she's took them in trade for a

119

clothesline and eleven feet of fence. Another one is hanging' in the greengrocer's smokehouse to pay for a busted-down door—"

"Wednesday—"

"An' Billy Joe is on his way to Dodge with a plain dozen that got bogged. How's it gonna look to Mr. Wentworth when he sends four hundred an' a few critters up the trail an' winds up with cash in hand for twelve? Don't you think he's gonna notice that?"

"Gentlemen," Howard said quickly, hoping to head off mounting hostility. "If you'd like to rest your horses a bit, we could go to the house and take tea."

"Do what?"

"Tea. And there are some little cakes there that Ambrose baked. Follow me."

Ambrose scurried ahead to get out the good tea service. It was seldom that there were guests.

"Sometimes it seems like the whole world is just plain goin' to hell," Pistol Pete complained as the two unsaddled their mounts at the barn. "Can't take my cows to Dodge because I can't find my cows, and I can't even lope over to Jubiliation an' get drunk about it because they've shut down uptown. Court injunction or some such. I don't see how they can do such a thing."

"It's like excavatin' a shrine," Wednesday Warren agreed.

"Desecrating," Howard noted.

"Yeah. That too."

Approaching the house, Pistol Pete and Wednesday stared at it, surprised at its dimensions. It seemed to be mostly roof, a lofty, high-peaked structure rising from stubby stone walls to soar aloft to a ridge like the cutting edge of an axe. The short walls from which the slants arose were not the walls of the

120

house, but sturdy fences of native stone outset from the house itself. The real walls were within them, under wide overhangs.

"Flying buttresses," Howard explained. "They anchor the roof from either spreading outward or tipping in a high wind. I got the idea from Gothic cathedrals. They're much sturdier than they look. The high peak dumps snow."

Behind him Wednesday Warren leaned close to Pistol Pete to whisper, "I really never believed about this place. I really never did."

Ambrose opened the door for them and Howard stood aside to admit his guests. They dusted their clothing with their hats, wiped their boots carefully, and entered, looking around. The main room was clean and simple, sparsely furnished—a maplewood table and four straight-back chairs, a brown velvet couch, hutches and chests here and there, curtained sunny windows, and a bright rag rug on a wood floor. But there was no ceiling. Instead a sleeping loft overhung half the room, while the remaining half soared up to the shadowed interior of the high roof. A large black and white tomcat glared at them from the seat of a rocking chair.

"That's Pericles," Howard said. "He isn't as mean as he looks."

Wednesday Warren shuddered slightly, wrinkling his nose.

Howard pulled out chairs at the table and they sat, the two cowboys perching gingerly on the fine-finished chairs. Ambrose came from the kitchen, carrying china cups and saucers and a silver teapot on a tray. Though he still wore his sweat-stained field clothes, he had put on a stiff collar and a dark coat. "Gentlemen, your tea," he said.

Wednesday Warren was aware of something moving against his leg. He flinched, and suddenly Pericles was in his lap, standing tall to stare into his startled eyes. The cat purred happily and rubbed its face against Wednesday's stubbled cheek.

"He's just doing that to annoy you," Howard explained.

Pistol Pete grinned. "Wednesday can't stand cats."

As though he understood the statement, Pericles dug wicked claws into Wednesday's midsection, climbed to his shoulder, and draped himself around the back of the man's neck. He purred mightily and began licking Wednesday's ear. Howard poured tea.

"We got those cows as far as the river," Pistol Pete said. "But that's where we lost 'em. We worked it out that they all turned around while we was busy, and headed back up the trail past Jubilation Gap. Then they turned off there an' went to town. But we don't know where they went from there. Me an' Wednesday, we been ridin' the river for sign. Some of the other boys are lookin' other directions. I guess we'll find 'em, but I sure don't know where they've got off to."

"There's a lot of country around here," Howard said. "I'm sure they're grazing somewhere nearby. Four hundred cattle—" He glanced at Wednesday. "If Pericles is bothering you, just tell him to get down."

Wednesday sat very still, his eyes wide. "Get—" he whispered. A large black and white paw flicked past his cheek to box playfully at his moving lips.

"—bound to turn up," Howard was saying to Pistol Pete.

"About your star-face Jersey," Pistol Pete said. "That sounds kind of like one that Mr. Wentworth has. Real good little milk cow. She came in with Mary a couple of years back. Best kitchen cow on

122

HW Connected. She might be yours, I guess. Mary ain't particular what critters she brings back."

"Get down," Wednesday whispered. Pericles had finished playing with his mouth and was washing his ear again with a tongue like coarse-grade sandpaper.

"—latest on Cole Yeager?" Pistol Pete was asking. "Rumors keep turnin' up that he's up around here someplace. They know he busted a bank over at Little Rock in the spring . . . thank you, I believe I will. Haven't tasted tea in a coon's age . . . and then later on he heisted a Wells Fargo box out of Fort Sill, and somebody thought they'd spotted him up at Wichita. But between times, folks say he keeps sort of homin' back on this area. Just no tellin' what that un's up to. He's a bad 'un."

Wednesday's fingers worked themselves to the butt of his gun, drew it slowly from its holster, and raised it, turning it in the general direction of his own head. Moving only his eyes, he tried to judge the cat's position on his shoulders. Sweat beaded on his brow.

The cocking of a hammer brought Pistol Pete's attention into sharp focus. In the instant while the sound still echoed in the room he was on his feet, his own revolver drawn, eyes searching. Then he frowned, thrust his gun away, and leaned across the table to wrench Wednesday's Colt from his hand. He let its hammer down gently, laid it on the table, and thrust his face within inches of Wednesday's.

"What the hell's got into you, Wednesday?" he rasped. "What kind of way is that to act? If you don't like tea, just say so. It ain't nothin' to shoot yourself about, for heaven's sake!" He turned to Howard. "Much obliged for th' hospitality, Mr. Sills, but I reckon we better go." To Wednesday he rasped, "You just get your hat on an' stop playin' with the gentleman's pussycat. My Lord, some folks just don't know how to act in civilized surroundin's—"

Excited voices erupted outside the house, in the near distance. A moment later they heard running feet and the shouts of several of Howard's young harvesters. Howard went to a window, peered out, saw nothing, and hurried to the door, Pistol Pete and Pericles right behind him. Outside they rounded a corner. Dust hung above Howard's fresnoed road beyond the gate and the boys ran to head off a galloping horse coming in, pulling Howard's spring wagon. The repaired wagon bumped and skittered behind the lathered animal.

They closed on it, brought it to a halt with two young athletes clinging to its headstall. The boys chattered and clustered there, then brought the rig on in. Howard and Pistol Pete met them at the gate.

"Runaway," one of the boys said. "Look at this horse. Might have run for miles."

It was one of Will Ambler's stable nags. In the yard it stood, trembling and head-down, while the boys loosed it from the rig.

"Rub that animal down," Howard told them. "Walk it around first and let it blow, then rub it down good. It looks half dead."

At first glance the wagon was empty. They looked again. There was blood on the wagon seat. It had pooled and dripped down onto the keeper box beneath.

Wednesday Warren came up to them, his gun in its holster, eyes glancing this way and that for any signs of Pericles, who had vanished.

"Somebody was drivin' this rig," Pistol Pete said. "But he ain't here now. Five'll get you a dime, though, that's his blood there."

Grim-faced, the men saddled their horses and

Sorry we could not buy your item.

OrderNumber:3229610
Reason: Mol
Date: 2024-07-03

00071657612

0007165 **7612**

Howard tossed his borrowed saddle onto Crowbait. With instructions to Ambrose and the harvest boys he rode out, Pistol Pete and Wednesday flanking him.

They found the body four miles out, where rolling hills rose from Bad Basin. He was about thirty, rough-dressed and tow-headed, and battered from falling from the wagon. But it hadn't mattered. The single bullet that had killed him had shattered his spine and entered his heart.

"Shot in the back," Pistol Pete gritted, removing his hat. Wednesday stood tall in his stirrups, surveying the surrounding countryside.

Howard dismounted and squatted by the dead man, looking at him. "Who was he? Do you know him?"

"Seen him," Pistol Pete said. "Don't know his name. He was a drifter, hired on for odd jobs here an' there. Seen him hangin' around Jubilation the last day or two. If that's your wagon back there with that smith's horse, then it'd be my guess the smith sent him to bring it home to you. You got any idea why somebody might want to shoot you?"

"Me?" Howard looked up, stunned. "What do you mean, want to shoot me?"

"Well, sir." Pistol Pete squinted down at the corpse. "Maybe not right up close, but a little ways away this fellow might have looked a lot like you."

XI

They brought the dead man to Jubilation in Howard's wagon, and crowds gathered on the street. The town was full of people, present for the City Council meeting and public hearing on the Prohibition question.

"Called himself Pete Swain," Will Ambler said. "He lost his stake in a game uptown so I let him fork hay and patch a gate, then sent him out to deliver Mr. Sills's wagon. He was supposed to bring my nag back."

"That horse was run half to death," Pistol Pete allowed. "Must have spooked when this fella got shot an' was still runnin' when it got to Howard's place. We was takin' tea at the time."

Marshal Ben Cutter glanced at the cowboy. "You were doing what?"

"Takin' tea," Pistol Pete repeated proudly. "Real elegant teacups an' all. If it hadn't been for Wednesday there havin' the bad manners to threaten to shoot hisself—"

"Don't start up again," Wednesday growled.

Ben Cutter walked around to look at the dried blood on the seat. "Anything missing?"

Ambler shook his head. "The wagon was empty. I just got done fixing that wheel and sent it back."

Howard reached in, drew the latch, and raised the lid on his keeper box. Inside was the same grimy accumulation of tools, spare parts, and odds and ends as usual. A pickaxe head with a broken haft, a set of windmill wrenches, a mallet, bits and pieces of wire, some tangled twine dark with grease, an old saddlebag, a forgotten rain slicker, a pair of discarded boots, a plaid-cloth bellows, some pieces of mica rocks . . . "Looks like everything's here," he told the marshal. "It's just some junk, but I don't think anything's gone."

The marshal peered past his shoulder. "What's that?"

"What?"

"That purse-looking thing. What is it?"

"It's an old windbag. For bagpipes. I sent off and got a new one. This one leaks."

"Bagpipes?"

Howard nodded. "It's a pastime."

"Bagpipes," the marshal muttered. He shook his head. "Well, since this fellow was shot 'way out there, it's outside my jurisdiction. The sheriff might want to look into it sometime. Ding Cox has gone to fetch Digger Moore. Who plans to pay for the burying?"

Will Ambler looked at Howard Sills and shrugged.

"I guess I will," Howard said. "It's my wagon." Visions of Uncle Chester's stern letter, his bill in Pleasant Valley, and his depleting bank account paraded darkly. It seemed the way of the world that whatever happened was going to cost Howard Sills money. Whoever Pete Swain had been, his funeral was on Howard Sills. Howard sighed.

They covered Pete Swain with a tarp to await the arrival of Digger Moore's old Black Maria, and the crowd began to disperse, seeking other entertainment. A Chautauqua tent had been erected in the pasture behind City Hall and the meeting was to start at six. The Pleasant Valley crowd had arrived, two wagons carrying courthouse minions and a surrey driven by a natty individual with slicked hair and gopher sideburns who paused for a moment to glance at the covered corpse in the wagon before proceeding down the street.

"That there is Justin Case," someone told someone else. "He's the Coleman County Attorney. He's the one got them women to get up that petition."

A grizzled rancher leaning against an awning support glared after the receding surrey. "Somebody ought to go down there an' shoot that scutter."

"You got some fair junk in there," Will Ambler told Howard. "That old pickaxe could be fixed up, and that looked like some good wire."

"Just junk," Howard said. He shrugged and opened the keeper box again. "Those mill wrenches, I use them sometimes. And the mallet. The rest is just stuff I picked up here and there. If you can use any of it, help yourself."

"Obliged." Ambler nodded. "Some things I could use, I guess. I can take 'em off your repair bill."

Digger Moore's hearse drew up and several men transferred the remains of Pete Swain, then stood back and removed their hats as the undertaker climbed to his high seat, turned his team, and trundled away.

Across the street a gaggle of young women passed, going toward the stores down the street. Howard was at his wagon again, watching Will Ambler remove things from the keeper box. The young women glanced across, one or two of them giggled, and they stopped there, a cluster of bright eyes, bright ribbons, and petticoats. Foot traffic flowed around them and young men lurked here and there, admiring.

"That's him," Betty Stapleton told others. "That's Howard Sills over there. Isn't he just the dreamiest thing?"

"And wealthy," Sally Spalding added. "My mother says he is from a family of Fine and Sears back east."

"Financiers," another corrected. "It's one word. Financiers. It means they have a lot of money."

"That's what I said. And he is such a marvelous dancer. He danced with Penelope, you know. Right here on this very street. Didn't he, Betty?"

Penelope's face reddened. "He did not!"

"He certainly did," Betty chirped. "I never saw anything so romantic. It was like . . . like those Spanish dancers at the Chautauqua last year. The flaming ones."

"Flamingos," Sally corrected. "They were flamingo dancers. But Mr. Sills is even better, I do believe."

"Flamingos are birds," another said. "Those were flamenco dancers."

"We didn't dance," Penelope insisted. "I don't know where you get such imaginations. Why, I hardly know Mr. Sills."

"That's what you say, Penelope Becket." Sally smiled sweetly. "But I know what I saw. It was totally romantic and charming. And after all, at your age—"

"There are things you need to think about," Betty concluded. "You are almost twenty, you know. Why, I expect by the time I'm almost twenty I should be married and . . . and all." She blushed.

"Me too," Sally said. "Except these boys around here are so terribly dull. Not like Mr. Sills at all. Why, wouldn't it be something if he came riding up to your house on a great white stallion and—"

"Sally, for Heaven's sake!"

"Well, a body can tell the man is desperately in love with you. I mean, it's obvious, after all. I do expect he might serenade you some evening. Oh! When he does that, can I come to your house and listen? Please, Penelope."

"Me too," Betty sighed.

"You're out of your minds," Penelope decided. "And I don't know why we're all standing her gaping. I have work to do. Mr. Thompson said if I don't write enough articles to fill the pages he'll print them blank. I have to interview Mrs. Twiddie and Mrs. Cox, and do a piece about the hearing. Then I'm supposed to pick up Mr. Gillenhauser's advertisement and interview Mr. Case—"

"Poo," Betty observed. "Totally dull. I heard Mr. Sills brought a murdered man to town. Why don't you interview him?"

Penelope paled at the thought. "I don't know how a person could interview a person who's been—"

"I don't mean the murdered man, silly. I mean interview Mr. Sills."

"Oh. No, I don't think—"

"Penelope, are you afraid of Mr. Sills?"

"Well, of course not!"

Puff McVey came out of the mill, spotted Howard, and hurried over to him, holding out some coins. "Here, this is yours. For the squish."

"The what?"

"Your squish. It got ripe an' blew up an' that little cussin' jaybird bought it. I took out for the mill fee."

Howard took the coins and looked at them, puzzled. "What did he want with it?"

"Damned if I know. Can't make heads or tails out of anything he says. But he paid good money, and I got to thinkin'. Nat Kinley says you got a lot of them turnips out there. Why don't you bring in a few more loads? We'll grind 'em and see if that little feller will buy them."

Will Ambler had his arms full of odds and ends extracted from the keeper box. He seemed pleased. "I can take these things off your hands, Howard, if you don't need 'em. These and that six bits you got there ought to clear your bill with me."

Howard handed him the money, more than a little distracted at what the miller had said. Someone had actually paid cash for stone-ground turnips.

"If it was me," Ambler was saying, "I'd put those windmill wrenches in that old saddlebag you got in there. Keep 'em from rattlin' around." He glanced past Howard and his eyes widened.

Howard turned, blinked, and his mouth dropped open. Arrayed before him were eight attractive young women, all bright-eyed and curious, all gazing at him intently. They stood in a close half-circle, neatly boxing him in, and directly before him was Penelope Becket. His breathing grew ragged and visions of angels swam radiant in a world gone foggy.

She held a pad and pencil before her, holding them high as though fending off phantoms.

"Mr. Sills," she asked, "would you care to comment?"

All around him men removed their hats and stared in open admiration. She wore a ribbon in her hair that precisely matched her eyes.

Howard gulped. "I . . . ah . . . what?"

131

"Comment," she repeated. "Do you have something you'd like to say?"

"Ah . . . I . . ." He felt he was locked inside her eyes and powerless to get away. "Um . . . it came to about . . . ah . . . ten to the penny. The profit, I mean. But that's more than . . ."

She looked down, starting to write, and the eye contact was broken. Howard looked around desperately, seeking escape.

"I don't really understand," she said. "What was the name?"

"It's . . . ah . . . Sills. Howard Sills."

She started to write, then stopped. "But that's *your* name. I mean the other one. The m-murdered man."

"The what?" Howard felt dazed.

Will Ambler cocked his head. "Called himself Pete Swain, Miss Becket. Are you doin' a piece for the newspaper?"

"Yes. Who, ah, who sh-shot him?"

Pistol Pete stepped forward, holding his hat in both hands, trying to look at all the girls at once. He was swallowing convulsively and grinning like the cat who ate the canary. "We don't know, Miss. We found him . . . Wednesday yonder, and me and Mr. Sills. That was after we taken tea at Mr. Sills's house an' Wednesday offered to shoot hisself. But it seems to me like whoever done him was after Mr. Sills. You can say that if you want to."

"Did you hear that?" Sally whispered to Betty. "Someone tried to kill Mr. Sills."

Betty hugged herself and shivered. "Oh, I just knew he had a secret past. Do you suppose they dueled? Maybe they fought over Penelope. Oh-h-h."

"Mr. Sills paid for the burial," Pistol Pete added.

Penelope wrote, then looked up at Howard again.

132

"He must have been a very good friend," she said. "I am so sorry."

"He . . . ah . . . I didn't . . ."

"He is absolutely gorgeous," Sally whispered in Penelope's ear. "See? Isn't this more fun than interviewing Mrs. Twiddie?"

Howard steeled himself and tried to keep his knees from shaking. "I have to go," he said.

"Right out back," Puff McVey pointed out.

"You must be going after the murderer," Sally chirped. "Oh, fantastic! Your friend has been killed and you are out to revenge his good name. Hurry, Penelope! Write!"

Wednesday Warren, by putting one foot in front of the other, had walked a complete circle around the covey of girls, admiring them. "I don't care about Mr. Wentworth's cows," he muttered. "I ain't goin' back anyhow. I'm staying' right here." Suddenly his eyes focused on a young townsman ogling the group. "You there!" he demanded. "Mind your manners! There's ladies present!"

"I have to go," Howard Sills repeated, panic-stricken. With a wooden lurch he turned, put a foot on Crowbait's hitch-buckle, and swung aboard. His disorientation grew to nightmare proportion when he couldn't find the reins, and even more when he realized there was no saddle, but by that time he had touched heels to the dapple and was proceeding smartly up the street among a widening sphere of curious stares.

The silence he left behind lasted for several seconds. Then Will Ambler coughed and said, "I guess he had to go."

"Why is he ridin' that horse?" Puff McVey wondered. "If it was me I'd ride in the wagon."

"Heard about him clear down in th' Outlet,"

Pistol Pete Olive said. "I guess there's just some things a man has to see to believe."

Nat Kinley came down the street, scattering pedestrians, his hat low over furious eyes. His tall sorrel had covered some ground and was still moving strong. At the bend he glanced aside long enough to recognize Howard Sills going the other way, then looked back again, mystified at why Howard was sitting on Crowbait instead of in his wagon. But Howard didn't look around. He was holding his hands over his face and heading out of town.

Down the street the sorrel plunged, then skidded into a haunches-down stop as Nat caught sight of Pistol Pete. Nat gave the HW Connected top hand a thunderous look and pointed an accusing finger. "You!" he barked. "What are you doin' in town? Why ain't you out tendin' to your cows?"

Pistol Pete gawked at him. "I don't know where they are, Nat. I . . . uh . . . we sort of lost 'em."

"Well, I know where they are! Or at least where they were! Lazy K is where, an' I've got a ruined cornfield an' a busted-down shed an' two banged-up brothers to show for it. I rode in home an' couldn't hardly believe my eyes!"

"Well." Pistol Pete spread his hands helplessly. "We'll go pick 'em up. We been lookin' all over for 'em, Nat."

"Yeah, well, I'm holdin' you personally accountable, Pistol Pete. Those critters is crazy!"

"What you ought to do," Elmer Wallace suggested from a doorway, "is step down an' shoot the scutter."

Pistol Pete looked extremely distressed. "I sure am sorry, Nat. I truly am. We'll leave right now, pick up the other boys, an' go get them critters."

"You better find 'em, is all I have to say," Nat snarled. "Else you an' me is going to have it out.

You find 'em and you get 'em the hell an' gone off my range, and I want my bull back."

"Your bull?"

"Conquistador, damn it! When your critters come through he took off with 'em!"

"You go on an' get those cows, Pistol Pete." Wednesday stood to one side, still gazing at the covey of girls assembled there. He wore a huge grin and his eyes danced as he tried to direct it at both Sally Spalding and Betty Stapleton. "I'll look after things here."

XII

Atop a hill several miles south, somewhere near the invisible line separating the state of Kansas from the Cherokee Outlet, Cole Yeager drew reins and looked back toward the Cimarron Valley. From here the wide swath of the Higgins-Wentworth Trail was a tiny, pale band diving between bluffs toward the valley's shadows, and the town of Jubilation was only a hint.

"If that was him, Cole, then where's the money?" Parson asked mildly. "Maybe we could at least have followed that wagon, seen where it was headed."

Cole Yeager turned to fix him with feral eyes and Parson flinched. Cole didn't like questions. Still, Parson had ridden with Yeager for two seasons now and felt he had some rights.

"I mean," he said, "it's well and good to kill the jasper that shied us into that pit, but it seems to me we ought to think about findin' that money we lost. Maybe he had it . . . if it was him."

Yeager's fingers toyed with the butt of his Colt. "Shut up, Parson," he rasped.

Eyes like dead slate scanned the distances, studying the terrain. "Maybe that was him, maybe not," he said. "Could have been him. And drivin' a spring wagon." He paused and raised high to peer across the miles. Out on the trail a tiny feather of dust moved, going slowly away from the town. For an instant he thought of a spring wagon, then decided not. It had been only a suggestion. The distance was too great to see. Some sort of drey, he decided. Rider on the horse, not in the vehicle.

"There's money in that town," he said. "Liquor and gamblin' money, and a bank. But the saloons are closed now. We'll wait for the right time, when there's payload money to be had."

"Jubilation is Iron Jack Fuller's town," Parson pointed out. Again those feral, slate eyes fixed him and he subsided. More than the others who rode with them today—four hardcases picked up along the trail—Parson knew about the outlaw Cole Yeager. He had seen Yeager kill—many times—for no more apparent reason than that he happened to feel like it. To ride with Cole Yeager was to ride with a coiled diamondback, fangs out and ready to strike. Only hours before—the man in the spring wagon— that had been sudden and unplanned, which often seemed Cole Yeager's way.

They had crossed the river and swung wide to avoid the town, heading south. Then there had been a man driving a spring wagon, coming across the trail. At Cole's signal they drew up and sat their horses there as the man approached. He passed them, nodded, and glanced at them curiously, and went on . . . another ten yards. Yeager watched him pass, then drew his Colt and shot him in the back. The wagon horse bolted and ran, but they let it go. Cole rode over to where the man lay and looked down at him.

"Looks a little like the jasper in the storm," was

137

all he said.

Sudden. That was Cole Yeager . . . sudden.

Now Parson's mouth went dry and he lowered his eyes.

"Any town I want is mine," Yeager said. "Don't make me tired of you, Parson."

"Sorry, Cole," he muttered.

Yeager took another long look to the north, then turned and headed south. The others fell in with him, following.

"This has gone on long enough," Iron Jack Fuller rumbled. He fanned, spread, and restacked the deck of cards in his large hand, then splayed the deck in an arc, face down on the table. He glanced up then, calm pig eyes under their bulging brow sweeping the room and its occupants before settling on the sweating man directly before him. "I wouldn't want to think you had let things get out of hand, Mayor."

"We have to have the hearing, Iron Jack." Mayor Twiddie held his hat in both hands, nervous fingers rolling its brim. "That court injunction is specific on that point. First a hearing, then the City Council has to act on an ordinance."

"You don't have to pass any ordinances, Mayor." Iron Jack selected a card and slid it from the splay, turning it in his fingers. Ace of clubs. "All you have to do is have a vote of the council. Nothing in the court order says the vote must be in favor."

"Iron Jack's right," Marshal Ben Cutter said. He stood in shadows to one side, only his white linen shirt and his white teeth clearly defined. "This is a democracy, after all. And you—all of you on the council—are duly elected officers of this fair city. The court can make you vote, but even the court can't tell you how to vote."

"But this hearing business," Twiddie protested. "My wife and her friends are all going to be there. They'll insist on a Prohibition ordinance. You've seen that petition."

Again Iron Jack looked up, fixing the mayor with his pig gaze. "Your wife is your problem, Mayor. The marshal is right. When council meets nobody can tell you how to vote —"

"Opal has it all written out. She even wrote the ordinance. That bastard Case helped her do it."

"Justin Case's jurisdiction is the county," Cutter said. "Jubilation is a legal municipality. You don't have to make an ordinance if you don't want to."

"I don't know what Opal's liable to do," Twiddie whined. "One time when she got mad she waited till I was asleep, then she filled my ears with butter. I thought I'd gone deaf."

"That's nothin' to what Ding Cox's wife done to him," Harry Patman said. "She dosed him with ipecac, then locked him in the tool shed. That woman is vicious."

"Ike Frazer's wife waits at the door for him, with a bucket of —"

"Shut up," Iron Jack rumbled. The room went silent.

Iron Jack selected another card. Ace of diamonds. "You hold your hearing, Mayor. No law says you have to listen. Then you convene the council and propose the ordinance."

"Nobody can tell you how to vote," Ben Cutter repeated proudly.

"You all vote no," Iron Jack said. "Then the injunction is satisfied and that's the end of it. I want uptown open again no later than Monday. Do you understand?"

Twiddie gulped. "Yes, sir."

"That's how democracy works," Cutter said shrewdly.

Iron Jack glanced at the marshal. "Send Leonard back up here. It looks better when he's on duty up here."

"Yes, sir," Cutter said. He glanced around. "Has anybody seen him today? I don't know where he is."

No one else seemed to either.

"When Florine Gosset gets mad at ol' George," someone offered, "she starches his underwear."

"You all recollect when Herb Woody had that broken arm?" another reminded them. "It was Sarah that done that to him. She got her back against the wall an' kicked him out of bed."

Iron Jack slid out the ace of hearts.

"Ever' time Joe White gets out of line his wife makes him wear a asafetida bag," someone said.

"That's better'n havin' your head shaved like Floyd Whisenant's wife done to him."

"Gettin' so a man ain't safe in his own house any more."

Iron Jack selected the ace of spades. "Shut up," he rumbled. In silence he swept up the deck and shuffled expertly. "As long as we're having this little meeting, there is a point I want to reemphasize . . . just so nobody forgets. Uptown Jubiliation has three commodities. Whiskey, gambling, and girls. You saloonkeepers provide the whiskey and handle the sales and keep books, and I get my cut. Your dealers handle the action at the tables and keep books, and I get my cut. Some of you keep girls, and you keep books and I get my cut."

"Everybody knows that, Iron Jack," Twiddie said. "Nobody would—"

"Shut up. You and your townspeople downtown

get the trade that all this brings, and I don't even ask a cut from downtown. Just behave yourselves and don't make too much trouble. I'm a reasonable person."

"We'll get this injunction business ironed out, Iron Jack," Twiddie assured him nervously. "Don't you worry about—"

"Shut up. As I said, whiskey, gambling, and girls. On those I get my share." He glanced at W.D. Tienert. "Your bank makes good money handling the money from uptown. Don't you make good money?"

"Of course we do," Tienert said.

"Then why would you want to, ah, bend the rules, Dub?"

"Bend the . . . I don't know what you mean, Iron Jack. I don't deal in any of those things. I just run a bank."

"The boys said Bert Thompson hasn't been feeling any pain lately."

Tienert blinked. "Oh, that. Well, that was just a couple of bottles of rye, Iron Jack. I need Thompson, and I doubt if he can set type sober. I doubt if he can do anything sober."

"No exceptions," Iron Jack growled. "I get my cut. And another thing, there are some cowboys over at Patman's right now," he said, glancing at Patman as the barkeep paled, "who have been playing poker since this morning without a house dealer. Who's keeping the books, Patman? How do I know how much is my cut?"

"But Iron Jack." Patman chewed his lip as the gambler and several of his somber associates looked at him. "Those are some of the H-Four crowd over there. I just figured as long as uptown's closed, if they want to be there and play a few hands I'd—"

"No exceptions." Iron Jack frowned.

"Besides, they threatened to burn the place down if I didn't let 'em in."

"No exceptions," Iron Jack repeated. "You figure my cut, and you pay."

"I'll see to it, Iron Jack. The Lord knows I wouldn't—"

"Shut up." Iron Jack riffled his cards again. "Now go away. The meeting is adjourned."

It was a morose and worried file of leading citizens that trooped down the slope toward downtown Jubilation a few minutes later. "Listen, Mayor," Tienert said, "I don't like having Iron Jack unhappy. I think you and the council had better get that court stuff squared away. It's time we got Jubilation back to normal."

"You know whose fault all this is?" Twiddie shook a finger at him. "It's—"

"It's your wife's fault as much as anybody's. Her and those We See To You'ers and their damned petition."

"No, it's Clarence Hanks's fault. That's whose fault it is. If he hadn't got himself killed in that stampede . . . that's what set off that court order and everything else."

"Don't be silly," Woolly Smith said. "There's killin's all the time uptown. You know that. Hardly a week goes by but what two or three—"

"Those aren't prominent men," Twiddie insisted. "Those are just customers. Clarence Hanks was a prominent newspaper publisher, and when he died that court just naturally jumped on the opportunity."

"Balls!" Ben Cutter remarked sagely. "Hanks wasn't anything but a drunken—"

"So look what's printin' the paper now," Twiddie

said. "The town drunk in a town full of drunks! It's all Clarence's fault!"

"We have to get Jubilation back to normal," Tienert said, persevering. "Hanks's brother should be here soon, so we won't have to worry about the newspaper. But the thing to do now is just what Iron Jack said. Hold the hearing, get it over with, vote against a Prohibition ordinance, and advise the court the orders have been completed. That part's up to you, Mayor. Be steadfast. Be a leader we can all look up to."

"Once when Opal was mad at me she washed all my best pipes," Twiddie lamented. "Then she sprayed cologne in my humidor."

Jack Maple, who specialized in dry goods, glanced north and stopped, bracing as some of those behind collided with him. He pointed. "What on earth is that?"

Some distance away, where the bluff's limestone face broke away above the sloping field behind Jubilation's clustered downtown, a tall mound of fresh dirt was growing. A spray of earth erupted from beyond it and landed on its top . . . then another and another.

"What is that?" a man asked. "I don't remember seeing that."

Leaving the path, the downtown delegation set off across the slope. Ahead of them there were muted chipping sounds, then a gout of rock shards flew up to land on the heap of earth. Another followed. Some distance above, atop the bluff, several cowhands from H-Four stood, looking down with attitudes approaching awe. Opposite but nearer, at the foot of the rise, the wide rear doors of the Jubilation Tribune's back shed stood open. A small, bearded man with a wool cap stood there, gazing

143

upward.

More faint chipping sounds, then more shards of rock shot upward to join the growing mound. These glistened as they flew, and were accompanied by a bright spray of water.

The downtown delegates raced around the mound of dirt, then stopped. Beyond was a hole. Sounds of chipping, grunting, and splashing came from the hole, then a cubic foot of broken rock soared upward from it, accompanied by spray. The rock rubble arced and fell atop the mound of soil.

Cautiously the delegates crept to the hole and looked in. Ten feet down, Leonard stood knee-deep in seeping water, chipping limestone bedrock with a battered spade. The crowd pushed back as he hoisted another spadeful of rubble and flung it upward expertly. Then Marshal Ben Cutter knelt beside the hole and shouted, "Leonard! What do you think you're doing?"

The deputy looked up, little eyes shining with satisfaction as he recognized his employer. "Digging this hole," he roared. "Stand back!"

He stooped to resume his work and Cutter snapped, "Leonard!"

Leonard glanced up again. "Yes, sir?"

"Leonard, why are you digging this hole?"

"There ought to be a hole here, Marshal," he thundered. "It's the Law!"

Mayor Twiddie looked at Cutter. "Do you know what he's talking about?"

"God only knows." Cutter sighed. "Leonard, come out of there!"

"I think he's tapped a spring," Slim Haggard allowed. "Even Leonard couldn't sweat that much."

"Not very deep for water." Woolly Smith frowned. "I had to sink my well thirty feet, an' even then I got gypsum. Leonard!" he called down. "How's the water?"

Leonard looked at him blankly.

"That water you're standin' in, Leonard. How is it?"

Leonard looked down at the water around his knees, then looked back up. "It's fine," he shouted. "It's in this hole!"

Ben Cutter swore under his breath. "Leonard! Come out of there!"

"Yes, sir! Stand aside! Make way for the Law!" He began to climb.

Woolly Smith chewed his lip, thoughtfully. "If he's cut a spring down there this could be a real good well. I wonder whose lot this is on."

W. D. Tienert glanced at the nearby back shed of the Tribune. Bloody Mare still stood there, watching. "Offhand, I'd say this is Hanks's property."

"Shame this hole wasn't here last week," Mayor Twiddie rasped. "Maybe Clarence could have fell in instead of goin' uptown and gettin' run down by cattle. Then I wouldn't be tryin' to figure out what Opal's liable to do to me. It's all Clarence's fault."

"The night them cowboys branded Martha's layin' hen I got home a little fuzzy," Slim Haggard said. "She made me sleep out on the porch. I'm still sleepin' there."

"It wasn't you that roped and branded her chicken," Woolly Smith pointed out.

Haggard sighed. "You go try to explain anything to that woman."

"They're all the same," another man said. "I got a brother up at Marysville. He was curin' out a bucket of guts to make stinkbait for catfishin' an' he just happened to spill it on his wife's parlor rug. Next thing he knew she'd knocked him down an' rolled him in that rug an' tied the ends with haywire an' hitched a buggy horse to him an' drug him down to the creek an' dumped him in. He like to drowned before she hauled him out of there, then she made him spend most of the night cleanin' up that old rug. Shoot. That man has give her a roof over her head an' eight kids. What more could she want?"

"Women can be mighty hard to please."

A dripping Leonard clambered from the hole and came to attention before Marshal Cutter, who sighed, shrugged, and ordered him uptown for street patrol.

With a few more admiring glances at the huge hole, the downtown delegation headed back toward the footpath.

On the bluff above, a cowboy replaced his hat on his head and looked at his pards. "I'm tellin' you, a man as had that deputy an' a good show rig could make a fortune."

At the Tribune shed Bloody Mare had disappeared. But now he emerged again, carrying a bucket and a length of rope. He headed for the hole.

XIII

One evidence of the current prosperity of Jubilation town was the fact that the local Chautauqua Society, headed by Wanda Wilkie and Emma Spalding as co-chairmen, owned a tent and a full set of bleacher benches. Normally these items were stored in the loft above Speck Mullins's stables. But now they were on loan to the city, and the tent stood rigged and ready in the pasture behind City Hall.

As evening crowds converged on the location for the public hearing on the town's proposed Prohibition ordinance, ladies of the Chautauqua Society worked the entrance, hawking tickets for the next scheduled Chautauqua. Advance tickets cost a dollar each, but they would be good for all three days.

This season's program, still being assembled by the society, would include lectures by a lady who had led her own safari in darkest Africa, two lyceum musical groups, inspirational readings by the famed Mercer twins from Minneapolis, Minnesota, special appearances by Miss Lilly White and the astronomer Dr. H. H. Fein, and a company of trained poodles from France. The ladies of the society promised other attractions as well, although there was no clear indication whether these might include readings from H. Rider Haggard's popular *King Solomon's Mines,* a favorite of Martha Haggard, or whether the bill of fare would be held to a higher plane. Mrs. Wilkie had been arguing strongly for a performance of excepts from *Savonarola.*

Betty Stapleton and Sally Spalding, drafted by their mothers to help sell tickets, were doing a land-office business with the assistance of Wednesday Warren. The cowboy was freshly bathed and freshly barbered and wore a collar so tight it made his face bulge, and had appointed himself guardian angel to the two girls. They wanted to sell tickets . . . he would see to it they sold tickets. His Colt rode low on his hip in a fresh-polished holster, and any gentleman who hesitated to buy Chautauqua tickets from Mistresses Spalding and Stapleton would have Wednesday Warren to answer to.

Sally and Betty were slightly mystified by Wednesday's techniques of persuasion, but were not inclined to argue. Their mothers had stressed the importance of selling tickets. By six-thirty the Chautauqua Society had sold 390 advance tickets. All but forty of these were sold by Sally and Betty.

"You know what would be exciting?" Sally suggested as she stuffed money into her apron pocket. "If Mr. Sills escorted Penelope to Chautauqua, that would be just lovely."

Betty's eyes brightened. "That would be romantic. It really would. But do you suppose he would consider that?"

"He danced with her, right in the street. I'll bet he would."

"I don't know. I've been thinking about what Penelope said, and you know what I think? I think the poor man is timid. Did you see his face when

Penelope interviewed him? He was pale as a goat."

"Ghost," Sally corrected. "Pale as a ghost."

"Whatever." Betty shrugged. "He was white as a sheep. I'll bet that's why he got on his horse and rode away like that when there was a perfectly good wagon right behind it. Don't you see? He is so dreadfully in love that it makes him bashful. He probably needs our help."

Sally grinned, inspired. "You're right. They both need our help."

"After all, what are friends for?"

"Right. What do we do?"

"I don't know. We'll think of something. First we need a pair of tickets, but I don't have any money. Do you?"

Wednesday Warren approached them, herding a distraught man through the assembling crowds. "Gentleman here needs some tickets." He grinned. To the man he said, "Buy several. They're small."

"But I can only use one ticket," the man protested. "And I don't even know if —"

Sally had an idea. "Additional tickets may be donated to the needy, Mr. Franscom. We can arrange that for you if you like."

"We're short two needies this very minute," Betty said, picking up on the idea. "Two of the very neediest. You have no idea!"

"Really, I —"

"Buy three tickets." Wednesday grinned wickedly. "Charity begins at home."

When the man had gone, still grumbling, Wednesday asked, "Who are those for? I was thinkin' about invitin' the both of you myself."

"Why, Mr. Warren." Sally blushed. "How sweet."

"These are for Mr. Sills and Penelope," Betty explained. "They're in love but they don't know it.

149

Do you know Mr. Sills? Oh, yes. You helped him bring in that murdered man, didn't you. Oh!"

"I taken tea at his house before that," Wednesday admitted with blushing pride. "Never in my whole life saw a place like that. I'd of shot his cat too, if I could have got a bead on it."

"Why on Earth would you have done that?" Betty was aghast.

He shrugged. "Can't tolerate cats. But that Mr. Sills, he's a fine gentleman, sure enough."

"And so romantic," Sally breathed. "Wouldn't you say he is romantic?"

"Well, Miss, I can't say as I noticed that—"

"Oh, but he is," Betty said. "And he and Penelope would make such a perfect couple. We're thinking about helping them."

Sally raised a fine brow, scrutinizing the young man. "How do you feel about romance, Mr. Warren?"

Wednesday's sun-darkened face took on a new tint and his grin threatened his ears. "I'm all for it, Miss Sally. I surely am."

"Then you can help," Sally decided.

"Yes, ma'am. Be my pure pleasure. Help what?"

"Why, help us arrange for Mr. Sills to escort Penelope to Chautauqua. Isn't that what we were talking about?"

Wednesday's confusion was interrupted by the approach of Ding Cox, navigating through the crowd and ringing a hand bell. Cox wore his official hat and his city clerk coat. He rang his bell for silence and barked, "Jubilation Town Meetin' is fixin' to commence, His Honor Mayor Twiddie presidin', everybody inside an' take a seat!" He wiped his mouth with his coatsleeve, rang his bell again, and said over his shoulder to Ben Cutter, "Let's get this foolishness over with an' get this town back to normal. I'm thirsty."

The city clerk and the marshal positioned themselves at each side of the double flap of the tent, Cox still ringing his bell. He pulled a dog-eared paper from his pocket, unfolded it, and read in a high, halting voice, "Hear ye th' Citizens of Jubilation Town, Coleman County, State of Kansas! By order of the City Council in compliance with directives of the 14th District Court of the State of Kansas, His Honor Judge Placid P. Goodrum—"

"Somebody ought to ride up there an' shoot that scutter," Elmer Wallace declared to some cronies in the crowd. "Never could tolerate that judge."

"—herewith assembled for the purpose of a public hearing to consider testimony pertinent to th' ordinances of the said Jubilation Town as they apply to th' dispensin' of alcoholic beverages within the municipal limits of said—"

"If I had me Leonard an' a medicine show wagon," a waddie from H-Four speculated, "I wonder what that yahoo would charge to do th' spiels."

"—it having been brought to th' attention of the said court of approved jurisdiction in th' form of a legal petition presented on behalf of th' Wednesday Ladies' Reading Circle of the said city properly executed an' filed by th' County Attorney—"

Justin Case beamed and straightened his tie. Opal Twiddie smiled archly and little Agatha Sturgis drew herself up proudly, then blinked as a half-dozen other ladies crowded against her, their hands clapping against her sides and back.

"For heaven's sake, Ding," Mayor Twiddie whispered, "you don't have to read the whole thing."

"This is downright pathetic," Nat Kinley allowed to anyone listening. "Like emasculatin' a shrine."

151

Wednesday Warren leaned close to Sally Spalding. "What did you mean, 'romantic'?" he whispered.

"What?"

"About that there Howard Sills . . . how come you think he's so romantic?"

"—th' City Council now bein' duly assembled at this designated meetin' place . . ." Ding Cox paused, glanced at the mayor, and whispered, "You fellows better get in there and get your chairs before I turn this bunch loose, Mayor. Sittin' targets is harder to hit." He cleared his throat and resumed. ". . . any an' all proper testimony will be heard so long as it pertains to th' issue of intoxicants." He glanced up then stepped back quickly as a pair of weaving, intertwined men shuffled out of the crowd and stumbled past him. Bert Thompson was grinning hugely, staggering and leaning for support on the skinny shoulders of a small man with a beard. Both of them carried skimmer pails in their free hands and as they approached Bert stopped, almost falling, and raised his pail for along, gulping drink from it.

He hiccupped, squared his stooped shoulders, and looked down fondly at the little man. "Lead on, MacDuff," he belched. "Twalyet in view. We shall overcome."

Bloody Mare grinned at the astonished crowd around them and raised his skimmer pail in salute. *"Za vasheto zdorovya,"* he wished them. Then, to the goggling ladies assembled by the tent, *"Dobr'iy vecher,* damn skinny. *Kak dela!"*

Ben Cutter whirled on Patman. "You told me all the stock was locked up!"

Puff McVey glanced at Will Ambler. "I thought ol' Bert ran out of rye two days ago."

"Would you look at that!" a man declared. "Them two is drunk as a judge!"

"Point me to the twalyet, Bloody Mare," Bert Thompson said urgently. "Whew!"

"It *is* locked up!" Patman insisted. "They didn't get anything uptown."

Opal Twiddie had hold of Justin Case's immaculate collar, slowly strangling the struggling lawyer as she pointed and shouted, "There! You see? Even a court order doesn't stop them! Those . . . those *saloons* are—"

"To pee or not to pee," Bert muttered. "That is the question." He tugged urgently at the Russian. "Vladimir! *Gdye* twalyet?"

"Po Russkiy!" Bloody Mare beamed. *"Khorosho,* Bert Tomsahn!" With a quick sip from his skimmer pail Bloody Mare grinned again at the crowd and led his large friend away. Admiring crowds opened before them and dwindled in their wake as men slipped away to follow, hoping for a clue as to what was in the pails and where it came from.

"In league!" Agatha Sturgis hissed. "They're all in league!"

In shadows beyond the periphery of the crowd several large, unsmiling men looked at one another. "Better tell Iron Jack about this," one said. "Somebody ain't keepin' books."

Mayor Twiddie thrust his head out of the tent. "Ding? What's going on out here? Let's get this hearing started."

Emma Spalding wrung her hands, her eyes wide with concern. "Oh, those poor men," she murmured. "They must be overcome from brewing solvent." Then, "Penelope? What are you doing?"

"I'm taking notes," Penelope assured her. "For the newspaper."

"Oh, but, dear, this isn't really—"

"Mr. Thompson said if it happens it's news."

Several of the H-Four waddies had trailed Thompson and Bloody Mare to the outhouse, where Thompson entered and closed the door. Now they surrounded Bloody Mare, peering into the skimmer pail he held. "What is it?" one asked. "It looks like water."

Bloody Mare grinned and handed him the pail. *"Vodka. Khorosho vodka.* Raw bear vodka. *Ya khochu."*

"Bless you," the puncher said, and took a sip. Then he took another. "It ain't water," he told the growing crowd of men. He tipped back his head and took a long drink. They watched him in silence. He licked his lips thoughtfully. A tremor seemed to go through him, as though transmitted upward from his boots. His eyes bulged and his mouth dropped open.

"If that scutter starts foamin', shoot him,' a grizzled rancher suggested.

The cowboy caught his breath. "Hoo-ee! That stuff'll take th' top of your head clean off!"

Eerie sounds now arose from the closed outhouse and a cowboy pulled the door open a crack to look inside. From the opening a voice rolled forth, rich and heavily slurred. "Hang out our banners on the outward walls! The cry is still, 'They come'—" The cowboy closed the door and looked around, confused.

"What's he hollerin' about?" someone asked.

"He's sittin' on the ground in there an' wavin' that pitcher around an' proclaimin'."

Dimly, from the outhouse, came Bert's voice: "Our castle's strength will laugh a siege to scorn!" There was a pause, then scrabbling sounds and the door opened. Bert Thompson stood tall there, the stoop gone from his shoulders, his eyes to the evening sky. "Tomorrow and tomorrow and tomorrow creeps in this petty pace from day to day—" He lurched forward and men caught him to keep him from falling. Someone eased the sloshing skimmer pail from his hand, looking into it, and sniffed it.

"What is that stuff!" Another asked.

"Out, out, brief candle!" Bert roared. His wandering gaze found Bloody Mare and he grinned crookedly. "Vladimir! *Khorosho gazechik! Schatluvogo,* you little son of a—"

The puncher with the other pail stood like one entranced. Then abruptly he blinked, howled like a wolf, and drew his revolver to fire three thundering shots into the air.

"Yee-hahhh!" another shouted. "Ain't any doubt about it! Uptown's open an' time's a-wastin'!"

In unison most of the H-Four crowd broke and ran toward the uptown trail. Townsmen stared after them, then by threes and fives began to follow.

"Where are they going ?" W. D. Tienert had just arrived on the scene, followed by Marshal Cutter. "Uptown isn't open. We haven't even finished the hearing yet." He stared at Bert. "Bert? Where did you . . . what have you . . ."

Thompson gazed past him at the marshal. "Yon Cassius has a lean and hungry look," he pointed out.

A short way off Ding Cox was ringing his handbell and there was a clamor of female voices: "George, where are you going? George! Come back here this minute!" "I can't believe this." "Martha, have you seen Tom? He was here just a—" "What do you mean, you just remembered an appointment?" "You just wait till I get you home, you—" "All in league. They're all in—" "Has the hearing started or not?" "Where are all those men—"

At the tent Mayor Twiddie peered at the throng

155

climbing the uptown path and Woolly Smith explained, "They've got it in their heads that uptown is open, Mayor. I don't know how, but that's what—"

"Uptown is *not* open!" Patman stamped his foot. "It *will* be, but first you have to comply with that damn court order."

Opal Twiddie stormed up to her husband. "Alfred, I demand you do something this instant! I have testimony to deliver."

Twiddie looked at her, speculatively, then leaned to whisper to Cox, "What's the quickest way to get this business done?"

"We got to have a hearing, then we got to vote on an ordinance."

"Then what?"

"Well, that's all the court order says. I guess after that you sign the order an' I certify it an' things get back to normal."

Ben Cutter arrived, almost running. "There'll be trouble up there if those saloons don't open, Mayor. The boys have got it in their heads that they are."

Twiddie strode to where Patman was standing, watching the trail. "You and the other owners get on up there, Harry. Stand by your doors. We'll get a signal to you." Striding past Cox then, he entered the tent, calling back over his shoulder, "Ding, commence the hearing."

Cox rang his bell. "This here hearing is hereby commenced! Citizens of Jubilation take the front seats—" He grinned wickedly at Polly Cox, who was heading for the opening. "And you women folks can sit over to the side."

Bert Thompson and Bloody Mare, coming up from the outhouse, staggered past trailed by several admirers. "Blow, wind!" Bert proclaimed. "Come, wrack! At least we'll die with harness on our back!"

"Mr. Thompson, do you have a Chautauqua ticket yet? They're just a dollar."

If Bert heard the question he ignored it. His entire attention now was focused on either reaching his bed or falling in the street, whichever came first. "O! that this too solid flesh would melt," he whispered. "Vladimir, I do believe thy brew surpasses the defenses of the senses. Whew!" His legs ceased to function then, along with everything else.

Several members of the Wednesday Ladies' Reading Circle witnessed the collapse of the knot of men pulled down by the sodden Bert. Opal Twiddie confronted Marshal Ben Cutter and pointed an imperious finger. "Marshal, do your duty. Those men are intoxicated."

Cutter cleared his throat, chewed on his mustache, and stood his ground. "Sorry, ma'am, but they can't be drunk. As you know, Jubilation is under a court order. There's no whiskey here."

Justin Case appeared at the tent flap. "Opal, if you ladies want to get a word in, you'd better get your . . . ah . . . come in and do so. Things are out of hand, it seems to me."

Inside the tent, chaos reigned, a dozen people were talking at once, trying to shout one another down, while the mayor and City Council sat at a bench in front of them. Twiddie pulled out his watch and shouted at Woolly Smith next to him, "How long does a hearing have to last?"

"What?" Smith cupped his ear.

"I said how long does this last?"

"The law says until everybody present has a chance to speak!"

"Do you see anybody in here not speaking?"

"No, I . . . oops, here comes your wife and the We See To Youers. And Case. They haven't spoke."

Twiddie shouted at the crowd and was drowned out. Ding Cox rang his bell and they subsided.

"Mr. Case," Twiddie said, wiping his brow, "do you wish to be heard?"

"I most certainly do," Case said.

"I heard him," Woolly Smith noted.

"And Opal, you and the other ladies wish to be heard?"

"I shall speak on behalf of the ladies," Opal said imperiously. "First, I have written comments that I shall—"

"Heard her too," Woolly said. "Get crackin', Mayor. All hell's fixin' to break loose up on that hill."

Twiddie slapped the table. "I declare this hearing adjourned," he pronounced. "Is there any other business to come before this council?"

Opal stood aghast, her eyes popping at him. "You what? Alfred, you can't—"

"Now see here, Mayor," Justin Case erupted. "You can't just—"

"I move for passage of the previously considered ordinance to prohibit the dispensation of alcoholic beverages in Jubilation Town," Woolly Smith said.

Opal relaxed a bit. "Well, as long as we're making this much progress, I—"

W. D. Tienert raised his hand. "Second the motion."

Justin Case stood with his mouth open, head swiveling to glare at first one and then another of them.

"Motion has been made and seconded that alcoholic beverages be prohibited in Jubilation," Twiddie said. "All in favor, say 'aye.'"

In the silence that followed Opal Twiddie's face turned white, Justin Case got his tongue tangled over a rush of wrath surpassing his speaking abilities, and there was a distinct thump in the vicinity of Agatha Sturgis. Penelope Becket scribbled as fast a she could write.

"No 'aye' votes," Twiddie noted. "All opposed, say 'nay.' Nay."

"Nay."

"Nay."

"Nay."

"Abstain."

Every eye in the tent turned to George Gosset, who reddened and gulped and looked pleadingly at the other Council members. "Look, fellas, you don't know how it is to have your underwear starched."

Distantly, from the top of Jubilation Bluff, came the unmistakable sounds of shouting, rioting, and gunshots.

Twiddie grabbed up a paper, scribbled on it, and passed it to Ding Cox, who signed it and swatted it with the city seal. "Done," he breathed. He handed the paper to an impassive court deputy standing behind the table. "All directives complied with," he announced.

Twiddie stood and waved at Ben Cutter. "Get out there and tell them to get those saloons open before we have a war on our hands!" He thumped the table top. "This meeting is adjourned."

Within minutes the big tent had cleared out, except for several ladies trying to reassemble Agatha Sturgis and sharing ideas to promote the misery of their men.

Opal Twiddie stood crestfallen in twilight before the tent, a sheaf of papers drooping in her hand. "I can't believe it," she muttered. "I can't believe they'd do such a thing. By heaven, if Alfred ever dares set foot in our house again I'll take a skillet to him."

Justin Case chewed his lip and stared up at the growing cluster of lights where uptown Jubilation was coming back to life atop the bluff. Sounds of revelry floated on the evening breeze. "It's a temporary setback," he decided. "All it means is, we must proceed to Plan Two."

Opal took a shuddering breath. "I don't know, Justin. What I've heard of Marshal Gault . . . well . . . I hesitate to involve his kind, even for a noble cause. I mean, well, I've heard some things that—"

"Tut," Case said. "Marshal Gault is a lawman, Opal. He has legal authority. I'm sure he wouldn't exceed it. At any rate, we already agreed, if this didn't work out—"

Across the street from City Hall and two doors up, Nat Kinley stepped from the front door of the Jubilation Tribune shop and closed the door carefully behind him. His eyes had the dazed look of one who has seen marvels beyond imagination. Much of what he had just seen was beyond his understanding, but he *had* seen it and so had a select few others. Puff McVey, Will Ambler, and Prosper O'Neil were even now standing guard in the back shed, where Bert Thompson slept like a dead man while Bloody Mare worked happily at his samovar, barrels, and coils, boiling off the last of his turnip squish amidst a glittering maze of copper coils and paraphernalia that had come from his mysterious box. Coils led from wood stove to samovar to barrel of water to barrel of charcoal, back to samovar, and then to a jury-rigged contrivance where steam condensed on a tray of metallic type to drip contentedly into a font tray and back to the water barrel. Beyond this a single, short spout of copper poured a brave small stream of high-potency vodka into a waiting whiskey barrel.

Nat licked his lips and took a deep breath. He had a feeling, somehow, that the world had shifted slightly and things might never again be quite the same. With a shrug he unhitched his sorrel, swung into his saddle, and turned the tall horse toward the uptown road. It was time to round up a committee.

Above him men shouted and cheered, shots rang out, and there was the clamor of several simultaneous fistfights. At least, he noted . . . at least for now . . . Jubilation was back to normal.

XIV

The abrupt normalization of Jubilation, followed by riotous adjustment from a week of enforced abstinence, tended to obscure a number of items that might otherwise have been of keen interest to several people.

One item was the report of Bert Thompson's mysterious inebriation, which had been on its way to Iron Jack Fuller. Iron Jack's henchmen, on their way up the bluff, were overrun and almost trampled by cheering cowboys from H-Four, followed by equally enthusiastic citizens and visitors expecting to find the saloons open for business. Within minutes the henchmen found themselves helping to guard the saloons until word came that they could legally open. By that time they had their hands full and had forgotten about Thompson, Bloody Mare, and the entire downtown episode.

Another item obscured as the days went by was the strange behavior of an oddly assorted handful of men whose attitudes and actions might have attracted extreme curiosity had the little town not had so many other curious things to wonder about.

Not since the evening of the hearing had Bert

Thompson been seen atop Jubilation Bluff, yet rarely now was he sober as he went happily about the typesetting and printing of the Jubilation Tribune.

Nat Kinley, who was known to come to town only to visit the high side of town, was in town almost every day now, riding his tall sorrel in and out of town on mysterious errands, but had not been uptown in more than a week.

There was some notice of the fact that crews from Prosper O'Neil's Warbonnet spread and Elmer Wallace's Circle-O had joined forces to erect tall slat bins next to the chute bay at Bunker's Mill, with the millhand Puff McVey supervising construction while Will Ambler provided chain and latching from his shop to rig a conveyor. It was noticed too that wagonloads of turnips had begun arriving in town to fill the slat bins, and that the mill was working almost around the clock. Some few even noticed that the demand for useable barrels had increased dramatically, with good used barrels bringing twenty-five to fifty cents apiece at the mill.

But such oddities tended to lose themselves in much more interesting subjects of conversation, including the fact that the entire City Council had taken refuge at the Drovers' Hotel while various members of the Wednesday Ladies' Reading Circle fortified their houses against their husbands.

Almost no one was aware that certain modifications were made to a deed of trust, whereby one small portion of the real property belonging to the estate of the late Clarence Hanks was transferred to a syndicate known only as the Greater Jubilation Research Society. And when a sturdy building arose on that property, squarely astride a large hole full of clear spring water, and wagonloads of sealed barrels rolled nightly from Bunker's Mill to this new build-ing, whose broad chimney belched white smoke, little note was taken of it. Far more attention was given to rumors about the activities of Justin Case, the county attorney. Some said he had gone to Topeka, others said he had gone to Fort Sill. Wher-ever he was, he was not in Coleman County.

Attention was diverted further when Pistol Pete Olive rode in to town seeking cowhands willing to cross the Cimarron for a night raid on a cattle herd two counties over. It would be tricky work, he admitted. He needed at least twenty top hands to filter into Dinsmore County, descend on a herd of more than 900 critters, drive them down to Ashley County, then cut out some 400 head of them and drive them to the pens at Dodge.

Wednesday Warren stood with the crowd of wad-dies outside Patman's and gaped at his sometime trail boss as Pistol Pete explained the problem. Then he pushed through to the front of the crowd. "What four hundred critters is that you're goin' after, Pistol Pete?"

"The very same ones we started out with. Once we get the herd out of Dinsmore County, we'll just cut out the HW Connected stock. The rest can drift back where they come from."

Wednesday stared at him in disbelief. "You mean you plan to rustle your own cows?"

Pistol Pete shrugged. "I have to. There's more'n five hundred head up there that don't belong to Mr. Wentworth, but they've sort of took up with ours. There's several ranchers pretty upset about that. They've got a cordon on that herd, an' the word is they intend to hang whoever shows up to claim 'em."

Wednesday shook his head. "Pistol Pete, if you didn't have your heart so set on trail bossin' I'd

164

suggest you look into some other line of work."

Pistol Pete turned away, ignoring him. "It ain't as bad as it sounds, boys," he told the crowd of waddies. "That ranchers' cordon is quite a ways back from the herd. They can't get very close because Nat Kinley's bad bull is with the bunch an' he don't tolerate anybody ridin' close. The herd's only been in Dinsmore County five days, an' word is more than a dozen hands from four different ranches has pulled off an' left without even collectin' pay, just because of that bull."

Penelope Becket's first issue of the Jubilation Tribune had been a trial for her. It was with trepidation that she delivered carefully written copy on the murder of the drifter Pete Swain, the legal hearing at the Chautauqua tent, and the City Council's decision not to prohibit spirits uptown. Although Penelope had penned a certain amount of poetry and quite a few letters to relatives, she was not at all certain whether she qualified to write news articles. Yet Bert Thompson seemed exceedingly happy with her writing.

"Marvelous." He belched, red-rimmed eyes running down the lines of her copy. He swayed slightly, and had neither bathed nor shaved in several days. Penelope might have suspected he was inebriated, except that there was no smell of whiskey about him.

The entire shop, in fact, was much more pleasant than it had been the first time she entered it with Emma Spalding. The air inside was rich with the fragrances of ink, machine oil, tobacco smoke, and unwashed Bert, but there was no longer the stench of cooking solvent. All that, he informed her, had been moved to a shed out back.

" 'Mr. Swain,' " he read aloud, " 'was said by witnesses to have looked the picture of good health except for that small flaw wherein entered the missile responsible for his tragic demise.' " He shook his head and giggled. "Remarkable! And this bit about the 'services paid for by the mysterious Howard Sills of Bad Basin, known for his musical inclinations and turnips,'—why, young lady, that is fine prose."

"Will it do, Mr. Thompson?" she asked, hesitantly.

"Will it do? Oh, mercy, yes. Clarence Hanks would have been astounded."

"God rest his soul," Penelope murmured.

Thompson glanced at her. "I doubt if He's had the opportunity."

Thus reassured, Penelope had gone on to bigger and better things. The resulting issue of the newspaper (Penelope was a bit puzzled at Bert Thompson's tendency to chuckle when he set type) sold out in record time. Penelope heard from friends that copies of the paper had found their way as far as Pleasant Valley.

No longer uncertain of her ability to write for the newspaper, she threw herself into the work with renewed zest and a surprising amount of help from her friends.

Avid readers learned that Mr. and Mrs. Fred Stockton had Mr. and Mrs. Boyd Mulvane for dinner Friday evening ('Cannibalism," Bert said, chuckling as he set the type, changing none of it) and that old Joe Forney had gone to the dentist at Pleasant Valley where he had "one tooth pulled and the other one filled."

Irate members of the City Council descended upon W. D. Tienert after reading at length about their enforced sojourn at the Drovers' Hotel. "Who's editing this rag?" George Gosset demanded.

"We don't have an editor," Tiernert admitted. "Not until Clarence's brother gets here."

"Well, I can't say I'm crazy about everybody in town knowing I don't want my underwear starched!"

"And that part about Mrs. Twiddie threatening me with a skillet," Mayor A. P. Twiddie blustered. "There's no call to put things like that in the newspaper."

"I was about ready to try to go home," Slim Haggard said. "Then Martha read that about me sayin' maybe her damned hen would lay fried eggs and now I don't know when I can move back in."

"Did you say it?" Tienert looked up at him, mildly.

"I might have," Haggard said, scowling. "But there's no call to put a thing like that in the newspaper."

"Somebody's makin' us look silly," Gosset allowed. "Do you know who's writin' all this stuff?"

Tienert glanced quickly away. "I suppose I can talk with Bert Thompson about it," he said. "I shall suggest discretion."

When they had gone, Tienert drummed thoughtful fingers on the polished top of his desk. He rarely read the paper, but he did read its operating reports, submitted weekly by a happy and staggering Bert Thompson. Since Clarence's death circulation had increased forty percent and advertising revenues were up by a third. Quickly assessing the value of the Jubilation Tribune as a property, the banker smiled and his eyes were large and liquid. He saw his executor's fee skyrocketing, and had no intention of doing anything to change such good fortune.

It was a piece of luck even better than the cash offer Elmer Wallace, Prosper O'Neil, and Ike Ferguson had made for that worthless hole on the back edge of Hanks's town lot. They were now building something out there, and Tienert was content to ask no questions. He had the money in his pocket and that was all he needed to know.

Atop Jubilation Bluff Iron Jack Fuller squinted at a copy of the Tribune and his pig eyes went hard. "What is this?" he demanded.

"What, Boss?" Packer and Hemp moved around to look over his shoulders at the incomprehensible rows of type. "It looks like a newspaper," Hemp added lamely.

"This right here." Iron Jack stabbed a finger at the page. "This business about '. . . reported that County Attorney Justin Case has journeyed to Fort Smith to visit friends there.' What friends? What's he up to?"

"I don't recollect Case havin' any friends," Packer allowed. "He's a lawyer. Maybe he's got family there."

Iron Jack ignored them, pursing his lips. Why would Justin Case have gone to Fort Smith? And how had the Tribune ever gotten wind of it?

"I want to talk to Bert Thompson," he decided. "Next time he comes up here, bring him to me."

"Yeah, Boss," Hemp said. "Funny thing, though. I don't recollect seein' Bert uptown for weeks now."

"Except Friday mornin's when he comes to make his payments," Packer added. "Funny thing . . . there's several of them downtowners that I ain't seen lately. Must be some teetotal goin' on down there."

Wednesday Warren personally rode out to Bad

Basin to deliver a copy of the newspaper to Howard Sills. He did so at the instructions of Betty Stapleton and Sally Spalding.

"You make sure he reads this part right here," Betty directed. "Where it says about local artists being invited to perform *ad interregnum* at the Chautauqua. That means between acts. I think."

"And you give him this letter." Sally handed the cowboy a folded and sealed paper. "It's from my mother, and it says he is invited to bring his instrument and perform. She always makes up a dozen of these anyway, so I got her to make one more."

"You tell him everybody is counting on him," Betty said. "Tell him that people who have heard him play never fail to comment on it."

"Drove a few flat to drink, the way I heard it," Wednesday pointed out. "What kind of instrument does he play?"

"He playes with his pipe," Betty said. "Mr. Ambler said so."

"Not pipe," Sally corrected her. "Pipes. You know, like Pan."

"Who?"

"He has hooves and horns and he dances through the woods playing pipes."

Wednesday's eyes went large. "Mr. Sills?"

"No, silly. Pan. I don't think Mr. Sills would do that."

"Well, I'd think not!" Wednesday snapped. "That's no way for a grown man to act."

"Anyway, you make sure he agrees. Don't take no for an answer. It's very important, Wednesday."

The young cowboy chewed his lip, thoughtfully. "I guess I could hold off shootin' his cat."

"Anyway," Sally continued, "when he agrees, you give him his Chautauqua ticket and get him to sign

169

his name on this card, right down here at the bottom."

"This is a blank card. It doesn't say anything."

"That's all right. Tell him the details will be filled in later."

"Oh," Betty sighed. "This is going to be so romantic."

Wednesday Warren arrived at Bad Basin in time to assist with the loading of a three-wagon convoy carrying turnips back to Jubilation.

"I never would have thought you'd find a market for them things, Mr. Sills," he admitted. "They payin' top dollar, are they?"

"In cash." Howard grinned. "Best crop I've had yet. I've already ordered more seed."

Wednesday shuffled his feet, looking toward the house. "I come on a errand," he said. "An' I was kind of thinkin' we might take tea like we done before . . . only maybe without the cat."

A few feet away Ambrose glanced at Howard Sills, then tied off the trap on a near-empty turnip silo and hurried toward the house to get out the tea service.

In the sun-spangled parlor of Howard's flying-buttress house they sat to tea and Howard puzzled over the invitation Wednesday had brought. "I really don't see how I would be appropriate. I mean, pipes normally aren't considered . . ."

Wednesday cleared his throat. "Mr. Sills, can I ask you something?"

"Of course. What?"

"You . . . ah . . . well, I don't see any woods around here. I mean, when you play your . . . ah . . . pipes . . . ah . . . well, do you dance or anything?"

Howard stared at him.

Wednesday blushed. "I mean, I don't know anything about pipes, only . . ."

"Oh. Well." Howard stood, crossed the room, and opened a cabinet. He pulled out an awkward contrivance which resembled a dead plaid goose impaled by many dark, elaborate spikes. Strings and tassels decorated the assemblage, and where the goose's bill should have been protruded a long ebony horn flared at the end. "Highland pipes," Howard explained. "I have to keep them locked away. The bag is treated with honey and if I leave it out the ants eat it."

Wednesday gazed in wonder at the unlikely contraption. "You make music with that?"

"It's really a fine instrument," Howard assured him. "My grandfather left it to me when I was seven. By the time I was ten I had my own apartment out in the summer house, just so I could practice."

"Can you play 'Yankee Doodle' on that? Or maybe 'Pop Goes the Weasel'? That's real pretty. I've sung it to cows many's the time."

"I don't think I know that one. How about 'Scots Wha Ha'e wi Wallace Bled'? That's one of my favorites. Or maybe 'Piobaireachd of Donald Dubh'?"

Wednesday blinked. "Pie broke what?"

"It's a march." Howard placed the goose under his arm, took one of the pipes between his teeth, placed his hands on the horn, and began to blow. The goose swelled, seemed to come alive. Several erratic squeaks sounded, blending hesitantly into a high screech like dry teeth on slate. Wednesday shivered.

A feline face appeared at a doorway and Wednesday's hand crept toward his Colt.

Howard tapped his foot, thumped the goose with his elbow, and suddenly the ear-piercing wail of tormented souls screaming in disharmony filled the room, rattling windows and cupboards. The cat disappeared. Ambrose, coming in with sweetcakes, turned tail and disappeared.

Howard Sills lifted his mouth from the blow-pipe and grinned happily. "That's got it unstuck. Now I'll try the . . ." He looked around. "Mr. Warren? Where . . . oh, there you are. Sorry about that. This is really an outdoor instrument. Would you like to hear the . . ."

Wednesday Warren, severely shaken, crept from behind a sturdy chest and holstered his gun. His eyes were huge. "I have to go," he said.

"That should do it nicely." Sally Spalding ran critical bright eyes over the completed invitation. In carefully printed letters it said:

"Mr. Howard Sills of Bad Basin requests the honor to serve as escort to Miss Penelope Becket of Jubilation upon the occasion of Summer Chautauqua next."

There could be no doubting its authenticity. The signature at the lower right was clearly that of Howard Sills.

"So what are you gonna do with it?" Wednesday wondered. "You gonna mail it?"

"Oh, heavens no." Betty giggled. "That would be so . . . ordinary. No, it will be delivered when Mr. Sills serenades her at her home."

"When he does what?" Wednesday was out of his depth. "How do you intend to manage that?"

"We'll think of something," Sally assured him. "It's what friends are for."

"I don't think he dances around when he plays that thing," Wednesday said. "Far as I saw, he just stomps his foot."

"That won't matter. It's the music that counts. I'm sure his music is quite eloquent."

"Matter of fact," Wednesday assured them, "I never in my whole life heard anything like it."

XV

The little junket line that ran a more or less twice-a-week schedule to Jubilation from Pleasant Valley in season was not exactly a stage line. Its owners had once owned a stagecoach but had lost it to a flash flood in the Cimarron Valley. The vehicle they used now was a converted hay wagon with slab seats and a tail boot for luggage. Bleached canvas of an afterthought canopy flapped and popped in the wind as the vehicle lurched up the road to Jubilation Gap, bounced and rattled along a section of the Higgins-Wentworth Trail, then turned to enter the streets of Jubilation.

From the window of his bank W. D. Tienert saw it pass, going toward the loading dock at Stapleton's store which was its regular depot. There were passengers, two men and a lady, and one of the men wore distinctly Eastern clothing. Tienert closed his desk, shrugged into his coat, put on his hat, and went to meet the arrivals.

Mentally, as he paced along the boardwalk, he recalculated the present assessment of assets of the Clarence Hanks estate, and decided that the sooner he could transfer said assets to their rightful owner the better it would be. The recent success of the Jubilation Tribune had pushed its value to an all-time high, and visions of healthy executor fees danced before his eyes. But he was nervous, and had become more so with each day of waiting for the arrival of Cornelius Hanks.

Better than anyone, W. D. Tienert knew the fragile transience of the Tribune's success. Real estate, equipment, and fixtures were a small part of its value. Its real worth rested shakily on a few weeks of accidental juxtaposition of the questionable talents of his niece Penelope and a few of her friends, and the barely perceptible skills of a town drunk and a Russian.

It was a wonder, he told himself for the hundredth time, that the Tribune had not collapsed immediately upon the death of Clarence Hanks. And it was high time that Cornelius Hanks had it unloaded on him, while there were still fees to be collected.

Ahead, up the street, Tienert saw the hay wagon stage pull up to Stapleton's dock to begin unloading. The first passenger to step down was the Eastern-looking man, and Tienert squinted, looking for family resemblance. The man did look a little like Clarence, he decided. At least his derby hat looked a little like Clarence's derby hat.

Passing the Tribune office, the banker paused, then turned quickly to open the door and peer inside. The place had a sour odor, but from here it looked fairly presentable. Creaking sounds from the shop stopped when the door's bell jangled, and the bearded face of Bloody Mare peered at him from the doorway, then broke into a friendly grin.

"Hollow stinking capitaliski," Bloody Mare greeted him cheerfully. "Cock de la!"

Tienert closed his eyes and breathed deeply. The

Russian had been bad enough before they started trying to teach him English.

"Horse piss on ya," Bloody Mare added, and went back to his press.

"A sooth!" The voice from the shadows startled Tienert and he ducked back, then turned. Bert Thompson sat cross-legged atop a galley table over by the fonts, sipping a glass of water—it looked like water—and blinking blearily at the banker.

"A sooth!" Bert repeated, and belched contentedly. "How like a fawning Publican he looks. There is some ill a-brewing if I'm right for I did dream of money-bags tonight."

Tienert glared at him. "Thompson, you're drunk!"

"O happy torment." Ponderously Bert unfolded himself atop the galley table, long legs searching blindly for the floor. He found it, staggered, and stood, clutching his sloshing glass. Squinting at Tienert he winked and laid a stained finger along his nose. " 'Tis nobler in the mind," he confided, "to suffer the slings and arrows of outrageous fortune—" He belched again. "Than to . . . to what?"

"Oh, for Heaven's sake!" Tienert strode past him to the inner door. "Bloody Mare!"

The bearded face appeared. *"Da?"*

Tienert pointed back at Bert. "Get him out of here!"

Bloody Mare tilted his head, confused. "Bert Tomsahn," he explained. *"Gazechik."*

"I know who he is," Tienert growled. "Just get him out of here."

"Izvinite?" the Russian said, puzzled.

"He's drunk!" Tienert was nearly shouting. He gestured. "Take him out. Back there. Out!"

Bloody Mare brightened. *"Da!* Hout! *Spasibo. Khorosho vodka,* hout-hout! Ya looble, you." He grinned and returned to the press.

"Oh, my Lord." Tienert sagged. Then he turned and went after Bert, who was now standing, swaying at the front window, watching some cowboys walk by.

"What ho!" Bert said. "What manner of men are these, who walk with their balls in parentheses?"

Without ceremony, Tienert grabbed him by cuff and collar and hustled him through the office, out through the shop and shed, and dumped him in the alley behind.

"Doe sweat on ya," Bloody Mare called cheerfully as the banker stalked back through the plant and out the front door. Tienert wished he had brought the transfer papers with him. He had visions of Cornelius Hanks taking one look at the Tribune shop, then climbing right back aboard the hay-wagon stage never to return.

On the boardwalk he mopped his brow, straightened his coat, and pasted a smile on his face. At Stapleton's dock the passengers had all disembarked and luggage was being handed down.

On closer inspection, the man with the derby looked almost nothing like Clarence Hanks, but Tienert had made up his mind. He strode past the other two passengers—a handsome woman of middle years collecting her luggage and a rough-hewn farmer shouldering a satchel—and thrust out a hand. "How do you do. I'm Tienert. Did you have a good trip?"

Guardedly, the man looked him up and down, then shook his hand. "Not bad, considering. Who did you say you are?"

"Tienert," Tienert repeated. "I received your wire a week ago. I suppose you'd like to look at the property. Or, if you'd like, we can directly to the bank. That might be preferable. All the papers are ready. Won't take but a few minutes. And if I may say so, a hearty welcome to Jubilation, Mr. Hanks."

The man raised a cautious brow. "Who?"

"Hanks." Tienert hesitated then, uncertain. "You . . . ah . . . I assume you are Cornelius Hanks, are you not? I knew your brother very well. Wonderful man, really, and sorely missed. Ah . . . you are, aren't you? Hanks, I mean? Cornelius Hanks?"

"Not that I know of," the man said, stepping back. "My name's Evans. Do I know you?"

"Ah . . . no, I suppose not. Excuse me . . ."

Tienert turned and almost bumped into the woman passenger, who stood now regarding him with gray eyes that barely suppressed their laughter. "Mr. Tienert?" she said.

"Ah . . . yes?"

She smiled, a smile controlled. Then she held a gloved hand out to him. "I beg your pardon, I overheard. I believe you are looking for me. My name is Cornelia Hanks. Clarence was my brother."

"It isn't very much as I had imagined it," Cornelia confessed, sipping tea in the spartan lobby of the Drovers' Hotel.

"The newspaper, you mean?" Emma Spalding asked. "Or our town?"

"Kansas in general, I suppose. I don't know quite what I anticipated, but . . . well, it is very . . . open, isn't it?"

"No place more than here." Opal Twiddie scowled. "Wide open, and that's the shame of it. We believe the men of the town have conspired to—"

"I think she means the terrain, Opal," Emma suggested. She smiled at the newcomer. "There aren't many trees, are there? Not like Illinois, I imagine."

"Oh, it isn't the trees so much. I've lived in prairie land, but there the grass was tall and there never seemed such distance. But let's talk about here. I picked up copies of the Tribune in Pleasant Valley, and I must say I'm a little confused. Just what sort of town is this?"

"A den of iniquity," Opal said, pouncing. "A running sore on the face of God's good earth. A place of corruption and—"

"It's the men," Agatha Sturgis declared. "They're all in league."

"It's a nice enough little town," Emma assured her. "But there have been a few problems."

"A few problems!" Martha Haggard snorted. "You see that hill up there? They say there are twenty-seven saloons up there. Of course, I don't know the exact number, but there's little doubt of what they do up there. Men come from all over, all the time."

"To carouse," Opal added. "That's what they do. They drink spirits and they carouse. Of course none of that's allowed downtown, but there it is, right over our heads!"

"I've heard some of the awfullest things," Wanda Wilkie confided. "I mean about . . . well, you know, gambling and carrying on. And painted women. That's what I've heard."

"Not even safe downtown," Martha assured her. "Some of them got loose up there and they came down and roped my chickens—"

"Actually," Emma said, "except for the noise every night uptown is pretty well contained."

"—and branded my best laying hen."

"Shame on you, Emma!" Opal glared at the offending woman. "We mustn't make allowances. We

179

must exercise undaunted zeal in the face of such abomination!"

"The problem is," Emma explained, "the town doesn't have an ordinance against distilled spirits. So there really isn't a law to enforce."

"That's what I gathered." Cornelia nodded. She glanced at Opal. "Your husband *is* the mayor, isn't he, Mrs. Twiddie?"

"That worm! He dasn't poke his head into my house, ever again. My husband, Miss Hanks, is a sniveling, spineless, traitorous worm! But yes." Her shoulders rose slightly with pride. "He is our mayor."

"I don't quite understand how there can not be an ordinance. As I understand it, the state constitution prohibits the dispensing of alcoholic beverages."

"It's very simple," Emma shrugged. "They just ignore it."

"The constitution?"

"The parts of it they don't like."

"How very strange."

"I do so hope you will join our Wednesday Ladies' Reading Circle, Miss Hanks," Wanda urged. "We meet on Wednesdays."

"Probably the only power standing between Jubilation and damnation," Opal Twiddie announced. "We do good works, of course. And we schedule literary reports —"

"You'd be such a welcome addition," Emma agreed. "You said you've taught school?"

"Elmhurst." Cornelia nodded. "It's a small academy for young ladies. I have taught there for quite a long time. I took leave of absence to come here. I don't know yet whether I shall stay. I had some misgivings about coming at all, but after I received Mr. Tienert's message —"

"About your poor departed brother," Opal sighed. "Such a terrible thing. Poor Clarence was a —"

"Clarence Hanks was an imbecile," Cornelia assured them. "I am just amazed that he managed to leave any estate at all. I must say the Tribune is an interesting paper, though. Rather unique, from what I've seen of it. Mr. Tienert was a little vague about who is running it, and the only person I met there doesn't seem to speak English."

"That one!" Opal snorted. "He speaks it well enough. You simply wouldn't believe what he said to —"

"He's Russian, I think," Emma said. "Actually he is very polite. But Mr. Thompson has been composing the paper."

"The town drunk," Martha said. "You'll want to terminate him immediately, I'm sure."

"Oh?" Cornelia glanced up from her tea. "I had the impression there might be quite a few . . . ah . . . inebriates here."

"So much the worse," Martha said, making her point.

Emma sighed. "Actually, Penelope Becket has been writing most of the articles since . . . well, since Mr. Hanks died. She has some young friends who help, and I try to look in on her now and then."

"Unseemly," Opal allowed. "Such associations for a young woman!"

"I think she is handling it rather well," Emma said. "I agree Mr. Thompson seems intoxicated most of the time, but it could be the solvent they use. At least they moved it out of the building. Those fumes —"

"Solvent?" Cornelia raised a fine brow. "Interesting."

"I suppose Emma could be right," Wanda Wilkie said thoughtfully. "I know Mr. Thompson is an educated man. Why, one evening when I threw out the wash water I saw him standing up on the edge of the bluff, and he was reciting. It was really excellent."

"Reciting?" Opal looked around at her, surprised. "Reciting what?"

"As best I could tell, it seemed to be the soliloquy from *Hamlet.*"

Cornelia's eyes widened. "All of it?"

"All of it. Unfortunately, when he finished, he lost his balance and fell off the bluff. He rolled quite a long way. I thought the poor man had killed himself, but he was downtown the next day. Limping a bit, of course, but all right."

Cornelia stared at her. "The entire soliloquy from *Hamlet?* Are you sure?"

"I think so. Two years ago one of our Chautauqua attractions was Mr. Byrne, the Shakespearean actor. He delivered it then . . . you ladies recall that, of course. But I swan, when Mr. Thompson recited it up there on the bluff, I believe it was even better than when Mr. Byrne did it."

"You say his name is Thompson?"

"Bert Thompson. He's the printer."

Cornelia looked down at her tea again. "Interesting," she murmured, then changed the subject. "I gather from the newspaper that turnips are a major crop here."

"Turnips?" The other ladies looked at one another.

"You were reading about Mr. Sills," Martha said. "He's over in Bad Basin. Really an odd young man, but he doesn't come into town much. He has grown some turnips and some of the men have been buying them to play with."

"Turnips? I wonder what they do with them?"

"I really don't know," she admitted. "They grind them at the mill, and carry them away in barrels. I suppose it gives them something to do."

"Ranchmen mostly," Opal added. "Well enough if it keeps a few of them off that bluff up there. Miss Hanks, something really must be done."

"They're all in league," Agatha Sturgis assured her.

"I do hope you'll decide to stay on," Emma said. "You'll want to meet Penelope, of course. Did Mr. Tienert mention that she is his niece? It was his idea to assign her to the Tribune, to keep the paper going."

And the value up, Cornelia thought, but kept her counsel.

"Penelope is a sweet, charming young woman," Emma added. "I believe you will like her. From what my daughter Sally tells me, Mr. Sills is quite smitten with her, and rightly so. She'll make some young man a wonderful catch."

In the evening, Cornelia Hanks ordered up a tub and water, and bathed in her room. She brushed her hair, hung her clothing in the wardrobe, and spent an hour reading the various documents she had received from W. D. Tienert. Then, wrapped in a long robe that touched her toes, she stood at the window gazing up at the top of Jubilation Bluff.

Stars appeared in a purple sky that deepened moment by moment, and a cool breeze flowed in from the prairie. Shadows deepened along the quiet streets downtown—quiet except for a bull voice somewhere shouting, "Stand aside! Business of the Law! Make way for the Law!"

With some exceptions, what she could see below her window was a sleepy little town, readying itself for bed. Yet above, on the bluff, lamplight winked and danced in myriad patterns, and the voices of men in full revelry drifted down on the breeze. There was a gunshot, then two more. Someone whooped in the night, and a dozen more responded. Pianos tinkled distantly, and laughter flowed like sea waves on the wind. Uptown was coming awake.

"Interesting," Cornelia Hanks told herself.

XVI

It was high morning when Bert Thompson dragged himself from beneath a pile of burlap pokes to come face to face with what had awakened him. Propped on one elbow, dirty and bleary from far too much of Bloody Mare's wonderful brew, he hung his head and shook it slowly from side to side trying to shake loose a few of the cobwebs that seemed to have muffled and mummified his brain. Then he opened his eyes . . .

To look into another pair of eyes inches away. In that instant he was jolted full awake. The eyes were those of Iron Jack Fuller.

But only for an instant. The snout in front of the eyes was not the snout of Iron Jack Fuller. It belonged to a pig. Even as he stared at it the pig nuzzled him affectionately, belched loudly, and fell on its side, rolling against him. Its porcine breath on his face was heavy with the stench of turnip squish.

"Oh, God," Bert rasped. He pulled himself up to a hunkered sitting position and ran a dirty hand across the beard stubble on his face. The pig grunted and heaved itself upright only to fall again. This time it tried to crawl into his lap.

Bert took a deep breath and tried to shout, but only a series of deep coughs came from him. He felt for a moment that he was strangling. He wheezed, coughed again, and spat. Then he tried again. "Vladimir!" he squeaked.

The pig in his lap sighed contentedly and rolled over, knocking him back against the pile of pokes. Before he could recover, it pounced on him belly-down and began to lick his face.

The press of a 200-pound shoat squirming sensuously atop him was too much. "Vladimir!" he roared.

The pig, stinking drunk on fermented mash, took the outcry as encouragement and pressed its admiring attention upon him, nearly smothering him with ponderous devotion. He pushed and pummeled, his feet drumming the plank floor. There were hushed, scurrying sounds, and voices. Then the door to the shop opened and Bloody Mare's face was there.

"Bert Tomsahn! *Dobroye Utra!*"

"Good morning yourself," Bert rasped. The pig was now lolling happily across him, nibbling at his ear. "Get this thing off of me!"

He had a glimpse of Penelope Becket, peering around Bloody Mare. "My goodness!" she said. "What are they doing?"

Penelope was pulled back and Emma Spalding stepped through, followed by another, slightly older woman in tailored clothing.

"Don't look, dear," Emma said to Penelope behind the door. "It seems rather suggestive." Then to Vladimir, "What on earth *are* they doing?"

Vladimir grinned at her, and pointed. "Bert Tomsahn," he explained.

Bert had his hands full. The pig was determined to smother him with affection. Emma came closer

186

and bent for a better look. "Why, it *is* Mr. Thompson. Mr. Thompson, please come out from under there. I want you to meet someone." She stood and turned to the other woman. "Cornelia, this is Mr. Thompson."

Even as he struggled with the belching pig, Bert had a glimpse of frosty gray eyes in a handsome—if somewhat severe—face.

"Which one?" the woman inquired mildly.

With a muffled roar Bert heaved his shoulders and pushed the drooling pig aside. It sat swaying on its haunches and gazed at him fondly. He got to his feet, braced himself against a shed rail, and glared at Bloody Mare and the women.

"It's delivery day," he growled. "I got to get ready for work."

"Mr. Thompson, do you feel ill?" Emma raised a brow, studying him with mixed sympathy and suspicion.

"Is this my printer?" Cornelia asked.

"Bert Tomsahn," Bloody Mare pointed at him. *"Khorosho gazechik."*

"I think he is ill," Emma said.

"I wouldn't be surprised. Mr. Thompson, my name is Cornelia Hanks. I own this newspaper. I shall expect you in the front office in one hour, sober and presentable. Then we shall talk."

He stared at her in bleary disbelief that faded as her gray eyes held his. She was half his size, but her stare was cold iron.

He wiped a dirty sleeve across his face. "The Ides of March are come," he muttered.

She blinked, but her icy stare didn't waver. "Ay, Caesar; but not gone."

When the stunned printer had lurched away in search of soap, water, and coffee, Cornelia led the others back through the shop. The befreckled Sims boys had arrived and were in the pressroom stacking papers for delivery. Bloody Mare joined them there. Penelope went to the order counter and picked up her advertisers' list. She glanced at Cornelia. "Usually Mr. Thompson has me call on these people on Thursdays to pick up their advertising."

"Then you do that." Cornelia smiled at her. "And by the way, Penelope, did you write this article?" She indicated a long, flowery bit of prose at the top of page four. It was eight columns wide, three inches deep.

"About the Autry ladies and their art? Yes, ma'am. They make such beautiful things. I thought it would be a nice piece. Did you like it?"

"What?" Cornelia glanced up from re-reading. "Oh, yes. I like the article very much. We might need to discuss poetic license, I suppose, but yes, it's very good. I take it they use things like dried flowers and thistles . . . only natural items."

"Oh, yes. Pods and bits of root, and burrs and pressed grass. Have you seen their work? They make table arrangements and wall plaques, just all sorts of things."

"Yes. Very good. Ah . . . did you also write the headline?"

"No. Mr. Thompson writes headlines. He said he might as well because nobody ever seems to get the character count right."

"I see. Thank you, Penelope. We shall visit more later."

As the girl left, Cornelia took a seat at the editor's desk. Emma looked over her shoulder at the headline. "I read the article," she said. "I thought it was well done."

"Oh, it is," Cornelia said. "It's just this headline

. . . I think I am going to have to be very stern with Mr. Thompson."

"Oh?" Emma read it again and shrugged. "It fits the page."

"Well, yes. But don't you see . . . no, maybe it's a matter of personal taste. Still . . ." She read it aloud. " 'Local Artists Prove Porcupine Prick Can Be a Thing of Beauty.' Well, I mean, really!"

"I do hope you decide to stay on in Jubilation," Emma said. She crossed to the counter, where her shopping basket lay. "I was . . . well, very impressed . . . I mean the way you addressed Mr. Thompson out there. I think a few of us might learn a thing or two from you, Cornelia."

The newcomer glanced up. "Why, thank you, Emma. What a lovely thing to say."

The front door burst open and suddenly the office was full of bright-ribboned girls—a rolling tide of bright-eyed enthusiasm engulfing the place. Eight in all, Cornelia counted, ranging in age from maybe twelve to possibly sixteen, and accompanied by a single, grinning young cowboy, freshly barbered and beaming his delight at the company he kept. Despite the weathered, sun-dark texture of a face pale only where his hat lived, she guessed him to be no more than sixteen or seventeen.

The crowd flowed around Emma at the counter, and a bright-eyed younger version of Emma said, "We've been looking for you, Mother. You just have to do us the biggest possible favor. You will, won't you?"

"Won't you, please, Mrs. Spalding?" Another chimed in. "It's almost a matter of life and death. Please?"

"I suppose," Emma said. "What is it? Oh, wait. Where are my manners?" She turned to Cornelia.

189

"Miss Hanks, may I introduce my daughter, Sally? And these are her friends . . . ah . . . Betty Stapleton, and Lillyanne Jones, and Peg Davis, and . . ."

One by one, subdued, they curtsied and said, "How do, ma'am."

". . . and this is Mr. Warren. Wednesday Warren. He works for one of the ranches."

Wednesday fumbled with his hat and grinned shyly. "I did," he said. "How do, ma'am. I'm thinkin' on changin' my trade. Cows just ain't a lot of fun any more."

"How do you do," Cornelia said to all of them. Then to Emma, "Well, Jubilation does seem to have a healthy younger generation. I am impressed."

"Thank you." Emma blushed.

"You're the lady from back East," Sally said.

"The one everybody thought was Mr. Hanks's brother," Betty added. "Oh, I think it is so romantic that you aren't!"

"I've taken tea with Mr. Sills," Wednesday confided. "Twice. At his house."

"My," Cornelia said, reacting.

"And I ain't shot his cat yet."

"My."

Emma sighed. "Sally—"

"So I don't want to work for Pistol Pete Olive any more," Wednesday explained. "I want to stay right here in town an' look after things."

"What was that favor you wanted, Sally?"

"Oh, Mother, just the simplest thing. We need for you to write a letter to Mr. Sills. It's only because he plans to play his pipes for the Chautauqua."

"He plans to . . . ?"

"He told Wednesday he would."

"He said that, ma'am," Wednesday agreed.

"So you simply must write him a letter and invite

him to bring his pipes in to town for a demonstration. We'll arrange it. I mean, that is the least that should be required of him, isn't it?"

Emma gaped at them. She was out of her depth. "Demonstrate? We haven't planned any demonstrations."

"Oh, don't worry. We can arrange everything. We just need for you to write him a letter so it's official. You will, won't you?"

"I'll be glad to deliver it," Wednesday said. "Maybe we can take tea again. An' maybe I can get a good look at that privvy of his." He turned to Cornelia, very serious. "Ma'am, if you an't heard, Mr. Sills has the world's strangest outhouse. There ain't another one like it any—"

"He is simply *so* romantic," Betty gushed.

"We need it today," Sally said. "The letter."

"But I don't know—"

"Oh, we've written it all out. Here. Just say this. Oh, Mother, I knew we could count on you. Come on, Betty . . . everybody . . . there is so much to do. Oh, won't Penelope be thrilled!"

A moment later the door closed behind them and Cornelia and Emma were alone in the office, accompanied by silence and the lingering scents of vanilla, lilac water, soap, and Wednesday Warren's bay rum lotion.

"I suspect," Cornelia said, "that you have no idea what that was all about."

Emma nodded "It seems I rarely do."

"If you'd like a suggestion," Cornelia said with a covert smile, hiding laughter, "write the letter. The chances are that whatever's afoot is relatively harmless."

"Probably. But how does one know?"

Cornelia shook her head. All the years of all the

191

crowds of bubbling pubescence, all the dreams and fancies and elaborate deviltries, quick young minds operating always at full gallop . . . all the years of teaching and coping and watching . . . suddenly Elmhurst Academy for young ladies seemed not so far away. "One never does. But one can learn after a time to outguess the little dears. Write the letter, Emma."

The door opened again and Wednesday Warren thrust his head in, pulling off his hat. He looked imploringly at Cornelia. "Ma'am, what I said about Pistol Pete Olive—well, I didn't mean any offense to him. I hope you understand that."

"Of course." Cornelia blinked.

"It's just that I got other things to do, you understand."

"I'm sure. Don't worry about it, Mr. —"

"An' what with him havin' to take to rustlin' just to get his herd up to Dodge, an' the way he come up with to get Nat Kinley's bad bull back to Lazy K. . . . I mean, it wasn't such a bad idea. Probably no other way it could of been done. But, ma'am, just the idea of drivin' a mean Mexican bull eighty miles with a blindfold over its eyes an' corks in its ears . . . well, I heard five of the boys will be laid up for a while, an' no offense to Pistol Pete Olive, but . . . well, I hope you won't go an' put anything I might have said in the newspaper."

Cornelia stared at him. "I wouldn't dream of it."

He sighed, vastly relieved. "Thank you, ma'am. If ever you need a hand, I'm your man." With a final grin he closed the door and hurried off to catch his herd of girls.

Cornelia shook her head. "Interesting," she said.

With Emma gone off about her errands, and Bloody Mare and the Sims boys out on delivery, she

192

settled herself to do some reading. There was so much about this place that she still didn't understand. And while the Tribune seemed to add more confusion than enlightenment, it was still her best source at the moment.

There would be an election soon, the key race being between Alfred Twiddie—whom she hadn't met, though she had met Mrs. Mayor—and someone named Hester, for the office of mayor. She had the impression it was a replay of past contests, and that no one really doubted the outcome, including Twiddie and Hester.

There was the puzzle about that recent hearing on Prohibition—no one seemed to know exactly how that had proceeded, but it had produced no change. Brief reports noted several shootings and a steady run of arrests atop the bluff—in that other, shadowy part of Jubilation—but there seemed no particular importance attached to these events. They received less attention than the price of beef or the recount of exhortations of one Brother Tall Paul Strothers at his recent revival meeting. Such an odd little town! Trying to digest the bizarre mix of daily happenings that seemed so much an accepted part of life in Jubilation, Cornelia felt disoriented. She went to the paned window and looked out.

It was a typical Western town, much as she might have envisioned it. Boardwalks and rutted streets, false-front buildings with their various signs and embellishments. A mill, tall silos standing beside it—all fresh wood and glimpses of turnips, a livery barn and blacksmith shop, a hotel, City Hall building, marshal's office . . . people on the street, morning traffic dappled as it moved by morning sun and the shadows of awnings . . . men on horseback, people in carriages, wagons going by . . . a group of official-looking men crossing the street toward her . . .

The door opened and she turned. Bert Thompson still was about as seedy-looking a man as she had ever seen, tall, slump-shouldered, and shuffling, everything about him suggesting defeat, cynicism, and a surly disregard for himself and the world around him. But at least, now, he was fairly clean and seemed relatively sober.

He glanced back over his shoulder as he entered. "Looks to me like you got visitors, ma'am. Jubilation's best, comin' to call. My, what an honor." He hawked and spat expertly into a grimy cuspidor beneath the composing table.

Cornelia nodded at him. "Have a seat, Mr. Thompson. We need to talk."

"I'll stand," he grunted. "Don't expect I'll be here very long. But I got six days' pay coming—"

"Mr. Thompson!"

"Ma'am?"

"Shut up and sit down!"

W. D. Tienert was in the lead when they came in, and Cornelia mentally identified the others as they entered. The pudgy one could only be Mayor Alfred Twiddie. And that would be the city clerk, Ding Cox, and Councilmen Smith, Gosset (she wondered whether his underwear were starched), and Haggard. The entire City Council, it seemed. The spotless, dapper man who closed the door behind them wore a polished star and a polished pistol on a polished belt. His face was perfect, his manner impeccable, his eyes searching and sardonic. She disliked Marshal Ben Cutter immediately.

Tienert made the introductions, ignoring Bert Thompson, then came right to the point. "These gentlemen and I have been discussing your . . . ah

194

. . . situation here, Miss Hanks, and we feel we would be remiss not to . . . ah . . . resolve your problem for you."

Cornelia looked at them, one after another. Her smile was cordial, her eyes hooded. "Indeed? How very thoughtful."

"Yes, ma'am," Twiddie said. "I mean, a lady alone like yourself, in a strange place . . ."

"It is that," she agreed. "But I'm not aware of any problem, really, except I need to learn more about your town, gentlemen. I've made no decisions so far."

"Well, I'm sure the ladies can fill you in on everything you might want to know, Miss," Marshal Cutter assured her in a voice as perfect as his profile. White teeth flashed reassuringly. "You'll be interested in the weather, of course, and the church and the school, and the social elements of the area. But of course you'll find little to compare with your home in Illinois."

"None of us realized Clarence's heir would be a lady, you see," Twiddie said. "So of course we want to help correct the situation. You'll be wanting to return home as soon as possible, I imagine."

"What we mean is," Tienert explained, "we think we can arrange for you to find a purchaser for the Tribune . . . a group possibly, that would buy it at a very acceptable price, and could put a man in here to run things. After all, a lady . . ."

He stopped, puzzled at the sparks he seemed to see in the Eastern lady's eyes.

"Definitely man's work, running a newspaper," Cutter added smoothly.

"I see," Cornelia said.

"If we had known," Tienert continued, "why, we would have made the arrangements ourselves, on

195

your behalf, and never bothered you to come all the way out here. As executor, I could simply have—"

"Not without my express permission," she told him. "I do know something of the law, Mr. Tienert."

"Oh, of course, of course." He raised his hands in protest. "But it could have been handled by wire. We feel we owe you an apology—"

"I'm beginning to feel you do too."

"For all the inconvenience. But we thought you were a man."

"After all," Cutter said with a dazzling smile, "running a newspaper is dirty work. All that ink and all, and writing about things that certainly are no concern of ladies."

She was silent for a long moment. "I don't think you gentlemen are making me feel very welcome here," she said.

"Oh, we don't mean that, Miss Hanks."

"Certainly not. Why, we'd be very pleased if you were to stay on in Jubilation. Possibly you'd want to consider teaching at our school? Or, with what I'm sure the Tribune can bring, maybe you could open a nice linens shop or something."

"Our only concern is for your well-being, Miss Hanks. We'll see to it that you have an opportunity to relieve yourself of this smudgy old newspaper."

"You can leave it to us. We'll take care of everything."

From the shadows where he sat, Bert Thompson's irritated voice lashed at them. "Why don't you just leave her alone! It's her newspaper. She can make up her own mind about it."

Tienert turned to him, only a glance. "We won't be needing your services any further, Bert."

"How times do change," Bert muttered.

Cornelia held her temper and her tongue, and a

few minutes later they were gone. She stood at the window seething.

"Let me guess," Bert said. "You've decided to stay in Jubilation and run the newspaper." He stood, sighed, and slouched toward the door. "Like I said, I got six days' pay coming. I'll pick it up in the morning."

She swung toward him. "Mr. Thompson, I'm becoming a bit weary of having my decisions anticipated for me. What do you normally do here on Thursdays?"

"Generally I clean type and set up ads for the next week's run."

"Then I suggest you do that, and stop wasting time!"

XVII

It was a busy Thursday at the office of the Jubilation Tribune. Bloody Mare and the Sims boys were in and out several times circulating newspapers, Penelope brought in advertising copy for Bert to set, and various citizens dropped by either to meet the lady editor—the men invariably certain that things would get back to normal soon, the women curious to size up the woman everyone had thought was Clarence Hanks's brother—and a few regular stringers brought in items of questionable news value.

Bert wandered past and glanced over Cornelias's shoulder as she read the deathless prose submitted by the widow Clara Moses. ". . . Mr. and Mrs. Delbert Wilson entertained the ladies of the Grange on Wednesday last . . ." He snorted. "What did they do, sing to them?"

She looked up. "Don't you have things to do, Mr. Thompson?"

"Yeah. I could be setting this drivel in type for next week's edition, except that I haven't got it to set because you have it all over here on the editor's desk."

Stubbornly he stood, waiting, until she shrugged

and handed him the sheaf of papers. He thumbed through them, squinting and shaking his head. "Garbage," he muttered. "Pure garbage."

She studied him. "Mr. Thompson, what is your assessment of this town?"

"It stinks," he assured her.

"And how long have you been here?"

"I don't know. Six-eight months, I guess."

"Well, if you think it stinks, why are you still here?"

He shrugged. "Haven't got anyplace better to be. Look, are you gonna fire me or not?"

"I haven't decided. Can you give me any reasons why I should keep you on?"

"Not a one."

"Do you like your job?"

"No. I only stayed on because Tienert paid extra 'til you got here. And for that I've had to babysit his sister's dumplin' and put up with every kind of rot the good folks here have to offer. Are you gonna fire me or not?"

"What can you tell me about . . . ah . . . uptown? What goes on up there?"

"I haven't been there lately."

"I saw you this morning, Mr. Thompson. You must have been absolutely drunk last night."

"I hope to squat I was. Look, tomorrow's payday. Are you gonna give me the wages Tienert's been payin' or do I get cut back to what that wart Clarence paid me?"

"Why do those gentlemen want to buy me out, Mr. Thompson? I'd like your opinion."

He sighed and swung a leg up to sit on the galley table. "All right. It seems to me they might be a little worried because you're a woman. I mean, they been expecting another Clarence Hanks to come along and step right in where the other one was, and everything just go along like it has been. They got a nice little town here, the way they see it, and they don't want any surprises. If you'd been another Clarence they'd have taken you uptown and fed you some free whiskey like they always did with Clarence, and pretty soon you'd all see eye to eye and everybody be just as happy as toads in a seep."

"Exactly what 'eye to eye' would they like me to see?"

"Oh, just go along, print a lot of garbage that doesn't stir anybody up too much, you know. It's a man's world, Miss Hanks, and they'd just as soon it stay that way."

"Then why do I get the impression you don't agree with them?"

"What do I know? I'm the town drunk. Ask anybody."

Having delivered all the advice he intended to, Bert swung down from the galley table and headed for the font shelves.

"Mr. Thompson?"

"What?"

"Your name. It seems to me I remember a Bert Thompson who was quite well—"

Bert clenched his jaws in irritation. "That wasn't me. Some other Bert Thompson. Anyhow, he's dead. Drowned in a flood, or something. That was years ago."

"I see," she said, puzzled. "And yet, this morning when you quoted from *Julius Caesar,* I—"

"From who?"

"*Julius Caesar.* Shakespeare."

"Never heard of either one of them." He got busy at the fonts, grimy fingers flying as he selected characters from their little bins, clicking them into the galley stick.

Cornelia returned to the front window. Traffic was still brisk in the street beyond, the town's stores and shops doing a good business. She had an impression of prosperity there, of bustling activity completely out of step with the town's appearance of a sleepy little place in the middle of nowhere. It was an isolated town, cut off from the rest of the world — she knew — by the vast Cimarron Valley to the north and the Cherokee Outlet lands to the south. Yet goods moved through the stores, many people were on the streets, and everywhere was evidence of brisk mercantile activity.

It was as though the world found its way to Jubilation and spent its money there.

"Mr. Thompson?" she said. Up the street a battered green spring wagon pulled up at the livery and a wholesome-looking young man stepped down to engage in earnest conversation with a group of men there. He had something in his hand, and he passed it around so they could all look at it. Distantly she saw puzzlement on various faces, heads being scratched. A man on a tall sorrel sat his horse beside the wagon and listened.

A man in the crowd pointed downstreet toward City Hall and others turned to look that way, then shook their heads emphatically. Someone else pointed toward her window. The tall young man turned and looked up at the mounted man, who shrugged and spread his hands.

"Mr. Thompson," she said again.

"What?" Bert demanded. "I'm busy."

"I heard the name Iron Jack Fuller mentioned. Can you tell me who he is?"

Bert blinked at her, seemed to pale beneath his whiskers and his stains. He resumed the setting of

201

type.

"Well?" she demanded.

"Well . . ." He hesitated, then turned sad eyes on her. "Well, I guess I've about changed my mind about you, Miss Hanks. I guess the best thing for you to do is sell out to those gentry out there and get on back home where you belong. I don't think you're cut out for newspapering."

The words startled her. "Why?"

"Because you ask too many fool questions."

The bell jangled and Bloody Mare came in, street sounds following him. He grinned at Cornelia. "Hollow damskin," he said cheerfully. "Cock de la?" Then to Bert, "Bert Tomsahn, ya rabota you, vermin itch squish." With another admiring grin at Cornelia he strode through and into the back shop. A moment later they heard the back door slam.

"He certainly stays busy," Cornelia muttered.

Penelope hurried in with a sheaf of papers, to impale them on the copy spike. "Mister Stapleton wants a half page this time," she called to Bert. "And the Tucker sisters said they'll buy a column for their new millinery lines if we can say something especially nice about their bloomers. Can you say something nice about their bloomers?"

Several bits of type slid off the galley tray and rattled on the floor. Bert seemed to be strangling.

"We'll attend to it, dear," Cornelia told the girl. Glancing out the window, she noticed a number of young townsmen lingering inconspicuously about. They had appeared there with the arrival of Penelope, shooting covert glares at one another and each pretending elaborately to just happen to be in the vicinity. Scowls appeared on some of their faces as the green spring wagon she had seen down the street pulled up at the Tribune's hitch rail and the young man climbed down to hitch his horse. The man on the tall sorrel arrived with him, and also stepped down. For an instant his hand swung near the butt of the gun at his belt, and several of the loungers backed away.

The young man hitching the wagon horse carried a parcel under his arm.

Penelope glanced curiously at Cornelia. "I was at the bank," she said. "My uncle said to hold the front page open for an article about new owners of the Tribune and a printer from Wichita . . ." She stopped, concerned.

Frost touched Cornelia's gray eyes and she blinked them to hide it. "Presumptuous," she breathed. "You go on about your work, Penelope. For the time being, we'll let your uncle run his bank and I shall decide what goes into the Tribune."

Penelope pursed pretty lips, then smiled. "I guess I was a little concerned. Well, I still have calls to make." She turned to the door, opened it, and stepped out just as the rider and the spring wagon driver stepped up to the walk. The first tipped his hat. The second goggled at her, caught his toe on the edge of the boardwalk, and fell flat out at her feet. The pouch under his arm sailed past her, propelled by his fall. It arced over the counter and thudded to the floor, skidding between the feet of Bert Thompson.

Penelope's eyes went wide and her hands went to her mouth. Cornelia stared open-mouthed. Wednesday Warren and his flock of bright girls had just rounded the corner and bustled to a halt, the girls gawking in delight and wonder while Penelope's coterie of admirers swiveled their heads to gape at them and Wednesday Warren, hand on his gun butt, stalked past scowling furiously at the young townsmen.

"Merciful heavens," Cornelia breathed.

Nat Kinley gazed ruefully at his sprawled friend. "Aw, Howard, for heaven's sake!"

Rattled and shaken, Howard struggled to his feet. He looked around for his hat, spotted it, and stooped to fetch it. He straightened, dusted himself off, and looked around, slightly dazed.

"You all right, Howard?" Nat asked.

"I'm fine," he allowed.

"It always happens," Betty whispered to Sally. "Oh, he is so romantic."

At their stifled giggles Howard looked around. Eight pairs of feminine eyes were fixed on him. "Oh, my . . ." He turned abruptly and Penelope bounced from him, tripping over the transom of the open door. "Oop," Howard muttered. A long stride and strong arms encircled her, catching her a foot from the floor as she fell. For a moment they were fixed there, face to face, and he was lost in the luster of astounded lavender eyes inches from his own. Awkwardly, still supporting her with one arm, he swept off his hat. "I pard your begon, Mill Penessiepie," he stammered.

In the gathering crowd Betty shrieked and Sally hugged herself with joy. "Marvelous!" she breathed. "Just marvelous!"

Wednesday Warren ceased threatening the young townsmen long enough to stare past Nat Kinley's shoulder. He glanced at the enthralled younger girls and then lifted a brow, studying the unlikely, theatrical posture of the pair suspended in the doorway. He would have to try that sometime, he decided.

Carefully Howard helped Penelope to her feet and backed away. She stared at him wide-eyed, panting for breath, then bolted through the door and ran.

Cornelia Hanks closed her mouth. She felt as though it had been open for some time. Then, as the young man fumbled with his hat, she cocked her head at him. "I have a feeling you must be Mr. Howard Sills."

He stared at her for a moment, composing himself. "Y-yes, ma'am," he said finally. "I need to see Mr. Thompson. I . . . I want to put an advertisement in the newspaper. About this pouch . . . this . . ." He looked down, noticed that there was nothing under his arm. ". . . about this . . ."

Nat Kinley entered, closing the door. "You tossed it back there, Howard."

Bert Thompson had not removed. He stood frozen at the font trays, staring at the floor. Beneath his feet an old saddlebag lay open. Scattered beyond it were stacks and bundles of currency. For once in his life Bert Thompson was speechless.

It took them several minutes to regather the money, and Howard Sills counted it while the others watched. "I guess it's all here," he said. "Close to twenty-eight thousand dollars. I found it in my keeper box. I think I—"

"We brought it all in to get a committee to think on it," Nat Kinley said. "That's a lot of money. Prob'ly belongs to somebody."

"You found it where?" Bert stared at the fortune on the counter.

"Keeper box. In my wagon. Seems like I tossed it in there sometime last winter, but I never had looked inside it 'til this morning. I was thinking I'd use it to keep my mill wrenches from rattling around, and here was all this money."

"So what do you plan to do with it?"

"Well, I thought I might turn it over to the marshal, but the men we talked to didn't think that

205

would be a good idea."

"Be a lousy idea," Nat concurred. "Ben Cutter'd steal his mother's teeth if he could get 'em without gettin' bit."

"So somebody said I might run a piece in the newspaper about it and maybe whoever it belongs to will come to claim it. Can I do that?" He looked at Bert.

"Talk to her." Bert indicated Cornelia. "She's the boss."

"We can run something, of course," Cornelia said. "But I hope you don't intend to leave the money here. We have nowhere to keep it. You should put it in the bank."

"That's a good idea," Kinley nodded. "Except make sure you get a receipt. And witnesses. Dub Tienert would steal his—"

"Slick thinkin'." Bert nodded thoughtfully. "Tell about it in the newspaper, every hooraw in six counties is gonna be on your doorstep tryin' to claim it. Why don't you just shut up about it and keep it?"

"It isn't mine." Howard shrugged.

"Howard's from Maryland," Nat explained. "Naw, the way to do it is put the money in the bank but keep the saddlebag somewhere safe. If anybody can't describe that bag to your satisfaction, it ain't his." He took off his hat and lay it on the bag. "Everybody's been lookin' at the money, none of us have paid any attention to the saddlebag. You look at it all by yourself, Howard. Memorize it, then put it away someplace."

They wrapped the bag in newsprint and tied it with a string. Then Howard gave Cornelia all the particulars he knew. He couldn't remember much about the bag, but he thought he might have found it the past winter. Snow and biting winds came to mind. "I pick up things all the time," he explained, embarrassed. "I never seem to remember where I got them."

"Well, there's one thing I'm rememberin'," Nat said. "And that's the fellow that got shot out there by your place. Pistol Pete said he looked a little like you, and he was drivin' your spring wagon."

"Yes?" Howard was puzzled.

"Do you have a gun, Howard?"

"I have a shotgun. I shoot ducks sometimes."

"Yeah. Well, we need to do something about that. It's a little funny to me that twenty-eight thousand dollars could be left layin' around, and disappeared all these months, and nobody has ever heard a word about it."

"You think whoever shot that man . . . Pete Swain . . . was trying to get this money back?" Howard felt a chill in his spine.

"It's a thought."

The back door slammed open and a breathless Bloody Mare appeared at the shop door. "Bert Tomsahn! Raw bear squish! Vermin itch! Hot kreetah! Horse piss on ya! *Ya kachinaya sevodnya!*" He glanced at the others, grinned and lifted his wool cap. "Hollow damskin. Nyetkin Lee, cock de la. *Dobr'iy den.*" Then to Thompson again, urgently, "Hot kreetah, Bert Tomsahn. *Vremya!*" Then he was gone, through the shop and out the back.

Bert already had his apron off. "Pardon," he told them. "I better go help." He followed the Russian.

"Some of the boys think that little fellow is a genius," Nat Kinley explained. "But it sure is a shame he talks like he does, because somebody's liable to shoot him about that."

Cornelia felt decidedly confused. She decided she had never encountered a town even slightly like this one. Leaving the two men at the counter she hurried through the shop and opened the back door. Some distance away Bert Thompson and Bloody Mare were hurrying up the slope toward the new-looking structures at the base of the bluff. A fortress-like building there pumped steady white smoke from its wide chimney. Beyond it ranked barrels stood in a pole shed. The entire complex was surrounded by a strong fence of bright new wire, and men worked there, repairing a hole in the fence while a lonely-looking pig stood outside, watching them.

A grizzled man with a gun let Bert and Bloody Mare through the gate, and they disappeared into the building.

Cornelia walked back through the shop and into the office. "Do either of you gentlemen know anything about that place out behind? I mean, up the slope, where those buildings are?"

Kinley's eyes became hooded. "That's the Greater Jubilation Research Center, ma'am. It's new."

XVIII

Had it not been for the late herd ghosted in by moonlight to fill the loading pens at Dodge — a herd showing one of the Cherokee Outlet brands but arriving from the southwest hazed by gaunt and hollow-eyed riders — Engine 49 would have hauled a short payload this run.

But the 400-odd HW Connected beeves added ten stock cars to the three already filled, and 49 belched and steamed as it clattered eastward on bright rails, pulling a respectable haul. Behind the old engine and her tender rolled four hopper cars piled high with bone, two passenger coaches, a barred and guarded express car carrying consigned currency from Denver, a pair of short-haul trucks to be shunted at Newton, thirteen loaded cattle cars, and a caboose.

Conductor Tuttle Beasley sighed his relief as the train steamed across the Arkansas bridge and lined out on open rail beyond. Even through the deck plate of the second coach and the scuffed soles of his brogans he sensed the tug of righteous mass that meant 49 was pulling at near-capacity. Even though Tuttle had no control over what went aboard his trains or the count of rolling stock, he was still the one who caught hell from the yard clerk at Atchison every time he flagged out a run that didn't tax his engine.

He swung out on the platform to squint ahead, where 49 chugged busily along, heading into a rising sun. Then he latched the gate, took up his billet pad, and entered the coach to account the fares.

Tuttle Beasley's contentment lasted for one hour and twenty minutes, the time it took 49 to leave Ford County, clear the Arkansas, and approach the stub trestle at Rattlesnake Creek.

Walter Flynn, 49's fireman, saw it first and shouted at the engineer as he hit the shut-down brake. Where there should have been a stub trestle, a half-mile out across the flat below Furlong Cut, rails lay twisted and broken on shattered timbers. Great clouds of steam erupted from her boiler jets as 49's deadman brakes locked in, screaming on tortured rails, drive wheels set against the momentum of 1200 tons of hurting mass.

When the juggernaut finally came to rest it was less than a hundred yards short of the blasted trestle, and it was a shambles. An avalanche of coal from the tender had inundated the engine cab where Flynn and his engineer worked dazedly to dig themselves out. The tender carried a good load of buffalo bone, the hoppers were short-filled, the coaches were strewn with tumbled passengers, the barred express car sat aslant between bent and frozen couplings, cattle bawled and protested along the line of slatsides, one of the shunt trucks had blown its timbers when its load shifted, and the caboose was deserted.

Tuttle Beasley crawled out from under a bench seat, bruised and shaken. He tried to stand and fell on top of a large moaning lady who immediately stopped moaning, cursed, and hit him with her purse. He scrambled away from her, sat for a moment on the unresisting belly of an unconscious drummer, then got to his feet again and staggered to the rear platform. There he peered around dumbly, then froze. Carefully he raised his hands. All around were masked and mounted men with drawn guns.

"Get them people out here," the nearest one told him.

Tuttle blinked at him. "Are you all robbin' this train?"

"No, we're sittin' around in the opry house back yonder playin' cribbage and thinkin' high thoughts. Get them people out here."

A passing rider paused, cold eyes scowling above his bandana. "Shut up, Parson. Get it done." Then he spurred away, up the line toward the express car.

By ones and twos, shaken passengers were descending from the cars. Tuttle herded them from the platform. "He ain't real cordial, is he?" he noted to the first robber.

"You might say that. Get 'em all out and line them up."

Tuttle did as he was told. "You fellows must be crazy, robbin' this train. Nobody robs trains anymore. Banks is the thing nowadays."

"We're behind the times," Parson said. "I don't suppose you've got a key to that express car back there?"

"That's a sealed car. The key's in Kansas City."

"Doesn't matter. We'll just blow it. How many men in there?"

Tuttle shrugged. He didn't know. At a flick of Parson's gun he started along the line of disembarked passengers, relieving them of their money, watches, and gems. "Somebody's gonna catch hell

211

about this," he said over his shoulder. From up ahead Flynn and the engineer stumbled back toward the crowd, herded by another bandit. A moment later a muffled explosion rocked them. Engine 49 lurched and sagged, boilers blown. Tuttle stared as smoke rose above her and water gushed from her rent seams. Moisture filled his eyes.

"You all didn't have to do that," he said.

The engineer stood stoic, but Walter Flynn stared at the engine's wreckage like one in a trance. As fireman, he had devoted eight years to old 49. The engineers came and went, and they set the pace and manned the throttle. But it was Flynn who had fired her boilers, patched her seams, and tended to her needs. Slowly he removed his cap. A tear coursed a path through the soot on his face.

"Get a move on," Parson told Tuttle. "We ain't got all day."

Back at the express car several riders had gathered, hard eyes on the guard ports. One of these eased open and a rifle snout emerged. Two of the riders aimed and fired, their shots entering the little port in unison. The rifle barrel tipped upward and hung there, suspended.

Up and down the length of the stock cars cattle bawled and lowed. In every car a few were down.

A rider approached the express car and hammered on its heavy door. "Come out!" he called.

There was no answer. But above the roof vent a wisp of smoke appeared and grew.

"They're burnin' the bills, Cole," a rider said.

Cole Yeager's gaze didn't waver. "Blow the door."

Satchel charges were suspended at the bolt mounts and short fuses touched off. The riders pulled back. The double blast rolled across empty hills and sent echoes booming back. In a cloud of smoke and debris the heavy door hung for a moment and then tipped outward and fell. As one they charged the car. A singed man staggered to the entrance, hands over his ears, and Cole shot him. Beyond, a scattering of bank notes burned in random small fires. Two riders swung from their mounts into the car and there was another gunshot.

Moments passed and they emerged, carrying canvas bags with heavy leather straps. "Small bills," one said. "A few thousand here. All the big stuff is burned, and they'd started on this. Sons a' bitches."

"Take what there is," Cole said. He turned hard eyes forward, where the conductor was handing a hat full of trinkets up to Parson. There were a dozen or so passengers lined up there, all bruised and shaken, a few bleeding. Three women among them, but none of interest to him. Two of his men were descending from the coaches where they had looted the hand luggage.

"I think we better get . . ." one of the riders started, then paused. There was an air about Cole Yeager—the intense gaze forward, the rigidity of his shoulders, the ice in his eyes—that some of them had seen before. One by one they backed away from him, silently. He ignored them and turned his horse, his gaze still fixed on the group outside the coaches.

"I hope you fellows ain't goin' back to train robbin' as a steady thing," Tuttle Beasley said as he handed the last of the loot up to Parson. "I never did like those times myself."

"Can see how you might not have," Parson allowed. He emptied the hat into a saddlebag, then tossed it into the brush where the passengers' guns had gone. A bare-headed cowboy among the passengers winced and marked where it had gone.

Parson turned at Cole's approach. "Ready

to . . . ?" He went silent. Cole walked his horse past him and drew his Colt.

"They burned most of the money," he said flatly. Ice eyes lit on the engineer. The Colt lifted and thundered. The man doubled and fell dead.

Cole scanned the white-faced crowd impassively. At random he selected another man and again the pistol spoke. The man was thrown back against the side of the coach, then fell limp on the tie-ends.

The ice faded from pale eyes. His shoulders lost their rigid set. He looked away as though nothing had occurred, and slid his Colt into its holster. "Let's go," he said.

The riders followed in silence as he rode away.

Tuttle Beasley's legs collapsed. He sat down hard on the ground, shaking and white-faced. One of the women screamed and fainted. For long moments the crowd remained motionless, then they began to stir. A cowboy ran for his hat, others for their guns.

Walter Flynn helped Beasley to his feet, and they went to look at the dead engineer, then the dead passenger. "That was Yeager," Beasley said. "Cole Yeager."

"We got to take care of these people," Flynn rasped. "We'll have to walk them out of here." His voice broke slightly. "Old Forty-nine ain't goin' any place. Not ever again."

Men were crowding around them now, stunned and angry, everyone waiting for someone to decide what to do. By the second coach the fainted woman was awake and wailing. In the stock cars cattle stamped and bawled.

"We shouldn't go off and leave those critters," Beasley decided. "They'll die in those cars. Maybe some of you men can let down the ramps and turn 'em loose. There's graze here, and water in the creek.

I guess somebody can come and get them later."

At the fourth stock car a one-horned cow, first out, stumbled on the ramp and then recovered her footing. Like the others, she bawled and danced skittishly away from the train, then found good grass and began to graze.

Being only a cow, it was not in Mary's nature to attach significance to events . . . or even to be particularly aware of them except as they might momentarily touch upon her bovine consciousness. Since she had left the train, the train no longer mattered to her except as a jumble of shapes in the distance. The people walking away, westward along the rails, were only moving creatures beyond the range of her instinctive reactions.

What did matter, vaguely, were the succulent grass and the sun on her back, the herd comfort of many other cattle around her, and the scent of water nearby. She lifted her head and ambled toward the creek. Others followed.

The bottom flats were lush with fat grass and she moved along the little watercourse from clump to cluster, grazing contentedly. By sundown she—and some half a thousand companions—were several miles south of the shattered trestle and the dead train.

Their need for water satisfied, the cattle drifted aimlessly along the creek's course and up into the hills beyond. The land here was stony and broken, long low dunes of winter-blown sand encroaching here and there into the lower places like slow-moving fingers of barren dun overreaching the green of the grasses. Each following its own path, the cattle spread over a square mile of country, then another. But as the blue of evening settled in and a cool breeze carried scents of ozone and moist dust, they began to compress again into a herd, barely moving as they grazed yet generally southbound. Massing clouds to the west deepened the blue and dimmed it toward darkness. Lightning flickered there, beyond the hills, coming closer on the wind.

A pair of wolves and a tribe of coyotes wandered about beyond the herd's perimeter, watching them intently. When they moved close the cattle nearest were aware of them and closed inward, bunching the herd even more. Yet the carnivores seemed no real threat, and when they moved beyond range of scent the cattle ignored them.

Gradually, Mary had gravitated toward the south edge of the herd, and since that was the general direction they were all going she became reestablished as leader. It was the infallible protocol of cows. If the herd were close about and moving, the one consistently in front became the one to follow.

A pair of range hands on tired horses rounded a low bluff and found themselves suddenly surrounded by critters. Those nearest them shied away, rolling their eyes. The rest ignored them.

The two men sat their saddles, tired and dusty, and stared perplexedly at the herd. Within moments each had arrived at a close head-count and an inventory of brands. The predominant mark was HW Connected.

The skinny one turned to the other. "I don't think none of these is ours, Slick."

Slick thought it over. "Reckon not."

Contentedly, tons of beef on the hoof crept past, circling only far enough to avoid bumping into their horses.

"Trail herd," Slick said. "They been drove, sure enough."

"Ain't been a trail herd through these hills in ten

years," Skinny allowed. "Last one was in seventy-six, I believe."

"Those ain't them. I make several for Rockin' A. That's Ferd Rutherford's spread out in Meade County."

"Mighty far to wander," Skinny said. "Ferd Rutherford tend to be forgetful, does he?"

"Not as I know of. You ever see that HW Connected brand?"

"Some, I reckon. That's Hiram Wentworth's mark, but his spread is 'way off down in the Cherokee Outlet. He drives up to Dodge, time to time, but nobody drives herds over this way any more. Last herd up here was back in seventy-six."

"That's right. I heard that somewhere."

It was growing dark. Gusts of wind whipped dustpats from beneath the hooves of the animals.

"You suppose we ought to do something about these here cows, Slick?"

Slick thought about it. "I reckon we could push 'em over into the valley pasture. They'd hold there."

"Take us most of the night to do that." Skinny frowned. "And I don't know if the boss wants somebody else's cows burnin' grass in his best pasture."

"Yeah. He might not like that. Maybe one of us ought to ride down to Mayfield an' let that sheriff know there's cows up here."

"I don't reckon that sheriff cares if there's cows up here or not. Besides, if they keep goin' like they are, they'll get to Mayfield by theirselves eventually. Won't matter whether we go down there or not."

"You're right as rain about that."

"Besides, it's fixin' to rain."

"You're right as rain about that too."

"Maybe there ain't anything we ought to do about

217

these cows."

Slick thought that over. "I reckon," he allowed.

The rain came with full dark, slicing cold and wind-blown. Lightning danced on hilltops and the cattle clustered in the lees of several low hills, waiting dumbly until it passed. Wolves and coyotes flanked them, creeping close under the storm, but were ignored. By midnight the sky had cleared and the herd was moving again, flowing together to stream slowly southward, following Mary.

XIX

Armed with the courage of his convictions, Coleman County Attorney Justin Case journeyed by surrey to the county seats of the four counties bordering Coleman. In each town he sought and was granted — what official governing body could do otherwise? — a commissioners' petition declaring that the open saloons of Jubilation were a blight on the surrounding region and urging strict compliance with the Prohibition Amendment.

Armed then with these documents and cloaked in righteous wrath, he entrained for Topeka, wiring ahead for meetings with the attorney general and the governor. There he sought and was granted — what officers of a dry state could do otherwise? — a letter of accord requesting judiciary reiteration of the principles of law involved in the constitutional mandates of sovereign states and the powers of federal officers regarding the borders of organized territories.

Armed with these and fortified by a profound

admiration for the usefulness of a complex structure of laws, Justin Case went then to Leavenworth, where, following three days of well-deserved relaxation at the discreet house of Madame Blanche — and one additional day to recover from a raging whiskey hangover — he went before a federal magistrate to present his documents.

"I must say you have been a busy man." The magistrate gazed at him over the tops of wire-rimmed spectacles. "Coleman County must be doing very well, to afford such ardent pursuit of a cause by its attorney."

Case permitted a self-deprecating smile. "I am funding my own travel, your honor. I feel an elected official such as myself must set an example of the duty of every citizen not to condone flagrant violation of the law . . . even if he must do so at his own expense."

"How very zealous of you," the judge admitted. And that's quite a speech you're rehearsing, he thought. I wonder what office you plan to run for next.

Finally then, armed with the power of the court, Justin Case set out for Little Rock in search of the legendary Marshal Frank Gault.

As with the succession of judges who had provided his principal employment for nearly thirty years, Marshal Gault's commission was for life. It was a license to do whatever he chose to do, for whatever reason, anywhere in the territories that were the jurisdiction of the court at Little Rock. And although he rarely now acted on behalf of that court, he did manage to stay busy. The territories were a magnet for wanted men. Robbers and renegades, killers and toughs, hardcases and scoundrels of every sort tended to drift into the territories seeking sanctuary and breathing room. Little law existed there, and natural hideouts were abundant.

For years Frank Gault had made it his business to know where these hideouts were and to keep track of who was using them. Wanted men carried rewards, and those rewards increased in proportion to their crimes. Frank Gault employed a small army of clerks, informers, and private gunhands working as deputies. Like a medieval gamekeeper he kept close track of the prize stags prowling his domain. When the rewards were right he harvested them.

Nor did he tolerate poaching. More than one lawman on the trail of a fugitive had disappeared in those territories, and many a bounty hunter had been planted by Gault's "deputies."

Seated in the parlor of the marshal's fine house on the edge of Little Rock, Justin Case studied the living legend seated across from him and was not impressed.

"You have everything you need right there," he said. "Court orders, warrants, even petitions from five counties in Kansas declaring their official backing. All you need to do is stop a few wagons."

"Haven't missed a bet, have you?" Gault rumbled.

"Not that I know of. When can you start?"

The marshal's weather-seamed face distorted itself into a slight smile. "Anytime I feel like, if I feel like it. But you ain't said the magic words yet, bub. What's in it for me?"

"It's your duty?" Case ventured.

The harsh smile planted itself more firmly on Gault's face, though Case noticed it never reached the old man's eyes. Gault dropped the sheaf of legal documents on the floor beside his easy chair. He leaned back and crossed his legs contendedly. "When did your mama wean you, bub? Yesterday? You want to talk duty, you get on back home an' talk to your county sheriff."

"He gets a percentage of the action."

"Yeah. Figured he did, or you wouldn't be here. Look, bub, what happens in Kansas is none of my concern."

"But the whiskey trade comes in through the territory."

"Sure it does. Bunch of teamsters carryin' goods from a legitimate warehouse at Fort Smith. Yeah, I know it says here I can stop them, but why should I? No skin off my nose."

Case played his ace. "Those wagons carry nearly three thousand dollars worth of liquor each, and there's nothing to say you can't confiscate every one of 'em. We can sell the goods in Missouri and I'll give you . . . say, twenty-five percent of the proceeds."

The smile disappeared and the eyes turned lethal. "Bub, I'm thinkin' I might take a notion to hand you over to a few of my deputies. They ain't had much fun lately, an' they do enjoy dandified lawyers. Ol' Pete, he uses 'em for target practice. Easy shootin' after Hubert gets done bustin' up some of their bones, because they don't run or nothin'. They mostly just lay there an' scream."

The color drained from Case's face. "What I meant to say was fifty per cent."

"Then there's Charlie. He's got this thin-bladed knife that he keeps whettin' all the time. He can slice pieces off a man that you can see daylight through."

"Well, what then?"

"The way I see it, you done handed me all I need to go out there an' take them wagons, an' I got plenty of contacts in Missouri to make my own deals. I don't need a partner, bub. Sorry."

Case was shaking visibly, his face a pasty white. "But I put all this together! You can't just cut me out like—"

"Sure I can," Gault rumbled. "I done did. But look at it this way, bub. You get on back to Kansas, an' when them wagons stop comin' in you can take full credit for dryin' up the source of damnation. You can be a hero. Hell's bells, you can be a legend in your own time if you can lie enough about it. Why, many's the man who's got hisself elected to the Senate on a whole lot less."

Case slumped in his chair, defeated and appalled. This old man . . . this beefy-shouldered, hard-eyed old man with his iron-gray hair and his piercing gaze . . . why, the man was a legend. And yet . . . "Have you no scruples at all?" he croaked.

The mild smile returned. "None whatsomever, bub. I recollect many a year ago I had a few of them. Kept 'em a while too, despite all good sense to the contrary. But I chucked 'em by an' by. Man with scruples don't generally have much money. But then you know all about that, don't you, bub?"

"But I thought . . . well, I just thought . . ."

"Oh, I know." Gault was almost genial now. "You thought you'd just put this all together an' come in here with these warrants an' I'd stand to attention an' salute the flag an' go roarin' off to make you a hero an' make you rich all at the same time. My, my. Wouldn't that be somethin'! Only trouble is, it don't work like that, bub. No, you ain't gonna get any money out of this at all. But if you're 'bout half as smart as you think you are, you'll come out just fine. I said you can have the credit. Fact is, I'll help you out. Ever' time I use these here warrants I'll make it my business to let it be known that this is the doin' of that fine, upstandin' young county

223

attorney, ah . . . what did you say your name is again?"

"Case. Justin Case."

"Justin . . ." The man grinned, then roared with laughter. Doors opened on both sides of the parlor and tough, dour men stood there with their hands at their gun butts. "Oh, my!" Gault subsided, still chuckling. "Your parents must really have been vicious. Justin Case, Hooee! Well, anyways, I'll see to it that everybody knows it was none other than . . . hee hee . . . Justin Case hisself that done dried up Jubilation. You can count on it."

When the deflated lawyer was gone, Frank Gault called in a deputy.

"Bo," he said, "you hear all that? Right. Get some of the boys together an' get a wire off to Fort Smith. We'll be doin' some ridin'."

"You gonna get that there lawyer kilt, Frank," Bo pointed out. "Jubilation is Iron Jack Fuller's town."

Gault gazed at him, his old eyes twinkling. "Do tell, Bo? My, my. I wonder if that fancy-pants lawyer knows that."

Still, Bo hesitated. "Frank, can I ask you a question?"

"Ask away, but be quick about it." Gault was at his gun case, loading a Winchester and a pair of well-worn Colts.

"Well, all that ridin' you've had the boys doin', up into Missouri to check on whiskey buyers, an' out into the territory to get routes an' schedules on the whiskey runners . . . Frank, did you know this was comin' off?"

"Know?" Gault blinked at him. "Why, hell, I been waitin' nigh a year for some yayhoo to do th' obvious thing an' line up all these warrants for me. You don't think that jaybird thought up the idea of comin' to me all by hisself, do you?"

It was Parson who found the newspaper at Pleasant Valley and read about Howard Sills's mysterious $28,000 find.

The band had drifted apart after their failure to score on banknotes in the train robbery. Every time he thought about those notes being burned Cole Yeager turned kill-mad all over again, and the rest had no interest in being anywhere near him on those occasions.

So when Cole heard about Marshal Frank Gault pulling in a lot of his deputies from down in the Strip, and decided to try his hand down there, most of the boys managed to get lost along the way. Parson was the first to drop out. Of them all, he had known Cole the longest. He knew Cole wouldn't be fit to ride with again until something came along to take his mind off his latest failure. So, somewhere in the flint hills, Parson just faded off from the rest and went looking for a quiet place to hang his hat for a time. Since he was a known man in some circles, such places were not easy for him to find.

That he turned up in Pleasant Valley was no accident. He wasn't known there. The only time he had ever been there was the winter before when they had tried to rob the bank and lost three men in a snow-filled pit. But the memory of that still bothered him, and he kept wishing he could have a better look at the town. Cole had been back several times, on his own, looking for the hooraw with the spring wagon, but Parson still was curious about the place. Besides, his contacts here and there told him that Pleasant Valley's menfolk were an oblivious lot and that the sheriff there was too nearsighted to spend any time reading reward dodgers.

All in all, a good place.

Parson put up his horse at the depot barn, had a meal at the hotel, and then rolled himself a smoke and sauntered along the street, just looking.

Pleasant Valley wasn't in a valley. It was located on a high flat from which the land receded into rolling hills in all directions. North were the flint hills, south was the Cimarron Valley, several miles away. The town had been named after an early settler, Jubal Pleasant, who—some said—had later moved across the river and founded Jubilation out of spite. There was now an ongoing hostility between the mercantile interests of the two towns. In the early days Jubilation had contended to be the county seat but had lost out to Pleasant Valley. The official reason was that when the river was on a rise nobody could get to Jubilation. The same reason accounted for Pleasant Valley's having regular stage service and ready access to rail-freight goods such as lumber, coal, and heavy hardware. It was the boast of Pleasant Valley's merchants that two out of every three dollars accumulated in Jubilation was spent in Pleasant Valley. It was the retort of Jubilation's merchants that without Jubilation's money Pleasant Valley would dry up and blow away.

None of which made any impression on Parson. He stood on the boardwalk outside a general hardgoods store and gazed longingly at the bank across the street. Next to it was a short, narrow alley leading to a shale pit. They had come that close. So close! Yet they had never made it to the bank. A wagon had entered the street, and an instant later . . . disaster. They had never had the chance to rob the bank. They had lost horses and men. Worse, they had lost the entire proceeds from their biggest haul, $28,000 still resting in Cole's saddlebag.

Parson shook his head, sadly. It *had* seemed like a good plan at the time.

Cole would be unhappy about his leaving, but Parson didn't know if that mattered. He wasn't sure he would go back. He'd had about all of Cole Yeager he could stand. It was one thing to follow a man who knew how to plan and execute high-stakes robberies. It was another thing being always around a jasper who took to shooting people at the drop of a hat. After a time, a thing like that got on a man's nerves.

Pondering the obliquities of fate, Parson wandered across and walked down the alley to look into the depths of the shale pit. Men were working down there. Pickaxes and wedge mauls sang a sleepy rhythm as hitched teams hauled lazily at dredges, fresnoes, and stone boats.

"Shale business goin' to the dogs this year," someone said. Parson turned. The elderly man beside him was one of the spit-and-whittle codgers he had seen on the mercantile porch.

"Pavin' contractors all usin' caleche these days," the codger explained. "It's cheaper an it smooths better."

"Paving?"

"Buildin' roads. You know. So's folks don't bog when it rains."

"Oh. I suppose they only work this pit in the summer."

"Yeah. Spring, summer, an' fall. Come winter it fills up with snow. Then the only activity is the drop-in trade."

"Drop-in?"

The codger grinned. "Can't recollect a spring thaw yet that they didn't find somebody down there

227

needin' buried. You leave a hole like that layin' around, people just naturally fall into it."

"Naturally." Parson shuddered.

"Past spring was th' best. Three men an' two horses, right down yonder. Nobody ever did figger out how they got there, but there they was. Right smart mess, it was."

"I can imagine. Ah . . . did they find anything else?"

"Not that I ever heard about. Ain't seen you before, mister. You doin' business here?"

"Just passing through." He turned away, the old man following.

"Reckon you're goin' to Jubilation then," the codger allowed.

"Oh? Why would I go there?"

"Not many reasons for a ridin' man to be passin' through Pleasant Valley. Generally them that does is on their way to Jubilation."

"I hadn't even thought about going to Jubilation." Parson shrugged. It was true. Riding with Cole Yeager, he had picked up some of Cole's habits. One of them was to avoid places like Iron Jack Fuller's town unless he had a good reason. But then, that was because Cole was known among some of the elements attracted to such places. As far as Parson knew, he wasn't known much at all.

"I think about goin' to Jubilation," the codger chatted. "Me, I think about it a good bit. Twenty-seven saloons they got there. *Twenty-seven* of 'em!" His old eyes gleamed at the glory of it. Then he added, sadly, "I can't go, though. Old woman won't let me. Damn ol' biddy. Says she'd let me go to hell afore she'd let me go to Jubilation."

"Many's the man that's been blessed half to death by a righteous woman," Parson allowed. "For the

228

Lord hath made it woman's lot to defend against wickedness and sin."

The codger squinted up at him. "You a preacher or somethin'?"

"No. I'm a notorious outlaw. I rob banks and trains."

The oldster squinted again and made a sour face. "I reckon," he said.

It was some time later when Parson returned to the hotel. He didn't intend to sleep there. He was short on cash and had staked out a place in the barn to throw his roll. But it was a good place to watch and listen, the hotel lobby, and for the price of a cup of coffee he could sit there a while. Several old newspapers were lying around and he picked one up and glanced at it. Then he looked again. There it was, right at the top of the page. Parson felt his scalp draw tight.

A sodbuster named Howard Sills had found $28,000 in a saddlebag. The saddlebag had been in the parcel box of his spring wagon. He didn't know how long it had been there or where or when he might have picked it up.

Twenty-eight thousand dollars. Parson felt a chill creep up his spine. A spring wagon. The buster drove a spring wagon.

"Where is Bad Basin?" Parson asked a seedy drummer.

The man scowled at him. "Beats me."

But another man nearby turned toward him. "I reckon you're readin' about Howard Sills and that there money he found. Don't that beat all?"

"Where is Bad Basin?"

"It's across the river, few miles out from Jubilation. But if you're thinkin' about that money, it ain't there. It's in the bank. Most everybody in the county done asked about that."

"What bank is that?"

"Why, the one in Jubilation, of course."

"That's a lot of money to keep in a bank vault. Must be an awful temptation to some folks."

"Only to the banker, I reckon," the man laughed. "Nobody ever robs the Jubilation bank. I don't think anybody's ever even tried."

Within the space of a minute, Parson found all his plans changed. If there was anything in the world that could improve Cole Yeager's killing mood — and get a man into the outlaw's favor — it would be news like this. As he saddled his horse at the depot barn and tied on his roll, Parson recounted in his mind the things he knew, and rehearsed how he would present them to Cole. The yayhoo with the spring wagon — he had his name and his location. The missing loot — he knew where it was. And maybe best of all — the bank it rested in was a bank in a big-money town, and a bank that had no experience at being robbed.

XX

Jubilation Post Office was a barred cubicle in the corner of Stapleton's Market. It did business three days a week, presided over by Morris Stapleton or a clerk in his postmaster cap. And on those days, Penelope Becket had discovered, the post office was the best place in town to gather news. Her logic was that anyone mailing a letter had something to say. Of the options available to her—uptown was off limits to ladies, the men at the mill and the feed store simply went silent in her presence, and Cornelia Hanks had forbidden her to hang around the barber shop—the post office was the best place to gather gossip.

It was there she had learned that Andrew Funt suffered from gout, that Bedelia Martin's sister in Iowa had twin boys, that Puff McVey's real first name was Shirley, that the Reverend Fennell Goodbody's brother was a resident of the federal penitentiary at Leavenworth and had found God there, that Prosper O'Neil was building a charcoal kiln in the valley a few miles below Jubilation Gap, and that Howard Sills reported regularly to his uncle, Chester Sills of Maryland, regarding the financial progress

231

of his enterprise at Bad Basin.

"Howard's right proud of this'n," Nat Kinley told her as he handed a posted envelope to Stapleton's clerk behind the bars. "Them turnips has got him over the hump. He's paid off all his bills, got money in the bank and a second crop in th' ground." He dusted his hat against his leg and grinned at her. "Whatever the rest of the place makes is gravy."

"Gravy?" She frowned.

"Pure gravy," he assured her. "I told Howard he ought to write to Uncle Chester an' tell him to mind his own business. Now Howard's gettin' rich like he is on turnips, it don't seem like he ought to have truck with some Easterner that wants him to come home an' marry Flutilla Culver, even if the dude is his uncle. I told him, I says, 'Howard,' I says, 'look at it this way. Would you kowtow to a man that abused his mules, or used whitewash on his face, or ate codfish?'"

"I don't believe I follow you," Penelope said, scribbling in her pad.

"That's just exactly what Howard said." Nat nodded. "But what I meant was, well, this Uncle Chester of his lives in Maryland. An' what's worse, he keeps tryin' to get Howard to go back to Maryland and marry Flutilla Culver, of all things. Me, I don't hold with people that won't better theirselves tryin' to get other folks not to either."

"What?" She looked up, confused.

"No law says Uncle Chester *has* to live in Maryland. I mean, he's had all his life to move, you see. It seems to me he prob'ly resents Howard's gumption."

"Gumption?"

"Get up an' go. Like Howard got up an' went, except his Uncle Chester has been on him about it ever' since."

"I see," she nodded. "I think." She resumed writing. "Turnips and gravy," she murmured. "That should make a news article. Who did you say Flutilla Culver is?"

"Some female Howard's Uncle Chester wants him to marry. But he don't want to, an' it's not just because of his delicate condition neither."

"What delicate condition?" she had stopped writing.

"Oh, you know how Howard gets. Around pretty women, I mean. Land, I never seen the like of it. Take you, for instance. You're a mighty fetchin' young lady."

She blushed. "Now, Mr. Kinley!"

"It's all right for me to say that," he assured her, "because personally I like women that's bigger an' solider, so to speak. But I can sure see what Howard sees in you."

"I haven't noticed he sees anything in me."

"Then you ain't been payin' attention, Miss Penelope. One look at you an' ol' Howard goes glass-eyed an' tongue-tied an' ain't got any more self-control than a possum eatin' yodelberries. I've saw critters on loco weed that make more sense than he does when you're around. But it ain't your fault, an' he can't help it neither. It's a . . . ah . . . a automoronic reflex. Somethin' like that. It's a condition."

She stared at him, dismayed. "That's the silliest thing I ever heard."

"Yes'm, but it's pure fact. Howard told me. That's why he has me bring in his mail, so he won't see you and make a plain fool of hisself anymore."

Even as she rejected the bizarre idea, Penelope realized it could be true. Howard Sills was, without doubt, the strangest-acting man she had ever encountered. Everybody knew he was weird. Sally and Betty talked constantly about him . . . but then Sally and Betty talked constantly about everything. And one never knew how much of what Wednesday Warren said could be believed. Yet everybody talked about the eccentricities of Howard Sills. Even the Reading Circle ladies whispered sometimes about his outhouse. He most definitely was odd . . . and yet everyone she knew liked him. They dismissed his aberrations as the natural result of being from back East, and generally found him polite, shy, and charming. Even the Reading Circle ladies accepted that he was a gentleman. People as widely varied as her Uncle Dub, Will Ambler, Bert Thompson, Emma Spalding, and Mr. Bloody Mare thought well of him and said so.

Yet every encounter Penelope had ever had with him had been either disastrous or absurd. She had become convinced the man was berserk. It puzzled her that she was the only one who thought so. Maybe there was something to what Mr. Kinley said.

Still, the thought was embarrassing.

"I don't know why you're telling me all this, Mr. Kinley," she said.

He smiled and shrugged. "Why, missy, Howard Sills is a friend of mine, an' he's got about all he can handle right now, what with strikin' it rich in the turnip business, an' every whistlebritches in th' county tryin' to lay claim to that $28,000 he found, an' the town ladies after him to play that thing he has at Chautauqua—he's been practicin' most every evenin' . . . did I mention that his cat run off? An' me an' some of the boys tryin' to teach him how to shoot a revolver so's he can defend hisself. Anyhow . . ." He paused, regarding her gravely. "What with all that an' tryin' to get his Uncle

Chester off his back long enough to lay in another turnip crop, why, ol' Howard's about at th' end of his wits an' he don't need to be lolly-eyed into a four-day conniption just 'cause some little honeypot don't know better than to. Sorry, missy, but that's how it is. Fine mornin' to you now, Miss Penelope."

Agatha Sturgis and Martha Haggard had been at Stapleton's bins selecting vegetables. As Nat headed for the door they glared after him and crossed to where Penelope sat by the post office.

"I don't think you should talk to people like that, Penelope," Martha said. "Nat Kinley is a known carouser. His name is prominent on Mrs. Mayor's list."

"What list?" Penelope shook herself aware, still deeply disturbed at what the Lazy K owner had said.

"Mrs. Mayor's," Martha repeated. "She has been making a list of the men who go uptown. We've all been helping her. Mr. Kinley appears on that list several times."

"They're all in league," Agatha pointed out.

"But I think all the men go up there sometimes, don't they?"

"Most of them, of course," Martha admitted. "But we all thought it would be a good idea to make a list. We intend to say some very harsh things about them at next week's meeting."

"Can I say that in the newspaper?"

"Of course you can, dear. But I hope you will be discreet. If you want to print the list you'll have to have Mrs. Mayor's permission."

"Very well." Penelope made notes in her pad. "I'll tell Miss Hanks about it. Ah . . . do you know whether . . . ah . . . Mr. Sills's name is on the list?"

Martha frowned, thinking. "Not that I recall. But he might be. It's a very long list."

"All in league," Agatha reminded her.

"We saw Miss Hanks moving into her brother's house last week. We must go and call. Do you know whether she needs anything, Penelope?"

"No, ma'am. She hasn't said. Just that she had decided to stay on in Jubilation for a while, and was tired of the hotel."

"Yes, and we're all just delighted. In fact, some of us took it upon ourselves to—"

"Only anticipating, of course," Agatha interrupted.

"Of course," Penelope agreed, wondering what they were talking about. They seemed, suddenly, downright furtive.

"It's only because the elections are so near, and there really hasn't been time for a proper social call. I do hope she will understand. You understand, don't you, Penelope?"

"Why of course I do." Understand what?

"And we have only just posted the notice, this very morning. Polly went to City Hall personally and tacked it up."

"Several of the ladies are standing guard there to make sure the men don't take it down," Agatha clarified. "They *are* all in league."

"We didn't even take time to discuss it with Mrs. Mayor," Martha said. "But of course she will agree. After all, our cause is hers, isn't it?"

"I'm sure it is," Penelope assured them. "But I haven't been to City Hall yet. I haven't seen the . . . notice. What is it?"

"Why, I thought just everyone knew," Martha said. "You must go see it, Penelope. Ann and Wanda composed the words, you know, and Fern Wickes lettered it with her calligraphy pen. She did it in blue ink. It looks just lovely."

"We're sure Miss Hanks will be very pleased. Don't you think so, Penelope?"

"I'm sure she will," Penelope nodded. "But what is — ?"

The front door of Stapleton's slammed open and Marshal Ben Cutter strode in, followed by two of those large, shadowy men who sometimes descended from uptown — Penelope thought of them as guards or special deputies, but had never been quite sure who they were or how many of them there were.

Cutter's face was red and he took a quick look around the store, glaring at the ladies by the post office, then walked across to the main counter where Morris Stapleton was counting carrots.

"Mayor Twiddie been in this morning?" he demanded.

Stapleton blinked. "Haven't seen him. You might try the Golden Rule. They get breakfast there."

"I'm going to get to the bottom of this," Cutter hissed. The large men with him glowered at all and sundry. "It's all part of a plot," Cutter added.

W. D. Tienert entered with a shopping basket. "Morning, Penelope," he said, then tipped his hat to the ladies. He stopped abruptly as Ben Cutter strode across his path, his furious gaze on the group at the post office.

"Somebody's way out of bounds," Cutter stormed.

The clerk behind the bars paled. "I'm supposed to be here, Marshal. Mr. Stapleton is the postmaster and he said — "

"Shut up," Cutter snarled. Hard eyes darted from Martha Haggard to Agatha Sturgis and back. "I want to know who put you women up to this!"

"Up to what?" Penelope asked.

"What's all the fuss?" Tiernert asked.

Cutter turned to him. "You're on the council.

Where's the mayor? What do you all plan to do about this?"

"About what?" Tienert stared at him.

"You don't know? Then you better get over to City Hall and find out! I never heard of anything so ridiculous in my whole life. A woman! Make a laughin' stock of my town . . ."

Penelope could stand it no longer. Tying on her bonnet as she went, she headed for City Hall. There was a clamor on the street and other people were heading the same way. Behind her she heard Marshal Cutter shouting, "Twiddie! Mayor Twiddie! Yeah, you! Where have you been? Get over to City Hall and wait there. I'll round up the others."

There was a crowd outside City Hall, people gawking at the bulletin board where legal notices were posted. Polly Cox and two other prominent members of the Wednesday Ladies' Reading Circle stood at stiff attention there. Polly held a cast-iron skillet and the others had rolling pins. Ding Cox, the city clerk, was dancing around just out of reach of his wife's skillet.

"—not legal till it's certified by the clerk," he protested. "You women can't just—"

"You come a step closer, Ding Cox, and I'll brain you," Polly promised. She pointed at a fresh-posted notice. "Is that the city clerk seal or isn't it? And that signature there, is that C. W. Cox or not? Now shut your mouth!"

Penelope edged through the crowd until she could read the notice. She read it twice. "Well, my goodness," she said to no one in particular. Getting out her pad, she started writing.

"You don't have to write all that down, dear," Martha Haggard said, coming up behind her. "We made copies. I'll give you one for the newspaper."

"And advertisements," Agatha Sturgis added. "Don't forget the advertisements."

"I'll get them to you," Martha told Penelope. "We're starting a campaign fund, but right now there's money in the WCTU and Mission fund to pay for the space."

W. D. Tienert and Slim Haggard had arrived, with Alfred Twiddie close behind. They shoved through and gaped at the posted notice. It was tacked to the board alongside Twiddie's proclamations setting the dates for Jubilation's Chautauqua and decreeing the penalty for horse racing on city streets. The notice was on crisp white paper, elegant with royal blue ink.

Ben Cutter herded Woolly Smith and George Gosset through the crowd and pointed a furious finger at the notice. "You read it," he told them. "Then we'll have a meeting." He turned to survey the crowd, hard eyes slitted and his immaculate mustache a-twitch.

"Oh, my God," Alfred Twiddie said behind him, staring at the notice.

"Is that legal?" Gosset asked. "I mean, a woman?"

"It's legal," Polly Cox assured him. "Has been since April."

Cutter addressed the crowd, his voice overriding. "I want the name of the man that put these women up to this! Whoever you are, it'll go easier if you step forward now. Whose idea was this?"

Penelope recalled suddenly what Martha had said about how pleased Miss Hanks would be. Backing from the crowd she turned and hurried up the street toward the Tribune office.

Bert Thompson stood in the doorway, red-eyed and weaving slightly as was usual each morning.

"Mornin', Penelope," he greeted her. "What's all the fuss down there? Somebody suddenly come to their senses at City Hall?" As she pushed past him Bert shook his head. "Naw, that's not very likely," he mused.

Cornelia Hanks had just arrived and was hanging up her bonnet. "Good morning, Penelope. My, you seem excited."

"Oh, Miss Hanks, I think it's just the greatest news! May I write the article, or do you want to do that yourself?"

"What article?" Cornelia raised a puzzled brow.

"Oh, then you really didn't know? I thought you probably did, even though Mrs. Haggard wasn't sure—"

"Penelope, calm down. What are you talking about?"

"Why, the notice on the board. At City Hall. About your being a candidate for mayor of Jubilation."

XXI

"I have to put a stop to this right now," Cornelia Hanks declared abruptly, shoving stacks of copy aside. "I should have gone straight over there and removed that notice the minute—"

"I wish you'd make up your mind," Bert Thompson fussed. "First you say we have to get all this folderah set up by noon so we can make printin' schedule, now you're goin' chargin' off somewhere. Are we gonna print a newspaper or not?"

"But I can't let that go on. All those people . . . they think I'm running for mayor. They've thought so all morning."

"Well, they can think it a while longer. It won't kill them. You're the one said we'd go eight pages, and you said you'd edit and block. I can't set up eight pages by myself."

Cornelia bit off words of exasperation, then settled for glaring at him. "You handled this newspaper for several weeks, Mr. Thompson."

"Not at eight pages, I didn't. Besides, that was before you got here and started imposing standards of procedure."

"Quality," she corrected him. "What I have in-

241

sisted upon is standards of quality. Adequate writing, neat composition, and proper captioning, that's all I demand."

"Sure, he muttered. "So instead of four pages of ordinary drivel, now we put out eight pages of *quality* drivel. What's wrong with runnin' for mayor anyway? You won't win, and it gives us something to fill that hole on page two."

She was silent for a long moment, poised over her stacks of paperwork. "What do you mean, I won't win?"

"Oh, come on, lady. Whoever heard of a female mayor?"

"And what is wrong with that idea?"

"Nothing. Fine with me. It'll just never happen, that's all." He slid a stick of type into a page form and worked shims between the lines to tighten it. "Are you gonna edit that copy there or do you want me to set it like it is?" He strode to the desk, lifted a sheet of correspondence, and glanced at it. "How about that! Some genius has decided it was Cole Yeager that stopped that train out of Dodge. Nice piece of detective work, considerin' there was a whole trainload of eyewitnesses to identify him. Uh-oh."

"Uh-oh what?"

He was looking out the window. "Now's your chance to put a stop to your candidacy, because here comes your constituency."

They came crowding into the front office, more than a dozen of the leaders of the Wednesday Ladies' Reading Circle accompanied by several of their daughters, bright-eyed, and Wednesday Warren.

Martha Haggard pushed forward and handed a sheet of paper across the counter to Cornelia. "Here is your copy of the posting, Miss Hanks. Penelope said you hadn't seen it."

"We're all behind you, Miss Hanks," Wanda Wilkie said. "We want you to know that. We are prepared to buy advertisements, put up posters, even go door to door to get people to vote for you."

Imogene Stapleton edged through the crowd, her daughter and Sally Spalding following and being followed in turn by young Wednesday Warren. "Some of us are working up a campaign platform for you to review, Miss Hanks. Of course, Prohibition will be the main plank . . . a plan to close all those . . . those *saloons* uptown. This really would be a much nicer town."

"A law and order platform," another chirped. "The very thing. Miss Hanks, we are all so—"

Cornelia raised a hand for silence. When she had their attention she gazed at them, one after another. "Ladies . . . I wonder . . . haven't you overlooked something?"

They exchanged puzzled glances among them. "Fund raising?" Polly Cox offered. "No, we've appointed a committee to—"

"We thought we would conduct a social," Belva Jones added. "We'll serve cake and—"

"A parade," Agatha Sturgis declared. "Parades are best."

"Ladies, please!" Cornelia shook her head. "Don't you think you might have discussed this with me first?"

"There really wasn't time, dear," Martha explained. "We only met about it yesterday evening, and you were so busy moving into your brother's house—"

"That's what brought the subject up," Polly said. "I mean, obviously you have decided to stay."

"And today is the legal deadline for posting filings," Martha finished. "There was so much to get done. Besides, the vote was seventeen to one. Clearly that is a mandate."

Seventeen to one? Cornelia glanced around again, noting absences. The most notable absence was Opal Twiddie. Mrs. Mayor. Of course.

"I am very flattered," she told them. "Really I am. And I think it is a marvelous idea. It really is high time that women got out of the kitchen and took a hand in things. But really, I am a newcomer in Jubilation. I have only been here a few weeks—"

"You own property. You're a legal resident. We looked it up."

"When we have the social you can make a speech," Imogene suggested.

Agatha Sturgis frowned and drew herself up ominously. "The men won't listen. They're all in league."

In shadows beyond the bins, Bert Thompson grinned and shook his head. "Talk about not listening," he muttered.

Cornelia signaled silence again. "As I said, I am flattered, but I'm not the one to run for office here. Surely, one of you ladies—"

"We thought about that," Wanda assured her. "But we can't. Our husbands would raise such a fuss."

"Let the old maid do it," Bert muttered to his type bins.

"I see," Cornelia said. "Well, ladies, I am very sorry, but I have no intention of running for political office."

Oblivious to the stunned silence around him, Wednesday Warren whispered to Sally Spalding, "I wish you'd stand still for a minute so's I can smell you. What is that?"

"It's almond extract," she whispered. "I put some behind my ears. Quit nuzzling me. What will people think?"

"But Miss Hanks, you must!' Martha erupted. "It's all arranged! What would everyone think?"

"They'll think you got almond extract behind your ears," Wednesday explained. Every face in the crowd turned to stare at him. He had forgotten to whisper. "Pardon," he whispered, turning bright red.

"Oh brave new world," Bert muttered, "that has such people in it."

Emma Spalding had kept her peace so far, slightly embarrassed at the situation. Now she caught Cornelia's eye. "We should have talked to you first, Cornelia, but some of us didn't even know about the vote until this morning. And anyway, you have said you agree with our goals."

"Of course I agree, but to run for public office —"

"I know, it sounds like such a bother, but think of the good it will do. Just having a Prohibition candidate on the ballot —"

"And it isn't as though you might actually win," Martha added. "We just want to get their attention."

Cornelia's gray eyes widened. "Now just a moment. If you ladies think I would consider running for office with the idea of losing . . ."

Emma shook her head. Martha, she thought, for heaven's sake! "Certainly not," she said. "It's just that it is such a novel thing for a lady to be a candidate. And Mayor Twiddie is very entrenched."

"The only way I would consider such a thing would be if there were a chance to win."

"Then you *would* consider it?"

"Definitely not. Not for a moment. Not under any circumstances."

"Lay on, Macduff," Bert muttered, "and damn'd

be him . . . her . . . that first cries, 'Hold, enough!' "

"Will you at least think about it?" Emma pleaded.

"We promise to do all the work," Wanda added.

"I really don't think so," Cornelia insisted.

Martha took this as a definite maybe. "Do think on it, dear," she said. "In the meantime we can start making posters and planning the social. Oh, and by the way, did we tell you that Mr. Hester has withdrawn from the race?"

"He withdrew this morning," Wanda added. "You should put something in the paper about that."

"Tell her why he withdrew," Bert called from the bins.

Emma was already herding them out the door. "Come along, ladies, we've taken enough of Miss Hanks's time for now. Sally, what is that . . . have you been into my extract again?"

The delegation filed out, trailed by Sally, Betty, and Wednesday. The cowboy crouched and bobbed, trying to compare the scents of the two girls' ears.

Cornelia sat down at her desk, still staring at the closed door. "I told them no," she assured herself. "Didn't I tell them no?"

Bert came out from behind the bins. "You talking to me?"

"No. Go back to work."

"I been working. You don't see me spendin' all morning talkin' politics. You gonna run for office or not?"

"Absolutely not!"

"Good choice. You'd just make a fool of yourself. Is that rewrite copy about ready? It's comin' on to noon."

"Set it the way it is," Cornelia sighed. Then, "What was that you said? About why Hester withdrew? Why did he withdraw?"

"Oh. Well, what he said was, he didn't mind runnin' against Alfred Twiddie now and again just to make a race of it, but he's damned if he'll humiliate himself by bein' on the ballot with a woman."

She stared at him. "He said that? How do you know he said that?"

"I just finished settin' type on it. He sent a written statement over. I put it next to the obituaries on page two. If you can write your withdrawal statement to make five inches of type I'll put it alongside with a single head—somethin' like 'Opposition Folds, Twiddie Wins' ought to fit. Then I can lock the page. I told Bloody Mare to be here as soon as he can go *gazyet-chick* the press. He's out fixin' a hole in the fence to keep Sweeny out of the squish."

First, Parson scouted Red Basin. The Sills place was easy to spot. It was the only place in Bad Basin with buildings. The rest was range land. But at Howard Sills's purchased claim morning sunlight swept across fields of corn and sorghum to glow on tall slat silos, a peculiarly awkward but sturdy-looking barn, a tall house that looked like playing cards slanted against each other, and various sheds and outbuildings, one of which—he wished he dared go closer, but he did not want to be seen—might have been a privvy except no privvy he had ever seen looked like that.

A large, carefully fenced plot was freshly tilled. From a distance Parson could see an old black man and two youths trudging along furrows, spreading seed. Beyond, near the barn, green of a fresh crop showed in a second fenced field. He recalled what he had heard of this Sills striking it rich in turnips, although nobody seemed to know who his buyers were.

Skirting entirely around the Sills spread, seeing what he could, Parson then set out east on a neat, fresnoed road that led up through hills beyond the basin to the broad expanse of the Higgins-Wentworth Trail. Off to the side was Jubilation Gap, where the trail dipped toward the Cimarron. Straight ahead was the two-tiered town of Jubilation. Shadows of the uptown bluff with its crown of roistering places still lay upon the elm-lined streets of downtown and a row of tiny wagons snaked up the inclined trail hauling fresh loads of spirits up from Arkansas through the Cherokee Outlet.

With the habit of many years of outlawing, Parson didn't go straight in. Instead he angled his mount to the left, rode through the first break of the gap, then bore hard right to flank the town, keeping just below the sheared limestone breaks that separated the town from the river valley. Two miles of careful riding, picking his way along the valley's upper slope, brought him to the shoulder of Jubilation Bluff where it plunged downward, jutting outward from the valley wall like the swell of a buried mountain. Far below was the shadowed valley of the Cimarron. Above, just visible, were the roofs of two or three of uptown Jubilation's refreshment stands. He heard the call of teamsters, coming closer, and a rattle of trace chain. He edged into a cleft and watched.

There were four wagons, sturdy overland vehicles with teams of mules. They crawled into sight around the thrust of the bluff, angling upward, and passed above him. When they were gone he spurred his mount up the rise and found a fresh-cut trail curving up around the bluff toward its high base beyond the valley's rim. Where rains had sagged fresh roadfill, creating a slight dip, the ground was littered with fist-sized lumps of black. At first he thought of coal, fallen from the wagons. But when he looked closer he found the fragments were kilned charcoal lumps. Some distance east, down in the shadowed valley, a businesslike plume of smoke rose to meet the winds atop the valley.

Somebody was making charcoal and hauling it to Jubilation by the wagonload.

The new road was as good as any. Parson doubled back on it, climbed around the thrust of the bluff, and entered wide pastures that narrowed toward the incline where uptown and downtown Jubilation met. Above and to the left was uptown on its hill. Ahead and sweeping in from the right were houses, barns, and the backs of a row of commercial buildings. Where the two features met stood a large, new building with expansions being built on both its wings. Sheds full of barrels huddled alongside it, and the wagons were there, unloading charcoal into hopper chutes of fresh-milled lumber. A strong fence surrounded the entire complex and the men he saw carried guns. This side of the place he saw no paths upward, so he reined to the right, toward the downtown center.

As he passed the fenced enclave he heard a commotion and saw a half-grown pig race around the main building, squealing in terror. A man with a stick was right behind it as it plunged across the intervening space and dived through a hole in the fence.

"Damn it, Sweeny," the man shouted, "you stay away from here!"

A grizzled man still further away shouted, "Somebody ought to shoot that scutter!"

The pig darted across Parson's path directly in front of him, then turned to look back, hurling grunted pig-insults. Off to Parson's right a back-shed door of a long building opened and a small, bearded man with a wool cap stepped out. He frowned at the pig and scolded, *"Svin'ya! Kogda izuyish' nye* squish? *Plokhaya svin'ya! Nyet!"*

The pig looked at the little man silently, thoroughly disgruntled, then sauntered to where Parson was passing and fell into step alongside his horse.

The little man lifted his cap and smiled at Parson. "Hollow Cossack," he said. "Cock de la?" He reentered the building.

Parson looked down at the pig. The pig looked up at Parson.

Behind him at the hole in the fence, someone asked, "Who's that there with Sweeny?"

"Never saw him before," someone else said.

Parson found a livery stable, put up his horse, and went out to look at the town. Two things in particular he wanted to see . . . the local bank and the local law. So far, the town looked to him to be a pushover. If it still looked that way after he had scouted it, he had a notion he might just help himself to that $28,000 — and whatever else he wanted — and not need to go look up Cole Yeager.

Eyes slitted and darting, Parson and the pig crossed the street together and began scouting.

XXII

Fewer than a dozen of Jubilation's buildings were made of brick. City Hall was one of these, and the Grange hall on the next street over. The houses of W. D. Tienert and his widowed sister, separated by a wide lot that served as a park, were brick, as were the homes of a few other substantial citizens. The house Cornelia Hanks inherited from her brother Clarence was brick veneer with clapboard overhang for its second half-floor. The newer part of Bunker's Mill was brick, as was the barn where Dutch Henry Vargas kept his racers.

But the most substantial brick building in town was the Jubilation Bank and Trust Company, an imposing two-story structure dominating the corner of Main and Peach. It was built like a fortress — one of the few things its founder, Jubal Pleasant, had ever done right. The thing W. D. Tienert had done right was to marry Jubal Pleasant's daughter and sole heir, who rested now in Eternal Peace Cemetery. Tienert had found himself possessed of a declining — if strongly built — bank and a brick house in a dying little town isolated by geography from the benefits of commerce. Those, and a worthless bluff.

When he sought to sell part of his holdings to pay off debts, a shadowy group of investors had come forward to call his bluff. From that day on, the prosperity of Jubilation had been assured. Uptown was born.

Now the brick bank on Main and Peach did brisk business. Just in the ten minutes Parson allowed himself inside—his pretext was to discuss valley range values with one of the clerks—he saw three men come in to deposit money. One was a merchant with a sack of coin and a few bills. The other two he took for uptown saloonmen, and the size of their deposits made his mouth water. Both were accompanied by large, watchful men with large, ready guns. It was Iron Jack Fuller's town, all right.

He also noted that the bank had two doors, both steel-riveted, one with an inner bar, the other equipped with a Sturgis Steadfast lock and a barred portal. Parson was impressed. Even more impressive was the safe, a two-ton Falstaff with three-point tumblers, stone-bedded in a key-lock vault. Such a safe could be cracked—any safe could—but not quickly. The bank guard was another large, watchful man with a ready gun. Parson decided he had seen enough. It was time to take a look at the local law. As he turned toward the door it opened and the two men entered. One was a tall, friendly looking man with well-fitted clothing and sun-bleached blond hair. The second was lean, dark-eyed, and sardonic, a rangeman by his dress and bearing, and the Colt at his belt was as much a part of him as the weathered hat on his head and the scuffed boots on his feet.

This one nodded at a clerk and flicked a thumb to point back. "Howdy, Harvey. Did you know there's a pig standin' watch out there?"

The clerk shrugged. "Howdy, Nat. Mr. Sills. I

guess that's Sweeny out there. Is he sober?"

"You mean the pig?"

"Yeah, 'bout half the time he's drunk as a judge. The other day he even tried to pick a fight with Leonard."

"Like to have seen that. Who won?"

"Aw, Sweeny was so drunk he fell down an' Leonard just stepped over him an' went on down to the marshal's office. He was totin' the Winslow brothers."

"Which ones?"

"All of 'em. They stick together, those Winslows."

The younger man walked across the lobby, through the swing gate and knocked at the door of the banker's office. The door opened and he went inside.

"Mr. Sills is doin' all right with his turnips," the clerk told Nat. "Gettin' to be one of our main customers."

"Not many problems a good committee can't solve," Nat agreed. He glanced around, furtively. "Any talk about how that pig comes to be drunk so much?"

"Not that I heard," the clerk said. "Found his way uptown, most likely."

The one called Nat looked relieved. "Yeah, most likely. I need to get in to town more often. Always somethin' new."

"Sure is. Did you know that there Miss Hanks is runnin' for mayor?"

"Yeah, heard that on the street a while ago. I bet Clarence is floppin' over in his grave . . . what's left of him."

"Mr. Tienert's been out all mornin' meetin' with the City Council about it. He just came in a bit ago. I guess some of 'em have gone to talk to her about it. Make the town look mighty silly to have a woman runnin' for office, you know."

"That's a fact," Nat said. He glanced around again and his eyes fell on Parson, who had paused to listen. "Howdy," he said. "Stranger in town?"

"Just passin' through." Parson nodded. "What's all that about a woman mayor? I never heard of a woman bein' mayor of a town."

"Not likely to happen." Nat shrugged. "Bunch of biddies put her name on the slate, tryin' to clean out uptown. But she's sensible for a woman. I expect she'll listen to reason."

"What do they want to clean out uptown for? I ain't even got there yet."

"I don't know." Nat shrugged. "They just don't hold with drinkin' an' gamblin', I guess. They keep tryin' to shut it down. Not likely, though. That'd be like evisceratin' a shrine."

"That's desecrating," Parson said.

"That's a fact. Plumb disgustin'."

The young man came out of the banker's office and crossed the lobby. "He says eighty-one people have laid claim to the money, but nobody's proved up on it."

Nat shook his head. "Sure has been a rash of people losin' twenty-eight thousand dollars around here. If they all find their money, nobody in Coleman County's gonna have any more problems." He grinned at Parson. "Howard here found some money and everybody in this part of the world is just now rememberin' that they lost it. Howard, this here is a tourist, passin' through. This is Howard Sills, Mr . . . ah . . ."

Parson tipped his hat and shook hands. "John Smith," he said. "Yeah, it is just amazin' what people will do for money. Me, I rob banks and trains."

Howard grinned. "I'd recommend turnips myself."

"Can't say I ever robbed a turnip. Nice to meet you, Mr. Sills."

The two turned away, heading for the door. "I mailed your letter for you, Howard," Nat said. "While I was there I told Penelope about your problem."

"You told her *what?*"

"How you get with women. Figured it was best if she knew."

They opened the door and went out. "Watch out for that pig," Nat was saying. "His name is Sweeny."

"You *told* her? My God, Nat, you can't just—"

The door closed behind them. Parson stared at it, musing, then raised a brow toward the clerk.

"They don't neither of them live here," the clerk explained.

"Whereabouts is the town marshal's office?"

"It's on down Main, other side of the street. You'll see it. It's got a sign. If you decide to do business in Jubilation, Mr. Smith, you just tell us what you'll need."

"Don't worry," Parson said. "You'll be the first to know."

Prosper O'Neil had come in to town with the latest load of charcoal. When his men had finished loading the hopper chutes he watched the wagons past the gate, then hitched up his britches and headed for the main building. Elmer Wallace was in the yard, cradling his shotgun while he rolled himself a smoke.

"What was that commotion while ago?" Prosper asked.

"Oh, that pig got in again. Busted another hole in the fence and was headin' for the squish shed when Ike chased him off. I told Ike he ought to shoot the scutter. Done it my own self if Ike hadn't got in th' way."

"Yeah, an' had half the town out here wonderin' what's goin' on. It's hard enough to keep this place quiet without you shootin' pigs, Elmer. It isn't like it's hid, or anything."

"Well, that's four-five times that shoat has busted our fence," Elmer pointed out. "Somebody ought to do somethin'."

At the main door Prosper's way was blocked by Ike Ferguson, brandishing a revolver. "Who goes there?" Ike demanded.

"It's me, Ike. I brought in some more 'coal. Let me in."

"What's the password?"

O'Neil glared at him. "Ike, dammit, it's me. Prosper."

"I don't care. You have to say the password if you want to come in. You know that. Everybody agreed."

"But dammit, Ike, it's embarrassin'!"

"Say the password or get off this property!"

"Oh, all right. *Cock dealer.* There."

"Come on in," Ike said, holding the door for him.

"I don't know why we couldn't have got ourselves a better password," Prosper fussed. "At least somethin' *decent,* for God's sake."

Ike latched the door behind them. "You know as well as I do it had to be something Bloody Mare would say. Hell, nobody's even been able to figure out how to tell him we *have* a password, much less what it is. An' where would we be if we didn't let him in? Do you know how to brew this stuff?"

The interior of the place was large, barn-like, and littered with distilling paraphernalia. Everything they had been able to beg, borrow, or steal that resembled a samovar had been brought here, modified by Bloody Mare and worked into the maze of coils, troughs, and pipes that ran from front to back of the factory. Cords of firewood lined the walls, alternating with barrels of various shapes and sizes, stirring vats, funnels, and bins. And over all hung the heady reek of fermenting turnip squish. Mostly, they had grown oblivious to it.

"It's just that I don't see why we have to have a password at all," Prosper argued. "I mean, there's only nine of us."

"Well," Ike said, shrugging, "it seemed like a good idea at the time. You remember what Bert Thompson said, that business about 'O conspiracy, shamest thou to show thy dangerous brow by night —' I forget the rest, but we all agreed."

"Bert Thompson was drunk."

"So was the rest of us. But it made sense at the time."

"I don't know how long we're gonna be able to keep this a secret anyway," Prosper growled. He went to a marked vat and lifted its plank lid. A dipper hung beside it and he took it down, dipped clear liquid, and took a long sip. His eyes closed, he rocked back and forth on his toes, and his face turned red. After a long moment he expelled a breath and sighed. "Hot damn, that's powerful stuff!"

"We better keep it a secret," Ike said ominously. "You know what'll happen if Iron Jack Fuller gets wind of this."

Prosper sipped the brew again. "I hear angels singing," he decided. Then he capped the vat and sat on it. "The wagons in?" he asked.

Ike gazed hungrily at the closed vat, but restrained himself. It was his shift on plant guard. "Two hours ago or better. Right on schedule. Elmer saw 'em goin' up the hill."

"An' they'll be here at dark?"

"That's what Nat said. Him and Twist made th' arrangements."

"Everybody know to be here to load?"

"Elmer's got the word out. Quit fussin' about it, Prosper. Everything's goin' to go off just as smooth as silk."

"It better. I got better'n eight thousand tied up in this venture so far."

"Same as me. So has Elmer, an' Will Ambler's out better'n five thousand. Since when wasn't you a bettin' man?"

Prosper lapsed into glum silence. After a few moments Ike went back to sit by the door. In the reeking interior of the Jubilation Research Center, Prosper O'Neil sat on his vat and pondered. Of course he was a gambling man, he told himself. He had gambled all his life. He had gambled on trail herds, gambed on the weather, gambled on feed crops and rises of the river. He had gambled on horse races and gambled on cards.

But never before had he gambled on something he couldn't even pronounce. What was it the Russian called it? Watka? Something like that.

Prosper examined his hand. He had the word of the town drunk of Jubilation that this stuff would sell if they could get it out of Kansas and past the territories. He had the word—in some obscure foreign language—of a strange little yayhoo who couldn't even talk American that he could keep producing the stuff in quantities to pay back a major capital investment. At least, he presumed he had that word. The town drunk told him so.

He had the word of a fast-draw squatter with a bad bull that there was a way to get the stuff to market. And he had the word of a seldom-sober millhand that he could keep on grinding turnips in his boss's mill as long as the money came in.

Never in the life of Prosper O'Neil had he entered into so strange an alliance. He, along with Ike Ferguson, Wallace, and the blacksmith, Will Ambler, had put up the money. He was providing the charcoal, Puff McVey the squish, and Nat Kinley and Twist McGuffin the connections. The Russian supplied the know-how, and Bert Thompson provided the Russian.

Am I a gambler? Prosper asked himself. He couldn't think of an appropriate answer.

In the alley behind Richardson's Refreshment Emporium, at the top of Jubilation Bluff, Iron Jack Fuller sat in his surrey staring down at the fenced complex at the bottom of the slope. Smoke came from a large chimney there, and a line of wagons that had delivered something bulky and black was disappearing northward along a new-graded path that led around the bluff and into the distant valley.

"I don't like it," he told the large men with him. "*Somebody* must know what they're doing in there."

"Yeah, Boss," Hemp said. "But we don't know who does, except them that are doin' it. And we haven't got our hands on any of them."

"Bert Thompson knows," Iron Jack growled.

"He don't come uptown any more. He just sends his payments. You want us to go get him?"

Iron Jack sat in thought for a long moment.

Then, "What was it you said about those wagons?"

"That was me, Boss," Packer told him. "What I said was, I thought it was funny those teamsters didn't stay around for a while like they usually do after they unload. They just delivered the whiskey, then turned right around and left. So I followed 'em. But they didn't go on into the territory. They only went a mile or so out, then turned off into the breaks and made camp. Seemed kind of funny to me, so I told you."

"I get the distinct feeling," Iron Jack muttered, "that somebody isn't keeping books. What did Cutter tell you?"

Hemp scuffed his toe in the yellow dust. "He said he doesn't know and he hasn't got time right now to check because he's got a woman on his slate and somebody's makin' a laughing stock of his town."

Iron Jack stared at him. "What does that mean?"

"I don't know, Boss. It's just what he said."

Iron Jack swore aloud, startling his thugs. "When I buy a lawman I expect him to stay bought! You get back down there and find out what he's doing that he can't look after my interests!"

"Yeah, Boss. Right away."

"And you," he told Packer. "You keep an eye on those wagons. If they move, I want to know where they went. And one of you tell Bert Thompson I want to talk to him. If he doesn't want to come, you bring him. But wait until after dark."

XXIII

"I think it must have started when I was twelve years old," Howard Sills told Nat Kinley. They shared a wall booth in the crowded dining room of the Golden Rule, the demolished remains of a pair of burned steaks, corn bread, and honeyed yams between them on the table. "That was the summer Mr. and Mrs. Cross came to visit Uncle Chester. They brought their daughters with them, and since the rest of the family was in Virginia for the racing season, Uncle Chester left it to me to entertain Letitia and Luella. I think it was the worst summer I ever had."

"Gave you a bad time, did they?" Nat asked, wrinkling his nose in sympathy. "Females can be a real bother."

"Letitia was my age. Twelve. Luella was a year or so older. I remember . . . ah, well." Howard's eyes went distant and sad. "They were really beautiful girls. I hadn't noticed girls much up to that time. The school I went to didn't have any, and when I was home I lived in the summer house and I used to play the pipes quite a bit and nobody much ever bothered me."

"Reminds me," Nat interrupted. "I noticed that bag in your wagon. That your pipes? Is this the day you're supposed to play them for the committee?"

"Yes." Howard sighed. "This evening. I don't much want to do that, but when Wednesday Warren explained how they were all counting on it, I really couldn't—"

"Sorry I can't be there to listen," Nat said. "I got other things to do. But what happened with the girls? When you were twelve, I mean."

"Letitia and Luella. Maybe it was just my age, but from the moment I saw them I forgot all about my pipes and my summer studies. I'm afraid I even neglected my animals, although Ambrose took over for me on that score."

"You had cows? Horses?"

"A dog and two chickens. Anyway, I'm afraid I became really smitten."

"First rut can be hell," Nat sympathized. "Which one did you fall in love with?"

"Both of them. And I suppose I never really got over it. They had dark-taffy hair and lavender eyes, and their gowns—especially Luella's, she was a bit older—sort of swelled outward about here."

"Yeah, I've noticed how they do that."

"But it was a disastrous summer, when I look back on it. Uncle Chester had specifically put me in charge. Have you ever been in charge of girls, Nat?"

"Can't honestly claim I ever was," Nat admitted. "Nor ever met another man that was either. Though many's the man that's tried."

"It started the day they arrived," Howard reminisced. "Letitia said, 'Well, we're here, what should we do now?' And Luella said, 'Let's turn the ducks loose.'"

"Ducks?"

"They were Uncle Walter's. A flock he had imported from Scotland. He intended to introduce a new strain of domestic duck. He had worked for years to cross them selectively with hardy native species and with the larger *Anatidaeus Breckii* developed by the Dutch for . . . but anyway, before I could object they had opened all the feeding pens and there were ducks all over Burgess Township. I was trying to catch them when Squire Trevaine's thoroughbreds bolted their pasture and frightened Mistress Oakes's dairy herd just coming in for milking. I never was quite sure what happened next, but the Squire's sulky driver became involved with the ladies of Holy Remembrance Mission, and a fishing punt was capsized off Sawtooth, and somehow Jason Hind's hayshed burned."

Nat was staring at him, glassy-eyed. "Ducks?" he whispered.

"Letitia and Luella were very energetic. Anyway, the time for explanation arrived and I didn't seem to be able to sort it all out satisfactorily. In fact, I don't remember even completing a sentence. But I was in a lot of trouble."

"Yeah." Nat blinked. "I can see that."

"And that was just the first day. As I said, it was a terrible summer."

"Seems to me like you'd have found a chance to explain."

"Somehow there never was the chance. I don't think I got a word in edgewise all summer long. But there were times I couldn't sit down. I remember those."

"Women!" Nat sighed.

"Yes." Howard smiled dreamily. "What a summer that was."

"That went on all summer? That kind of thing?"

"Every day. After the first week or so I tried to stay out of their way. I even hid several times, but they always came and found me. They didn't want me to miss any of the fun. By the time I was packed off to Cold Ridge Military School for a year I had a fractured tibia and I was considered a hellion and vandal. And I had almost lost the ability to speak."

"That's terrible!" Nat goggled at him.

"Yes, in a lot of ways it was. I'm afraid it took years for Uncle Chester to restore the Sills Family of Maryland to its proper reputation. On the other hand, though, I know I'll never forget Letitia and Luella. Nat, you just wouldn't believe what exquisite creatures they were. Just lovely . . . like angels."

Nat raised a curious brow. "Like Miss Penelope?"

"Yes, very much like . . ." Howard gulped and took a deep breath. "So you see how it is."

Nat nodded. "I'm glad I got my problems an' not yours," he said helpfully.

"I wish you could come along with me tonight," Howard said. "For moral support."

"You'll be all right," Nat assured him. "Probably be a couple of biddies there, maybe a leadin' citizen or two that they've drug in. Where's it gonna be, at the school?"

"No, in an open lot. Sort of a park between houses. Two streets over. It's a good choice. Bagpipes are an outdoor instrument."

"How'd Wednesday Warren get hooked up with the Chautauqua Committee, anyway? That button's a fair hand with cows, but I'd never have figured him for culture."

"I don't know. But he's been carrying the invitations." They looked up at a commotion at the door. Marshal Ben Cutter hurried in, grabbed a pair of young waiters, and set them to moving tables and chairs, clearing a space in a near corner where three tables could be set together as one. As this was being completed, Mayor Alfred Twiddie pushed open the door and held it for Cornelia Hanks, who entered followed by Twiddie and Councilmen Gossett, Haggard, and Smith. They headed for the created table and Ben Cutter held a chair for Cornelia.

"Well, they're fixin' to put a stop to that nonsense." Nat nodded.

"The thing about running for mayor?"

"Yeah, they'll explain to her how the cow ate the cabbage. She'll drop that idea soon enough. Woman's got no business gettin' involved in politics. It ain't natural." He turned to squint at the big clock between the lace-curtained windows. "I need to be up an' about, Howard. Business to tend to. By the way, how'd you get that broke trivia?

"What? Oh, you mean tibia? When Letitia and Luella were — ?"

"Yeah. How'd that happen?"

"It was toward the end of their visit." Howard shivered visibly. "They decided to see if I could be trained to fly. Nat, I really wish you hadn't mentioned anything to Miss Penelope."

"Can't hurt. I figure if she knows you got this pathetic condition maybe she'll let you alone. Least I can do for a friend." Nat saucered the last of his coffee, fanned it with his hat, and drank it down. "Obliged for the steak," he said.

Noonday trade had swelled the crowds on Jubilations' main street to sizeable proportions. Townsmen and ladies thronged the boardwalks, mingled with grangers and their extensive families in for the day, while carriages, commerce wagons, and riders vied for passage along the street. Standing on the corner in front of the bank, Nat Kinley tipped back his hat, enjoyed an after-dinner belch, and observed the spectacle. Never before, until the happy convergence of Howard's turnips and the arrival of Bloody Mare with his coils, had Nat paid much attention to downtown Jubilation. Downtown always had been just a place to be passed through on the way uptown. But he studied it now and realized it had a life of its own, quite apart from the routine roistering atop the bluff. The town was like two towns in one, operating by two sets of rules side by side. The rules uptown were simple and masculine. A man went there to have as good a time as he could afford. He was expected to pay for what he bought and do no more damage than he could cover with the cash in his poke. Don't shoot an unarmed man without good reason, don't kick a man when he's down unless you have to, knife-fighting to be kept to a minimum at all times, don't get caught cheating at cards, no shotguns allowed in general brawls — simple rules that a man could understand and abide by. The visible law uptown was Leonard, and it was commonly understood that it was a hanging offense to shoot Leonard. Short of being shot, Leonard could take care of himself.

Downtown, though, seemed to Nat far more complex. Here the rules came in layers, and it was hard to know just what a man could and couldn't get away with. The visible law downtown was Marshal Ben Cutter, and it was generally conceded that Cutter wasn't worth shooting. But here also were the intricate rules of propriety, civility, courtesy, and those subtle combinations of organized charity and veiled hostility that characterized town life.

266

It had to be different, Nat realized. Most of the people downtown lived here. Most of those uptown just came to visit.

Nat saw Wednesday Warren threading his way across the street, surrounded by a bevy of giggling girls. Wednesday's arms were full of ribbons, streamers, and banners that fell about his shoulders and streamed behind him in the breeze. Atop these was a huge, string-tied bundle of Chinese lanterns six or seven feet in all directions. Wednesday was walking blind, leaving it to the girls to guide him and get him through the passing traffic.

Lately, Wednesday had taken on part-time jobs at the feed store and the mill, and gotten himself a bed at Gilpin's Boarding House. He kept himself shaved and barbered and always smelled of rose water. Nat thought he had never seen a young man look so out of place and so happy all at the same time.

From where he stood Nat could see a large group of riders—more than thirty in all—hazing along Elm Street, heading for the road uptown. It looked like most of the crew of Warbonnet, with maybe some of Rocking M's hands thrown in. Behind them, shouting and waving their hats as they spurred to catch up, were at least two dozen H-Four riders, fresh off the summer count and on their way uptown to get an early start.

All along the rising trail up the bluff were riders, some alone, others in groups. But by nightfall there would be hundreds of customers up there. It would be a pleasant evening.

A dusty, trail-worn group appeared on Elm, paused at the intersection, and then turned left to make their way along Main. Nat watched them come and recognized them. As they came abreast the lead rider nodded, then veered aside and swung down from his tired mount. He handed the reins to another, and the rest headed for Ambler's to put their horses on graze in his back pasture.

"Howdy, Pistol Pete." Nat nodded. "You all look tuckered."

Pistol Pete swatted dust from his clothing, gazed sadly at the wreckage of his hat, then replaced it and stepped up on the walk. "That's a fact, Nat. I don't ever want to have another drive like this one's been. But we got 'er done. And I promised the boys I'd stand the first three rounds uptown as a bonus. But first I got to feed 'em so they'll have their strength tonight. We saw H-Four comin' in ahead of us, an' my boys won't be happy till they've drunk with 'em and beat hell out of 'em."

"Naturally." Nat nodded. "I want to thank you for bringin' Conquistador back, Pistol Pete, even though it was your critters that took him off like that. Give you much trouble, did he?"

"Not to mention, considerin'." Pistol Pete shrugged. "Willie Bright is still in the hospital at Hays, an' Tom Needmore is laid up at Springdale with a widow woman tendin' him, an' we hauled Slim Shinton and Wally Purvis up to that doctor at Hillsdale. He says they'll live. Scat an' Elvis wasn't that banged up, so I just paid them off an' sent them on home."

"That's not too bad," Nat agreed. "Conquistador has done worse in his time. I reckon that blindfold helped."

"It did for a fact. You seen Wednesday around here, Nat? I said I'd pick him up on the way back to HW Connected."

"He's around. Does he have pay comin'?"

"Some. Why?"

Nat grinned. "That button's plumb lost interest in

cows, Pistol Pete. But he's workin' hisself a fine string of heifers."

The cowboys came across the street afoot, dusty and worn, down-at-heels and dragging their tails the way their boots dragged their spurs. It had been a hard trail. But their eyes gleamed with visions of uptown as Pistol Pete herded them into the Golden Rule for their feed.

A large black and white tomcat paused at the corner of Bunker's Mill to rub its face luxuriously against the rough brick exterior. It arched its back, yawned, and stretched, then crossed the street, darting through openings in the traffic. It went in the direction Wednesday Warren and his girls had gone.

Far down the street Nat could see the tough-looking stranger from the bank, lounging outside Stapleton's place, across from City Hall. Sweeny sat beside him, idly watching traffic go by.

"Thing about towns," Nat Kinley told himself, "the best way to tell the critters from the folks is see which ones wear hats."

"This is going to be the romantickest thing I've ever imagined," Betty gushed as Wednesday Warren crawled out on a swaying elm limb above her to hang a Chinese lantern on a string winch. "It will be just like in *Hamlet*. A bit further out, please, Wednesday, past that fork."

The limb swayed, dipped, and groaned as Wednesday worked his way along it.

"That wasn't *Hamlet*," Sally said, correcting her. "It was *Romeo and Juliet*. Hamlet's the one that digs up dead skulls and talks to them. Not that branch, Wednesday. It will look better to the right. Yes, there. Oh, that's perfect. Hurry, now. We still have fourteen more."

Some of the younger girls were lugging benches into place near the front of the lot, angling them to the Becket side.

"Penelope will be just thrilled to death," Betty said. "Are you sure she will be able to hear his pipe from her window, Wednesday?"

"Pipes," he corrected from above, squirming to turn himself at a fork. "Yes'm, she sure will hear them all right. I don't think there's any problem there at all. Ouch!"

"What's the matter?" Sally called.

"Oh, I got my gun hung up on this branch an' I'm stuck. Oof!"

"That silly thing! Must you wear that all the time, Wednesday?"

"I generally do."

"Well, it isn't appropriate for climbing trees. Take it off and drop it to me. I'll hold it for you."

He hesitated, then unbuckled his gunbelt. Swinging it out, he let it drop. Sally picked it up, wrinkling her pert nose as she studied it at arm's length. Then she hung it over her shoulder and pointed. "Tie a bit of the festoon there too. We'll drape it to the next tree."

"Yes'm."

"Are you sure your mother will be here with some of the ladies, Sally?" Betty asked, worried. "He might not play if there aren't some ladies here. He thinks that's who he's playing to."

"She said she would," Sally assured her. "I think Miss Hanks told her she should humor us because we are at an awkward age. What's wrong now, Wednesday?"

"Nothing. My hat slipped over my eyes is all. I got it. What's goin' on down there?"

Some of the younger girls had finished with their benches and were oohing and cooing at a large black and white tomcat sauntering through the park. "Nothing," Sally called. "You'd better come down, now. We need to do three more trees. Be sure those string things —"

"Slings," Betty corrected.

"Be sure those string sling things are loose so we can lower the lanterns to light them, then lift them again."

"Yes'm."

"We have a lot of this yellow bunting left," Julie Linden called. "Why don't we tie it around the main trees here and make big bows?"

Sally and Betty went to see. After a time they looked around for Wednesday Warren.

"Did he ever come down?" Betty asked.

"Maybe not," Sally said. "I still have his gun."

They hurried back to where the lantern had been hung, and looked up. Wednesday was where they had left him, but no longer lying along the branch. He sat upright now, ashen-faced, staring back toward the trunk of the tree.

At the base of the limb he was on, gazing back at him with a look of immense satisfaction, sat a black and white tomcat.

XXIV

Last sun of evening glowed red on Jubilation Bluff as W. D. Tienert closed the door of the Jubilation Bank and Trust Company behind him and carefully locked it. He hadn't meant to spend the day in the bank, but what with first one thing and then another . . . well, sometimes things could be hectic when deposits were coming in. He thought of the amount of hard cash locked securely in his vault and it gave him a good, warm feeling. Life might have its irritations, but there was a real satisfaction in having that much money safely stored in one's keeping, ready for transfer to profitable use.

He stretched, smoothed his coat, and turned just as a neat surrey with polished woodwork and a handsome, spirited black pacer in harness turned the corner, pulled up, and stopped. He looked, blinked and looked again. The driver was Cornelia Hanks, handsome in tailored habit, bonnet, and driving gloves.

"Ah, Mr. Tienert," she said cordially. "I did so hope to find you before the day was over."

"Miss Hanks," he smiled. "I've just closed, but we can remedy that. Do come in. I have been hoping we might discuss again the offer for your properties — "

"We can talk here," she said. "I suppose you are aware of the meeting I attended today, with Mayor Twiddie and some of the Councilmen and Marshal Cutter?"

"Why, yes," he assured her. "We discussed the matter earlier today among us. I had hoped to be present, but . . . well . . . the press of business. I'm sure you understand."

"Oh, I certainly do." Her gray eyes were steady and unreadable. His smile elicited no answering smile and he had a twinge of guilt. He should have been there. He could have softened the comments, made them easier for her to understand. He could have protected her from the abrupt shock of facing reality. But then . . . "And I told the gentlemen I would seriously consider all they said," she added. "But I really wanted to know, Mr. Tienert, are you in full concurrence with their sentiments? I mean, after all, as my brother's recent executor, and as my banker, it is important to me to know where you stand."

"As well it should be." He nodded. "If a lady cannot seek guidance from her banker, where is she to turn? Yes, Miss Hanks, I do agree with them. I'm sure you know that all of us hold you in the highest esteem, and are interested only in what is best for you."

"No question about it," she said. The mild tone of her voice touched a nerve in him somewhere, but he couldn't identify it.

"Then I assume you have considered the gentlemen's recommendations?"

"I certainly have. Just to be sure we understand each other, I can give you a brief recapitulation of their comments — "

"That certainly isn't necessary. I know—"

"But I insist, Mr. Tienert." Something like ice—or cold fire—seemed to have sprung aglow in her eyes. "First, Marshal Cutter was very insistent on knowing the name of the man who conceived the idea of my running for the office of mayor."

"Marshal Cutter can be abrupt at times, but his concern is for our town."

"When I assured him that no man had ever suggested the idea to me, he said he realized that, that it was something the ladies' organization had done, but he thought I might happen to know the name of the man who—as he said—put them up to it. When I suggested the ladies might have thought of it themselves, Mr. Gosset assured me that was unlikely because . . . if I understood him correctly . . . of the scientifically accepted hypothesis that original thought is a phenomenon exclusive to the masculine gender."

"I didn't know George Gossett knew words like that," Tienert mused.

"I'm certain he doesn't," she said. "But I do. However, it was Mayor Twiddie himself who made the most telling points. He explained to me that, as a newcomer, I lack experience in the protocols of Kansas society—"

"Alfred said that?"

"More precisely, what he said was that in Kansas ladies don't fool with politics and stuff like that. He also reminded me that I really have no stake in this community, and that the serious work of guiding its destiny is best left to businessmen. He assured me that the reason for everyone's concern with my candidacy is purely business, and nothing personal."

"That is a fact," Tienert said, suddenly feeling a twinge of dread.

"To be specific, he predicted that having a woman's name on the ballot for mayor of the city would make a laughing stock of Jubilation and that business would suffer accordingly. It was a very well-thought-out argument, I must say."

Tienert now had a definite sinking feeling. There was something about the steady gray gaze of her eyes, the way she held herself, the steadiness of her hands holding the pacer's reins. "We wouldn't have approached you at all if it hadn't been important," he assured her.

"Thank you, Mr. Tienert. I appreciate your concern. Do you have anything you'd like to add to what the other gentlemen had to say?"

"Ah . . . why, no. Not really. I believe they summed it up nicely. And I'm sure, Miss Hanks, after you have thought it over—"

"Oh, I already have. I just wanted you to be the first to know. Do you like this surrey? And this fine horse? I hope you do, because I just bought them this afternoon, Mr. Tienert. I did so because I intend to stay on in Jubilation and I shall need transportation. Particularly since I intend to run quite an active campaign against Mayor Twiddie, with the full intent of becoming mayor of the City of Jubilation. And I must tell you what my campaign will hinge upon, Mr. Tienert. I intend to promise that, if elected, I will bring about ordinances to enforce the constitutional mandate prohibiting alcoholic beverages. And I will see to it that they are enforced uptown as well as downtown. Good day, Mr. Tienert. Have a nice evening."

Lifting a victorious chin she turned, flicked the reins, and was half a block away before Tienert realized that his mouth was open. He closed it and put on his hat, still staring after the receding surrey.

Finally he turned and started home, confused and deflated. What had gone wrong? He shook his head as he walked. The reasoning of women was totally beyond him.

As he trudged along Peach Street and turned left on State he was aware of distant bright color — ribbons, festoons, and ornaments decorating the far corner of the park lot beyond his house. And there were people there, doing something. As he came closer, approaching his house, he saw glows begin as colored lanterns were lit and lifted, suspended from the branches of shade trees. It was across the lot, nearer the Becket house than his. Vaguely, he wondered whether his sister might be having a party. No, not Maude. His sister was still back East. Then maybe Penelope was having a party.

What had gone wrong? Surely Cornelia Hanks could see the logic of their arguments. Surely she wouldn't go through with such a thing. Surely she had *some* reason about her.

The banker sighed, climbed the stone steps to his porch, and turned the key in his lock. At least he did have *something* pleasant to think about this evening. There was all that money in his vault, money that would make more money. At least there was that.

He stepped into his foyer, closed the door behind him, and crossed to the parlor. There was a special jug of very good whiskey locked in his cupboard, one he had saved for a special occasion. He felt the need of it now. In the dusk of his parlor he turned up the wick of a lamp, struck a match, set the flame, then lowered the mantle and placed its hood. A pleasant glow illuminated the room, striking highlights on the polished leather of his favorite chair, the polished woodwork of his cupboard, the polished brass at his fireplace, the polished Colt .45

pointed at him by a tough-looking man standing in shadows.

"Sit down, Mr. Banker," Parson said quietly. "It's a mite early yet, but come full dark you and me will take us a trip down to that bank of yours so you can open the safe for me."

South of Jubilation in cool of evening Finn, Whaley, and the other teamsters broke camp and hitched their teams.

"You know somethin', Finn?" Whaley asked as they checked harness on their rigs, pulled side by side facing north along the whiskey trail. "It's about time we made ourselves some money. Man can't go on forever on company wages."

"Free enterprise." Finn nodded. "You know that keg of brandy we got stashed down at Rattlesnake Bend? Well, when we get down there I want to break that out. We'll pour us all a cup, then I want to propose a toast to the good health of them two saints, Nat Kinley an' Twist McGuffin, for puttin' us on to this deal."

"Amen," Whaley agreed. "Wasn't for them, we'd be haulin' back to Arkansas empty again, just like we always done, just to pick up wages an' wait for the next company haul. Course, I do miss spendin' a few days at Jubilation, gettin' drunk like we usually do."

"Price a man pays." Finn shrugged. "Them few days is what gets us to Missouri to cash in, then back to Arkansas on schedule."

"What is that again that we're haulin' to Missouri?"

"Dunno. Nat called it 'fatky' . . . somethin' like that. All he said was take care of it an' don't spill any. Him an' Twist got the buyers lined up, whatever it is. You ready?" He looked at the purpling sky. "We better roll. They be lookin' for us at full dark."

Five empty wagons snaked out of the breaks and up the whiskey trail as late dusk streaked the western sky. Above them on a flat-top spire Packer squatted on his haunches, watching them go. He scratched his head, then went to get his horse. They were headed back toward town. Mystified, Packer followed at a distance. Iron Jack wasn't going to like this, he was sure. He didn't know what was going on, but he knew his boss. Iron Jack wasn't going to like it.

Although Iron Jack Fuller moved his collections around from saloon to saloon, a procedure which allowed him to keep a visible presence in each place and an eye on all of them, his main office was a fortress-like room in back of Lester's House of Leisure. Dusk was fading from the sky and uptown Jubilation was coming alive as Hemp, dragging a bruised and sodden Bert Thompson, knocked at the alley door and was admitted. Marshal Ben Cutter followed him in and turned to close the door, but not in time to keep Bloody Mare out. The little Russian flitted through the opening and grinned at him, removing his wool cap.

"I see you brought them both," Iron Jack rumbled, sitting at his desk. He squinted and pointed. "Who's that?"

"I don't know, Boss," Hemp shrugged. "He followed us. We couldn't get rid of him."

"What do you want?" Iron Jack demanded of Bloody Mare.

The Russian blinked, then smiled and strode forward to the desk. He thrust out a hand. *"Dobr'iy vecher,* Commissar. Bloody Mare Nickle Eye A Bitch Melon Cough." When Iron Jack refused his hand, staring at him, he tapped himself with a thumb. *"Gazechik,"* he explained. *"Mne zovut* Bloody Mare. *Ya zhdu* Bert Tomsohn. *Yakhochu . . ."*

"Bless you," Hemp muttered.

Bloody Mare turned to glare at the big man. "Cossack!"

"Is he crazy?" Iron Jack erupted. "What's he saying?"

Bloody Mare pointed at the sagging Bert, who was upright only because Hemp had hold of him. "Bert Tomsahn," he told Iron Jack seriously. "Horse piss on ya."

"I hear he's a Russian," Ben Cutter explained. "Whatever he's saying, it isn't English."

"It better not be," Iron Jack rumbled.

"Cutter says he don't know what those men are doing in that building down there," Hemp said, "so I brought along Bert Thompson, like you said."

"Why don't you know?" Iron Jack glared at Cutter. "You're the town marshal. You're supposed to know. And you're supposed to tell me."

"I've had my hands full, Iron Jack," Cutter blustered. "You don't know what it's been like down there. And now there's a woman tryin' to run for mayor. Something's got to be done."

"Shut up," Iron Jack growled. "Can't you keep a lid on them people? What do you think I pay you for, Cutter?"

"I *am* keeping a lid on," Cutter objected. "That's why I haven't got time to—"

"Shut up," Iron Jack repeated. "I want to know what's going on at that new building down there."

"Well, I don't know. Why are you asking me?" He

pointed at the smudged and bleary Bert. "If he knows, ask him!"

Iron Jack fixed pig eyes on Hemp. "You knew I wanted to talk to him. Why did you knock him out?"

"I didn't, Boss. He was already like this. I punched him a little, but I didn't do this. I'd say he's drunk, but I don't smell any whiskey on him."

"That doesn't make sense, Hemp."

"Well, that's how it is. Do you want to smell him?"

"Shut up." Iron Jack stared at Bert. "Can you hear me, Bert?"

A silly smile planted itself on Bert's unshaved face. He lolled, dangling down from Hemp's hand, and rolled his eyes. They refused to focus.

"Bert!" Iron Jack roared.

"Hark!" Bert slurred. Wavering eyes came to rest on the face before him. "The bird of dawning singeth."

"What?"

"Something is rotten in the State of Denmark," Bert pointed out.

"What in hell did you do to him?" Iron Jack demanded.

"Nothin', Boss. All I did was punch him a little."

"I bear a charmed life," Bert decided.

"On pit vodku," Bloody Mare explained.

"The play's the thing," Bert reasoned, "wherein I'll catch the conscience of the king." Wrenching himself upright, he turned to the hulking Hemp and took the big man's face in gentle, grimy hands, gazing at him sadly. "O! what a noble mind is here o'er-thrown."

Loud noises erupted outside, growing in volume. Hemp jerked free of Bert's hands and backed away, his eyes wide. "Boss, I need to punch him some more. Is it all right if I—"

The door burst open and a man poked his head in. "Trouble, Boss," he said.

Iron Jack took a deep breath. "What now?" Outside, the sudden commotion had become a riot of sound.

"H-Four and HW Connected are both in town at the same time," the man said. "And they just found each other."

Distantly the bull voice of Leonard thundered, "Stand aside! Make way for the Law! Make way!"

"Get them out of here," Iron Jack graveled at Hemp. "You too, Cutter. Out!"

Beyond the open doorway dusk had deepened to full dark. Gunshots echoed and uptown Jubilation rang to the harmonies of hundreds of cowhands, farmers, and miscellaneous customers in full cavort.

XXV

It was late when Penelope Becket finished the last page of prose which was her copy for today and planted it on the spike.

It had been an exhausting day, beginning with gathering news at the post office in Stapleton's store, then the excitement about Miss Hanks being posted as a candidate for mayor, and the uncertainty whether she would accept—she had said hardly a word to anyone after returning from lunch, then had left in mid-afternoon to shop for a horse and buggy. And over it all, like a tenuous bright mist muffling everything else, was the strange, puzzling, and somehow exciting information Mr. Kinley had given her . . . about Howard Sills's peculiar condition.

She didn't know what to make of it. She had never heard of such a thing. Even more, she didn't know what to make of the way she felt about it. All the rest of the day's events as she reviewed them had an unreal, obscured quality that seemed to result from that strange mist in her thoughts. At times it was a cold mist, touched with dread. But when she tried to analyze it, to think about Howard Sills, the mist became warm and cozy.

"Are you ready to go home?" Betty Stapleton asked as she spiked the last sheet of copy. Penelope jumped. She had forgotten that Betty was there, waiting for her.

That was another puzzling thing. Beginning about mid-afternoon, her friends had been dropping by. Not for any particular reason, they had just stopped in, one at a time, to say hello and then sort of hang around until another came by. Sally had been there, and Roberta and Lilly, and Julie—even Wednesday Warren had happened by. And now it was Betty.

With Miss Hanks off to buy a horse and buggy, and Bert Thompson and Mr. Bloody Mare disappeared somewhere, Penelope would have coped with the office alone. Except that she had not been alone once, all afternoon.

"If you're ready to walk home, I'll walk with you," Betty said. "It's a nice evening for a walk."

Penelope tied on her bonnet, got her shawl and her bag, and put out the desk lamp. In evening shadows they stepped out onto the boardwalk. She locked the door and they turned left toward Maple. It was the supper hour and, though some stores were still open, there were few people about on the streets.

They walked in silence along Main, then along Maple toward State. Or it would have been silence, but for Betty's stifled giggling. Finally Penelope stopped. "Betty, is there something you want to tell me?"

Betty gazed at her with eyes the color of innocence. "Not that I can think of," she said. Then she giggled again. Penelope shook her head and walked on. At State she started to turn right, but Betty caught her arm. "Let's go on, Penelope," she urged. "It's such a lovely evening. We can go down the alley."

By the time Penelope had tried to reason that out—and failed—they were past the corner. "Betty, is something going on that I should know about? Why are you behaving this way?"

Betty seemed about to collapse from stifling giggles. She breathed deeply and kept her face turned away. "I just felt like walking you home, Penelope. When we get to your house can I come in for a little while? You shouldn't be alone, you know."

"I shouldn't . . . Betty Stapleton, I don't know what you're talking about! Mrs. Haskell is there. She lives there, remember?"

"And she bakes the best cookies! I'll just go in with you to see if Mrs. Haskell has baked any cookies. Ah . . . here is the alley. We turn here. Do you suppose your bedroom window is open, Penelope? One should always keep one's bedroom window open in warm weather. We'll check on that. I'll be glad to help. My, it's almost dark." Again, she giggled.

Wednesday Warren came for Howard Sills at the hotel, where he had taken a room for the night. "They sent me to fetch you," Wednesday said. "Your cat ain't here, is it?"

"Pericles? I haven't seen him in several days. But I'm sure he's around the farm somewhere. Why?"

"I . . . I just wondered. Are you ready to go?"

"As ready as I shall ever be, I suppose." Howard collected his pipes out of their bag, checked them over, and put on his hat. It was nearly dark as they headed up Peach Street. "I hope no one is making a big thing of this," Howard said. "I mean, not everyone likes the sound of pipes, so I've only planned to play two or three selections. Do you suppose that will be enough?"

"Far as I'm concerned it will," Wednesday assured him. "It's just sort of like a picnic, Mr. Sills. Some of the . . . the people strung some lights and things in the park, and there's benches. The thing is, you play a couple of tunes, then we'll have pie and coffee."

As darkness closed down on the hills and prairies, Packer rode near the wagons entering town. He followed them in on the south trail, sat in shadows as they eased off the trail, one by one, and headed along the sloping base of Jubilation Bluff. He was more and more mystified. Ahead, torches burned at the south gate of the Greater Jubilation Research Center. From the foot of the uptown trail, beyond the light, Packer watched as the wagons rolled through the gates, circled, and pulled up. Men came from the shadows with trundles and slings and began loading barrels onto the first wagon.

Packer had seen enough. He hauled his reins and eased right, onto the uptown trail, then put his horse into a lope up the incline. Whatever was happening was happening now, and Iron Jack would want to know. Ahead and above, where lights reflected in smokes to halo the crown of the bluff, men's voices were raised in revelry.

As he reached the cutback, the noise topside seemed to double and redouble, hundreds of voices shouting and cursing. He decided the evening's first brawl had begun. But before he reached the crest and entered the streets of uptown Packer realized this was more than a routine brawl. It sounded like everyone in town was getting involved. Here and there gunshots punctuated the general din. It reminded him of the time, two or three seasons before, when the H-Four crowd from Higgins's spread and the HW Connected bunch from the Wentworth ranch had both arrived at Jubilation simultaneously. That had been some kind of night. It had taken weeks to clean the place up.

Suddenly Packer remembered. He had seen H-Four ride in as he headed out to check the wagons. And, from atop his vantage spire, he had seen horsemen enter town that looked to him like some of Pistol Pete Olive's trail crew . . . HW Connected.

He spurred his mount over the crest and into the spreading melee of a general knock-down-drag-out brawl that seemed to fill the entire street. Far away, above the ear splitting din, he heard Leonard's voice: "Stand back! Make way for the Law! Somebody ain't keepin' the peace here! Stand aside!"

A thrown cowboy slammed into Packer's horse, almost knocking it down. Another aimed a fist at a friend, missed his aim, fell, and scuttled backward under the belly of the animal. Packer and his mount were awash in cursing, punching, heaving tourists. One climbed directly over his saddle, gasped, "Beg pardon," and dived from there into a knot of men on the other side.

Hemp emerged from the fray, followed unsteadily by a weaving, proclaiming Bert Thompson and a wild-eyed Bloody Mare, crouched and trying to look all directions at once.

"Where you been?" Hemp demanded. "We got trouble up here."

"Those wagons the Boss wanted to know about," Packer shouted. "They're down at that place, loadin' somethin'. Where's Iron Jack?"

Hemp glanced around at the fight ensuing around

286

them. "Can't get to him now," he said.

"Then get your horse, and any of the other men you can find. We got to stop those wagons." A bullet sang through his hat brim as a cowboy almost directly under him fired his revolver into the air. Packer swore, hauled reins, and backed away.

By the time Hemp came from the stables, mounted, Packer had rounded up two more men. The four of them set off down the trail. From the cutback they could see the Research Center, below and to the right. The gates were open and wagons were just coming out.

"We're in time," Packer shouted. "We'll stop 'em at the foot of the grade."

Nat Kinley and Twist McGuffin closed the gates behind the last wagon. "Well, that's it," Twist said. "There goes our fortune, on its way to bein' made. You sure we shouldn't be ridin' guard with 'em or somethin'?"

"Just call attention to 'em if we did," Nat said. "No, those boys been haulin' whiskey long enough, they know how to stay out of trouble. Best thing we can do is just wait, and get Bloody Mare started on another batch." He looked toward the top of the bluff. "Boys are really feelin' their oats tonight. Sounds like a war up there."

Doors closed around the facility, lights were doused, and Will Ambler, Prosper O'Neil, Ike Ferguson, and Elmer Wallace joined them one by one in the ruddy light of the gate lantern.

"God go with 'em," Ike said, looking into the darkness where the wagons had gone. "Where's Bert an' Bloody Mare? How come they wasn't here to help load?"

"Makes no difference," Wallace sneered. "Thompson's been stone drunk since five o'clock, and that little jaybird ain't worth a dime for fetchin' an' totin'."

"He doesn't have to be," Prosper said. "He's a genius. Tell you boys what, we still got our private stock in there. How about a drink to celebrate?"

Nat was still looking toward the top of the bluff. "I don't know about you fellows," he said, "but I ain't been uptown in a while an' the night's still young."

"Be a shame to miss the kind of fun them boys is havin'," Twist agreed.

They all stared upward. "Can you imagine anybody tryin' to shut down a place like that?" Nat breathed. "Why, it'd be like segregatin' a shrine."

In the big brick house on State Street Parson parted the drapes of a side window to look at the activity across the park. Somebody was having a lawn party. There were colored lanterns in the trees, and ribbons with bows, and benches pulled up, and more than a dozen people milling around.

"What are them people doing over there?" he asked.

W. D. Tienert stared at him. "I . . . I don't know. They didn't tell me."

"Well, it won't matter. We be leavin' here now, goin' up to make that withdrawal from your bank. Here's how it goes. I got a horse right outside, an' you've noticed I got this big gun in my hand. We'll step out your front door, and you'll stand right still while I get on my horse. Then you'll walk an' I'll ride, and we'll just head on over to the bank. You make sure you got your keys now. You surely "wouldn't want to get there without your keys."

"No, I wouldn't want to do that," Tienert agreed dazedly.

"That there's the spirit! All right, it's dark. Now you stand up an' put on your hat . . . that's the way . . . an' away we go."

In darkness at the foot of his steps Tienert stood immobilized while Parson led his horse from the shrubbery around the corner. Parson smiled at him.

"We're gettin' along just fine, ain't we?"

He put his foot in the stirrup and swung aboard.

"They're comin'," Packer said. "See, there they are. Five wagons. What we do is wait till they're right here, just pullin' onto the trail. Then we just close around 'em nice and easy, and stop 'em."

"What do we do with 'em when we get 'em?" Hemp wondered.

"What else? We take 'em uptown an' let Iron Jack decide. He'll want to see what's in them barrels they're carryin'."

The wagons were coming on. They could hear the rattle of chain, the voices of the teamsters. Two men to a side, they eased off the trail and into the shadows.

"This really worked out very well, Mr. Sills," Emma Spalding said as Howard looked around at the colored lanterns, the decorations, the ranked benches, and the more than a dozen people present. "You see, we had planned—Wanda and I and a few others—to get together to begin planning for the Chautauqua posters and things. Then when the young ladies suggested you might play for us, well, it

289

just fit right in. And they have done so much of the arrangement themselves. Aren't the decorations pretty?"

"Yes, ma'am, they are," he assured her. "Ah, what do you want me to do?"

"Well, we thought you might do a brief recital for us, just to begin things, you know. Then we'd love to have you stay for refreshments, and possibly a bit later you might want to play again. We might even arrange accompaniment. Wanda has a guitar, and Mr. Haggard—they should be here later—is seldom without his harmonica. And it is a beautiful evening."

"It really is." Howard had been introduced to most of those present, consisting of three women, two men, and a gaggle of youngsters, mostly girls, who seemed to form a sort of flock around the ecstatic Wednesday Warren. The oldest of these was Mrs. Spalding's daughter, Sally.

Howard chose an area beneath the trees, in front of the benches. He stamped his foot a few times, pursed his lips, then unpacked his pipes. People clustered around him, marveling at the unlikely contrivance with its plaid bag and burnished dark-wood extensions.

"That looks more like some critter that's been mutilated than it does like something to make music," Mr. Spalding observed.

Howard grinned. "Oh, it makes music, all right. I'll show you."

Eagerly the audience arranged itself on the benches. Wednesday Warren faded back into the shadows, his hands over his ears, and Sally Spalding edged around the corner of the house, then ran up the steps and banged on the front door. Penelope Becket opened it, with Betty Stapleton right behind her. "Betty," Sally said, "have you looked to see if Penelope's bedroom window is open? It's really a beautiful evening." She winked an exaggerated wink and hurried away.

Penelope turned to Betty. "What was that all about?"

"She is exactly right," Betty assured her. "We must go up to your bedroom and check that window. Hurry, Penelope. We mustn't stand for musty."

Howard checked over his pipes. In the distance, a ringing din told of hilarity uptown, but here the night was soft and quiet, touched only by the breeze and the faint sounds of a window being raised.

He placed the bag under his elbow, placed his fingers on the chanter at his waist, and began blowing, filling the plaid goose. It seemed to come alive under his arm, and a series of improbable squeaks and thin squeals arose from it.

He stamped his foot, he bumped the bag with his elbow, the upstanding drones came alive with the din of earth primeval, the chanter howled, and Howard Sills began to play.

XXVI

For sixteen years of his life — which was more than
two-thirds of it to date — the Great Highland Pipes
of his grandfather had been a challenge and a
comfort to Howard Sills. The old instrument had
been his inspiration on foggy days, his companion
through lonely evenings, his artistic obsession, and
his idle hobby through the years. Many there were
who might strike a tune on the chanter, but Howard
Sills was a serious piper. He skirled in the realms of
the masters.

Though he had never set foot on the soil of
Borreraig in Skye, nor tested to the MacLeods of
Dunvegan, Howard had graduated in his fifteenth
year from perfecting the chants and ditties of the
brigades to studying the classical Ceol Mor composi-
tions, including those of the Piobaireachd fashion.

His reeds were tuned and tight for volume, his
hemping carefully waxed, his bag honeyed, and his
lungs had the force of one who, through long
practice, can blow even after meals and suffer no ill
consequences.

If the population of Jubilation was not prepared
for Howard's pipes, the shortcoming lay with them
and not with him. He was a master. He could
double-key to seven pitches, waver nuances of vi-
brato with his elbow on his goose, and stir the

primitive soul and bring tears to the eyes of the unsuspecting two counties away downwind. Some might have said, despite the heresy of it, that Howard Sills was a match for any MacCrimmon.

It would never had occurred to him to say such a thing himself, but he did know he was pretty good and it pleased him to have a small skill he might share. His thought was to begin lightly, with the sweet, sad "Flowers of the Forest," then break to a more lively mood with "Highland Laddie" and possibly "The Nut Brown Girl," before demonstrating for his audience the rigorous craftsmanship of "Piobaireachd of Donald Dubh" . . . and possibly close with "The Rowan Tree" or a lively few bars of "Inverness Rant." He didn't want to overdo it.

With his bag filled and blowpipe firmly in his teeth, Howard slapped the plaid goose expertly with his elbow to snap the stiff reeds into full voice, allowed the instrument a split second of unrestrained blast to wash the atmosphere free of interference, then launched into the tune that had buried kings. By the expressions of those before him, his selection had been good. They sat clinging to their benches, wide-eyed and open-mouthed, transported by the ecstasy that only the pipes can bring.

His fingers flew upon the chanter, doubling and trebling the tender tones of the haunting old ballad, while Chinese lanterns trembled in resonance, paint peeled on the eaves of nearby houses, distant livestock bawled, and a large tomcat broke from cover in the brush to streak away, a black and white blur in the darkness with wings on its feet and distance on its mind.

In her window above, Penelope Becket stood transfixed. Behind her, Betty Stapleton dived for shelter beneath Penelope's bed.

Outward and away the music flowed, a tidal wave of perfected harmonics unimpeded, building, cresting, and climbing as it went.

In the darkness in front of W. D. Tienert's house Parson had one foot in the stirrup and his leg in upswing when the horse under him bolted. In an instant the outlaw was in full flight, left foot caught in left stirrup, both hands clenching the flailing right stirrup, his spine meeting the horse's pounding rump on occasion and his right leg straight up above him. By the time his cocked Colt hit the ground, discharging on impact to shatter the little window in Tienert's front door, Parson and his horse were sailing into a haunches-down turn onto Peach Street.

W. D. Tienert stood rooted on his walk, staring absently after his departed nemesis, stunned to paralysis by the lilting melody that rattled his teeth and softened the mortar in his brick house.

A half-grown shoat came from beneath the porch to stand enthralled, porcine snout high and little eyes glowing with excitement. The wailing, skirling sound crashing about him struck chords in Sweeny akin to racial memory of his most ancient ancestors.

A cluster of late riders from Warbonnet, ambling along Elm Street toward the uptown road, froze at the sudden sounds that seemed to come from all directions. Hard hands on tight reins, they backed their mounts into a rump-to-rump circle. Each rider drew his gun and their eyes scanned the darkness about them. They were still there when a runaway horse pounded past, shadowy and terrified, a man clinging upside-down atop it.

At the uptown fork the wagons had reached the trail and were turning onto it. Finn was in the lead, Whaley bringing up the rear, the other three teamsters between. The trail was a lighter dimness in the dark and Finn breathed more easily as his wagon eased on to it and he heard the others follow. He had worried about the open field, but he knew the trail. He raised his leads to snap the team into an easy trot and tall shadows appeared from the darkness on both sides of him . . . horsemen with drawn guns.

"Hold 'em right there," a voice said. "This is—"

Whatever else the man had to say was lost then, drowned beneath pounding floodwaters of pure sound, leaping and cascading on the night air, an omnipotent disharmony that seemed not to rise and fall at all, but to hang motionless while the galaxy danced around it. Finn was almost thrown backward into his load as his team bolted and ran. He clung desperately. Dimly, behind him, like highlights in the fabric of sound roaring across him, he heard the other teams keeping pace.

A riderless horse passed him, running belly-down in the gloom, and he glimpsed another veering away toward the breaks. He tried to glance back, saw wagons behind and around him, Whaley's rig with its powerful team coming up on the left, the other three close-packed to the right as it passed.

He had no idea who the riders had been or where they had gone. He clung to his bench, powerless to control the pounding team ahead of him, stunned by those awful waves of eerie sound that carried them all along, dismasted on a tide that must crash somewhere against a battering shore.

On the uptown path Nat Kinley and Twist McGuffin came within a hair of gunning down Elmer Wallace. The grizzled rancher was walking behind them when the music came and they both whirled — instincts acting with reflexes of their own — drew and fired.

"Jesus Christ!" Wallace screamed and fell face down. His hat flew away in the darkness, fresh bullet holes through the brim on both sides. No one helped him get up. The others stood transfixed, stupefied by the undiluted glories of "Flowers of the Forest" played unannounced on great highland pipes.

Atop Jubilation Bluff the biggest melee of the season was in full swing. It had begun mildly enough, with Pistol Pete Olive poleaxing Shorty Love, the six-foot-two top hand of Higgins's H-Four spread, at the bar in Patman's Pleasure Palace. But it had grown. Before Shorty Love had finished skidding across Patman's floor, a wrangler from H-Four had HW Connected's fence boss pressed back across a card table and was pounding him across the face. A pair of HW waddies took the wrangler off the fence boss and were in turn decked soundly by a mass of H-Four manpower. Seeing an uneven situation, three hands from Warbonnet dived in, then two more and a tough rigger from Double Deuce. Within a minute the fight had become a real social occasion. It spilled from Patman's into the street, from the street into Richardson's and the Loving Arms, and as it expanded it grew. A bottle flung by a Warbonnet hand bounced off the skull of a passing farmer, who spun around and charged a pair of drovers. One of them fell against a Cherokee Peak settler, who broke a chair over the head of his oldest friend and tried to brain a Whisenhunt Mercantile teamster with a rung of it.

There were several hundred men atop the bluff on this night, and within moments every one of them was totally involved.

Leonard emerged from an alley, roaring at the top of his lungs, to find himself wading hip-deep in brawling humanity. He began collecting them. "You're under arrest!" he bellowed. "Everybody here is under arrest! It's the Law!"

Abruptly, then, all activity ceased as the ear-splitting din of Howard's pipes skirled among them, shrieking and mourning in massive cadence, the tune of the silver-toed chanter dancing through the fabric of huge disharmony delivered by the great drone and its companion tenor drones. Men froze in place, fist to jaw, boot to ribs, thumb to jugular, men standing, men fallen, men piled atop other men. The primordial tones, so reminiscent of rending planets, blending the forces of Creation with the subtle nuances of a primal scream, tore at them and found their souls.

Slowly some of those still standing went to their knees. Many removed their hats, some recounted their sins, and a few wept. For many among them it was a stunning and beautiful moment. For some it was at least a solemn occasion, and for a few it was a religious experience. Few if any realized just then that they were hearing the mighty voice of the only musical instrument ever officially classified as a weapon of war.

It was a blessing to Leonard. With single-minded determination he went about collecting prisoners, but he had only a few to carry. The rest of those so designated fell in behind, hats in hands, and humbly followed him as he started down the hill.

At the far end of downtown Polly Cox and Fern Baxter stood guard by lantern light, faithfully preserving the posted notice on the public board. As Howard's serenade reached them they stiffened, blinked, and glanced at each other.

"Great heavens," Fern breathed. "They've branded another of Martha's hens."

In the distant depths of the Cimarron Valley

wolves paced nervously, rabbits awoke and darted away, night-flying bats lost their sense of direction, and numerous lower life-forms responded to a sudden urge to mate.

With good wind in his bag Howard ended "Flowers of the Forest" with a crescendo of pitched pipes, held the final, sorrowful tone for a moment, then launched into the spritely "Highland Laddie," doubling his tempo as he did. It was high time for a change of pace. He noticed that while some of his audience remained frozen and glassy-eyed, others had tears on their cheeks. "Flowers of the Forest" could do that.

He noticed also that there were a lot more people than there had been. They seemed to be coming from all directions. "Highland Laddie" quickly broke the spell. He was glad to see that some of the newly arrived men were putting away their guns. Emmett Wilkie released his stranglehold on his bench and seemed to become convulsive for a moment. Then he whooped, sprang to his feet, swept up his wife, and launched into a stomping, swirling, high-stepping dance. A moment later two more couples were spinning among the trees. Around the blowpipe clenched his teeth, Howard grinned.

He was into the third part of "Highland Laddie" when he happened to glance upward. His breath left him, his fingers froze, and for a moment only the pressure of his arm maintained the pipes alive. There at a window just above stood Penelope Becket, captured in lantern light, angel eyes aglow, white teeth glinting in a soft mouth that oohed with awe. Howard found he could not look away. He gasped, swallowed, and fed more wind to the bag, catching it just as it threatened to fade. He couldn't remember what he had been playing, nor did it matter. All those others around him suddenly were shadows and meaningless forms. He gazed into lavender eyes that all his life, it seemed, had left him speechless, and found suddenly that he could speak. A tangled tongue was no impediment to the playing of the pipes. His fingers moved again and the tune that arose, full and clear in the night, was "The Nut Brown Girl'—but played as possibly "The Nut Brown Girl" had not been for centuries. It was the same sprightly song, but with a different soul.

Not since Culloden Moor had "The Nut Brown Girl" been presented as a love song. But now it was, and mute listeners whose ears were attuning themselves to the ancient power of the pipes found themselves awed and haunted by the beauty of it.

He played it full and he played it rich and he played it to mean all the things the confusion of years had stolen his power to say to a lovely girl. For a frozen time the highland pipes became the heart of Howard Sills, and that heart sang to Penelope Becket.

"He's doing it!" Sally Spalding said over and over to herself and those around her. "He really is doing it! Oh, he is! He's serenading her!"

Wednesday Warren leaned close to shout in her ear—between delighted breaths of almond extract, "How about this invitation you rigged up? How do we get him to give it to her?"

"Give me that!" She took it from him, folded it, and put it away. "Just listen to him, Wednesday. Look at her. Oh, did you ever see anything so . . . so . . ."

"We ain't going to matchmake them two at Chautauqua?"

"Silly! Don't you know when the cake is done to stop baking?"

"Only thing I ever baked was biscuits," he admitted. "An' they never come out good. They always squat to rise an' bake on the squat."

Betty Stapleton, thoroughly daunted but resurrected now from under Penelope's bed, crept from the house to huddle beside them. Her eyes were huge and moist. "I never ever heard anything like that," she submitted.

"I reckon most everybody hardly ever has," Wednesday assured her.

Finally, Howard Sills managed to tear himself from gazing up at Penelope and looked around. A richer world regarded him than had been before. With a sigh that sweetened his bag he let "The Nut Brown Girl" peal down and stamped his foot, establishing the beat of "The Rowan Tree." The pipes skirled, shrilled, and sang, and people danced under the trees by lantern-light. He didn't even try the intricacies of "Piobaireachd of Donald Dubh." He felt strangely elated but deeply confused. He was in no shape right now to play Ceol Mor.

A few easy selections and he folded his pipes, put them away, and accepted an excited flurry of handshakes and gushings before wandering away in the darkness toward the hotel. Behind him someone strummed on a guitar and someone else struck up a tune on a harmonica.

But Howard Sills wanted to be by himself, to sort things out. Two things he was certain of: tomorrow would not be the same as any tomorrow before, because a commitment had been made and life would not be the same again; and, though he was only foggily aware what had happened, it involved Penelope Becket, and he had a feeling that from this point on everything in his life just might.

On a limestone shoulder below the rim of Jubilation Bluff Bert Thompson and Bloody Mare sat listening to the silence. After a time Bert belched and shuddered. "Every room hath blazed with lights," he pointed waveringly at the town below, "and bray'd with minstrelsy."

Bloody Mare nodded. *"Da. Balalayka chudesnaya!"* He stood, stretched, and yawned. *"Ya idu spal'nyu. Ya lozhus' spat'."*

"Good night, good night!" Bert proclaimed. "Parting is such sweet sorrow, that I shall say good night till it be morrow." Without another word he fell over on his side and began to snore.

Bloody Mare looked at him sadly. *"Dobr'iy vecher,* Bert Tomsahn. Horse piss on ya."

Under the seat of a green spring wagon beside Will Amber's shed a large tomcat slept. Hiding there once had brought Pericles a trip to town and many hours of high adventure. Hiding there again would get him home to Bad Basin.

Beyond the breaks five loaded wagons rolled in the night, their teamsters once again in charge. They crossed the Kansas line into the Cherokee Outlet and turned east a mile beyond. It was a route the drivers knew, one as likely as any to take them safely to Missouri.

On the Higgins-Wentworth Trail a battered outlaw, disarmed and bruised in unlikely places, turned his exhausted mount south and went in search of Cole

301

Yeager. Parson now was a believer. The town of Jubilation was not what it seemed. He would not again try to take the place alone.

Cornelia Hanks sat at the open window of her house, enjoying the night breezes and distant music as she finished a bedtime cup of tea. No sounds came now from uptown. The roistering there had been interrupted and would take time to recover. Cornelia sipped her tea and savored the memory of the music she had heard. Not in a very long time had she heard the pipes played so. "Interesting," she told herself. Then her thoughts returned to the announcement she must write for the Tribune, the statements of intent, the campaign material. Time was short and she had a great deal to do. "Interesting," she whispered again.

Penelope Becket had hesitated to go outside where all the people were. She was afraid of her feelings, confused, and strangely shy. She was afraid Howard Sills would be there. But when she went out he was gone, and she was disappointed and didn't know why.

For a time she mingled with the people in the park, then she retreated to her front porch to sit in shadows alone on the porch swing and watch the moon rise over the muted bluff.

XXVII

Mary's herd kept moving vaguely south, more or less following the Rattlesnake Creek watershed, spreading over a square mile or more at times, bunching again when graze or water warranted, but always moving.

Their presence was noted, but rarely so in this wide range country. People expected to see cattle here, and those who saw casually gave them little thought. The size of the herd fluctuated, but generally tended to grow. During the weeks of their migration across Archibald Gaines's Sawtooth spread, a dozen or more Rocking A brands wandered away, along with several HW Connecteds. But forty or fifty Sawtooth critters joined them, as did a small bunch from the neighboring T-Cross and three or four animals that had wandered up from the Sleeping 6. In their journey across the isolated Deep Hole range and its barren surroundings they picked up thirty-five Deep Hole brands, seven buffalo, a mule, and a small flock of sheep. By the time they reached Castle Rock and the perimeters of the Diamond Ranch, they had been joined by a herd of antelope and a cowdog named Bone, who took it upon himself to guard their flanks.

Bone's efforts resulted in the herd staying closer and moving faster. By the time the herd had crossed Diamond range and was in sight of Mayfield, their number included nearly fifty registered Hereford breeding animals, a gaggle of goats, and a red rooster.

It was possibly the largest exodus that had ever gone unnoticed in Kansas history.

On the outskirts of Mayfield men gathered to peer northeastward in failing light.

"It's cows," they told one another. "Whose cows do they suppose them are?"

Some of them would have ridden out for a better look, but for the thunderheads accumulating in the west and the scent of ozone on the wind. If there was a storm coming they had other things to do.

"We can look at 'em in the mornin'," they told one another. "They still be around."

"Could be stole cattle," one said. "That Cattlemen's Association up at Kinsley's been puttin' out broadsides about rustlers. Lot of cattle been disappearin' up thataway."

"Well, if they's rustlers out there I sure don't aim to go ridin' in on 'em," another allowed.

They went about their business, men bringing in their stock, women battening their shutters, children laughing and playing in the streets, the younger ones circle-dancing to the latest childhood chant: "A B C D puppy? L M N O puppy. O S M R A puppy! C M P N?"

The storm broke at dusk. In the north pastures Bone responded to the rain on his face by deciding to drive the cattle in.

Between the growing storm and Bone's yipping and circling as he moved them along, the animals were nervous. But the majority were thoroughly trail-broke critters by now and had no inclination to stampede. The Herefords and the buffalos took comfort from their attitudes and plodded along amiably.

Bone worked with a will, aiming them at the little town. He had learned his trade through teamwork with men, and the tending of a large herd alone was new to him. But he had looked them over carefully and decided there were no men here. And *somebody* had to be in charge.

At point Mary tossed her single-horned head in irritation, but kept moving. Cutting back to deal with the dog would have meant losing her place in line.

But while the cattle and their cousins remained calm, others did not. As they approached the town a pair of deer came up from a brushy draw and found themselves surrounded by creatures. They bolted, and the idea caught on. Before the little street of Mayfield was even fully wet with rain, people were scattering before a stampede. First it was an undulating flow of graceful pronghorns, racing along the street followed by two deer. Bleating sheep came next, half a hundred of them, with goats running among them. Lightning danced on Cemetery Hill, and the people of Mayfield peered from behind closed doors. A mule went by, followed by a furious red rooster and the sheriff's best saddle horse.

"Yonder goes the sheriff's horse," people told one another.

"And yonder goes the sheriff," others noted. In the rain and darkness a portly, mustached man dressed in hat, boots, and longjohns pounded down the muddy street just ahead of a Hereford bull. For a time there was silence but for the rain, the thunder, and the barking of a distant dog. People peered out, then withdrew and slammed their doors. The street was full of trotting cattle—all kinds of cattle—and here and there a buffalo.

With the herd brought safely to town, Bone loped along the streaming street and found refuge on a sheltered porch. A cowdog's work was never done, but a fellow had to sleep now and then.

By the time the storm passed over, Mary's herd was well into the sandhill country, miles from any-place where people were. They rested there, content, but the morning's sun brought problems. Here there was little graze and no water.

They moved out, and again the direction was south. It had long since become Mary's habit, when not being driven, to take the morning sun on her left flank. Thus when Mary chose a direction to wander it was invariably south.

Petticoat politics, as the weeks rolled by toward Jubilation's municipal election, became a source of zealous fervor to a few, of disgruntlement to some, and of hilarity to many.

Despite Cornelia Hanks's assurance that the Jubilation Tribune would publish fairly all statements and arguments of the Twiddie campaign, in emergency session the City Council had declared the official newspaper of Jubilation to be the Pleasant Valley Enterprise. City officials took turns journeying across the valley to Pleasant Valley to deliver statements, diatribes, and advertisements to an elated editor there, and to bring back enough copies of each week's Enterprise to distribute throughout Jubilation.

For her part, Cornelia steadfastly refused to engage in any exchange of printed insult or slander. Instead, each week's issue of the Tribune carried on its front page a thoughtful and well-reasoned editorial in favor of law and order, constitutionality and sobriety.

It rankled her that Bert Thompson, setting the type for these high thoughts, was seldom sober and never without sarcastic comment. She could always tell when he came to her best points of logic by the nasty laughter emanating from the typography corner.

"If you don't enjoy working here," she demanded of him, "why don't you leave?"

"Why don't you fire me?" he retorted. "If I was you, I would."

"If you were me," she snapped, "you would have the decency to remain sober, at least long enough to do the work I pay you for."

"It gets done, doesn't it? Ma'am, do you ever read this drivel that you write? Man has to set this stuff he's better off drunk. Listen to this. 'No community can prosper,' you say, 'whose very economy is rooted in sinful behavior.' Why, if I was to set that sober I'd laugh myself to tears."

"What's wrong with it?" she demanded.

"What's wrong? Why, Miss Candidate, ma'am, look around. What do you think Jubilation does best? Prosper, that's what. Why, even this election business with you — a woman — runnin' for mayor . . . why, business has increased by a third around here just since you was filed. It breaks the monotony and folks are comin' from miles around just to say they been here. Don't you know that's what the mayor's campaign is all about? Where have you been all your life, woman?"

She paled at the thought. "You mean Twiddie and

307

the rest . . . they aren't campaigning against me?"

"Why would they do that? You can't win. It's just that Twiddie's got his back up an' everybody else is makin' the most of it."

"You think I am making a laughing stock of Jubilation too, don't you, Mr. Thompson?"

"No more'n usual," he assured her. "Jubilation's always been a laughing stock. You're just makin' it real profitable to be that way."

"We'll see." She glowered. "We shall just see."

For his part, Bert was not wholly content with the entire situation. The increased activity uptown was keeping Iron Jack's thugs perfectly busy for the moment, and Iron Jack was making enough money that he hadn't got around to looking further into the Jubilation Research Center. This in turn left the Research Society free to concentrate on producing more wagon loads of Vladimir's wonderful brew before the wagons returned on their next whiskey trip. And when the wagons came they would bring the money from the first haul. While Bert's fee from the proceeds would be minimal—barely covering nuisance value—it would be enough to pay off his debt to Iron Jack Fuller and a little left over.

And, in the meantime, he had ready access each evening to the marked vat that the partners kept as domestic stock. Not once since that first spout flowed had Bert Thompson been truly, painfully sober.

But it was too good to last. Nothing good ever lasted. And right now Bert was pretty sure when it would end.

He frowned, big clumsy fingers choosing type and setting it with the casual ease of habit. The good times would come to a screeching halt. Even if he paid off Iron Jack, he knew Iron Jack would get to the bottom of all this, and some people likely were going to get hurt. He was pretty sure he would be one of them.

Unless . . .

Bert shook his head. The thought was ridiculous. Even through his fumy clouds he knew that. Still . . .

"Miss Hanks, you're serious about this mayor thing, aren't you?"

"I am quite serious about it, Mr. Thompson."

"Well, if you *was* to win . . . I mean, that's preposterous, but just supposin' you did. You certainly wouldn't go on an' try to *be* the mayor, would you? I mean, mayoring *is* man's work, after all—"

"I most certainly would! Will! I intend to be elected, Mr. Thompson, and when elected I intend to perform actively as mayor of this city."

He put down his type stick and tray and came to the desk to peer at her. He was hung over, grimy, and had a three-day growth of beard, as well as bad breath, and she drew back.

"And all this drivel about ordinances and enforcement of Prohibition and total teetotal uptown and down? You're really serious about that?"

"I most certainly am."

"Why?"

"Because the situation here now is an abomination. Besides, if . . . when I am elected, it will be by those good people who want sobriety brought to this town. And I will work to enforce the wishes of my constituents."

A huge grin split his homely face. "My," he said. He returned to the fonts, still grinning happily. Even if every woman in town came out on election day and voted for her, Cornelia Hanks didn't stand a chance of winning the election. But that wasn't what

309

Bert Thompson was thinking about.

"All the world's a stage," he crooned. "And all the men and women merely players."

"Mr. Thompson?"

He turned. She was staring at him. "I asked you once before about your name. There was a Bert Thompson who—"

"That was another Bert Thompson," he said, cutting her off, crossly. "He died. Hanged by a miners' court at Leadville. That was years ago."

He snorted, then returned to his trays and his crooning.

"—men and women merely players: they have their exits and their entrances—"

"And one man in his time plays many parts," Cornelia Hanks responded smugly.

As evening sun left its last blush on the teeming top of Jubilation Bluff, that magic span of moments when first night-birds sought the sky to flit on pleasant evening breezes and the stillness was not yet shattered by cicadas in the elm trees and tourists on the bluff, Howard Sills and Penelope Becket sat side by side on the porch swing of her house.

At the hitch post in front, Crowbait waited patiently in harness before the spring wagon, which was loaded high with supplies for Bad Basin.

The two on the swing sat at arm's length, Howard holding a bouquet of purple flags clenched firmly in both hands. He was freshly shaved and barbered, and the white linen collar threatening to throttle him was spotless. He stared straight ahead, his jaws clenching and unclenching as he swallowed spasmodically.

"I really am so glad you came to call," Penelope

chattered. "I'd love to introduce you to my mother, but I can't because she is still visiting back East. Her cousin took a turn for the worse. Of course, I could introduce you to Mrs. Haskell. She lives here. But I suppose she would rather I didn't. She enjoys peering out from between the curtains. Are the irises for me?"

"Yes, I . . ." He swallowed again and thrust them at her, still staring straight ahead.

"Oh, they're lovely," she said. "So thoughtful of you. I just love irises in season. Don't you? I've been wanting to tell you, Mr. Sills, I have heard just so many lovely compliments on your performance for the Chautauqua Committee. Everyone says they never heard anything like it. I managed to write a whole long piece for the newspaper just based on what people had to say about your music. Oh, but I'm sure you know that. You probably read the paper."

"I . . ."

"Everyone does, it seems. Especially since Miss Hanks decided to run for mayor. Did you know that the circulation of the Tribune has nearly doubled? And that on top of those gentlemen bringing bales of Pleasant Valley Enterprises into town every week and passing them around. I don't think that is very farsighted of them, do you? I mean, it seems to me people should support their local businesses, and a newspaper is a business even if its publisher is running for office."

"Yes, I . . ."

"I'm glad we agree. Do you plan to vote for Miss Banks? Oh, but then I suppose you can't vote in a city election, can you? Not living in the city, you know. And that reminds me. Mr. Warren told some of my friends about your house and they were

311

describing it to me. Betty Stapleton said it had flying buttocks, but Sally Spalding said that wasn't right, that it was flying mattresses. I have been meaning to look that up."

"No, it's . . ."

Nat Kinley and Twist McGuffin, riding along the street, pulled rein in front of the gate and tipped their hats.

"Evenin', Miss Penelope," Nat said. "Howdy, Howard. I'm proud to see you took my advice. How's it comin' along?"

"Well, I . . ." Howard said.

"Good." Nat nodded. "Man's just got to take some initiative in these matters, because it's the man that's got it to do. Right, Twist?"

"Right."

"You're on the right track," Nat assured Howard. "Just remember what I told you. Build up easy, like, till you reach the right point, then tuck that tailbone tight between them legs an' go for it. It's the only way."

"Should I know what you're talking about?" Penelope inquired.

"No, miss, you shouldn't. It's man talk." He tipped his hat again. "Sorry we can't stay around to visit, but me and Twist has got business over to the Center. Somebody called a meetin'. That second turnip crop is lookin' good, Howard. Ought to make a yield before frost, an' the market's ready an' waitin' for you. Puff's hoppers are low an' Ike says they've already mixed tailin's into the last six vats of squish. Evenin', folks. Have a nice time."

They turned and rode away, down the street.

"Those are nice gentlemen," Penelope said. "Sometimes I think the ladies here are a bit premature in some of their judgments. And Mr. Kinley is such a friend to you. I'm sure you know that, Mr. Sills . . . ah, Howard. Is it all right if I call you Howard, Mr. Sills? You may call me Penelope. Or Miss Penelope, if you prefer. That's what you have called me before. At least, I think that's what you meant."

"I . . ."

"The reason I know he is your friend is because he told me . . . well, about you, you know. I can't for the life of me understand what would have caused such a problem, but I think it's wonderful that you have recovered from it. Ah, would you like to sit just a bit closer? I think it may become cool."

"I, ah . . ."

"Mrs. Haskell is extremely nearsighted," Penelope assured him.

On the back street that led to the Research Center Nat Kinley chewed his lip thoughtfully. "I don't know whether Howard's really got the hang of courtin' yet," he admitted to Twist. "But then, there ain't no time like the present to learn."

XXVIII

"You want us to *what?*"

Although the voice belonged exclusively to Prosper O'Neil, there was no doubt the words reflected the sentiments of seven of the eight other men in the room. The eighth was Bloody Mare, who was busy in the far corner, happily stirring corn tailings into fresh squish to make it ferment.

The rest of them stared at Bert Thompson, incredulous.

"I said I want you to figure out how to get Miss Hanks elected mayor," he repeated.

In silence they looked at him, then at one another.

"How much of that stuff has he had this evenin'?" Twist McGuffin wondered.

"All in favor of shootin' the scutter say 'aye,' " Elmer Wallace growled.

"That'd be like constipatin' a shrine," Nat Kinley allowed.

"A *woman?*" Ike Ferguson goggled.

"You ought to swear off, Bert," Puff McVey urged. "You ain't makin' any more sense than that little jaybird over there."

Will Ambler's eyes went from wide to narrow. He stoked his pipe and puffed on it. "I don't suppose you'd mind givin' us a reason, would you, Bert?"

"The reason is, he's drunk," Prosper decided.

Bert drew a deep breath and shook his head. "Misery acquaints a man with strange bedfellows," he muttered. "Here will be an old abusing of God's patience and the king's English."

"What?" Prosper demanded.

"May shoot th' scutter my own self," Elmer Wallace declared.

"Let him talk," Will urged.

Bert eyed them all. "Do you know what's going to happen when Iron Jack Fuller gets wind of what's being done here?"

"He probably ain't gonna like it much," Ike Ferguson admitted. "But he don't know yet."

"That's because he's been busy. But the election is coming up. When it's over things will be back to normal and he'll sort this out quick enough. You know what his rules are, don't you? In Jubilation, whiskey, girls, and gambling belong to him. He gets his cut. Anybody offered him a cut of this business?"

"That's uptown," Twist protested. "This is downtown."

"Sort of in between, actually," Ambler conceded.

"No whiskey downtown," Prosper said thoughtfully. "But what we're makin' ain't whiskey, and we're not sellin' any of it in Jubilation anyways."

"Big difference that's going to make." Bert grinned. "When that election is over, Iron Jack is going to land on you fellows like an avalanche. The way he'll see it, you've broke every rule he has. He won't just stop with takin' over here. He'll send thugs to visit Bullseye." He glanced at Wallace. "And your Lazy K, Nat, and Twist's place, and Ike's. You think you can stand them off in the valley, Prosper? How about you, Puff? Where will you hole up? Bunker's Mill?"

He had their full attention now. Mostly, they hadn't thought too much about it. They hadn't wanted to.

"What do you care, Thompson?" Wallace blustered. "You ain't a partner. All's you get is a finder's fee for gettin' that cussin' jaybird started off."

"Iron Jack Fuller is not a man to make fine distinctions," Bert pointed out. "I don't want my legs broken any more than anybody else."

"We might have time to get one more load out before the election," Will Ambler said. "Maybe we ought to do that and then liquidate our assets."

"Do what?"

"He means shut 'er down," Prosper explained to Wallace. "I hate to do that, though. I got a lot of money tied up here."

"Well, either way you're going to lose it," Bert told him.

"Them yayhoos come lookin' for Nat Kinley, they better come shootin'," Nat said.

"Likely they will," Twist assured him.

"So what's all that got to do with tryin' to elect a woman as mayor of the town?" Ambler pursued.

"That's the point," Bert said. "You all know the platform she's running on. 'We See To You and Teetotal Too.' She doesn't call it that, but I do. First thing she intends to do if she gets elected is shut down uptown."

"That's ridiculous," Prosper pointed out.

"No way in the world," Ike seconded.

"Be like defoliatin' a shrine," Nat allowed.

"That's desecratin'."

"It sure is."

Bert shook his head and spread imploring hands. "It doesn't make any difference! We all know she couldn't do that even if she tried. But it would keep

Iron Jack busy for a while, and Ben Cutter and the council. Meantime you could go on makin' vodka. And sellin' it. And makin' money. And givin' me some."

"But electin' a woman as mayor!" Prosper shuddered. "My daddy would turn right over in his grave."

"Don't see how we could do it anyway," Ambler said. "There's only so many people in this town to vote, and the men outnumber the women about two to one, an' they plain aren't gonna do it."

"How about the uptown crowd?" Bert suggested softly.

"You mean Patman and Richardson and them? Well, they do think this whole business about a woman runnin' for office is funny as a toad in a turkey-shoot, but they sure ain't goin' to vote for her."

"I don't mean them. I mean the customers. Think about it."

Bloody Mare finished stirring in the dried, sprouted grain tailings. Several vats of squish by the far wall, treated earlier, already were beginning to bubble and reek. He added wood to his samovars, then went down the line, checking coils, peering at spouts and vessels, testing the level of liquid in charcoal drums, humming to himself as he went. At the final great drum, from which was suspended the payload spout, he lifted a lid, sniffed the contents, and nodded. He came to where the others were gathered.

"Ya khochu—"

"Bless you," some of them said.

"Ya khochu kopit sakhara," he persisted. *"Mne nuzhno dengi."*

Absently Prosper O'Neil counted out a few dollars

317

and handed it to the Russian.

"*Spasibo,*" Bloody Mare said.

"You're welcome," Prosper said. "Bert, them boys up there don't even live here, most of 'em. They come from all over."

"To vote, you have to have a place of residence here," Ambler added. "And register."

"*Khorosho vodka,*" Bloody Mare told them, pointing at the great drum. "Horse piss on ya." He put on his wool cap and headed for the door, turning to wave. "*Do svidanya.*"

"Doe sweat on you too," Elmer Wallace called, deep in thought. "Cock dealer."

"And even if they was residents, how many of them hooraws do you think would go to the polls and vote for a woman for mayor of the town? No man in his right mind would do that."

Nat Kinley gazed at the great drum, the line of barrels waiting to be filled. "I just might have an idea," he said.

Twist McGuffin was looking at the stacks of unused lumber under the loft. "I wonder if you're thinkin' what I'm thinkin'," he mused.

"Have to clear this whole place out," Will said. "We'd need every bit of room we could get."

"It won't work," Ike Ferguson protested.

Bert Thompson went to the great drum, opened it, took down a dipper, and took a deep slug of colorless liquid. He shuddered, closed his eyes, and leaned against the drum, his head rocking back and forth. "Whoooo!" he said.

"You know," Nat Kinley said, "it might just work if we had Leonard."

It was a nervous and apologetic Bo who came

before Marshal Frank Gault in the back room of a tavern at Fort Smith. In all his years of riding with the old marshal, Bo had never seen him quite so angry.

"I talked to the boys, Frank," he said. "They told me how it was."

"Five wagons," Gault rasped, his eyes blazing. He had been mad for two days, waiting for Bo to sort it out for him, and he was still mad. But he clenched his jaws. "All right, Bo. Tell me how it was. I'll listen. But it damn well better be good."

Bo pulled up a chair and straddled it, his heavy arms across the back of it. "The boys done just like you said, Frank. They put scouts on the trail to follow the wagons back across the Outlet and signal ahead. You know them whiskey haulers, Frank. They don't have any schedule to speak of. So without gettin' a bead on 'em comin' in, we wouldn't have knowed where they'd load up or when they'd head out again. It was all set up, to take 'em at Salt Fork on their way to Jubilation."

"I know how it was set up, Bo. So what happened?"

"Nothin', Frank. The scouts never saw 'em. They must have come back a different route."

"All this time they been goin' an' comin' the same way, like ants on a honey track." Gault glared at the deputy. "So why, just now, would they change their habits? Did somebody tip 'em off? That's what I want to know."

"None of the boys did, Frank. I'll swear to that."

"Even if we didn't follow 'em in, somebody should have known when they got here an' loaded up. Somebody should have known they were on the way."

"Frank, we had people in town and outside town

319

at the line and on all three trails. I checked. Seems they didn't come in through the territory at all. They came down from Springfield."

"Missouri? What the hell were they doin' in Missouri?"

Bo shook his head. "That's the strangest thing, Frank. Nobody knows. I can't find anybody that has the least notion why five empty whiskey wagons from Kansas would go to Missouri, less'n it was to pick up a load of hooch, and they didn't have any load of hooch. They come down from Springfield empty and went to Felstein's warehouse and loaded up with bond whiskey, then they took off for Jubilation again just like always."

"And we missed 'em."

"Yeah, Frank. Since nobody knew they was on the way, we only had two men at Salt Fork instead of twenty. And you know how that is."

Gault knew. Teamsters traveling the territories unescorted tended to carry a lot of guns and have little hesitation about using them. A whiskey convoy was not a target for two men in the wilds.

"They done their best, Frank," Bo said. "They chased 'em close on six miles before Bill took a ball in his wing and Ferris got his horse shot out from under him." He chewed his mustache and rolled his hat brim in sad fingers. "Sorry, Frank, but that load's on its way to Jubilation right now and we ain't got any way to catch 'em."

"It was the same bunch? Finn and Whaley and them?"

"Yeah. Same ones. Our boys knowed 'em."

"Then they knew our boys too. You know what that means. They'll make this haul, then they'll change their routes, or go to ground, or change their line of work, or something. We'll be damn lucky if

320

we ever get another chance at them. That one load would have been all we got anyhow, but it would have bought us all some pretty good times."

"Yeah, Frank, I know. Sorry."

Gault sat scowling, sipping at his brandy. "So none of our boys tipped anybody. So who else knew about it?"

"Who else?"

"Just one. That fancypants lawyer. The popinjay. What was his name?"

"The Case jaybird?"

"Yeah. Case. Justin Case." Gault opened a satchel and pulled out a stack of papers. "You know, he done a fine job linin' up all these warrants an' everything. Not worth the paper they're writ on now, though. You know, Bo, I reckon I might ought to take a personal interest in Mr. Justin Case. Why don't you get on the wire and see what all you can find out about him."

Bo breathed a sigh of relief. "Yeah, Frank. I'll do that. I'll keep lookin' till I find somethin' good."

"Never knew a man in my life that hadn't did *somethin'* illegal," Frank Gault said.

More than two hundred miles southwest of Fort Smith, Parson rode a tired horse along a brushy draw. At a place where sandstone outcroppings rose high on both sides he halted and raised his hands.

"It's me," he shouted. "Parson. Comin' in to see Cole."

"Come on in, Parson," a voice answered. "Cole's been thinkin' about you a lot lately."

Parson was sweating by the time he rode into camp, but he kept his face calm and his hands in plain sight. Cole was lounging beside a cutbank, thumbing fresh loads into his Colt. As Parson stepped down, Cole closed the port on the revolver and spun the cylinder.

"I'm prob'ly gonna kill you dead, Parson," he said.

"I hope you don't, Cole, because I know where there's a bank just stuffed with money, and part of it's that twenty-eight thousand dollars we lost last winter. I know where the fella with the spring wagon is too."

In evening shadows a pair of horsemen dismounted at Will Ambler's barn, stood for a moment looking down the street — where lanterns shone on the standing crowd in front of City Hall and the strident voice of Mayor Alfred Twiddie was raised in all its eloquence — then crossed the street and turned to walk along Peach.

They were a mismatched pair, one lithe and slim, walking gingerly as one who is most comfortable in the saddle, the other sturdy and barrel-chested and not as tall. Both were shaved and barbered, and both were uncomfortable with their task. But they had all drawn straws.

At the salt-box house of Slim Haggard they hesitated, then opened the gate, crossed the dooryard, and stepped up on the porch. The taller one knocked on the door. When it opened, spilling bright lamplight on them, Nat Kinley smiled his best smile and said, "Evenin', Mrs. Haggard. My name's Kinley and this here is Mr. McVey. I wonder if we could come in and talk to you ladies for a minute or so."

Martha Haggard scowled, holding the door. "What do you want here?" she demanded. "My husband isn't home."

Polly Cox peered around Martha's shoulder, perplexed. "I know you," she said. Then she pointed an accusing finger at the flustered Puff McVey. "I know him too. He's a drinking man and a carouser. His name is on our list."

From inside the lighted sitting room the strident voice of Agatha Sturgis announced, "Don't let any of them in here, Martha. They're all in league. Make them go away."

"Your cowboys violated my chickens," Martha accused.

"No, ma'am." Nat shook his head solemnly. "Those were some of the boys from H-Four. I'm Lazy K."

"He's still on the list," she said.

"I reckon he is," Nat admitted. "I prob'ly am too, but that ain't what we need to talk about. Can we come in?"

"What for?"

"Well, ma'am, it's like this." He lowered his voice. "Some of us has seen the error of our ways an' decided to help Miss Hanks win the election. But it ain't goin' to be easy, and we need your help."

"Halleluya," Puff McVey added.

"Don't believe a word of it, Martha," Polly Cox warned.

Nat looked at her, mustering all the innocence he could manage to display on a somewhat sardonic face. "I hope you'll believe us, Miz Cox, because part of what we need is the borry of your husband."

Where the footpath came down from Jubilation Bluff three men and a pig gathered, shrouded by closing darkness. Sweeny wore a new harness, to which had been affixed a shiny metal star, and was on a leash held by Ike Ferguson.

"You sure this is gonna work?" Prosper O'Neil asked. "How do you know he'll do it?"

"I been trainin' him for a week," Ike explained. "Just like we said, every evenin' at dark, I've let him in at the gate an' let him get to the fixin's. Last night when I run him off he was so drunk I had to hold his back legs for him an' steer him like a wheelbarrow. You damn right he'll do it. Pigs is critters of habit."

"All right," Will Ambler said. "Let's try him and see, because tomorrow night he goes to work. Election's just four days off."

Solemnly they gathered around the shoat, and Ike knelt to release his leash. "Go get 'em, Sweeny," he said.

Sweeny headed for the Jubilation Research Center, the other three following. The nearer they came, the faster the pig went, until the men were running all out to keep up. When they arrived at the Center Sweeney was there, oinking and scratching at the gate, and Twist McGuffin was coming across the yard to let him in.

"I guess," Prosper panted. "I guess maybe it'll work. But Leonard's goin' to have to hump it to keep up with that pig."

"What if Ben Cutter gets wind of any of this?" Will wondered. "You think he'll stand still for—"

"Ben Cutter's gonna be busy," Ike promised. "Nat Kinley said he'd see to that."

XXIX

It had become habit with Cornelia Hanks to arrive at the office of the Jubilation Tribune no later than seven each morning, which gave her a quiet hour to review correspondence, bring the ledgers up to date, proofread galleys, and do the myriad other tasks associated with printing a newspaper on a weekly basis, before Penelope Becket showed up with copy and ad orders from her early rounds, or the ladies came calling to gush with enthusiasm about what they were doing in her campaign, or any of the other interruptions of the day began.

Of the parts of the day, she had always preferred morning. Mornings could be hectic at times, she had discovered—publishing a newspaper in a Western town was a far cry from educating young ladies in Illinois—but they were good times for her. One of the things she liked best about them now was that she could always count on several pleasant hours before her printer came staggering in, smelly, hung over, vile-tempered, and disreputable, to bless the shop with his sour and distracting presence for the rest of the day. She wondered a dozen times a day why she hadn't fired him yet—and if she forgot to wonder about that, he invariably reminded her—and each day she seriously considered doing so. And yet, somehow, it was never quite the time. Despite being as nearly despicable as any human being she had ever encountered, still, sometimes he puzzled her, and now and then—just once in a while—she wondered if Bert Thompson didn't just possibly make more sense than anyone else in this strange little town. She didn't care to think about him. The man was an absolute disgrace, and a constant embarrassment. But sometimes . . . well, sometimes she found him interesting.

At any rate, she did enjoy that part of the day before he showed up, and she counted on it.

So, on this morning, when the door opened at half past seven, it took her a long moment to recognize the man who entered.

He was freshly bathed, scrubbed free of ink and smudges. He was freshly shaved, and his dour, creased face, without its usual gray stubble, looked severe and unnatural. He wore a clean suit of dark broadcloth—only slightly threadbare—and a clean linen shirt shone white between his lapels. His boots were blacked and polished, his hat cleaned and shaped, and there was spring to his step.

"I hardly recognized you," she said after a long study of him.

"I hardly recognize me either," he admitted, scowling darkly. "Being awake and sober this time of day is no pleasure, and I do not intend to make a practice of it."

"Then why—?"

"You said you are serious about winning this election. How serious are you?"

She blinked, confused. "Well, I am quite serious in my intent, Mr. Thompson. Of course, it's hard to know how such a thing will come out."

"No, it isn't. There's no question about it. You're going to lose, and you know it. You don't stand a chance. If every woman in Jubilation goes to the polls and votes for you—and even if a hundred of them could convince their husbands and grown sons to do the same, which not a dozen will—you will still lose at least two to one."

She stared at him stonily. "I am quite aware the chances are slim, Mr. Thompson. Why are you saying all this to me?"

"Slim? Lady, you don't have the chance of a snowflake in Dante's down-under, and if you don't know it, it's time you did. You think just because you're new in town and a bunch of pea-brained women have shoved you into the arena to be their sacrificial lamb, that miracles are going to happen and lightning is going to strike and God's wonders are going to unfold on earth and you're going to come forth victorious and lead all these people to glory."

The color drained from her face. She didn't remember standing, but she was standing now, and her nails dug into her palms as she clenched her fists at her sides. "I don't think any such thing!" she blurted. "How dare you—"

"Shut up," he said. "You look like you've been bleached. What's the matter . . . can't you take the truth? Politics is a man's game, Miss Hanks, not some genteel sport suited to drawing rooms and tea parties. There's no convenient powder room to retire to while the gentlemen call time out and wait for you to freshen yourself. No, ma'am. Twiddie and the council and most of the men in town are having themselves a high old time these days. You and those women have given them the opportunity of a lifetime. Handed it to them on a platter. Three days from now they will have proved once and for all that this is a man's town, and will have put an end once and for all to all this We See To You nonsense. The women will have had their chance and lost and that will be the end of that. They'll go back to their kitchens and the Wednesday Ladies' Reading Circle will go back to having ice cream socials and gossiping about whoever isn't there and Jubilation will be back to normal . . . once and for all. You've given them that, Miss Hanks. Are you proud of yourself?"

"Mr. Thompson! I . . ." She found herself speechless, almost strangled by her fury. Her eyes blazed at him and he smiled in contempt.

"You see?" He nodded. "A great point is being made, right here in Jubilation. We're about to prove that women are only good for one thing . . . and of course, you haven't done that, either, have you . . . *Miss* Hanks?"

"You're fired!" she hissed. "Get out!"

"I've been wondering when you'd even have the gumption to do that. My, my. Just look at you. Hasn't anybody ever in your whole life told it to you like it is? That's a real pity." He mocked her now, and she was too furious even to wonder how this man—this laughingstock town drunk who was invisible most of the time because he was beneath notice—could so mold inflection, so lash her with wounding words, so master the nuances of speech, expression, and posture that his very presence intimidated her.

"But maybe I have misjudged," he said, raising a cynical brow. "Maybe the Eastern lady knows exactly what she's doing. Maybe this whole business is just to raise the value of your brother's estate and the cash market for the Tribune. They did offer to buy

328

you out, didn't they? Well, lady, if that's your game I admire it. You'll probably walk away with twice what you could have got honestly, and never look back. Why should it matter to you how many people get hurt in the process? This isn't your town, any more than it's mine. Is that how it is? If so, I must admit you make the rest here look like pikers when it comes to cold-blood cash and carry."

Without thinking she raised a hand and lashed out at his face. He blocked the slap casually, grinning now in a different way.

"Out!" she breathed. "Get out of my shop! I'll . . . I'll . . ."

"My," he said, suddenly gentle. With a shrug he reached out a large hand and wiped it across her cheek. Then he looked at it. "Will you look at that?" He turned his palm to her. It shone with moisture. "Tears. Real, honest-to-God tears."

She could hardly see him for them. They flowed and she raised her apron to dab at them. "Mr. Thompson, I don't understand. Please . . . why are you doing this to me? What have I done to you?"

He waited in silence for a moment while she found a kerchief and blew her nose. Then he took her shoulders gently and sat her in her chair. "Nothing," he said.

"Then why—?"

"You said you want to win this election. I believe you. And maybe there's a way to do that. You won't like it, but maybe there is. But first . . . well, there's something I just had to know."

"What?"

"Whether you are the dried-up old maid they're making you out to be—Twiddie and that bunch—all prim and proper and scrubbed and empty, or whether you got the juice in you to be worth taking

329

chances for."

"I don't know what you're talking about."

"It doesn't matter. You've got juice, Miss Hanks. I've held it in my hand. You'd better go and wash your face now. You're a mess. I'll be back in a little while, with your horse and buggy."

"With my . . . why?"

"Have you ever been uptown, Miss Hanks?"

"Certainly not!"

"Well, if you plan to be mayor of this town, don't you think it's high time you saw the rest of it?"

He turned, opened the door, stepped aside to admit Penelope, then left, striding along the boardwalk toward the stables.

"Thank you," Penelope had said, absently, but now she was at the window, leaning to peer after him. "Mr. Thompson? Was that Mr. Thompson? Miss Hanks?"

The polished surrey made good time up the uptown trail with Bert at the reins. The black pacer was fresh and alert, high-stepping up the long incline, doing a smart turn at the switchback, and cresting the top with high spirits to enter the morning streets of Uptown Jubilation. Three armed men rode escort, and as they topped out and turned left onto the packed expanse of caleche that funnelled into uptown's main avenue—commonly known as Halleluya Row—they fanned out to flank the surrey in regal fashion. Nat Kinley rode to the left and Twist McGuffin to the right, both wearing spotless new black hats and broadcloth coats. Wednesday Warren brought up the rear.

"That place is called the Loving Arms," Bert pointed out to Cornelia. "One of the first places up here, they say. Old Jubal put it up himself after he found out what they wanted with this bluff they bought from him. Over there, that's Patman's Pleasure Palace. Lot of the ranch crews from nearabouts favor that place. Sort of consider it their private club. And over there is Richardson's Refreshment Emporium. Caters to the gentry, so to speak. The last time I saw your brother alive was in there. He was so drunk he could hardly stand up. No offense, Miss Hanks, but your brother was a little wart and that's about all he was."

"I know all about my brother," she said quietly, staring about at the long, double row of buildings which curved away out of sight on the crescent street. Other streets climbed away toward the bluff's low-dome crest.

Word had gone out, and men came from most of the buildings to goggle at them as they passed. Among them were a few women. Some of the men removed their hats.

"Those women," she asked. "Are those . . ."

"Yes, ma'am. They are. Now that one comin' up, with the feathered red nightie, that's Flossie." He tipped his hat as they passed. "Mornin', Flossie. And over there on the walk, that's Gert . . . and the one in the window above, that's Jade. The fellow in the funny hat, with garters on his sleeves, that's Jiggs. He's Richardson's best bartender but he fills in as a waiter most evenings. The skinny man there is Jackie Diamond. He's a dealer. And there's Max Bigelow. See the two big men by the alley coming up? They work for Iron Jack Fuller. The red-nosed one is Hemp. The other one is Packer. Sort of jacks-of-all-trades, you might say. Iron Jack has several more just like 'em. Did you ever see anything like this, Miss Hanks? Come night, there'll be anywhere from two hundred to maybe eight hundred men up here. May be half that many now, sleeping it off someplace. Uptown accommodates its marks . . . uh, its customers. Ah. Look who we have here!"

As they neared the alley a harnessed red bay stepped out, drawing a buggy larger than Cornelia's little surrey and bright with brassware. The man in the seat was large, solidly built, and cruel-faced. He drew rein and stared at them. Bert pulled up, swept off his hat, and mimicked a courtly bow and sweep. "Good morning to you, Iron Jack. Isn't it a beautiful day!"

The man eyed him sourly, his gaze darting to Cornelia, then to the solemn riders around them, then back to Burt. "What is this, Thompson?" he demanded in a voice like gravel falling in a hole. "Have you gone crazy?"

"Iron Jack, it's my very great pleasure to introduce Miss Cornelia Hanks. Miss Hanks, Mr. Iron Jack Fuller. Miss Hanks is running for mayor of Jubilation, Iron Jack. I'm showing her around."

"I want to talk to you, Bert," Iron Jack growled. Packer and Hemp stepped forward threateningly and the hands of Nat, Twist, and Wednesday went to their guns.

"Why, I'd be glad to chat with you, Iron Jack," Bert said happily. "Would you like to take the reins, Miss Hanks? I'll only be a moment. I suggest you drive on down the street here to its end, then turn around and come back. I should be ready to rejoin you by then." He stepped down, handed her the reins, and nodded to her.

Somewhat confused, she snapped the reins and the pacer high-stepped along the street, Twist and Wednesday following. Nat Kinley sat his tall sorrel in mid-street, silent and watchful. Bert walked over to

Iron Jack's buggy.

Iron Jack glared at him suspiciously. Something was going on here that he didn't like. "What's got into you, Bert? You know better than to bring a . . ."

"A lady," Bert prompted. "She's a lady, Iron Jack. And she hadn't seen uptown."

"Get her out of here. I'm about fed up with you, Bert. One of these nights you might have some callers."

Bert stared at him with eyes that made the uptown boss blink. He had never seen Bert sober before. "How much do I owe you now, Iron Jack?"

"Seven dollars, Bert."

"Seven dollars. And I suppose the payoff on that is thirty-five dollars?"

"Interest is interest, Bert. What are you getting at?"

"Would you be interested in another wager, Iron Jack? I wanted you to have a chance to see Miss Hanks. You know she's running for mayor, I suppose. Against Twiddie."

"Of course I know. It's ridiculous, but it doesn't affect me. What about it?"

"Why, she's running on the Prohibition ticket, Iron Jack. The first thing she plans to do is shut all this down." He grinned.

"Yeah, and an ant can look at an elephant with rape on its mind too, but it just isn't going to happen. Get to the point."

"Very simple, Iron Jack. What would you say the odds are against her winning?"

"A thousand to one. Count the voters."

"Would you give that kind of odds against her?"

"I've been giving twenty to one. Drunks'll bet on anything. You want a piece of it? Is that what you

333

want? How much?"

"Well . . ." Bert tugged at his chin. "Twenty to one isn't very interesting, Iron Jack. I mean, for a man in my position, all or nothing is best. You understand?"

"You have gone crazy. What are you offering? The thirty-five dollars you owe me?"

"Of course. But how about fifty to one, Iron Jack? Think of me as a preferred customer."

"You know what's wrong with you, Bert? You're sober."

"What's the matter, Iron Jack? You think you'll lose?"

"I never lose," the man snapped. "All right. Double or nothing on what you owe, only at fifty to one."

"And another hundred at the same odds."

"Where would you get a hundred dollars?"

"I can borrow it."

"Done. And I'd advise you to stay sober until the election is over, because if you get drunk and realize what you've done and come whining to me to call it off, you can forget it, Bert. I'll enjoy putting a hundred and seventy dollars worth of you in my pocket, whether it's cash or broken bones."

Cornelia's surrey was coming back. As it pulled abreast Bert climbed aboard and took the reins. Nat Kingley swung his sorrel to fall in behind.

"Have you seen enough?" Bert asked.

"I certainly have. It's unbelievable. Do you know there's a open field back there covered with men? I don't know how many of them, just strewn all over the ground—"

"The boys call it Potter's Field. But don't worry about them. They're just sleeping it off. Most of them will recover. A lot of them will be back on the street tonight. Now over there, that big building, that's the pokey. That's for the ones that get too out of hand."

"Mr. Thompson?"

"Yes?"

"I know you brought me up here for a reason. Do you want to tell me what it is?"

"No reason not to, I guess. I wanted you to see this. There's just an off chance that you will be mayor of Jubilation very shortly . . . no, don't ask why I think so. I told you before you wouldn't like it. Anyway, I wanted you to see this. Being mayor is well and good, but you aren't going to close this place, and if you try you'll only get hurt . . . and so will a lot of other people."

"I have made promises," she said.

"I know you have. And I know you'll try. But remember what you've seen up here, Miss Hanks. Remember it clearly. It wouldn't be a good thing to try *too* hard. Uptown Jubilation is an institution, and it's the life blood of this town whether the ladies understand that or not."

"Mr. Thompson, I am no hypocrite!"

"Miss Hanks, you're in politics. Just remember what you've seen, and what I've told you. Think about it."

XXX

It was Thursday evening when the cowboys began to disappear.

Each evening for more than a week, the crowds had grown atop Jubilation Bluff. In the arable valleys across the river harvest time was done. The farm boys and the seasonal field hands had their wages and nothing much to do, so they gravitated to Jubilation. On the big spreads south, summer cuts and counts were complete and herds broken up and put to fresh pasture. Ranch hands and grubliners alike had their wages and nothing much to do. They gravitated toward Jubilation. From Pleasant Valley, Sparta, Holmburg, and places as remote as Chesterton and Dodge, townsmen with time on their hands and money in their pockets gravitated toward Jubilation. The traffic was further swelled by throngs of curiosity-seekers who had never been at an election where a woman was running for public office. But of all the divergent groups of men homing on Jubilation Bluff, by far the most numerous were the cowboys.

For at least a hundred miles in every direction, the land was prime rangeland. And where there was rangeland there were cattle. And where there were cattle there were cowboys. H-four was back in town, in force, and plenty of hands from Warbonnet, Star V, XOX, Rocking A, Snake-eyes, and half a hundred other spreads. Not in years had uptown been in better voice.

For their first test, cautiously, the Jubilation Research Society selected a knot of early-whoopee veterans up from the distant Shiloh spread and a cluster of Warbonnet lads weaving along the street toward Madame Fifi's sporting house.

The choice was based on three deciding factors: it was nearly dark, the two groups were about the same strength, and their paths would cross at a point somewhat remote from the heart of activities.

They drew straws. Twist McGuffin stared at the short straw and muttered, "I hate this part." Then he shrugged in resignation and hurried to catch up to the staggering Shilohs just passing by. For a moment he paced along behind them. Then as their path and that of the Warbonnets came together he stepped forward, pushed through the Shiloh crowd, shouted, "Son of a bitch!" and cold-cocked the nearest Warbonnet waddy.

The instantaneous retaliation by the waddy's nearest buddy sent Twist staggering backward into the arms of several Shilohs, who surged forward joyously to do combat. By the time Twist crawled from the melee he was a mass of bruises and had several loose teeth, but his success was complete. More than thirty men were engaged in a full-fledged brawl.

Ike Ferguson skidded from a sidestreet, turned, and waved a beckoning arm. "There they are! They're breaking the law. Do your duty."

Coming around the corner at a pounding run, Leonard charged the fray. "Stand aside!" he roared. "Make way for the Law! You're all under arrest in the name of the Law!"

337

Twist had scuttled free, but a bloodied bulldogger fell headlong over the sprawled body of a grubliner and grabbed his ankle. In an instant, Twist was dragged back into the pummeling mass of humanity.

"Twist, get out of there!" Ike urged him.

"It ain't like I ain't tryin'," Twist assured him from somewhere within. "Jeez, I hate this part!" Knuckles thudded on bone and Twist erupted from the heap, rolling. Ike helped him to his feet. Leonard had arrived and waded right in.

"Under arrest! Make way for the Law!"

Twist and Ike backed into shadows, then hurried to the head of the downhill path. Puff, Prosper, and the pig waited there. Sweeny's star shone brightly on his harness. "He's comin'," Ike puffed. "Y'all ready?"

"As we'll ever be. Whose crazy idea was this anyways?"

"Let's see if it works, then we'll decide."

Slowly the sounds of the fight fragmented and ceased. Moments passed. Then there was movement atop the path.

Ike and Twist crouched in the shadows. "My Lord," Ike breathed, "I believe he has 'em all!"

"Stand aside!" a bull voice roared. "Make way for the Law!"

The mass that hove into view, silhouetted against the sky, seemed a great, writhing octopus sprung with various many arms and legs and surrounded by shuffling men on foot. One way and another, Leonard had collected his miscreants and was on his way downtown.

"Stand aside!" he shouted.

Prosper O'Neil stepped in front of the mass. "Leonard? Is that you in there?"

"Make way for the Law!"

"I believe that's Leonard, all right," Puff allowed.

"Leonard, you hadn't ought to take these men downtown," Prosper said.

Leonard paused. "Why not!" he roared. "It's the Law!"

"Because Marshal Cutter is all tied up down there and hasn't got time to look at 'em," Prosper assured him. "What the marshal did was, he sent his proxy."

"He sent his Proxy!" Leonard roared.

"That's right, Leonard. You see that star there? That is Marshal Cutter's proxy."

"That's a pig!" Leonard shouted.

"Well, that pig is Marshal Cutter's proxy. See there, he's got a star."

"What you ought to do is follow that pig," Prosper advised. "He knows where to go."

"Follow that pig!" Leonard agreed.

Prosper nodded. "That ought to do it. Slip Sweeny loose, Puff."

Puff slipped the leash. For a moment Sweeny stood, looking questioningly about him. Then he ambled off down the path, his star twinkling in moonlight.

"Follow that pig," Prosper pointed.

"Follow that pig!" Leonard roared, and started after him, escorted and burdened by his coterie of combatants. As the mass passed Prosper noticed that most of them—those afoot—where connected in various ways by belts, shirtsleeves, peggin' strings and other devices, and all were connected to Leonard.

The pig was picking up speed. Leonard stepped up his pace and those assembled about him had no choice but to do likewise. A pounding monster of many legs and thrashing extremities hurtled away down the incline.

"Make way for the Pig!" Leonard was shouting. "Stand aside! Make way! That Pig is th' Law!"

The men atop the path watched them all the way down the slope, out across the skirt of the incline, and to the lantern-lit main gate of the Research Center.

"I believe maybe it's gonna work," Prosper admitted. "When do we go again?"

"Soon as Leonard gets back, I guess," Twist reasoned, "and somebody goes after Sweeny. But it's somebody else's turn to open the ball next time. I hate that part."

At the Research Center Elmer Wallace and Will Ambler persuaded Leonard to place his charges in their care so he could go get some more. The culprits were herded quietly into the interior of the main building, whose walls now were lined with makeshift bunks, five deep. In the center of the space a stove was glowing, a huge vat of stew atop it, and alongside a row of barrels with dippers atop them.

"Come in, gentlemen," Bert Thompson welcomed them. "Welcome to Election Central. Good beds, good food, plenty of political advice, and the best snakebite tonic you ever tasted. Haul your boots off an' plan to stay a couple of days."

In the shed alongside, Elmer Wallace allowed Sweeny a brief guzzle at the fermented squish, then hauled him around to the gate. "You come on back later, Sweeny," he assured him. "You can have some more then." He saw Ike coming with the leash.

Atop Jubilation Bluff the evening was just getting into full swing, and Elmer shook his head and took a deep breath. It was going to be a long night.

In the ripe two-holer behind City Hall Marshal Ben Cutter sat fuming in the darkness, muttering to himself and now and then letting loose with a string of curses. An hour of pounding, hammering, and shouting had accomplished nothing. He was trapped, and well aware that he might be here until morning. Sometimes, distantly, he heard voices. But all the shouting and pounding had brought no one to get him out.

He felt totally helpless, and was resolved to kill someone if he could ever discover who the culprit was. Vaguely, he suspected some of the waddies from H-Four. After all, they were the ones who had a record of escaping from uptown and bringing their hilarity downtown. What they had done to that biddy's chickens, he had found amusing. But there was nothing amusing about this.

He had stepped out for his evening relief, had stepped into the outhouse and closed the door. What happened next he could decipher only from the sounds he had heard. There had been an abrupt pounding of hooves, the whir and swish of a thrown lariat, then the little building had shuddered and seemed to tighten around him as hoofbeats sounded outside, going around and around the privy, and rope scraped and snugged against wood.

The outhouse was lashed now as tightly as the feet of a thrown calf, and Marshal Benjamin Cutter was trapped inside.

His polished Colt was fifty yards away, hanging in his quarters in the rear of City Hall, along with his good hat, his good suit, his linen shirts, and string tie. Of all his natty apparel now he had only his boots. These he wore with a long nightshirt and a dangling nightcap.

Again he heard distant voices, and raised his fist

341

to pound again, then hesitated. They were women's voices. He kept his peace, fuming. He didn't want to be found by women. He'd never live it down.

Resigned, Ben Cutter sat in the high dark of a lowly outhouse, waiting for rescue. Several times, far in the distance, he heard Leonard's voice, and waited for the big deputy to show up bearing prisoners. Leonard would let him out. It was the Law.

But as the hours wore by, though he heard Leonard's inane bellowing several times, Leonard never came.

In the wee hours of Friday morning Nat Kinley stepped out onto the porch of the hotel. It was the quiet time in Jubilation. Downtown slept soundly and most of uptown had passed out. A riding moon in the west cast slivers of silver on rustling trees, still rooftops, and darkened windows.

Nat yawned and stretched, easing the kinks of the stiff hotel bed he had occupied for a few hours, wondering idly whether Flossie's featherbed was in use atop the bluff. It was going to be another long day.

He turned and walked down the street, toward City Hall. Past the dark windows of Linden's Dry Goods he turned into a narrow alley, walked its length, and turned right again.

All was dark and still behind City Hall. On soft boots Nat approached the outhouse, and paused for a moment to listen to the rhythmic snoring coming from inside. Then, silently, he removed his ropes, recovered his lariat, coiled them, and headed for Ambler's to deposit them with the rest of his gear.

In the time before dawn Opal Twiddie came abruptly awake and sat bolt upright, eyes wide and nostrils twitching. Something was wrong. She felt it. She crawled out of bed and went to the window, a nameless dread crowding into her mind. She opened the sash and peered out. The town slept. Night breezes had stilled to a pre-dawn hush, and here and there a bird was clearing its throat. Somewhere far off she heard the rattle of Lowell Hampton's milk wagon beginning its rounds, and a sleepy rooster rasping its first crow.

From the direction of City Hall came a flat slap, as of a plank door thrown open, followed by the sound of a man cursing.

Unnamed suspicions crowded Opal's mind. Something was wrong.

Mrs. Mayor had been in a snit for weeks now. She felt betrayed. She felt left out. She felt things had gotten thoroughly out of hand. She simply did not understand how her friends could have done such a thing to her. To follow her lead toward righteousness and universal sobriety was one thing. To come up with a candidate for her husband's position was quite another. She did not know when, if ever, she would be on speaking terms with most of them again. It was a direct affront, and where had they found the nerve?

She had even let her husband move back into the house in protest, though he was still relegated to sleeping in the guest bedroom. Part of the reason was his sash. During his latest term of office, Alfred had taken to wearing a red sash on ceremonial occasions. Somewhere he had picked up the idea that it was traditional for a mayor to wear a sash, and that it lent honor to the office. Opal had not minded that. As Mrs. Mayor, she favored all the dignity the office could handle.

But Alfred had changed since . . . that woman
. . . had posted for his job. If it had been a slap in
the face to Mrs. Mayor, it had been a kick in the gut
to His Honor. He had taken refuge behind his sash
and was seldom seen without it.

As a matter of principle, Opal objected to his
wearing it in her bed.

Now, though, she stalked into the guest bedroom,
grabbed the mayor's shoulder, and shook him.

"Alfred? Wake up."

"Mbzgup?"

She shook him again. Eyes still closed, he reached
for her. "Mmph. Gert . . ."

Opal chalked up another score to settle with her
husband. She avoided his clutch, climbed over him,
got both arms under him and rolled him out of bed.
He thumped and howled.

On hands and knees she glared down at him.
"Alfred? Are you awake?"

He sat up, bleary and stale, whiskey lingering on
his breath. "What the Hell . . ."

"Mind your language, you spineless twit. Are you
awake?"

"Yeah. What's the matter?"

"Alfred, I'm having an intuition."

He blinked at her in the dimness. "So go back to
bed and sleep it off. It'll pass. Woman of your age is
bound to —"

"Alfred!"

"Well, you ain't any spring chicken, Opal."

"Will you shut up and listen to me!"

"Of course, honey pot. What's the matter?"

"Alfred, there is something going on."

"There usually is."

"I mean especially, Alfred. Something definitely is

344

wrong."

"Do you have gas, Opal?"

"Alfred! I'm trying to tell you, somebody is doing something they shouldn't and I know it and I want you to put a stop to it."

"Yes, dear. I will. First thing in the morning."

XXXI

It was nearly noon when the spring wagon pulled up in the yard of Howard Sills's place in Bad Basin, full of beribboned and bright-eyed passengers and followed on horseback by Wednesday Warren.

Ambrose came from the house as Howard climbed down to hitch Crowbait at the rail. Wednesday dismounted and looped his reins alongside. "Howdy, Ambrose." He waved. "We come out with Mr. Sills to take tea. That there on the seat is Miss Penelope Becket. The two in the back is Miss Sally Spalding and Miss Betty Stapleton. They're girls. Ladies, this here is Ambrose. He's black."

Ambrose bowed courteously to the young ladies, grinned at Wednesday, and peered at Howard. "Th' good service, Mist' Howard?"

"Yes, Ambrose, please. Ah, you see, I was in town and the young ladies expressed a desire to see the place, so I thought—"

"Mist' Howard, you want me to listen to you 'splain or you want me to put on th' tea?"

"Put on the tea, Ambrose. Thank you."

Ambrose hurried away to don proper uniform for serving tea to guests.

346

Wednesday planted a boot on the spring wagon's hub and began unloading girls. Howard went around and offered his hand to Penelope, turning bright red as she took it and descended. Howard had turned red a lot in the past hour or two. All the way out from Jubilation he had tried to resist sneaking glances at Penelope, sitting on the seat beside him. His attempts had failed. He could barely keep his eyes off her, and each time he looked at her, she looked back and he blushed and looked away. The two in the back had giggled a lot. He suspected that they were aware of his nervous condition, though he couldn't imagine that Penelope had told anyone.

But then, if Nat Kinley had told her all about it — he still was appalled that his friend had done such a thing — there was no telling who else Nat had educated. Maybe he had told Penelope's friends. Or maybe he had told Wednesday Warren and Wednesday had told them. For that matter, maybe Nat had called a town meeting and simply told everybody. It was embarrassing. Still, Howard had to admit that Nat's advice had been sound. Any man who is going to be unhappy about a woman, the cowman had told him sagely, might as well go ahead and be downright miserable and get it done. In other words, court or cut bait.

"Oh, my," Penelope exclaimed. "What an interesting place!"

"That's his house," Wednesday pointed out. "It's got flaming fortresses."

"Buttresses," Betty corrected him. "Flaming buttresses."

"Flying," Sally said. "My land, I don't believe I ever saw a barn built just like that one. And those . . . what are those tall things, Mr. Sills?"

"Oh, those . . ."

347

"Them is silos," Wednesday explained. "That's where he stacks his turnips when they're ripe." He gazed across the huge field of succulent greenery. "I believe you're gonna make that second crop. They're comin' right on up, aren't they?"

"They . . ."

"My father says he'll buy some more of your greens, Mr. Sills," Betty said. "My mother showed some of the ladies how to cook them with vinegar and side meat, and my father made a good profit. What people didn't buy he sold to Mr. Ambler for bale fodder."

"You see yonder," Wednesday pointed out. "Where it looks like there's a little hill with a lid on it? A body might not think so, but that there is a storm cellar. Did you ever see anything like that? An' the best thing of all, we got to get Mr. Sills to show you ladies his—"

"I don't—"

"Is it really true about your house?" Penelope wondered. "I mean, that the roof isn't fastened to it?"

"Well, it really—"

"That's right," Wednesday told her. "It's *on* the house, but that's just because the house is built under it. But it ain't attached."

Howard shook his head. "That isn't—"

Ambrose, wearing his dark coat and stiff collar, stepped out onto the porch and held the door wide. "Tea is served," he said.

Sally and Betty headed for the door trailed by Wednesday Warren. Penelope took a step, then hesitated. "May I take your arm, sir?"

The question startled him and he looked directly into her lavender eyes, then blushed furiously. "Of c-course. I . . ."

348

She lay a dainty hand on his arm, elegantly, then for an instant was close against him. "Don't worry," she whispered. "I've discussed you with Miss Hanks. She feels you can recover fully."

Howard wondered if there were anyone in Coleman County who didn't know by now that he had an affliction.

As Ambrose set out the service—steeped tea and sugar cakes—the girls gazed in wide-eyed curiosity at the house around them.

"There isn't any ceiling," Betty said.

"Except over there, I'll bet that's a ceiling for the rest of the house, but what do you suppose is up there? Maybe," she whispered, "it's his bedroom."

"That is totally romantic," Betty breathed. "Just totally."

Penelope circled the main room, seeing everything, her eyes shining. "Oh, I wish my mother could be here," she said.

Just at that moment, so did Howard.

They took seats then at the table and Ambrose poured, wearing his best imitation of the expression he had seen on the face of Squire Sedby's English butler in Maryland. On Ambrose it lacked something, but he persisted.

"Tomorrow will be a busy day," Penelope chatted. "It's election day, you know. And this year I shall vote. I intend to be at the polls early, to vote for Miss Hanks. I think it's exciting, the idea that she is running for public office."

"Seems a shame to me." Wednesday had dribbled tea into his saucer and was fanning it with his hat. "All this bother she's goin' to, an' no chance for her. That's what I heard. I told some of the boys if I's old enough to vote I reckoned I might vote for her. They all figgered I'd ate loco weed but I would.

349

Seems to me *somebody* ought to."

"My mother says all the ladies are going to," Sally advised.

"Yeah, but that's just women. I reckon it'd be a mercy if she had some real votes too. But I ain't heard from anybody that admits they might."

"Well, Howard would if he lived in Jubilation," Penelope assured them. "Wouldn't you, Howard?"

"Yes, I . . ."

"Miss Hanks is the 'spearhead for our fight against John Barleycorn,' " Betty said. "I read that in the newspaper."

"Oh, yes. I wrote that. It was what Mrs. Haggard said at the last ladies' meeting. Do you know, they had prepared a list of men who go to the saloons and things like that? It was quite a long list, and very distinguished . . . although some of the ladies were severe in their commentary, I thought."

Wednesday's eyes lit up. "Was I on it?"

"No, I don't believe you were, Wednesday."

He frowned. "Recognition don't come easy when you're new in town." He saucered some more tea, then seemed to freeze where he sat. A moment later the head of a large tomcat appeared above his knees, and then the entire cat was in his lap, standing tall to rub its cheeks against his jaws, first one side and then the other. Its purr was unrestrained.

"Oh, look," Sally blurted out, absolutely charmed. "Pussy likes Wednesday. Sit still, Wednesday, don't frighten the dear thing."

Wednesday wasn't about to move a muscle. White-faced, he sat frozen and thought about his gun. It was beyond recovery, though. The cat was standing on it.

With the attention of the rest otherwise occupied, Penelope edged closer to Howard, her hand resting

350

on his. "Do you know what I'd like?" she whispered to him.

"I . . ."

"I'm sure the others wouldn't mind. We could just slip away for a time, if you'd like."

"No, I . . ."

"Or right here, if you prefer, Howard."

"Here? We . . ."

"Oh, yes, Howard. Please?"

"Well . . ." He nodded, avoiding her eyes. Then he arose, went to the cupboard, and took out his bagpipes.

At their first preparatory wail dishes rattled in the back, there were hurried footsteps, and the back door slammed. The cat went out a window. Wednesday's hands went to his ears and Betty shuddered.

With his pipes skirling he could meet her eyes. As the great tones grew he could draw meaning from them and return it to her tenfold.

Howard stamped his foot, thumped his goose, and launched into "Piobaireachd of Donald Dubh." Nat Kinley was right about courting. A man simply had to take matters into his own hands and guide his drive along trails of his choosing. It was time to play the Ceol Mor for Penelope Becket.

In all, it was a magical afternoon at Bad Basin. Summer's end lay gentle upon the rolling land, sweet breezes whispered from the hills, and lazy clouds in a deep blue sky cast patchwork shadows on the world of greens and golds.

After the first round of Ceol Mor, Ambrose suggested—in fact insisted—that they all go outside.

Howard moved the rocking chair from the porch out to the meadow where a spreading elm cast pleasant shade, and there he played for Penelope the concert range of the pipes. "Scots Wha Ha'e Wi' Wallace Bled" rose high to set the clouds a'tremble. She laughed and applauded at "Inverness Rant," listened gravely to "The Green Hills of Tyrol," fumed with him at "The Carles wi' the Breeks," and had tears twinkling in her eyes at the sad, solemn majesty of "Flowers of the Forest." With the last of his wind he stood before her and played again "The Nut Brown Girl."

Wednesday had been giving the girls a tour of the outhouse. Now they stopped and listened, and Sally clasped her hands.

"He's serenading her again," she breathed. "Oh, that's just beautiful."

Betty's eyes were huge. "When he plays like that, it's . . . it's just . . ." She leaned close to Sally to whisper. "I don't imagine a person could have babies from that, do you?"

"Had me a juice harp one time," Wednesday said. "Maybe I'll get me another one."

Even Ambrose came to the door of the house to listen.

Howard and Penelope walked across the meadow, along the wagon path flanked by his fields, and up to the crest of the basin ridge. Beyond, sweeping away to blue distance and shadowed depth, lay the great cleft of the Cimarron Valley. Along its floor, threading among groves and thickets, the river was a winding ribbon of gold.

"I've never seen it like this," she said. "It's beautiful."

"Maybe . . ."

"See the colors! It sparkles, doesn't it?"

"It . . ."

"How many miles do you suppose we're seeing,

352

Howard? Oh, look! A golden eagle!" She turned to him, looking up at his eyes. "Howard, say something."

"What?"

"I don't know. Anything. You started to say something, what was it?"

"I . . ."

He waited and there was no interruption, only the encouragement of wide lavender eyes.

"I started to . . . say . . ." He swallowed. "To say that if you haven't . . . seen it . . . like this . . . well . . . maybe you should be here more often. I mean . . ."

"Yes. I'd like that."

"I . . ."

"Go on."

"I . . . haven't seen you . . . like this, either. You're . . . well . . . your eyes . . ."

"Oh, I know. Mr. Kinley told me about Letitia and Luella. They must have been perfectly horrid. What a rotten time that must have been for you. Mrs. Spaulding and Mrs. Wilkie both said they've heard of things like that—people confusing people so. Even Mr. Ambler has been concerned. He wanted to know if he could help. But Miss Hanks said the best thing is to just let matters take their course—"

"Damn!"

"What?"

"I said damn. Pardon. But does everybody in that town think I'm some kind of a cripple or something? If Nat Kinley were here right now I think I'd punch him right in his big mouth. What business is it of anybody's that I get the cold shakes every time I look at you, and my tongue won't work and my knees go shaky and I can't sleep for thinking about you and I keep making up reasons to go into town

353

just so I might see you somewhere and then when I do see you I want to run and hide because I don't know what else to do and the whole reason I planted turnips to start with was because I was thinking about Penelope Becket when I should have been thinking about seed! And all those times when . . ."

"I . . ."

". . . I saw you on the street and all those young men were following after you and I wanted to follow after you too but I couldn't because if you had looked at me I wouldn't have known what to say. Uncle Chester always said I wasn't very bright and maybe he was right but I'm out here and I'm going to make it and if he doesn't like it he can take the whole Sills Family of Maryland and—"

"Howard, I —"

"—and do something improbable with them because I'll be hanged if I'll marry Flutilla Culver of the Shasta Plantation Culvers or that needle-nosed Mimrose Finch or anybody else Uncle Chester might have in mind. If he wants them, he can marry them! And as for—"

"Howard—"

"—reporting to him on my finances, I've had it up to here with that. This is my place, not his. I'll run it the way I choose—"

"Howard Sills!"

"—ah . . . yes?"

She stared at him. "My, once you get started, you're really something. But let's don't use it up all at once. We have a great deal to talk about."

"I . . ."

"And don't start going fuzzy again, Howard. I'm not your Uncle Chester. And I'm not Letitia and Luella either, or anybody else. I'm me, and I intend to be dealt with on my own behalf, not as a proxy for someone you—"

"Penelope—"

"—think I might resemble. And I'm not a child either, although people keep trying to treat me like one. I get so mad at Uncle Dub sometimes, telling me to do this and do that and don't worry about a thing. Heavens, Howard, I'm twenty-one years old and so far I've never even—"

"Penelope Becket!"

"—ah . . . yes?"

"Shut up! Pardon, but I have a lot to say to you that I've wanted to say for a long time, and if you keep interrupting I might not get half of it said. Do you know that I milled a whole load of turnips and broke my wagon just because you were . . ."

He stopped then because she was on tiptoe, tight against him, her arms around his neck, and even if he had remembered what he wanted to say he could not have said it for the soft lips pressed against his own.

In the barnyard where Wednesday Warren was explaining Howard's unlikely barn, Sally Spalding glanced northward and gasped. "Oh," she breathed. "Oh, Betty! Look!"

Atop the distant ridge, silhouetted against a golden sky, two figures seemed to have become one.

"They're kissing!" Betty sighed. "Oh, just look. I've never in my whole life seen anything so . . ."

"This is all working out better than I thought it might," Sally decided. "Probably we should go up there now and chaperone, do you think? I mean, Mother says these things can get out of hand without chaperones."

"How about that!" Wednesday stared at the distant couple. Then he looked at the girls and grinned.

"Wednesday Warren!" they backed away. "You

behave yourself!"

In the evening, after a buffet meal served under the elm by Ambrose, Howard hitched up Crowbait and they set off for Jubilation. Tomorrow was election day and Penelope had promised to cover the polls.

Ambrose held the gate for them. "Don't forget, Mist' Howard," he reminded him. "When you gets home you got to write to your Uncle Chester."

Howard pulled up, looked down at him thoughtfully, and said, "Ambrose, if you feel Uncle Chester should be written to, you write to him." He twitched the reins. "Giddap, Crowbait."

Ambrose closed the gate and leaned on it, watching the spring wagon recede in the evening light along the fresnoed road. Howard and Penelope sat on the seat, closer than its width required, and the other three were in the back. Wednesday's horse trotted along behind. Five voices blended in harmony to the strains of "Shall We Gather at the River." Ambrose shook his head. "He knows I can't write," he muttered.

Dusk lay upon the land as the spring wagon crossed the Higgins-Wentworth Trail with Jubilation just beyond. Because of the westering breeze no sound came here from the bluff, but even now its lights were being lit and its evening had begun.

A group of riders approached them, coming from the town. Five men on horseback, indistinct. Then they were near, and passing. The four who nodded their direction and tipped their hats all wore dark masks. The fifth was Marshal Ben Cutter, hatless and gunless, a gag across his mouth and his hands tied behind him.

"Evenin'," one of the masked riders said. "Evenin', ladies."

Then they were past, and Penelope turned to stare after them. "That sounded like Mr. Kinley."

"Believe it was," Wednesday agreed. "Wonder what them boys is doin' with the marshal?"

Howard also was peering back, at the cluster of receding silhouettes against the western sky. "I guess they're taking him for a ride," he said.

XXXII

Election day Saturday dawned on scenes of general confusion. Uptown, those still standing were remarking on the number of fights there had been the past two nights. General brawls had erupted with clockwork regularity on both nights, and it was noticeable that Leonard, putting himself to bed in the hayloft behind Patman's, was bleak and drawn with fatigue. Never had so few worked so hard for so long to arrest so many.

The confusion came about when it was noted that there wasn't a soul in the pokey, and hadn't been for two days.

That in turn got some to wondering about the wagons that had come and gone during the early hours of morning, hauling off collapsed bodies from Potter's Field.

Downtown, there was the confusion of setting up polls at the schoolhouse, with pollwatchers and election judges scurrying to get in place and ready to open the polls at seven.

The task was complicated by the fact that no one could find the city clerk. Ding Cox was among the missing, and a check of his office revealed that his seal and his supply of printed voter registration forms were gone.

"Something is going on here, Alfred," Opal Twiddie declared ominously. "I told you so yesterday, didn't I? Somebody is doing something."

"Doesn't matter whether Ding is here or not," the mayor assured her. "City clerk has nothin' to do with elections except to register voters, and as far as I know everybody in town that ought to be already is."

"With all those forms gone, what's to keep whoever has them from voting several times?"

"Opal, for heaven's sake! This ain't that big a town. Hardly anybody here doesn't know most everybody. Nobody can vote for somebody without everybody knowin' it and that goes for anybody."

"What?"

"I said . . . oh, never mind. Quit worryin'. If it hadn't been for you gettin' them women all stirred up, this'd just be a peaceful election like we always had before."

The confusion was heightened when Marshal Ben Cutter walked into town, hatless, weaponless, limping, and furious, with a story about having been kidnapped by masked villains and detained most of the night at an abandoned shed several miles out of town.

It was the second morning in a row that the marshal had shown up with a wild story of personal harassment, and some people were beginning to wonder about him.

A little before seven Cornelia Hanks unlocked the door of the Jubilation Tribune, opened the blinds, hung up her shawl and bonnet, and straightened the pile of correspondence on her desk. Beyond the paned windows the street was unusually busy for a

Saturday morning. Election day had brought the people out, and most of the merchants had opened early to attract their trade. Cornelia went to the big wall clock, wound it as she always did on Saturday morning, and noted the time. In a few minutes the polls would be officially open. Outside, much of the foot traffic was heading down the street toward the school.

The door opened and Penelope Becket came in, said an absent-minded "good morning," and deposited a sheaf of notes on the writing table. Cornelia glanced at her, and glanced again. Always a stunning young woman, Penelope looked absolutely radiant on this morning, high color in her cheeks, eyes sparkling, hair piled high in a loose bun on which perked a ridiculous little cap. Penelope picked up a galley proof, stared at it distractedly, put it down again, picked up some of the notes she had brought in, took them across to her desk, changed her mind, replaced them on the writing table, then went to the window and stood looking out.

Cornelia shook her head. The classic symptoms, to the letter. "Penelope," she said. There was no response. She said it again. "Penelope?"

The girl turned. "Yes? Oh, Miss Hanks. Good morning."

"You already said that, dear. Ah, if the clock is right, the polls will open shortly."

"Yes. I'm sure."

"Penelope?"

"Yes, ma'am?"

"You did say you'd be at the polls when they open, didn't you, dear? To note the attendance and all?"

"I . . . oh, yes, I did. Oh, heavens, Miss Hanks, I almost forgot."

"I can imagine." Cornelia's smile was hidden as she turned away. "Have you seen Mr. Sills recently, Penelope?"

"Oh, yes! Oh, my, yes. Yes, I have."

"Really. And is he getting along all right, dear? Is he doing well?"

"Wonderful," Penelope sighed.

"I see." She saw. "Well, I am glad to hear it. He seems a very nice young man."

"Wonderful," Penelope sighed.

"Penelope, have you seen Bert lately?"

"Who?"

"Mr. Thompson. Do you have any idea where he might be? I haven't seen him since Thursday. I know I fired him, but I'm sure he knows I didn't mean it. Usually he comes around on Friday to set the forms and clean the press. Vladimir did that alone yesterday."

"No, I don't think I've seen him."

"Well, he certainly behaved strangely that day. Do you know he very nearly promised that I would win the election?"

"That's nice," Penelope sighed dreamily.

"But what it has done is force me to recognize that it just isn't possible. I thought at the time he was being terribly cruel . . . and he was! But maybe it was the only way he knew to make me face reality."

"That's nice," Penelope murmured.

"And I don't know why he should care, one way or another. In most respects, Bert Thompson really is a despicable person."

"That's nice," Penelope said.

"Penelope!" Cornelia gave up. "The polls, dear. Please?"

"The . . . oh, my! I don't seem to be myself today.

I'm going right now, Miss Hanks." With businesslike bustle she was out the door, then turned, still holding it. "Ah . . . did I say good morning, Miss Hanks? I think I did."

"Yes, dear. You did. Go!"

"Yes, ma'am."

Cornelia gazed at the closed door. "Ah, me," she sighed. "Young love."

"*Da. Lyubit*," Bloody Mare said from the shop door. "*Khorosho lyubit. Dobroye utroo*, damn skinny. *Gde* Bert Tomsahn?"

"*Dobroye utroo*, Vladimir," she greeted him. "I don't know where he is." At his blank gaze she tried again, shaking her head. "*Nyet*. Bert Thompson *nye* . . . ah . . . here." She shrugged.

He grinned and mimicked her shrug. "Bert Tomsahn," he said, as one practicing patience. He turned and was gone. She heard the back door close.

"This is the strangest town," she told herself. She began her attack on the correspondence pile. Later, when it was done, would be time enough to go to the school and cast her vote for herself as mayor of Jubilation. She did not want to seem, well, unseemly by arriving too early.

The latest issue of the Pleasant Valley newspaper, distributed as usual by Mayor Twiddie and his cronies, had advertisements urging all upstanding Jubilation residents to come forward and vote the "Peace and Prosperity" ticket, to assure that Jubilation retained the "keen quality of municipal leadership for which it has become noted." In the same paper, headlines heralding the special election in "our sinful sister city to the south" gave vent to more than half a page of heavy-handed wisdom and wit designed to leave no aspect of Jubilation or its election unslandered.

362

"Although the movement to add bustle to the business of government in our neighboring den of iniquity has obvious merit," the writer extolled, "the efforts of the ladies there to cast out demon rum seem doomed to defeat. It is unlikely that we shall see sobriety surface soon in Jubilation. Though we question the integrity of those noteworthies presently in power there (whose recent unprecedented patronage this newspaper deeply appreciates and whose political advertisements we proudly display, having received cash in advance to provide the space) it is obvious that we shall see no significant change as a result of Saturday's vote. There are not enough sensible and sober citizens in all of Jubilation to unseat Alfred Twiddie, even if the candidate on the Prohibition ticket were a man. We prophesy without fear of folly that the hamlet under hiccup hill is no more destined to have itself a mayoress than frogs are destined to fly."

There was more. Cornelia read it, wondering at the mentality of men who would carry such a flag into battle. Unfortunately, she conceded, the writer was right. And so was Bert Thompson, in his own twisted way. Now, in the cold light of election day, she knew there was no conceivable way she could win, and Alfred Twiddie's victory—because of her—would be the final blow to the ladies and their crusade. She should have said no. She should have stayed out of it. She knew so little of this strange town. She had let herself be manipulated into a contest that never should have happened. It would set the cause of decency and sobriety back by years, and it was her own stubborn pride that was to blame. The ladies had flattered her, the town council had insulted her intelligence, and she had reacted in exactly that mindless fashion that always infuriated her when others did it.

In a part of her mind, she began composing a statement of concession. She would publish it on the front page, part apology to those who had shown faith in her, part congratulations to those whose point was won, and part endorsement of the need for sobriety in Jubilation because it was the law. Maybe in defeat she could salvage something.

She glanced through the rest of a newspaper, noting items to rewrite for the Tribune. One of the newspaper's best sources of material was other newspapers ... a fact she had learned by doing in picking up the reins of her dead brother's enterprise.

Stock disappearances had been reported in several counties to the north. There appeared to be a growing epidemic of cattle rustling. The culprits — as yet unknown — had even taken sheep, chickens, riding stock, and assorted other animals.

There was also a long article about the circus coming to Pleasant Valley. The two most noted festive occasions in Coleman County annually were Jubilation's Chautauqua and Pleasant Valley's circus. Each town tried each year to outdo the other in the quality of its entertainment. This year's visiting show would be Doctor Dimwater's Traveling Extravaganza, humbly touted as "The Biggest Little Show on Earth." It specialized in aerial artists, clowns, performing ponies, and trick riding, and had a menagerie that included "the finest exotic creatures of Africa, Asia, and several other countries." Show dates would be announced upon arrival of the company, which was expected within a few days.

A rash of violent crimes had broken out in the federal territories. Robberies and murders were reported ranging from the Cherokee Outlet to the Neutral Strip. Settlers were demanding a return of deputy marshals to the area. It was noted vaguely that there were no legal settlers in those lands, but that did little to diminish their plight.

In a little item from somewhere in Missouri was mention of a new alcoholic substance which Prohibitionists in that state considered the devil's own concoction. It was, they claimed to have heard, colorless, odorless, almost tasteless, and capable of depriving any man of his senses in a fourth the time of honest corn liquor. Its use had caught on in the hills of Missouri.

The correspondent had heard the substance called "fawdky."

"What a world we find ourselves in," Cornelia murmured to herself. "Outlaws and trapeze artists, amazing creatures imported from the far corners of the earth and amazing liquids appearing from who knows where, people robbing banks, cattle mysteriously disappearing, and it all gets second billing to a one-post election in a town nobody ever would have heard of had it ever learned to behave itself. "Oh!" she added more loudly. "What men may do! What men dare do! What men daily do, not knowing what they do! Now where did I get that? *Much Ado About Nothing,*" she reminded herself.

She wondered what had become of Bert Thompson.

Would any of the men vote for her? Possibly a few. The voting booth was a private place. But not many. It was unthinkable.

No, she decided, there was nothing to do but hold her chin high, cast her ballot, thank those who voted for her, and accept defeat graciously, as a lady should.

Elephants and aerialists, outlaws and elections, sobriety and imbibery and Shakespeare on the side.

365

What a world! Uptown rowdied and downtown howdied and politics proceeded oblivious below a hill where they racked sleeping drunks like cordwood. And where was Bert Thompson?

Vladimir was back. He burst through from the shop, grinning and beckoning. "Damn skinny, *izvinite, prizzhete!* Cossacks *prizzhayut!*"

In her time, Cornelia had developed a mild fondness for the little Russian. She tried to understand a few words of his language. But here she was out of her depth. It just didn't seem likely that he could be trying to tell her the Cossacks were coming.

Still, he was beckoning excitedly. She followed him through the shop and out the back door. He pointed.

Beyond the back lot, beyond the new road, in its pasture on the slope of Jubilation Bluff, was the fenced and silent complex of the Greater Jubilation Research Society. But now it was not silent. The doors of the main building were open and men were issuing forth from them, a line of laughing, shouting, cavorting men that seemed to go on and on. There were hundreds of them. She shaded her eyes and squinted. There was a quality about them . . . unbidden, words came to her mind: *What ho, what manner of men are these, who* . . . she blushed. Where had she ever heard such a thing? But by that aid she identified them. They seemed to be cowboys. The line went on and on, beyond count. The place seemed to have been packed to improbability, and now they were loose.

Shouting, laughing, singing bawdy songs, prancing and staggering, weaving, pushing and shoving, the line of men wound from the building across the fenced yard and through the north gate, there to veer to the left toward the downtown business area.

Those at its point already were cutting across Stapleton's wagon yard and disappearing toward the street.

"What in the world?" she said.

"Cossacks," Vladimir explained. "*Khorosho* Cossacks."

Cossacks? Cowboys? "What are they doing? Where did they come from?"

Of course he didn't understand her questions. Yet he knew they were questions and his shrug and grin were eloquent. Who could explain the behavior of Cossacks? They were Cossacks.

Hitching up her courage and her skirts, Cornelia ran to intercept the line of raucous young men. Several saw her coming and stopped, their hats in their hands and silly grins on their faces.

"It's her," one announced. "That there is the woman 'at's goin' to save our stompin' grounds."

"Howdy, yer highness," another slurred.

The one next to him elbowed him in the ribs. "It ain' her highness, Slim. It's her grace. Lord, I buy you books an' you jus' eat the pages."

This set them off into peals of laughter, and Cornelia realized that they were inebriated. Yet, coming close, she found no scent of whiskey about them. They didn't smell good, but neither did they smell of whiskey.

"What . . . what are you gentlemen doing? Where are you going?"

They stared at one another blearily, then at her. "Ma'am, we're going to do our duty as citizens," one explained.

"Th' right to vote is a sacred oath," another assured her.

Again he got an elbow in his ribs. "That's solemn duty, Slim. Sacred oath is that other part. Remember?"

"You're going to vote?" She gaped at them. "In the city election? But you're not—"

"Yes, ma'am, we are," one assured her. He dug into a pocket and produced a crumpled bit of paper. "Says right here, we been sanctified as presidents—"

"Certified as residents, Slim."

"Yeah. An' we're all registered."

"To vote. See, what we got to do is line up an' go in an' make our marks where it says . . . ah . . ." He stared at the open palm of his hand. "Here. Like it says here." He displayed his palm before her. Written on it with proofing ink was, "2) C. Hanks," and a large X.

"We're countin' on you, ma'am. You run th' rascals down."

"Out, Slim."

"Out. Got to go now, ma'am. Soon's we vote we get to go back in that there new pokey for 'nother shot of . . . whatever that is."

They turned and hurried on. Others going by grinned and tipped their hats. Cornelia's mouth hung open.

"Told you you wouldn't like it," a voice at her shoulder said. She turned.

"The evil that men do lives after them," Bert Thompson intoned, watching the passing parade with huge cynicism. "The good is oft interred with their bones." He shrugged. "So let it be with Caesar."

The Bert Thompson of the past Thursday was gone. Cornelia stared at the mocking, half-drunk printer and shook her head. "I must say your change for the better didn't last very long."

"Long enough." He jerked a thumb at the line of roistering registered voters. "Congratulations, Miss Mayor. You got what you wanted."

"Mr. Thompson, what have you done? Those men shouldn't vote. They don't live here."

"Sure they do. Certified and legal. Place of residence right yonder. Didn't you know they knocked out the time in residence statute when they tried to run the poll tax through in Topeka? Twenty-four hours qualifies, Miss Hanks."

"But those men . . . they're intoxicated."

"They are? Well, my, my. An' there they all go, staggerin' to the polls to vote dry. Ah mischief, thou art afoot, take thou what course thou wilt."

"You've made a mockery of this election! I can't condone—"

"You said you wanted to be mayor."

"But not by such means as . . . oh, mercy, I'm ashamed."

"No, you're not. You're just confused. You'll get over it." He turned and walked away.

After a moment she hitched up her skirts again and stormed after him. "I'm not going to stand for this, Mr. Thompson!"

"What are you goin' to do, fire me?" He kept walking. "You already did that."

"I won't accept the office! It's an outrage!"

"Public office always is. So you'll just betray all those good, decent, sober people that voted for you, is that it? You know who's in line down there with those cowboys, waitin' to vote? I mean besides Twiddie's chums? About a hundred people who really believe in you. What about them?"

"Well, I . . . I can at least refuse to vote. This election is a travesty!"

"Aren't they all." He grinned. "Just imagine . . . a bunch of drunks electin' a woman mayor on the Prohibition ticket! Now that's got style. Beats the hell out of a bunch of drunks reelectin' Alfred

369

Twiddie, which is what was fixin' to happen. At any rate, they're all down there votin' now, Miss Hanks. You're bein' elected mayor of Jubilation by about five to four, is my guess. Maybe better. What you do about that is your problem. I left some things in your shop. I'll just pick 'em up."

She followed him into the back shop, then hurried on through to grab her bonnet and shawl, and headed for the school.

An ecstatic Emma Spaulding led the group that met her there. "Oh, Cornelia, you're winning! Just look, all those men! They're all voting for you."

"And," Polly Cox added with a cryptic smile, "they are legal voters."

"Definitely legal," Martha Haggard declared smugly.

Cornelia blinked at them. What had they been up to? Were they party to this? Yes. Instinctively she knew they were. But not Emma. Emma brimmed with surprise and enthusiasm. And not Wanda Wilkie, or Imogene Stapleton. They had seen a miracle.

"I've decided not to vote," she said, deciding.

At sundown Alfred Twiddie conceded. A half-hour later the Wednesday Ladies' Reading Circle held a spontaneous punch social which Cornelia Hanks declined to attend. It was just as well. A group of H-Four waddies, paying their agreed-upon return visit to the Jubilation Research Center after doing their civic duty, had spirited away the holding vat from Bloody Mare's huge still. Then, in honor of the occasion, before resigning their citizenship in Jubilation and heading home to dry out and plan their next visit uptown, they visited the punch social.

The capacity of the vat was somewhat more than all the punchbowls the ladies had brought, but by judicious — and covert — mixing they managed to alter the contents of every bowl to something that still looked a little like fruit punch but had its roots in other kinds of ingredients.

Uptown Jubilation was no match in revelry for downtown Jubilation the night Cornelia Hanks became mayor of the town.

XXXIII

By waning moonlight five laden wagons crept up the back trail from the valley and rattled along the sloping vee between a downtown that was mostly asleep and an uptown that was mostly passed out. Where streets became the uptown road they turned hard left, climbed to the switchback, turned hard right, and plodded on to the top of the bluff.

Harry Patman was asleep when his swamper pounded on his door. He emerged disoriented and cursing roundly.

"Need you downstairs," the swamper said. "Wooskey wagon's here."

"Now?" Patman rubbed his eyes. "What time is it? What's wrong with them drivers?"

In the back of the saloon Finn had roused Patman's barmen and had them unloading cases and kegs. He handed Patman a paper and pencil. "It's all here. Just sign here 'cause I got two more stops to make."

"Have you gone crazy, Finn? What kind of hour is this to make deliveries?"

"It's when we got here," Finn said levelly. "And it's just as near as we can make it to when we leave.

372

Sign here."

Grumbling, Patman signed the receipt. "All right, but by God from now on—"

"May not be any 'from now on,' Harry. Whaley an' me, we're not sure we'll come back this way. Nor the rest either."

"You what?" Patman was awake now, abruptly. "What do you mean, not sure you'll come back? Who's going to haul our supplies? What's going on?"

"I sure don't know, Harry. But bein' chased an' shot at never was part of our deal, and if Frank Gault don't want us bringin' whiskey across the territories, that's somethin' we got to think about."

"Gault? The marshal?"

"The same. Couple of his stars waylaid us, give us a run before we put 'em down. Far as we're concerned the trail from Fort Smith is off limits until somebody shows us different."

"You put down . . . Gault's deputies?"

"Nothin' else to do. Well, you're stocked. See you around sometime. Good night."

Finn climbed aboard his dray as Patman ran out after him. "Wait! I don't know what this is all about—"

"Neither do we, Harry, but we don't sign up to fight Frank Gault. Sorry."

"Does Iron Jack know about this?"

"Haven't seen him, and we ain't got time to go lookin'. If you want Iron Jack to know, you tell him. Good night."

For a time Patman stood in his alley door, sorely puzzled. He heard other deliveries being made, other wagons and teams. And then he heard the empties rolling away in file, over the crest and down the hill. And about then it occurred to him.

"That woman!" he swore. "She done it! I don't know how, but she's done it!"

At the Jubilation Research Center four sleepy partners, hastily assembled, heard the wagons roll by coming into town. A little later they heard them return, and Prosper O'Neil went to the gate to let them in. "You fellas keep th' damnedest hours," he allowed.

"Surprised to find anybody here," Finn told him. "But it's a good thing. We didn't want to wait 'til morning."

"You bring our money?"

"Sure. And if you got another haul ready right now, we'll take it. But somethin's goin' on, Prosper, and we don't like it. I don't know when we'll be back."

"It's ready. I guess we can get you loaded. But what's the matter?"

"We got hijacked in the Strip. Some of Marshal Gault's men. We won't take that trail again."

A weaving figure appeared in lantern light at the door of the main building, carrying a leather case. Seeing the light at the gate, he came toward them. He could barely walk. At the gate he grinned loosely at the men, gazed at the wagons and teams, and squinted at Prosper. "Nice night," he allowed. "Ought to be 'bout time for 'nother sip."

Prosper shook his head. "There ain't any more sips, Ding. You better go home and sleep it off."

"I'm celebratin' . . ." Ding Cox said.

"Yeah, I know."

". . . 'cause Jubilation has . . . pardon . . . groaned tremess . . . tremendous . . . got bigger an' you know who did it?"

374

"Sure I . . ."

"I did it," Ding said proudly. "Lots an' lots of fine new citizens. I got to tell Twiddie."

"Oh, he knows," Prosper assured him.

Finn and Whaley gazed at the staggering city clerk. "He's not in very good shape," Finn allowed.

"He just needs to go home an' sleep it off. Ding, you go on home now. You'll feel better tomorrow."

"Feel jus' fine," Ding assured him. "Le's have 'nother sip."

"There ain't any more sips. You better just go home. You know how to get there?"

"Course I do." He drew himself up proudly. " 'S my house."

"The barrels are all over there in the shed," Prosper told the teamsters. "There's lanterns there. You can start loadin' if you want. We'll be there directly."

"Sure," Finn agreed. He handed down a satchel. "Here's y'all's money. We already took our pay. Receipts are in there. Ah, how's come you all are out here this time of night anyway?"

"We got a hurt man in there. Bert Thompson. He's messed up pretty bad and we're tryin' to patch him."

"The printer? What happened."

"Don't know for certain," Prosper said. "Ike an' the pig found him while ago, over yonder by the bluff. All we know is, he went uptown the past evenin' lookin' to collect a gamblin' debt from Iron Jack Fuller."

There were sounds in the night and a neat surrey with polished woodwork rolled into the light, drawn by a handsome black pacer. Bloody Mare tugged the reins. "*Gde* Bert Tomsahn?"

Beside him Cornelia Hanks, in tied robe and nightcap, leaned toward Prosper. "Mr. O'Neil, can you tell me what is going on? Vladimir came to my house, with my rig, and he pounded on my door, and I don't know what he's saying."

"*Gde* Bert Tomsahn?" Bloody Mare demanded.

Prosper pointed. "He's in there. You see, miss, Ike an' the pig found Bert—"

Bloody Mare slapped the reins against the pacer's rump. "Gee-yap!" he told the horse. "Gee-yap!"

At the main building he halted the rig, climbed down, and beckoned imperiously. Cornelia followed him. Beyond the wide doors the building was barn-like and murky. Lanterns lit walls lined with new-built bunks, piles of lumber, and heaps of sacking, clutter everywhere. The air reeked of stale men and old turnips.

"It's some kind of bunkhouse," Cornelia declared. To the right, men were gathered around one of the bunks. Tugging her, Vladimir pushed through and pointed. "Bert Tomsahn, damn skinny. Bert Tomsahn."

She looked at the figure on the bed and her hands went to her mouth. "Oh, my Lord in heaven!"

Rose gold of first dawn grew above Jubilation Bluff as the saloon owners and Ben Cutter emerged from Richardson's and trooped across to Lester's House of Leisure to rap at the side door of Iron Jack's office.

Packer opened the door. "Too early. Go away. Boss is sleepin'."

"We need to see Iron Jack," Cutter said. "We have a problem."

"*He* has a problem," Harry Patman clarified.

"Nothin' that can't wait." Packer glared, holding the door. The knuckles on his visible hand were bruised and crusted.

"Tell him there won't be any more whiskey comin' in," Max Bigelow said, loudly. "That woman mayor has . . ."

"I told you it can't be her," Cutter hissed. "She ain't even sworn in yet."

"I told you to go away," Packer repeated. He opened the door and stepped out. Hemp appeared in the doorway behind him. Hemp also had fresh-scarred knuckles. Packer stepped down from the narrow stoop, crowding them back. Hemp stepped out.

A gunshot roared and echoed in the alleyway. Splinters flew from the sill an inch from Hemp's shoulder. Ben Cutter dived under the stoop, Packer whirled, searching, and saloon keepers scattered like quail. While echoes still thundered, another gunshot scarred the pillar post behind Packer, a third thudded into the wall, another gouted dust between Packer's feet and ricocheted to take the heel off Hemp's boot, throwing him backward into the office. Two more shots in crashing cadence took out an upstairs window and shattered a door hinge. These last were almost drowned by Iron Fuller's roar, "What the hell is going on out there?"

Packer had fallen, rolled, and in one motion dragged Ben Cutter from beneath the stoop and scudded in to take his place. Cutter shrieked and ran, disappearing around a corner. Sprawled inside the open door, Hemp was struggling to get to his feet. Packer was stuck, halfway under the stoop, his legs thrashing.

In shadows up the alley, hidden by a rain barrel, Bloody Mare stared sadly at the empty revolver in his hand. Six shots! Six shots and no villains. He hadn't hit anybody. Muttering dire comments in dark Russian, he turned and ran.

Cole Yeager heard the shots and wondered about them. In the dimness of the portage way beside the Golden Rule he knelt, studying the bank on the corner by first light. Since midnight he had scouted the town, studying its streets and ways, trying to understand it in the way a hunter tries to understand his game. He had watched in darkness as a strangely chaotic social broke up at the schoolhouse, people of various descriptions wending off in various directions, many of them unsteady on their feet. One birdlike little woman sipping from a porcelain cup had stopped within a yard of his hiding place, giggled inanely, and then uttered an improbable word when something thumped on the boardwalk. Balancing her cup carefully, she gathered her skirts with her free hand, stepped high, and emerged from what seemed to be a whalebone corset standing on the walk. She turned to peer at it. "All in league," she muttered. Then she turned haughtily and proceeded along the street, cherishing her cup and singing portions of a church hymn.

He had spotted the local law, a natty individual with enough polish on his leather that a man could shoot him in the dark. He had followed this law for a time, trying to see his patterns. Then the law had gone uptown with someone else, whispering worriedly as they went.

Scouting around he had noticed activity at a fenced complex below the bluff — wagons and people and a surrey coming in — but it was a clear area and there was lantern light. He had not gone close.

Mainly, though, he had studied the bank. In the dark of morning he had explored its exterior, waiting

378

for enough light to confirm what he had determined. This was not a bank to be blown, it was a bank to be taken. Once he had faded into shadows to watch a huge bull of a man stomp past, shouting at the top of his lungs and carrying three smaller men.

And now, after a time of quiet, he heard six gunshots in quick succession, atop the bluff.

He needed to back off and think about this. Parson had babbled about this being an unusual town. That didn't mean much. Parson was not long on spine. But those comments, plus the erratic things he had seen, plus knowledge that this was Iron Jack Fuller's town, made him edgy. He had left the gang holed up at a deserted shack partway down the valley slope and several miles east. He would go back there and make his plans. He had learned enough to have some ideas.

Doctor Dimwater's Traveling Extravaganza, deposited at a rail siding west of Coldwater to await the arrival of wagons and official escorts from the town of Pleasant Valley, greeted the dawn with its usual chorus of animal sounds, clattering pans, and quarreling voices.

Junius Dimwater, impresario extraordinaire (alias at various times Alonzo the Great, the Amazing Abelard, Merlin the Magnificent, and—in some unforgiving areas of the east—Light-fingered Louie), sputtered and snorted and watched dreams of sybaritic delight dissolve into the reality of another day on the dismal prairies. For a minute or two he buried his face in his grimy pillow and tried to go back to sleep. But it was gone. He groaned and admitted awareness.

The thin walls of his gaudy caravan did nothing to muffle the sounds of morning. Somewhere nearby a lion roared. Further away Rajah trumpeted and set off a chorus of screams among the peacocks. Horses whinnied and dogs barked and the Flying Fenaglios were on the verge of killing one another, screaming insults as they prepared their breakfast. He heard Sandy rousting the roustabouts and smelled the aromas of coffee and hot, rancid grease drifting from the mess tent.

Junius Dimwater yawned and rubbed his eyes. Without glancing her way he elbowed the recumbent female next to him. "Get up," he ordered. "I need some coffee."

"You know where it is," she muttered.

"Least you can do is go out and get me some coffee," he insisted.

She didn't move. She lay facing away, her face buried in bedcovers. "Why don't you go mumble yourself," she suggested drowsily.

Junius sighed. Lazy bitch. Lady Marie Antoinette —the present Lady Marie Antoinette, ballerina of the high wire—was a sooky he had picked up in Arkansas because she could overflow a costume and she came cheap. He had made up his mind that the next Lady Marie Antoinette would at least be from someplace civilized. He started to sit up, then was thrown backward as the rear of the caravan suddenly rose high in the air. Lady Marie Antoinette shrieked and fell out of bed.

"Hercules!" Junius roared. "Damn it, put us down!"

The caravan dropped with a bone-jarring thump. "Sorry," a voice said. "I forgot you was in there."

"Go practice somewhere else," Junius shouted. "How many times must I tell you—"

"Okay, okay! I said I'm sorry. Jeez!"

He heard footsteps scuffling away, then the voice again. "Hey, Willy! Look over there. What is that?"

"Where?" a nasal voice responded. "Oh. Jeez, will ya look at that! Antelopes or somethin'."

"Yeah, I guess. Man, look at them buggers go! Hey, isn't that a horse? Over there, look! What the bejeez *are* all those things?"

Other voices were chiming in now, queries overlapping.

"Goats? Yeah, goats. Right there. And sheep."

"Hey, look over there! The other way, dumb ass. Is that cows?"

"Willy, what do buffaloes look like?"

"That's a rooster. Them over yonder is buffaloes. Out there where that mule is. Some deer too. Look!"

A murmur like low, distant thunder resonated through the earth and up through the caravan's running gear. Lady Marie Antoinette, not very dressed, opened the hatch and stepped out. For a moment she stood there, then she screamed and ran. Julius was trying to get his pants on. One leg was pulled inside out and he couldn't decide which one it was. He glanced at the doorway and blinked. A cow was there, looking at him. A lot more cows were beyond it, a sea of cows and . . . other things . . . flowing into the distance.

Something jolted against the caravan and Junius's feet went out from under him. The caravan heaved to one side and his Merlin trunk teetered, swung open, and fell forward, engulfing him in silk scarves and paper flowers. He surged upright, was rocked again, fell, and the trunk rolled over and snapped shut with him inside.

It took Junius several minutes to escape the magic trunk. By the time he was free and strode out pantless to survey the wreckage of his camp, whatever had caused all this was gone.

Sandy came with a damage estimate and a mug of coffee.

"It was animals," he explained. "Cows and buffaloes and who knows what. They just came right through. The mess tent's down, and it'll take us a while to patch the crew tops . . . few other odds and ends. I've got the roustabouts working. Some of the draft stock is scattered, but they won't go far."

Junius sipped his coffee, listening to the clamor of lion's roar, peacocks' shrill, and the Flying Fenaglios blaming everything on one another. He sighed.

"There's just one more thing," Sandy added. "We can't find Rajah."

"You can't find Rajah," Junius repeated. He turned full around, surveying the rolling, treeless landscape. "Sandy, do you see anyplace around here that you think an elephant might hide?"

"No. I sure don't. But we can't find him. He isn't here and nobody saw where he went."

XXXIV

Cornelia Hanks attended her swearing-in ceremony with ink on her hands and a smudge on her nose. Distractedly she repeated the oath of office, signed the city's file copy, accepted the congratulations of those present at City Hall, and gave her first administrative orders.

Through the formalities, Marshal Ben Cutter stood at the back of the crowd, spotless and polished, gazing at his new boss with eyes that were the soul of honor and duty, smiling now and then with a mouth that wouldn't melt butter.

Her office now in hand, she turned to him. "It is our stated intention, Marshal Cutter, that the prohibition of alcoholic beverages be enforced in Jubilation. I expect you to attend to that promptly."

"Yes, ma'am . . . ah . . . Miss Mayor." He nodded. "No liquor to be sold downtown. I'll see to it."

"I mean uptown as well, Marshal. You know precisely what I mean."

"Miss Mayor . . . ah . . . Mayoress Hanks, I can't do that. I'm only the town marshal. I can't enforce anything that isn't the law."

"Prohibition is specified in the state constitution,

Marshal."

"But it ain't in the ordinances of Jubilation, Mayoress . . . ah . . . Your Honoress. You give me an ordinance and I'll enforce it. Best I can do, ma'am."

She took a deep breath and counted to ten. "Mr. Cox!"

"Yes, ma'am . . . Mayor Ma'am."

"I will expect to see an ordinance drafted for presentation to the council at the next meeting."

"Be fine with me, Miss . . . er . . . Madame Mayor. Who's going to do it?"

"You are going to do it, Mr. Cox."

"Ah, Miss . . . Lady Mayor, I don't do ordinances. I'm the clerk. Ordinances is did by the council. I guess you could write it if you want to."

One by one, she looked at the bland faces of the City Council members. Tienert, Smith, Haggard, and Gosset returned her gaze silently.

So this is how it's to be, she told herself. Very well, gentlemen, we shall play hard marbles.

"Polly, dear." She raised a brow toward Polly Cox. "I really believe the city clerk might be able to draft a suitable ordinance, don't you?"

A hard gleam came into Polly's eyes. She grinned. "I most certainly do."

Ding Cox went pale.

She picked out Martha Haggard and Florine Gosset. "There is a fine old American tradition known as lobbying. It is the process by which constituents suggest to their elected officials how they might vote on certain issues. I believe some of our councilmen have constituents in position to be quite influential. I'm sure you ladies agree."

Their smiles were angelic and enthusiastic. George Gosset stared at his wife and wondered what came after starched underwear.

"If you will all forgive me now," Cornelia said, "I think matters are well in hand here, and I have a newspaper to print."

"That woman is vicious," Woolly Smith whispered to W. D. Tienert.

"I don't know how Iron Jack is going to take this," Tienert said with worry. "First that Gault business . . . now this."

"I thought Patman and them got another supply."

"They got some boys to run some in from Wichita. Bootleg stuff. Poor quality and the supply is uncertain. They have problems."

Back at the Tribune office Cornelia found Penelope and the Sims boys, ink to their elbows, trying to lock a plate into the press while Wednesday Warren, Sally Spalding, Betty Stapleton, and little Ruth Ann Vargas presided over the type fonts.

"Where's the A's?" Wednesday asked. "I can't ever remember where the A's is."

"Are," Betty corrected him.

"They're right there on the left," Sally pointed out. "Pay attention. Which piece are you setting?"

"The one about that blastin' powder that somebody stole from Wisenant's ground vault. What do you suppose anybody would want with a keg of blastin' powder?"

"I haven't the vaguest idea. Wednesday! Will you set type and quit trying to hold our hands?"

"Sorry. I was lookin' for the X's."

Penelope heard the door close and looked around. "Miss Hanks, do you want me to write something about your taking office? I didn't have a chance to go, but—"

"I can do that," Cornelia said. "It won't be a

major story anyway. Did the article about Mr. Zimmerman's prize turkeys come in?"

"Yes, ma'am. We already set it up. I'll get you a proof if we can ever get this blasted . . . oof! There. You boys tighten those bolts now. Whew! When Mr. Bloody Mare locks these in it looks easy. Miss Hanks, have you seen him? He hasn't been in."

"I'm sure he'll show up. How about the market reports from Dodge? They were supposed to be here yesterday."

"On the spike." Penelope pointed. "Oh, and that pile of stuff, that's all the material on the Chautauqua. I looked through it. There are some articles, and advertising. They want us to print some posters too. I said we would."

"Very well." Cornelia thumbed through the materials. Chautauqua had to be the big article on page one. It was almost upon them, and the committee was working frantically to get things ready.

Some changes had been made in the bill. The safari lady from darkest Africa would not be present. She was recovering from injuries sustained on a lecture trip to Pittsburgh. But the famed Mercer twins from Minneapolis, Minnesota, would be present, along with two lyceum musical groups, a company of trained poodles from France, and special appearances by Miss Lilly White and the astronomer Dr. H. H. Fein.

It was Dr. Fein's contention that Halley's Comet, not Moses, had led the Children of Israel out of bondage. Dr. Fein was not a favorite of Brother Tall Paul Strothers.

The dispute over whether to feature readings from *King Solomon's Mines* or excerpts from *Savonarola* had been resolved by scheduling Mr. Howard Sills of Bad Basin for a performance of the pipes.

"So Howard is going to play," she mused.

"Yes'm," Wednesday said. "I'd say he didn't have much choice in the matter."

"Oh, he did so," Sally said. "Actually, Mother says he was very gallant about it. He said he would love to perform."

"Way I heard it, Miss Penelope did his talking for him."

"Sometimes that's best," Cornelia pointed out.

"Howard can speak for himself very nicely," Penelope said defensively. "It was just that he had hiccups that day."

"So did I," Wednesday said, trying for a sniff at Sally's ear as he searched for the H font.

"It was the day Betty made doughnuts," Sally explained.

"We got an ad from the circus that will perform at Pleasant Valley," Penelope said. "They've lost their elephant."

"Is he still carrying that gun everywhere?" Cornelia asked.

"The elephant?" Betty blinked.

"Yes'm, he is," Wednesday assured her. "And a good thing too. Nat Kinley says he's got a hunch."

"I really wish he wouldn't." Penelope frowned. "He seems so . . . awkward with it."

Betty cocked a pretty brow, trying to imagine Mr. Kinley being awkward with a hunch.

"The boys have had him practicin' ever' few days. He's got so he can hit paper now an' again. It was that feller tryin' to rob Mr. Tienert that got Nat to thinkin' about it."

"About robbing Mr. Tienert?" Betty wondered.

" 'Cause that same feller had been in to ask about the found money. Nat heard about that from the clerk at the bank. An' there's been a rumor around—"

"Most men carry them," Penelope conceded. "It's just that Howard is so—"

"My mother says men carry rumors just like women," Betty pointed out. "She says they gossip to love."

"You mean love to gossip," Sally corrected her. "Wednesday, if you're going to set type I wish you'd spell words the way they're written. There isn't any 'f' in 'prophet.'"

"Was last time I set it. That rumor is that Cole Yeager is back in Kansas—"

"I said it just the way Mother said it," Betty assured Sally.

"—and Nat got to rememberin' that it was twenty-eight thousand dollars that Howard found, which is the exact same amount that Cole Yeager took from that bank at Hays City last winter. So he got to thinkin', what if Cole Yeager was who lost the money Howard found, an' then happened to hear about Howard findin' it."

Penelope had gone pale. "But that's ridiculous. Besides, the money is in my uncle's bank."

"Yes'm, but Howard ain't."

"But no one would just . . . shoot a man, would they?"

"Somebody shot that drifter, Pete Swain. An' he was drivin' Howard's wagon at the time. 'Scuse me, Miss Sally, I was tryin' to find me a S."

"Now your gun is tangled in my apron. Oh, Wednesday!"

"Oh, dear," Cornelia murmured. It was a wonder she was able to publish the Tribune at all these days. Her eye lit on the latest stack of mail and she leafed through it, then stopped, selected an envelope, and opened it. It contained several neatly folded newspaper clippings, from various places, and a note from Dean C. W. Billings of Chesterfield College. She smiled at memory of the bright-eyed old man. He had done so much for her in Illinois.

The note was brief and cheerful. The dean was delighted to have heard from her, and pleased that she was embarked on a new venture. He hoped the enclosed would assist her with her inquiry, and he hoped she might write again when time allowed.

The clippings were meticulously annotated with source and date, and she spread them in chronological order to read. The first was twenty years old, a review of the performance of the Warner Repertory Company, giving high acclaim to its cast, singling several out by name. She smiled a secret smile, nodding.

The second was a notice from Chicago, two years later, about the breakup of the Warner Repertory Company and the financial difficulties of several of its principals. Again there were names. This was followed by two clippings, only months apart, one about two men injured in a brawl in a Chicago restaurant and the jailing of their assailant, the second dealing with a bankruptcy hearing in which criminal charges were filed. Both named names.

Then there was a somewhat longer clipping from Denver, a detailed story about the episode that had closed the Diamond Jubilee Opera House once and for all. It had been a gala evening, and the crowd was assembled for a performance of *Henry IV*, when a large number of armed men, most of them miners, had gathered outside. Midway through Act II, the toughs had invaded the Opera House and created a general melee. Some among them were members of a vigilance committee with a grudge against the owners of a cluster of mines. Most of them were simply drunks.

The interruption began as Sir John Falstaff proclaimed on stage, "Go hang thyself in thine own heir-apparent garters . . ." and grew quickly to a full-house brawl complete with screams of ladies and roars of guns. The stage emptied, except for Falstaff, who glared at the interlopers and their brawl, strode to stage front, and roared, "Strike! Down with them! Cut the villains' throats!" Taking up a fallen pikestaff he leapt from the stage and waded into the fray, shouting, "Hang ye, gorbellied knaves, are ye undone? No, ye fat chuffs, I would your store were here! On, bacons, on!" Bruised and shaken gentlemen of the audience had rallied behind him, beating the vigilantes and drunks back, finally evicting them. But a lot of people had been hurt.

Only a few of the vigilantes were ever captured, but most of the drunks and the roaring actor were jailed, on charges of mayhem.

The actor's name was Bert Thompson.

In a gleeful sidebar a long-forgotten wag had fancied that the Shakespearean was jailed as much for bad acting as for anything else, in that his behavior had seriously distorted the Bard's intentions for the character of Sir John Falstaff.

One final clipping remained, a mention from the Tombstone Epitaph of a town marshal at someplace called Shinbone Flat who had been fired for drunkenness.

Cornelia put the clippings away, blinking back moisture. "Ah, Bert," she whispered. "That must have been the unkindest cut of all."

"I'll be going home for a little while," she told Penelope. "I think you have things well in hand here, though I do wish I knew what has become of Vladimir. We'll need him to feed the press."

"He was at my father's store yesterday," Betty recalled. "He bought a pair of iron pots."

"He was over at Ambler's buyin' stove bolts," Wednesday added. "Where's the Z's?"

Bedecked in bonnet and shawl, Mayor Cornelia Hanks walked along Main Street looking at her town. Traffic was heaviest up the street where wagons rolled in from Bad Basin, bringing in loads of Howard Sills's second crop to deposit at Bunker's Mill. A pair of ranchers were there, directing cowhands in the barreling of squish.

Cornelia shook her head. So much activity, so seemingly random, yet the patterns were so consistent. She knew now what they were doing, the men involved in the Greater Jubilation Research Society. She knew about Howard Sills's turnips, and Bunker's Mill, and Vladimir's marvelous inventions, and why the fenced complex out there under the bluff smelled the way it did.

What she didn't know was what should be done about it. Anywhere else in Kansas, such an operation would be blatantly illegal. All that protected it here was the maze of distorted ordinances and civil structures that had been developed over several years' time to allow for the existence of uptown. To an extent, she agreed with the ladies of the Reading Circle. Uptown was a sort of abomination, a unique institution based on the lowest appetites of men, and yet it was the life blood of Jubilation. Isolated and remote, cut off from anywhere else by the Cimarron Valley to the north and the Cherokee Outlet of Oklahoma Territory to the south, Jubilation was a town with one industry . . . and that industry was uptown.

Until now.

She had promised to close uptown. She wondered

391

whether her constituents realized what that meant, or whether in their zeal they had overlooked their dependence. But she had promised, and a promise to Cornelia Hanks was a promise.

Turning the corner, heading for her house, she looked back at Bunker's Mill, where still another wagon load of turnips had pulled in, awaiting its turn at the chute. People passed on the street: ladies doing their marketing, merchants coming and going from their shops, cowboys on their way to the Golden Rule, people arriving from other parts of the country to pick favored spots at the Chautauqua campground . . . in all ways a prosperous and vital community, she thought.

But things were going to have to change. No matter how contrived the election had been, the voters had spoken. The law must take its course in Jubilation.

Westward beyond the mill, where the town sloped away to distance, feathers of dust marked the approach of a cattle herd coming up the Higgins-Wentworth Trail.

She found, to her continuing surprise, that she cared about this strange little town. With each passing day, thoughts of a return to Illinois—to the old, quiet life of schoolmistress to successive crops of little darlings destined to produce new generations of little darlings and wonder what else life was all about—became more remote. Her involvement now was here.

The first lady mayor of Jubilation found herself faced with a dilemma as old as the history of towns . . . how to protect her town against its own best interests.

"Interesting," she told herself.

At her gate she stopped, frowning at the man who

sat in a rocking chair on her front porch. One side of his head was swathed in plaster and muslin bandages. His left arm was in a sling, and what was visible of his face was a mass of healing bruises. She pushed open the gate, went through, and climbed the steps. "You shouldn't be out here," she said.

Bert Thompson returned her critical gaze. "If I have to spend one more daylight hour cooped up in that guest bedroom of yours, Cornelia, I think I'll go out of my head. I'm not one to complain, mind you, but that is the worst wallpaper I ever saw in my life. And as to the bed in there, I've slept on saloon floors that are more comfortable than that bed."

"You're better," she decided. "Come into the house. I'll make sandwiches and tea. I need to talk to you about something."

"Yes, ma'am."

He still limped painfully, but he no longer leaned on a cane when he walked, and despite his injuries he seemed healthier than she had seen him before.

"What are you looking at?" he demanded.

"You."

"Well, quit. I'm a mess."

"Yes, you are. But I think I might find a use for you."

XXXV

"So you're going through with it." Bert munched at a sandwich and regarded Cornelia sadly. "Even though you know what it'll do to this town."

"I promised. I gave my word."

"You gave your word. Marvelous. Do you know how many people make their livings because uptown is here? You dry it up, and what reason will any of the ranch crews and the farmers and the drifters have to come here? Nobody comes to Jubilation except to go to the saloons. They go up there and spend their money with Harry Patman and Max Bigelow and Jackie Diamond, or with Flossie and Jade and the rest. Then all those people use the money to buy things from Will Ambler and Morris Stapleton and Bunker and the Gossets and all the merchants, and they pay wages to other people so they can turn around and buy the things they need, and all these people swappin' money makes a nice market for Prosper O'Neil and Elmer Wallace and Nat Kinley to sell some crops, which gives them spending money to put back into Alfred Twiddie's shop and Slim Haggard's store and Woolly Smith's barber shop, so they can support their families and give their wives the freedom to go to Reading Circle meetings and cook up plots to turn the whole thing off."

"I know!" She glared at him. "We've been through all this before. What I don't know is how to make it all come out for the best."

"Easiest way would've been to back off an' let the council outvote you on Prohibition ordinances. But no, not you. You put the cork in it this morning, Mayor. Yeah, I heard. Dutch Henry Vargas was by. You showed those ladies how to finish the job they started. There'll be no stoppin' them now. So tomorrow, whatever ordinance you set in front of those poor jerks will become city law. Oh, yeah." He shushed her with a raised hand. "You'll have a majority vote. Those men are only human. You've put George Gosset and Slim Haggard in a box and there isn't any way out. Tienert and Smith will vote against you, but the other two won't. And you know what will happen to them, don't you?"

"What?"

His eyes turned hard. "Same thing that happened to me. In this town a man doesn't cross Iron Jack Fuller."

She had been starting to pour tea. Now she stopped, staring at him. "You mean . . ."

"Exactly. Iron Jack doesn't keep those thugs on his payroll for their exquisite beauty. By tomorrow night, Mr. Gosset and Mr. Haggard are going to be in bad need of a doctor. Oh, no, don't be afraid. They won't hurt you. You're a woman. Even Iron Jack stops at threatening women. You're safe enough, but I pity those poor souls who don't have skirts to hide behind. They're going to get hurt."

"But Marshal Cutter—"

"Oh, come on, Cornelia. Who do you think Ben

Cutter works for? You? He's on Iron Jack's payroll just like those thugs are."

She nodded. "I thought as much. He isn't likely to enforce the ordinance even after it's passed, is he?"

"No way under the sun. You can forget about that, and it's probably best. If you *did* shut down uptown, this town might as well just dry up and blow away. That's what I've been telling you."

"It isn't that simple."

"It isn't any other way. Be honest with yourself, at least. You can't shut down uptown. Let it alone."

"But I intend to shut it down. I promised."

He stared at her. "You are the stubbornnest woman I ever saw. Doesn't any of this mean anything to you? By God, Cornelia Hanks—"

"By God, yourself, Bert Thompson! Mind your language in my house. I think there's a way around all this."

"Oh? My, wouldn't that be nice," he crooned. "She has a plan. What is this plan of yours, Mayor?"

"Vodka."

"What?"

"I said 'vodka,' Mr. Thompson. Certainly you know about vodka."

He sighed. "You know about that then."

"Yes, I know about that. I'm not blind, Bert, and I'm not stupid. I think it is amazing that you and those others have kept the secret as well as you have for as long as you have."

"I guess you're going to write it up for the Tribune? And probably send Cutter to shut them down, I guess."

"How many of you are there?"

"Nine, altogether. Plus some teamsters, but they don't know what they're hauling. And of course

Howard Sills for the turnips, but he doesn't know what we're doing with them. Well, I'm sorry you found out. You can add Will Ambler and Puff McVey to the list of people about to get hurt. Iron Jack won't stand still for that. He might not go after the ranchers, if they stay out of town. I can take off for parts unknown, and maybe take Vladimir with me. But Will and Puff, they're stuck here. They'll take their beating, just like I did."

"Of all the places to build a distillery, Bert, *why on earth* did you put it in Jubilation?"

"Well, it started out because Howard had turnips and Vladimir showed up. And Nat Kinley and the rest of . . . well, it's where all of us happened to be, and it's the only place in Kansas where it isn't exactly illegal."

"Liquor *is* illegal *downtown,*" she pointed out.

"Only if we sell it. We don't sell it. We just make it and ship it to Missouri. Nothing illegal about that. Not here. But I guess you'll fix that, right along with everything else."

"I said I'm working on a plan, Bert."

"It's just a damn shame! What those fellows have done—Will and Puff and that crazy Russian and those ranchers—could have been one of the best things ever to happen to Jubilation. But just because what they're making isn't lemonade, you're going to bring it right down around their ears. You ought to be real proud of yourself, Mayor."

"Will you shut up?" she gritted. "I happen to agree with you."

He blinked. "You do?"

"I do. I see nothing whatever wrong with a town having an industry, and as far as I am concerned I can overlook the product of it as long as it is sent someplace legal for sale."

"Then what are we fussing about?"

"We are *fussing*," she explained, "because you are a stubborn, pig-headed, long-winded, arrogant, cynical, semi-civilized, intolerant, ungrateful, cowardly—"

"Now hold on! I am *not* cowardly!"

"—whining, disruptive, and often unpleasant man with a lot of very bad habits, the worst of which—"

"Who says I'm cowardly?"

"—is running away any time things get a little tough."

"I do not!"

"I have quite a long reference file now on Bert Thompson," she said quietly. "Would you like to see it? It dates all the way from the Warner Repertory Company."

"That was some other Bert Thompson. He died, years ago."

"Yes, I know. You killed him, didn't you? And you've been burying him ever since. That's why you are a coward."

"I am not!"

"Methinks he doth protest too much," she said. "When is the last time you stood up for something you believe in, Bert? Was it at the Diamond Jubilee Opera House in Denver? Was that the last time?"

"Lot of good that did me," he muttered, bitterness in his eyes. "Hell, I stood up to Iron Jack Fuller, didn't I? And look what it got me."

"You didn't stand up to him. You went up there drunk and tried to collect a stupid bet."

"Will you leave me alone? I'm tired of this."

"Oh, yes. You're tired of it. So you'll just sneak away from Jubilation before Iron Jack Fuller decides to notice you again. It is really decent of you to think about taking Vladimir along. Of course, you'll leave all those others here to get hurt, but that doesn't matter as long as you can get away and start drinking again and forget all about it. You're a coward, Bert Thompson. Somewhere between Denver and Shinbone Flat you became one, and you've groveled ever since."

"That's enough, Miss Hanks." He stood, his face very pale. "I am indebted to you for nursing me to this point. But I won't burden you any further—"

"Shut up and sit down! My, you can dish it out, but you can't take it, can you?"

"I'm—"

"I said sit down!"

He sat.

She poured tea, then gazed at him speculatively. "All right," she said, finally. "We are even. As I said, I have a plan. I think I can keep my promise to my constituents, and still preserve the economy of the town. I intend to write an ordinance that will prohibit once and for all the activities uptown. But that same ordinance will protect and legalize the *manufacture* of beverages here. I've studied the constitution. There is a way it can be done, legally and above-board. All I shall need is the agreement of the Greater Jubilation Research Society to develop and expand their enterprise, and provide legitimate employment to the people displaced by Prohibition. With the full support of city government, of course."

He stared at her, amazed. "Of all the devious, hypocritical—"

"You named me hypocrite once before. Don't do it again."

"Well, you've overlooked one little detail."

"Which is?"

"Iron Jack Fuller."

"Oh, I haven't overlooked Mister Fuller. That's why I wanted to talk to you. I expect you to attend to him for me. I believe you can find a means to do that."

"I need a drink."

"No, you don't. You need to think. Soberly. I shall leave you to that task."

"Even if I could, what's in it for me?"

"Your pride, I should think. If I had lost mine, I believe I'd try very hard to regain it."

Coming in from Lazy K, Nat Kinley stopped off at Bad Basin to check the harvest of Howard Sills's second turnip crop. Approaching through the meadow, he paused, marveling again at the changes Howard was making. The marvelous barn had a fresh coat of red paint, the windmill sparkled with painted struts and polished brasswork, the legendary privvy sported fresh shingles, and rose bushes stood around the raised cellar.

"Off hand," Nat said grinning, "I'd say the young feller is fixin' to find hisself a bride."

The first turnip field had grown. Faced with abundant sales, Howard had expanded it to nearly forty acres, a vast carpet of lush green tops where young men worked now, getting the crop to market.

He rode toward the house, where Ambrose — in stained coveralls — was putting fresh whitewash on the dooryard fence. Ambrose looked up, saw him coming, put down his brush, and ran into the house.

Nat reined in at the fence, stepped down, and tied his reins. Cupping his hands he shouted, "Howard! You here?"

The door opened and Ambrose stepped out, resplendent in spat breeches and a brand new tail-coat.

His white hair was crisp and brushed, his linen shirt and silk cravat immaculate, and the expression on his black face was haughty and severe. Ambrose was in his element.

"Good day, sah," he intoned. "How may I help you?"

Nat shook his head, impressed. He had never seen an English butler, but he had heard about them, and he realized suddenly that if the lands south of the Cimarron could be single-handedly civilized, Ambrose was the man for the job.

"Mist' Howard is out in the field," Ambrose told him haughtily. "If you'll kindly wait here, I will announce you." The feigned haughtiness faded and the black man grinned. "Cold buttermilk over at th' wellhouse, Mist' Nat. Help y'self."

Howard was sweat-stained, sun-baked, and enthusiastic. Nat noticed with approval that he wore his Colt, and had become accustomed to its presence.

"I hope you never need that," Nat told him. "But if you ever do, you use it."

"I don't know . . ." Howard started.

"No, a fella never knows. Some things have to be found out the hard way. I'm headin' for Jubilation, just stopped by to see if you need anything."

"I guess not," Howard said. "If you see Miss Penelope, tell her I'll be in tomorrow evening. We won't have this all done by then, but I'll need to go to the bank."

"You're makin' good money, ain't you?"

"Good money! Nat, I never dreamed I could make so much. And mostly from turnips! It's fantastic. I've paid off Uncle Chester, I've fixed the place up, I've paid all my bills—"

"Bought Ambrose a monkey suit—"

"Yeah. He really likes that. And when this crop is

in I'll have enough in the bank to . . . ah . . ."

"To ask for somebody's hand in marriage?"

"Yeah." He reddened slightly, and grinned. "Do you think a woman might like this place, Nat? I mean, with it all fixed up pretty?"

"Only one way to find out. Ask her."

"Well, I intend to."

"And wear your gun," Nat said.

"To propose?"

"All the time. I got this hunch that's botherin' me, Howard. You remember that feller we met at the bank that time? The day you went to town to play your pipes?"

"The one who said he robbed banks and trains?"

"Yeah, that one."

"His name's John Smith. Stopped by day before yesterday, just sort of looking around. People do that sometimes."

Nat felt his hackles rise. "He came here? Why?"

"He just stopped by. No reason. Come to think of it, Ambrose said he'd been here once before too. Couple of months ago. Just looking around. What's the matter, Nat? You think he—"

"I sure do." Nat was on his feet, surveying the hills around. "Was there anybody with him?"

"No. Well, yes, I saw two more men, but they didn't come in. They just stayed out there on the ridge."

"You keep that gun handy every minute, Howard. I mean it."

There were cattle on the Higgins-Wentworth Trail. Nat crossed ahead of a fair herd, then stepped his sorrel up onto a knoll to watch them pass. HW Connected stock, summered out and fat for market.

Hiram Wentworth was doing well down in the outlet. The trail boss, riding upwind flank on the herd, saw him there and swung his horse to lope up to where he sat.

"Howdy, Pistol Pete," Nat called. "Been seein' a lot of you this year."

"Howdy, Nat. Yeah, Mr. Wentworth got top dollar on that last bunch that we had to rustle to get back, so he decided to clear his range for the calf crop and sell off these critters. We got two hundred an' a few here. Ought to make Dodge in a couple of weeks."

"Mr. Wentworth's foot ever heal up?" Nat shaded his eyes, scanning the herd. "Whatever become of ol' Mary? I don't see her."

"He's limpin' some, but he gets around. No, it's too bad about that cow. She never showed up after the last drive, so I reckon they finally got her loaded up. By now she's took that great train ride to Kansas City." He removed his hat solemnly.

"Hiram Wentworth had himself a prize in that cow." Nat nodded. "Any chance you might stop off for a shot or two, Pistol Pete? I got things to do, but I'd sure stand a round."

"Can't do it," Pistol Pete said sadly. "Mister Wentworth got charged for some doctorin' after the last time we was here and he said a mite about it. He said he'll shoot the man that stops in Jubilation afore these cows is sold, an' horsewhip the man that stops off afterward."

"Hiram Wentworth is a hard man."

"Heard you fellers is doin' right well in the research business here, Nat. Also heard Jubilation has got itself a lady mayor now."

"That's a fact on both counts, Pistol Pete. Things been right interestin' this summer. Wish you could stop over to visit."

"Right sorry I can't, Nat. But this herd is movin' right on through to Dodge with no stops. I still ain't lived down losin' that other batch. Wednesday Warren still around town?"

"Sure is, Pistol Pete. He's got himself about three payin' jobs and six or eight girls and you never seen a happier button in your whole life."

The cattle plodded along toward the gap, and Pistol Pete Olive settled his hat on his head and lifted his reins. "I'm takin' point across that valley, Nat. There isn't anything gonna happen to this herd if I can help it."

Twist McGuffin met Nat at the end of Elm Street, spurring his mount to catch up to him. "I'm glad you're here, Nat. I was lookin' for you. Prosper and Ike are roundin' up the rest. We got to have a meetin'."

"Now? What about?"

"Bert Thompson called it. He showed up at the place and said to get everybody together because he's gonna bring Cornelia Hanks to meet with us. Before Prosper could get the gate open to stop him, he'd limped off down the hill and gone into the newspaper shop."

"He's bringin' the mayor to *the place?* Has he gone crazy? We got the stills runnin' again in there. He can't show her—"

"Well, he's fixin' to. He says she knows all about it an' wants to talk a deal."

XXXVI

In late afternoon Mary came to the Higgins-Wentworth Trail where it crested the north rim of the Cimarron Valley. A dim sense of familiarity worked its way into her bovine brain and she tossed her one-horned head, stretched her neck, and lowed softly, comfortable at the presence of a path she had trod before. For a time she grazed at the trail's edge, where tall grass stood lush from recent rains. Then she caught the scent of distant water and stepped out on the wide slope angling through deeper and deeper canyons toward the valley floor.

The vast, placid array that moved after her was a dark carpet of moving creatures, flowing over the crest on a front nearly a quarter mile wide, scattering, regrouping, clustering, and sundering, each creature a law unto itself but all now accustomed to the journey and to following Mary.

Antelope like yellow ghosts flowed past her to scatter on the slopes, then fell in behind again as the main herd passed. The little flock of sheep clustered to one side, less inclined than cattle to spread out, but caught up in the drift of things and going along where the herd went. Goats danced and browsed at random, but seldom wandered far.

The deer remained aloof, remote always, but where the herd went they were never far away. The mule and two horses had formed a society within a society, seeking one another's company as they accepted the direction of the cattle. As for the buffalo, all seven of them had become so thoroughly absorbed into the herd that they mingled freely with the cattle as though that was what they were.

The red rooster had taken to riding on the elephant's head, only flapping down now and then to peck gravel for its craw or goatweed for its dinner . . . or to hurl insults at the several geese and sandhill cranes trailing along behind. In one way or another, every bird in the herd had come to regard Rajah as its own personal elephant.

Longhorns, crosses, and range cattle, the main body of the movement now numbered nearly a thousand head, plus the fifty registered Herefords among them. The count of other species in the mass fluctuated from moment to moment, but there were a lot of them.

It was the elephant and the rooster who broke ranks in blue of evening as the herd flowed into the lush bottom lands of the valley, heading for the river. The elephant's dim eyes picked out the shape of groves of trees alongside the trail, and he raised his head high, lifted a questing trunk, and tasted the air. There was a scent of cottonwoods. Rajah trumpeted his joy. The sleeping rooster on his head jerked awake, blinked fierce eyes in the dusk, and crowed. Disinterested cattle eased aside as six tons of hungry elephant and six pounds of irritated red rooster headed for the trees.

Rajah's gregariousness had cost him in his time with Mary's herd. Accustomed to 500 pounds of hay and 60 gallons of water each day, he had lost weight since leaving the circus. He needed to strip some bark and chew some branches.

Followed by a flock of cranky geese and sandhill cranes and a few frolicking pronghorns, Rajah and the rooster entered the riverbank groves several hundred yards ahead of the main herd.

For a time Rajah gorged himself among the cottonwoods, ripping and browsing while the chicken on his head clung determinedly and clucked its disapproval. Finally he was satisfied, and stood for a while in deepening twilight, chewing his meal. The rooster thrust its head under its wing and went back to sleep.

Fed and content, Rajah wandered down successive shallow banks to the ford of the river and began to drink. Sated, he raised his trunk again to test the air. Dim eyes told him of movement in the distance, across the shallow stream. His proboscis told him of smoke, and his heart was gladdened. Smoke meant people, and people meant fresh baled hay. Thinking happy thoughts and wearing a sleeping chicken, Rajah set out across the river.

Pistol Pete Olive and four HW Connected drovers had moved the little herd slowly, once past Jubilation Gap. Here tall grasses rippled gold in the breeze, lush graze to take the trail's strain off their critters and plump them for the windy hills ahead. They moved them loose and easy, giving them time to graze until dusk, then brought them down to the river to water and bed them.

Pistol Pete was taking no chances with these 200 head. This drive would go like clockwork, and he intended to have no surprises.

Thus, in the dark of evening, when the valley's whispering peace was shattered by strident trumpeting from somewhere across the sandflats of the stream, Pistol Pete and the four came to full alert, ready for most anything. The rooster crow that echoed the trumpeting was a puzzling note added to a puzzle. Something across the shallow stream had made a loud and unusual noise, and must be investigated.

Scat and Elvis, on fresh mounts, were with the bedding herd, calming them, as Pistol Pete, followed by Willie Bright and Tom Needmore, cut mounts out of the remuda and saddled up. All four were waddies selected by Pistol Pete. All were veterans of the disastrous last drive and all carried the marks, as he did, of bringing home Nat Kinley's bad bull. Seasoned men, he reasoned. Men who would keep their heads no matter what faced them.

Mounted, they checked the loads in their Colts and waded into the lazy water of the ford. Here the riverbed was wide and flat, a quarter-mile of pale sand with ribbons of clear water lacing it.

Pistol Pete's horse, a high-strung bay filly, shied and danced at water's edge, then stepped out in the lead with the other two following. Pistol Pete squinted ahead.

Deep purple dusk lay on the valley, sombering the greens and grays of the groves on the far bank while the meanders between shone with the reflected crimsons of cloud-tops in the west. There was movement in the distance, dark against the dark of foliaged banks, but he couldn't make it out. It was coming their way, crossing the bottoms.

"Is that a wagon yonder?" Willie asked, beside him.

"Could be a wagon," Tom agreed. "High load or

carryin' a cover. Who you suppose it is?"

Nearer the approaching silhouette they reined up. "I ain't so sure that's a wagon," Tom pointed out.

Pistol Pete was squinting, looking beyond the tall shape at the still-distant bank. There was more movement there now . . . a lot of it.

"I think it's bigger'n a wagon," Willie said.

"I'm pretty sure it ain't any wagon," Tom decided. "I don't think it's got wheels. I think it's got feet."

"There's a bump on top of it," Willie noticed.

Then the silhouette, only a dash away now, changed. It grew taller suddenly, much taller, sprouting an extension that reared high above its bump and wavered there, and a blast of joyous sound erupted from it as it sprayed water from beneath massive feet and broke into a lumbering trot.

Willie Bright's horse reared, whinnied, and swapped ends so fast that Willie was still sitting his saddle after the saddle had left. He landed on his back in ten-inch water, shooting dark spray that drenched Pistol Pete to his ears. Tom Needmore was a hundred yards away in the other direction, clinging to a crow-hopping mount and yelling at the top of his lungs.

Rebounded from the river, Willie was running upstream faster than Pistol Pete had ever seen a man move. Somewhere behind him he heard shouts and the drumming of hooves.

Then the monstrosity was on him, looming over him, and its trumpeting voice rang in his ears. It blared three huge notes, and in the ringing silence that followed it clucked angrily.

The bay had not moved. Through the moment's madness the filly had stood like a horse made of stone. As the leviathan loomed above him, thundering, Pistol Pete went for his gun . . . and the bay

409

suddenly unwound and left for Texas.

In an instant Pistol Pete found himself bouncing, skidding, and scudding across stinging wet sand, then skimming through flying water that curled over him as he fought to free his foot from the stirrup. He hit dry sand again and his boot came off. He rolled, somersaulted, and saw the bay disappear up the riverbank and into tree shadow.

Dazed, he got to hands and knees, swinging his head to clear his senses. Somewhere cattle lowed nervously, and somewhere else he heard geese talking. All around him shapes flowed past. He raised his head, then ducked as a goat sailed over him. He heard the unmistakable baaing of sheep, looked up, and blinked at the curious buffalo cow that blinked back and then moved on. He tried to stand and pronghorns scattered from him. Against a huge flow of cattle dark against pale sand and afterglow he saw sandhill cranes taking wing to settle again in the nearby brush. A steer jostled him and he yelped, then stood frozen as hundreds of head of range stock trooped by, feeling their heat, smelling their odors. Vaguely he noted that not all the cows were cows. At least one cow was a mule.

An imperious white goose honked at him, then marched between his legs. He leaned down to look after it and another goose, trying to follow, nipped him sharply on the ear.

It was the worst time of Pistol Pete Olive's life.

Somehow, then, the massive herd was past and flowing up the north bank leaving him standing ankle-deep in murked water, hatless, gunless, and wearing only one boot. He wandered around distractedly for a time, staying to the sand bottoms, trying to recover his senses. The first two or three times he found his hat it wasn't his hat, and he kept heading for the water to wash his hand. Finally he found his hat, reshaped it as best he could, and crammed it onto his head. Then he got his bearings and headed for camp.

He found where camp had been, but there was no camp now. He limped to where the herd had bedded and there was no herd. He sought out the remuda and it was gone. He heard voices and Scat and Elvis came in, riding double on one horse. They were jibbering and chattering and he ignored them. Willie came from somewhere, soaking wet, leading the bay filly and carrying its saddle. Then, a few minutes later, Tom Needmore rode in on a limping, exhausted mount.

Pistol Pete Olive looked at them, counted them, strode among them. "We come down here with two hundred head of Mr. Wentworth's best critters," he said quietly. In the gathering darkness he was aware of their nods. "We put them to bed right over yonder," he added. "A few minutes ago they was all right over there." They nodded. He paced before them. "I just looked," he said. "They ain't there any more."

"Don't look like it, Pistol Pete," Willie agreed.

"Do any of you boys have any idea where they might have went?"

They looked at one another, blankly. "We sure don't, Pistol Pete," Tom said. "We don't even know what . . ."

Pistol Pete Olive nodded. Reverently he removed his hat, stared at it for a moment in the gloom, then with a roundhouse swing he threw it to the ground. "Damn!" he roared. "God All Mighty Damn!"

The others turned their eyes away. It was always embarrassing to see a trail boss stomping on his hat.

* * *

Working by lantern light in the reeking squish shed behind the Jubilation Research Center, Vladimir Nicolayevich Malenkov put the final touches to his contrivance. All the high skills of eight years with *Narodnaya Volya* were here displayed, all the teachings of Ivan Petrunkevich and Vera Ivanova embodied in a device that would have made them both very proud. Next to the distillation of vodka, the thing Vladimir Nicolayevich did here was his noblest skill. He hummed to himself as he tightened stove bolts adjoining the rims of two iron pressure vessels and tested the springs on the fusing trap. Alongside, on the workbench, stood a slender vial of glass and wax, an intricate and wholly reliable time-fusing device that he himself had perfected many years ago, following the unfortunate demise of Gregor Mikhailevich Puchik of the weak kidneys.

The keg he sat on as he worked had once contained blasting powder. Now it was empty. All the blasting powder was packed within the shell created by the two pressure vessels.

Ah, to have had such a bomb in the old days. It saddened him to recall the pitiful rubble of the bathhouse on Romanov Square, dusted to oblivion while the great house of General Trepov—and General Trepov himself—remained unblasted.

Far better things could be done in America. Here there were decent tools to work with.

Vladimir had nothing against Cossacks, as such. Cossacks were Cossacks. They couldn't help being Cossacks. But here, just as in Russia, there were *khorosho* Cossacks—good Cossacks—and there were *plokho* Cossacks. These, the bad ones, always seemed to be found in the employ of either Commissars or the *Rosiiskaya Imperiya*. So far as Vladimir

412

Nicolayevich could determine, there were no *Rosiiskaya Imperiya* in Jubilation. There was, however, a Commissar, and his Cossacks had done severe and unwarranted damage to Bert Tomsahn.

The lessons of Ivan Petrunkevich returned to him. When one sees a wrong one must right it, and in civilized society the accepted way to do that is to either shoot someone or blow someone up with a bomb.

Vladimir Nicolayevich had never been good at shooting. But he was good at making bombs.

The hole now was an abandoned shack under the rim of the Cimarron Valley, a few miles from Jubilation. In dim of evening Cole paced the hidden expanse before the shack and studied the western sky. He sniffed the air, his cold eyes speculative and distant as he read minute changes in the blend of temperature and odor and considered the piling cloudbank far away fading now from crimson to dim rose.

They were unnoticed here, and well provided. Yet they had been here too long. Cole was moody and restless. He had been making plans, awaiting the right time to move, and now he sensed it was at hand.

He turned and entered the shack. "That bank at Jubilation, we hit it tomorrow," he told them. "Then get the sodbuster."

There was no argument, but Parson had been watching too, watching the weather build. "You thinkin' rain, Cole?" he asked.

Cole only glanced at him. "What I think is my business. But if there's rain it will help. Either way, we go in."

413

They nodded and waited. He would tell them what he wanted them to know, when he wanted them to know it. No one argued with Cole Yeager.

In the alley beyond Lester's House of Leisure, men clustered in shadows, waiting. Uptown Jubilation was coming alive, and it was time to act if ever they were going to. Twist McGuffin peered at Nat Kinley. "You sure there ain't any easier way than this, Nat?"

"Not that I can think of," Nat said, hushed, watching the side door. "You know as well as I do how many of 'em there are. The mayor said it would be all right if we was to even the odds a little, as long as we was gentle about it."

"Gentle!" Twist snorted. "This idea is about as gentle as—"

"Hush!"

The side door opened. They flattened themselves against the alley wall, peering out, while Prosper and Ike knelt silently behind them, each clutching a mass of tow sacks and rope.

"How come I always draw the short straw?" Twist whispered.

"Hush!"

A large man stepped out of the door and closed it behind him.

"Which one is it?" Nat whispered.

"How do I know? These bruisers all look alike in the dark."

"All right. It don't matter. Do your stuff."

"God, I hate this part," Twist muttered. He stepped out of the deep shadows, walked to where the bruiser stood, tapped him on the shoulder, and then, as he turned, hit him in the belly.

The bruiser cursed, Twist ran, and the bruiser was at his heels. Twist dived into the alley and stopped. The bruiser grabbed him, raised a ham-sized fist . . . and collapsed to his knees as the butt of Nat Kinley's gun collided — gently — with his skull.

"That's one," Nat said.

XXXVII

Rarely was Iron Jack Fuller seen downtown. The boss of uptown preferred his little world on the bluff, where he could move almost invisibly from office to buggy to back door and thus seldom be seen on his feet. Sitting, Iron Jack was a big man. He arranged to be seen always in that position, and was comfortable manipulating both uptown and downtown through other people.

Yet on Friday, when Cornelia Hanks arrived at City Hall early to prepare for the meeting of the City Council, Iron Jack Fuller already was there, seated in the middle of the front row of chairs, a dark robe draped across his lap and hiding his legs.

Several other men were in the assembly room, some seated, some standing, and she recognized faces from uptown. Two of the large men flanking Fuller were the same two she had seen the day Bert Thompson took her uptown—Mr. Packer and Mr. Hemp. She also recognized Harry Patman and one or two others from the bluff. She was not surprised. She had announced publically what she intended to do.

"Gentlemen, good day," she said cordially. They

416

glared at her.

Marshal Ben Cutter, immaculate in dark suit, bright linens, and high-polished armament, stepped out of the city clerk's cubicle and swept off his hat. "Ah, your honoress," he fawned, casting a smirk at some of the watching men. "I was hoping you'd get here early. I just had a look at that proposed ordinance you made . . . ah, had . . . Clerk Cox draw up. Good thing I did too. We all know your heart's in the right place, Miss Mayor, but you probably don't understand that once an ordinance gets passed, it has the force of law . . . no matter what it says."

"I think I understand that, Marshal." She gazed coolly at him.

"Well, that's good," he assured her. "Because I'm sure that on second thought you really won't want to make law out of what that says there. I understand how fine, educated ladies like yourself can get all carried away with an idea now and then, but let me explain to you just exactly what that really says. In plain language, I mean. It says—"

"I know precisely what it says, Marshal. I gave serious thought to every word of it."

For a moment his mustache twitched uncontrollably, then he rearranged his handsome face into a smile carefully designed to melt the heart of any female. "I am sure you did, Your Mayorship. And I think it's just grand. But not as law, you see. Why, the first part of that—if it was law, of course—why, it would just about shut down one whole major section of the business community here. I don't imagine you've took any training in economics, of course, bein' a lady, but the way things work in economics is—"

She shook her head. "Marshal, why don't you go

and sit down. After the meeting I shall give you your instructions."

His eyes widened and a pallor crept into his cheeks. "You will give me my—now look, lady, I'm here tryin' to do you a favor, keep you from makin' a big mistake. I don't hold with women takin' that attitude toward me. Not even women mayors. Not for a minute, I don't. 'Specially when I'm tryin' real hard to be civil."

"Civil?" She lowered her voice. "Marshal, you are making an absolute ass of yourself. Now go and sit down."

"Ass?" He almost shouted it in his fury. "Lady, do you know who you're talking to?"

She raised a quizzical brow. "Yes, I do. Do you?" She strode past him and when she glanced back he was crouched beside Iron Jack Fuller's chair, deep in whispered conversation. The mayor of Jubilation smiled to herself.

Others had entered the room. Behind his plasters Bert Thompson grinned sardonically and whispered to Will Ambler, "Sign of a real lady, Will. Always gives tit for tat."

"That marshal," Elmer Wallace growled. "Takin' that tone of voice to a lady. Somebody ought to just plain shoot that scutter. Can't hardly tolerate him anyhow."

George Gosset and Slim Haggard entered, accompanied by their wives and surrounded by a phalanx of severely clad women, all carrying skillets, rolling pins, or axehandles. The two city councilmen looked miserable.

At sight of them Packer and Hemp stood, started to intercept them, and were confronted by a picket line of determined women brandishing blunt objects. The toughs stopped in confusion. Nat Kinley, just coming in, edged up to them and said, mildly, "I wouldn't argue, boys. Man could get hurt real bad."

Packer stared in disgust at the tiny woman directly before him, brandishing a rolling pin. He reached to push her aside and was clouted painfully across the wrist.

"Mind your manners," she scolded. "You're all in league."

With a muttered curse he doubled a fist and froze, staring into the muzzle of Nat Kinley's Colt.

"Man that raises a hand to a lady is just askin' to be plugged," Nat advised him. When the big man backed off, Kinley holstered his gun. "Like she said, mind your manners."

As he moved away, Bert Thompson eased over beside him. "How many are left?" he whispered.

"Just these and one more—that Cooley. He's uptown tryin' to find his playmates, but they ain't there."

"You got five of them?" Bert was impressed.

"Yeah. We might have got Cooley too, but Twist swore off drawin' straws."

"Everything ready out at the place?"

"I reckon. You know somethin', Thompson? Life sure was easy before we all taken a notion to go into business."

"Way it goes." Bert shrugged. Then, noticing that Packer and Hemp were still involved in a staring contest with the Wednesday Ladies' Reading Circle, he stepped up beside Iron Jack Fuller's chair. "You owe me six thousand, seven hundred and fifty dollars, Iron Jack."

Pig eyes in a powerful face glared at him. "You're lucky the boys were gentle with you, Bert. Next time they won't be."

"Tomorrow you'll owe me six thousand and nine

hundred dollars, Iron Jack. I don't amortize interest, it's a flat hundred and fifty a day, starting now. When do you want to pay me?"

"The day hell freezes over, Bert."

Bert nodded. "I just wanted to be clear about that, Iron Jack. I wouldn't want to start spreading the word that any man is a welshing son of a bitch unless he has told me himself that he is."

With a growl of fury Iron Jack came out of his chair . . . and stopped, realizing every eye in the room was on him.

Standing carefully beyond reach of the powerful arms, Bert Thompson looked down at him and his eyes went sad. "You know something, Iron Jack? You've got more to be ashamed of than any man I know offhand. Isn't it a shame that the only thing you're ashamed of is an affliction you couldn't help?"

"I'll kill you, Thompson. So help me—"

Packer and Hemp saw what was happening and started to intervene. But they were surrounded now by skillet-wielding ladies, with Nat Kinley acting as referee.

"Climb up on that chair again, Iron Jack," Bert said. "I don't want to humiliate you. I just want my money."

W. D. Tienert and Woolly Smith had come in and taken their seats at the table. The council was complete. Cornelia emerged from the city clerk's office, trailed by a pale Ding Cox, with Polly Cox running close escort. She looked around at the assembled mob, then took her place at the center of the council table. She glanced at Polly Cox, who put a sharp elbow into the ribs of Ding Cox, who rang his bell.

"If everyone will be seated," Cornelia said, "I shall

call this meeting to order."

Cooley, a bruiser who could almost have doubled for either Hemp or Packer, edged into the room and went to crouch beside Iron Jack. "I can't find the rest of the boys, Iron Jack," he whispered. "You got any idea where they are?"

Iron Jack frowned, suspiciously. If Cooley couldn't find them, they weren't there. So where were they? He glanced at Packer and Hemp, who shook their heads.

"I ain't seen most of 'em since yesterday," Packer whispered.

"Never mind," Iron Jack rumbled. "You three know what to do."

"Yeah, boss." As one, they grinned evilly and focused their attentions on Slim Haggard and George Gosset, who squirmed in their seats.

Cornelia rapped on the table. "This being a special meeting, we can dispense with the reading of minutes. I'll accept a motion to declare a quorum present."

She looked to right and left. Woolly Smith blinked back at her, innocently. W. D. Tienert looked away, pretending not to have heard her. Gosset and Haggard stared straight ahead, sweat shining on their faces.

"Do I hear such a motion?"

Standing behind her husband, Florine Gosset leaned to whisper in his ear. He went pale. "So move," he gulped.

Slim Haggard jumped as though prodded from behind. "Second." Directly behind him Martha Haggard smiled, a smile of innocent pride in her husband, and covertly replaced the knitting needle in her sleeve.

"We have a motion and a second," Cornelia said.

"All in favor say 'aye.' "

Outside in the sunlit street, a buggy pulled up, its traces audible in the meeting hall.

"Aye," George Gosset said, as one ordering a last meal.

After a moment's silence Slim Haggard jumped again. "Aye," he yelped.

"All opposed, signify by saying 'nay.' "

"Nay," Tienert said.

"Nay," Smith added.

"Aye," Cornelia said. "The vote is three to two. I declare a quorum. Now I'd like the city clerk to read the ordinance proposed for passage at this meeting, for which consideration this council is duly assembled."

The street door opened and a woman in traveling clothes entered. Penelope glanced up from her notes, then stood and hurried to her. "Mother," she whispered, hugging her. "I didn't expect you until this evening."

"Well, there was a coach available, so I . . ." Maude Becket peered around, her eyes adjusting to the indoor gloom. "Oh." She lowered her voice. "Is there a meeting, dear? Mrs. Haskell didn't tell me. Just that you were here. My, but your letters have been just fascinating, dear. I hardly know what to make of everything you've told me. And the young man? Is he — ?"

Penelope put a finger to her lips. "Hush, Mother. Come and sit down. Mayor Hanks is trying to have a meeting."

"Mayor Who?" Maude squinted. "Oh, my goodness. Dear, I thought you were joking. Why, is she really — "

"Come sit down, Mother. I'll tell you about it later."

They found seats and Cornelia shrugged and rapped the table again. "A quorum being declared, we shall proceed with the reading of the ordinance. Mr. Cox, if you please?"

"Uncle Dub just voted against a quorum," Penelope whispered.

"He did?" Maude counted noses at the council table. "How could he do that? The whole Council is here except Mayor Twiddie—ah, no, he isn't mayor any more, is he? They are all here." Raising her voice she said, "W.D., you should be ashamed of yourself. A banker certainly should be able to count."

Tienert sank down in his chair. "Hello, Maude," he said.

"Order, please!" Cornelia said. "Mr. Cox?"

Polly Cox whispered to her husband, who blanched, gulped, and stood. He began to read from a sheet of paper.

"As of this here date it is hereby proposed that the followin' ordinance be enacted, to wit: declaring domestic commercial distribution of distilled spirits to be henceforth prohibited throughout the corporate limits of the City of Jubilation—"

"My," Maude Becket whispered. "We certainly have made progress since I left, haven't we?"

"—and creating a charter commission to address and regulate any operations of saloons, gaming houses, and taverns, so-called refreshment stands, houses of prost—prosti—" He blushed. "I can't say that word in mixed company, but I swear it's in here. Anyhow, also to wit: such prohibitions are to be rigidly enforced from this day forward—"

In the back of the room Nat Kinley bowed his head in sorrow. "It's just like despicatin' a shrine."

"That's desecrating," Bert Thompson said.

"That it is."

"—provided," Cox continued, "that no provision herein is to be construed as prohibiting or interfering with the conduct of legitimate enterprises for the purpose of deriving, transporting, and exporting to legitimate market of extracts, essences, antidotes, and solvents licensed for the purpose of giving employment to our citizens."

All around the room, people looked at one another.

"What in hell do you suppose that means?" a man wondered.

"It means we have reasoned together," Bert muttered.

Nat nudged him. "Time for me to join the boys around back, Bert. You better get goin' before this place comes unglued."

With a nod, Bert followed him out the door, then headed for the Research Center. He hoped Bloody Mare would be there. Nobody had been able to figure out how to explain to the Russian what was about to happen. Not that it would matter to him, but Bert didn't want him wandering around where he might get hurt. He was such a harmless little guy.

"You have the recommendation," Cornelia told her council. "Is there a motion?"

Slim Haggard and George Gosset looked at each other, each willing the other to go first. Before them, right in the front row, the hulking forms of Packer, Hemp, and Cooley sat, glaring at them, smirking, and cracking their knuckles. Just behind them Iron Jack Fuller sat and stared, expressionless, murder in his eyes.

Haggard turned to look pleadingly at his wife. "Martha, this just ain't worth it. You're fixin' to get me hurt real bad, honey. Who's gonna take care of you if—"

She had her knitting needle half out of her sleeve, but she stopped there. "A man," she whispered. "A man with the backbone to do what's right when he sees it right there in front of him. Do it, honey."

George Gosset nudged him. "We ain't got any choice, Slim. Besides, you know what them ranchers promised. We just got to trust 'em."

"Well, I'd feel better if we was all in this together. Hell, I feel like I haven't got any clothes on." Again he glanced around at his wife. Damn her branded chicken anyway . . . but she *was* his. "So move," he muttered, staring at the table. Then, more loudly, "So move."

Beside him George took a deep breath. "Second."

"There is a motion and a second," Cornelia said. "Is there any discussion?"

W. D. Tienert came to his feet. "Yes, there is. For the record, I wish to lodge a stern protest against the manner of this assembly . . . and against the entire proceeding, which poses a serious economic threat to our community . . . indeed, which could mean the death of our fine city as surely as if we had—"

"Uncle Dub isn't in favor of any of this," Penelope whispered to her mother. "He intends to vote against Prohibition."

"I'm not in the least surprised," Maude whispered. With a sigh she stood, clasping her purse. "Forgive the interruption, your honor," she said. "I have to be getting home, but I want to say something to my brother. W.D., when you finish here please meet me at the bank. I intend to make a withdrawal."

"You intend what?"

"I intend to withdraw my funds, W.D. It may be your bank, but most of the money in it is my money, and I don't care to do business with you any more.

425

Good day."

The banker went chalk white. "Maude . . . Maudie, please. I don't understand."

"Why, W.D.! What a fib! Of course you understand. You know exactly how I feel about certain things. Good day."

"You were saying, Mr. Tienert?" Cornelia asked.

"Nothing." He sat heavily, leaning his head on his arms.

"Mother!" Penelope whispered. "Do sit down! I'm sure he will behave."

Maude Becket sat.

"Is there further discussion?" Cornelia asked. In the audience men shuffled their feet and coughed, but no one spoke. They knew how the deck was stacked.

"If there is no further discussion, all in favor of the motion say 'aye.' "

"Aye," Slim Haggard said, staring clamp-jawed at Iron Jack Fuller. Packer thumped a fist into a hand and grinned.

Martha Haggard knelt behind her husband. "Maybe you'll do," she admited.

George Gosset said a silent prayer and nodded. "Aye."

"All op—" Cornelia began.

"Aye," W. D. Tienert said in a stricken voice.

Woolly stared at the banker, unable to believe his ears. What was he doing, leaving him odd man out? What if they managed to enforce this farce, and only one man had voted against it? What would happen to his business? Suddenly Woolly Smith saw himself outnumbered and outgunned. Odds shifted and he saw his town on one side and Iron Jack on the other.

"Aye," he said.

Cornelia closed her mouth, trying to hide her astonishment. She rapped the table. "Very well, it is unanimous. Aye. I declare the ordinance in force, and direct Marshal Ben Cutter to undertake its enforcement immediately, allowing of course a minimal time for the owners of establishments closed to make other arrangements . . . though not to dispense or sell locally during the interim."

Cutter stood at one side, speechless. He had expected a split, been ready to play on it. The rug was no longer underfoot. "Ma'am, I can't . . ."

Iron Jack pointed at him. "Cutter, don't forget who butters your bread!"

"But Iron Jack, I . . ."

Cornelia pinned him with cold gray eyes. "Marshal Cutter, do you accept your instructions?"

Cutter glared at her, then looked around the room in panic. He sensed a shifting of priorities in the crowd, a feeling ranging from resignation to acceptance to a sudden, awakening civic pride. Sides were being chosen here, and he realized with a start that when it came down to it, these people would unify if they had to. One face after another told him—it wasn't just uptown versus downtown, it was more than that. In a pinch, the *whole* town outranked either of its parts.

But there was Iron Jack. Iron Jack was Iron Jack. Inside Ben Cutter, something wilted.

"I just don't see how I can," he told the Mayor. "You all have made a big mistake here, and I'm not fixin' to get cut up over your doin's. Now if we could just back off a while . . ."

"Would you care to resign?" Cornelia asked quietly.

"Resign? Don't be foolish, woman. I'm the law here. Who do you think is gonna take care of you

427

folks if I don't?"

"You may resign if you wish," Cornelia repeated. "But you will either walk out of here and do your duty *as instructed,* or walk out without your badge."

Cutter turned to Iron Jack, imploring. "Iron Jack?"

"Give the biddy the damn badge," Iron Jack said. "We got work to do."

Solemnly, Ben Cutter removed the badge from his vest and dropped it on the floor. He fixed a malevolent stare on Cornelia Hanks. "You wanted to see a town without law, lady? Well, take a look."

Iron Jack smiled. "All right, boys. Break 'em up good."

Packer and Hemp stood, followed by Cooley. All three stepped toward the council table, relishing what came next. A revolver's hammer was drawn, two crisp clicks that hung in the shocked room.

From somewhere, Cornelia Hanks had drawn a Colt .45. She held it easily and expertly, watching the men before her. "Sit down, gentlemen. This meeting has not been adjourned."

Elsewhere around the room other guns were drawn as townsmen realized the world had changed and they were committed.

"Who do you think is gonna be your law?" Cutter snarled.

Cornelia ignored him. She nodded at some of the women, who formed a cordon around the table, escorting the four councilmen to the back door. Two of them—Tienert and Smith—had no idea what was going on, but were too busy to argue.

Outside, armed ranchers awaited them, falling in as escort. "Come on," Nat Kinley said. "You'll be all right as soon as we get you away from here."

When the door was closed Cornelia put away her

gun and rapped on the table. "Meeting adjourned," she said.

Beside her mother, Penelope was scribbling as fast as she could. "Isn't this exciting, Mother? And just wait until you meet Howard."

XXXVIII

The plan was simple, direct, and full of gaping holes. But it was the only plan they had. It required a presence of law downtown until a new marshal could be found, a keeping of the peace uptown long enough for the saloon owners to study the ordinance and figure out that they hadn't been hurt as much as they thought they had, and protective custody for the city councilmen until things cooled down a little.

In the great maw of the Jubilation Research Center W.D. Tienert, Wooly Smith, Slim Haggard, and George Gosset gaped at the pipes and coils, skimmers and vats, boilers, filters, drums, flues, and samovars of a startlingly original vodka distillery. Pure water from an enclosed well fed the process and cooled the coils. Hard charcoal from Prosper O'Neil's enterprise filtered and refiltered the process. Cords of firewood from the groves of Ike Ferguson's spread stood ready to fuel the boilers and samovars, and great quantities of turnip squish bubbled and reeked in vented barrels, awaiting conversion. Trusted hands from four nearby ranches operated the system and cheated at cards for the honor of taking a turn as brew tester. The most recent brew tester snored happily on a cot in a dark corner.

"What is it?" Smith asked, his eyes wide with awe.

"It's a solvent factory," Bert Thompson explained.

"Extracts and essences," Prosper O'Neil clarified.

"Antidote for what ails 'em in Missouri and points east," Nat Kinley added.

"It's a distillery," Cornelia Hanks said. "These gentlemen have perfected the distillation of vodka from turnips."

"Bloody Mare invented it," Nat pointed out. "We just kind of adapted it."

"Vodka." Tienert stared at the process. "So that's where you fellows are getting all that money."

"Behold an entrepreneurial endeavor," Bert waved his good arm.

"Enough to make a man humble and sort of proud," Elmer Wallace assured him. "Beats hell . . . pardon, ma'am . . . beats heck out of makin' a honest livin' off cows."

Tienert raised a brow, gazing at Cornelia Hanks. "You knew about this when you drafted that ordinance."

"Our mayor is a devious and conniving woman," Bert assured him.

"Of course I knew," she said. "You gentlemen have been so busy trying to run things Iron Jack Fuller's way that you haven't noticed what else was going on here. Jubilation has a productive new industry."

"This is what that second part was about."

"Yes."

"The women are going to lynch you when they find out about this."

"Oh, I don't think so. All they really wanted was to keep their husbands relatively sober and impose some constraints on that wildness uptown. Women can be very reasonable people, Mr. Tienert."

"As long as they get their own way," Bert added.

"Well, you . . . we . . . have certainly opened a can of worms now. Iron Jack and those saloon owners—"

"I think the saloon owners will come around," Cornelia said. "We printed detailed explanations of the new ordinance yesterday. They're being distributed right now. We're not closing the saloons, we're only prohibiting whiskey."

"Amounts to the same thing."

"Not exactly. Beer isn't a distilled spirit. Neither is wine."

"Men don't drink wine."

"And we didn't outlaw the gambling places or— any of those other enterprises. Yet."

"It's going to occur to Patman and Richardson and a lot of the others that they have some valuable properties up there and there are other ways of making money off of them," Bert suggested. "Benjamin Harrison intends to open the Cherokee Outlet to settlement. Can you imagine a town anyplace that's better located to outfit settlers moving to Oklahoma?"

"Somebody ought to go up to Washington and shoot that scutter," Wallace allowed.

"To where?" Smith asked.

"Oklahoma. They're calling the whole territory that now."

"Times change," Prosper decided.

"That still leaves Iron Jack," Tienert pointed out. "He isn't going to stand for any of this, you know. He's up there right now, getting ready to come down on us." He shivered.

"Yeah, I been worryin' about that," Nat agreed. "He's a little short-handed right now, but that won't

432

last. But Mayor Hanks has a plan."

She blinked at him. "Well, not really. I left that up to Mr. Thompson to take care of."

Bert turned pale. "Is that all? That's it? I thought . . ."

"You *have* taken care of the problem of Iron Jack Fuller, haven't you?" she asked him levelly.

"Well, I . . . no. I mentioned it to Nat, but we got kind of busy on other things. Nat, you said we'd come up with something."

"We did," Nat said. "We cut the odds down a little. But I thought . . . well, you said Miss Hanks had a plan."

As one, they turned to her, their eyes wide.

She shrugged. "I can't think of everything. Anyway, just what is it you think he will do? He doesn't have the law any more . . . just a few toughs. What can he do?"

"She don't know," Nat said bleakly.

"I thought you knew, Cornelia." Bert Thompson took a deep breath and expelled it. "I guess I thought you had help on the way, state law or somebody. I assumed it."

"No. Why, what can he do?"

"It isn't just his bruisers, Cornelia. Iron Jack Fuller hires killers. He has a whole network. That's why nobody ever crosses him. Everybody knows what he'll do."

"If there isn't state law on the way now," Nat said, "then it's too late. Because his guns are on the way, an' you can count on that."

His spring wagon piled high with fresh-harvested turnips, Howard Sills drove out his fresnoed road, crested the rim of Bad Basin, and reined in to look

433

around. High thunderheads stood in the sky just west of the meridian, behind him, blocking the lowering sun behind a curtain of purple gray where rain squalls danced in the distance. Shadowless light of early dusk amplified the pale colors of the Kansas hills, making of them a patchwork of bright greens, crisp yellows, near-whites, and somber browns. It was exhilarating, and Howard felt an elation that came from more than the beauty of the land and the ozone in the air.

His pipes were beside him and Jubilation was ahead of him, and this was the evening he would propose to Penelope Becket. He had long since made up his mind. He would play for her, he would walk with her, and he would ask her to marry him. They would be married during Chautauqua.

Not far north of him he saw horsemen, a group of them heading for town. Waddies from some spread, he thought, in for the evening. Beyond them, where the land dipped away toward the valley, the brief horizon seemed to ripple and flow with movement, and he squinted to make it out. Animals . . . quite a lot of them, probably being moved.

Cool, errant breezes from the west wafted across, picking up the clean, crisp scent of fresh turnips to add to the stimulus of the air.

Whistling, he slapped rein and Crowbait set out for Jubilation, bright in the distance across the Higgins-Wentworth Trail.

He had covered nearly a mile when he looked to his left again and saw that the animals were much closer. Oddly, they seemed to be coming up the trail from the valley. He had never seen a herd move south on this trail, and was puzzled. Even more puzzling, the herd of cattle didn't seem to be all cattle. There were other things too. Buffalo? And a

434

mule and some horses? Possibly part of someone's remuda. But there were smaller things as well, and one vastly larger. He would have sworn it was an elephant.

But where were the riders, the drovers?

Reminded, he peered around to see where the group of riders had gone. They were angling toward him, a little way behind, and as he turned to see around the heaped turnips he saw one of them stand tall in his stirrups and point, and he recognized him. It was the rough-looking man from the bank, the one who had joked about robbing banks and trains.

Suddenly he recalled what Nat had told him, and cold realization crept up his spine. He saw a man drawing a revolver, and knew instinctively that he was looking at the man who had killed Pete Swain. The man spurred his mount and raised his gun. Howard snapped his reins, ducked low, and shouted at Crowbait. Turnips exploded atop his load, and he heard the roar of a gunshot.

Crowbait surged, found his footing, and ran, the spring wagon jolting after him, flinging turnips. Another shot echoed and bits of shattered turnip stung Howard's head and shoulders. More shots. A bullet sang off the iron tire of his nearside front wheel. Splinters flew from the box frame of the wagon. The ivory toe of the great drone of his pipes shattered and was gone.

Howard shouted. He drew his revolver, turned and emptied it at the closing band of horsemen. One of them disappeared from atop his horse. The rest scattered aside, receding abruptly as Crowbait found a source of new strength in the sting of box splinters across his rump.

Holding the reins in his teeth, clinging to his seat with bent knees and wedged boots, Howard struggled to feed new loads into his Colt.

Hitting the main trail, the wagon bounced and caromed, flinging turnips as it went.

He dropped several cartridges, but got a few into the cylinder and turned. They were coming again, closing rapidly.

He fired wildly and heard bullets singing around him. The man in the lead, a cold-eyed, hard-looking man, raised his gun and took careful aim at him . . . then discharged his shot into the air as his racing mount sidestepped. An antelope flitted past under its nose, followed by several more.

The wagon bumped and sailed and Howard clung desperately. He heard shouts and curses behind him, distantly. At a smoother stretch he looked back again. The horsemen were some distance back, awash in milling, turning cattle. And buffalos. And deer, horses, geese, sandhill cranes . . . Howard bounced high as the wagon sailed out of another rut, and clung for his life. Turnips flew.

Crowbait's run began to tell on him as they went up the slope beyond the trail, and Howard reined him to an easy lope. He put away his revolver, looked himself over for wounds, found none, and turned his attention to his payload. More than half his turnips were gone, and the ivory toe of his great drone was a wreck. He shook his head. The toe's bow lent a flow to the tone of the drone, and its absence didn't help the pipe's appearance.

Probably, Penelope would notice.

Almost at the verge of town the wagon jounced across a diagonal rut and its remaining load shifted. Between small groves of elm and cottonwood trees Howard reined in, still holding his offended pipes, and stepped down to rearrange his turnips. He wiped down the lathered horse with a bit of sacking, then walked back to the shoulder of the trail to see what had become of his attackers. There were animals everywhere, mostly cattle but other things too. He saw sheep now, and goats . . . and the drift of the herd was reorienting itself, beginning to flow toward him. In the lead a one-horned cow lowered its head to sniff at a fallen turnip, then collected it and came on, seeking others.

Abrupt sounds behind him brought Howard around, and he stared. An elephant had stepped out of the trees, and Crowbait stared at it. But only for an instant. With a shriek of equine disbelief the horse dug in his heels and bolted, the spring wagon bouncing along behind, showering turnips in its wake.

The elephant watched it go, then turned ponderously and ambled along after it, chewing on a turnip. Atop its head a red rooster clung, wings outspread for balance, and glared back at Howard.

Cattle behind him, an elephant ahead, and his horse and spring wagon receding now up Elm Street, Howard began the walk into Jubilation. Early antelope bounded by him, and a goat trotted happily at his side, sniffing at his windbag. Howard kept his eyes forward and walked, fully expecting that sooner or later he would find a rationale to account for the past hour of his life.

At the Jubilation Bank and Trust Company a surrey, fresh off the trail, pulled up and its driver stepped down to tie his hitch. The gunbelt at his hips and the derby hat on his head were at contrast with the railroader denims and scuffed brogan shoes he wore, but he carried himself with severe dignity as he entered the bank.

"I need to see the man in charge," he told the clerk. "My name's Walter Flynn. I represent the Atchison, Topeka, and Santa Fe Railroad Company." He pulled a wallet from his vest pocket and held it open, showing the silver signet of railroad inspector.

"Mr. Tienert's our president," the clerk said. "Him and the rest of the City Council is holed up over at the Research Center today because they voted the Prohibition law in and they figure Iron Jack Fuller won't take that kindly."

"Well, can you send somebody for him? I haven't got all day."

The clerk shrugged. "Reckon so. What'll we tell him it's about?"

"You're holdin' some found money here. It might be railroad funds stolen from Hays City last winter. The amount is right. I'm supposed to check the serial numbers on the bills."

"Yeah, Howard Sills found that money someplace. I'll send Joe to fetch Mr. Tienert. Do you always dress like that? I'd have thought railroad inspectors would wear suits."

Flynn shrugged. "I was a fireman until recently. I tended Old 49 for more'n eight years. Then some bastard came along an' robbed us an' blew the old lady's boilers. I just didn't have the heart to take on another engine, so they gave me this job."

At the Jubilation Research Center, Packer arrived carrying a white flag on a stick. At the gate he told Elmer Wallace, "I got a message from Iron Jack Fuller, for all them inside. Get 'em out here."

Wallace covered him with a shotgun while Ike Ferguson went to get the rest. They assembled inside

438

the gate—the entire City Council and most of the Jubilation Research Society.

"Iron Jack says to tell you he's takin' over this town," Packer said. "Says to tell this here woman mayor she's got three days to pack up and go back where she came from. Says to tell Bert Thompson an' that Russian they got three days to see how far they can get from here before he turns some friends of his loose to find 'em for a price. Says you city councilmen got until tomorrow to bring him the ledgers an' tax records an' the city seals. From now on Iron Jack is the mayor in this town, an' City Hall is uptown at his office."

"But that's—" Cornelia erupted.

"Shut up. Iron Jack says you ranchers can clear out, but if you show your faces around here again you'll wish you never was born. And them boys you took, he wants them back right now, undamaged. That's all he had to say, except you might as well come out of here because we're gonna burn this place down in a little bit."

Cornelia stared at him. She looked at those around her and saw it on their faces. They had lost. Iron Jack could make good on his demands, and they knew it.

"We've been a bunch of damned fools, Cornelia," Bert whispered. "I'm sorry."

"But how can he . . . ?"

"He can."

"You men . . . you're all armed. Can't you—?"

"They're armed," Bert said quietly. "But they're not gunmen. Even Nat Kinley, he's just a rancher. The men Iron Jack can bring in are another matter entirely. You don't know about them, Cornelia. How could you?"

"We can still fight. We can . . ." She stopped, her

chin quivering. No, they couldn't. Most of them had wives and families. This town was their home. "Oh, God, Bert. What have I done?"

He saw the moisture in her eyes, the frustration, the shock, and the dread. She had planned everything . . . except the one little detail she had left to him. With a start he realized she had been serious about that. Not knowing a thing about it, she had just assumed he knew and that he could take care of it. Take care of Iron Jack Fuller, she had said. Such a small detail, in the fabric of her plans for the liberation of the town.

She had counted on him.

Having delivered his message, Packer strode away. They stood there, looking at one another, and Bert saw abruptly how small she really was . . . and how lost, alone, and innocent in a land she did not understand.

"I need a drink," he muttered. He left them there by the gate and went inside to find the dipper, the vat, and oblivion.

Iron Jack Fuller. The son of a bitch. The bastard. Bert drank, and drank again. Iron Jack Fuller had made Cornelia cry.

From the Research Center Packer hurried toward the uptown trail. Iron Jack would be waiting with further orders. He had never seen the boss so furious. This was going to be fun.

At the foot of the trail Ben Cutter sat tall and sleek in the saddle of a prancing roan, waiting for him. Five men afoot were with him, two of them holding an object that looked like a big iron egg, two feet in diameter at least, with bolted seams.

"You found them," Packer said. "Where were

they?"

"Same place those yayhoos kept me the night I was kidnapped," Cutter told him. "Old shack under the ridge. I figured they were there. Somebody had hit 'em all on the head an' tied 'em up in burlap bags an' dumped them there."

"Anybody there with 'em?"

"Not when I got there, and I didn't wait around. Figured Iron Jack might need 'em."

"Well, this gives you somethin' to crow about, Cutter. What's that thing there?"

"I don't know. We was just headin' up here when I saw that little Russian jaybird draggin' this thing out of a shed. We took it away from him. Thought Iron Jack might like to see it."

Cutter riding, the rest walking, two of them carrying the iron device, they headed up the path and turned onto uptown's front street. Men watched them pass, curious but not about to interrupt. Cutter didn't much worry anybody, but the others were six of Iron Jack's toughest goons.

At the fortified office behind Lester's House of Leisure they grouped while Ben Cutter tied his horse and knocked on the door. It opened and they entered, the last two carrying their iron egg. The door closed.

From behind a rainbarrel down the alley a wool-capped head peered out. Bloody Mare had blood on his brow and a badly cut lip. One eye was swollen almost shut, but the other gleamed with pure delight as he saw the door close.

Do svidanya, Cossacks," he murmured, contentedly.

The grin that split his face as he turned away was painful, but it was worth it. His hurts would heal. Memories of the Commissar and his Cossacks would help them heal. He glanced at the sky, where blue deepened to violet above massed and marching storm clouds. He estimated the time and grinned again. He had just time enough to get down off the hill.

He scurried along the alley, turned at a street corner, and stepped into a street where traffic was beginning to increase for the evening, then stopped at the sound of a familiar voice shouting. His good eye went wide. He turned and ran, back to the alley, along it, then skidded to a stop.

Outside the fortified office, Bert Thompson stood spread-legged, one arm in a sling, the other hand holding a revolver.

"Fuller!" Bert shouted. "Iron Jack Fuller! Foul villain! Knave! You get your butt out here! I'm goin' to teach you a lesson about how to treat a lady!"

He swayed slightly on his feet, brandishing the gun.

Bloody Mare started for him. "Bert Tomsahn, *nyet! Ya sdelal bombu! Otkryta,* Bert Tomsahn! *Bomba! Bolshaya bomba!*"

Bert turned to him, swaying drunkenly. "Ah, Vladimir! Good and faithful Vladimir, whose potent lotions steel the heart and loft the spirit, giving shame to all of lesser potions." He giggled. "That's pretty good." He turned toward the door again, raised his pistol, and fired a shot through its center. "Iron Jack Fuller! Come out, come out! Let no man ever say that even the lowest of the dogs was not allowed his day!"

Running, Bloody Mare had almost reached Bert when the heavy door swung open and men boiled out. Bert had lowered his pistol, and had no time to raise it again. Heavy hands mauled him, fists thudded into him, and large men threw him to the ground and swarmed over him. Bloody Mare hit the tangle and was thrown aside. He tried again and a fist doubled him over. A boot to the ribs sent him rolling, to slam against the side of a building.

In the doorway Iron Jack Fuller stood, squat and monstrous. "Bring him inside," he thundered. "I want him in here."

Huddled in deepening shadows, Bloody Mare gasped for breath and tried to get his feet under him. He could barely move. He saw them lift Bert Thompson, saw him carry him into the office, and heard the door close with a thud of finality.

"Bert Tomsahn," he whispered. *"Pochemu? Otshego?"* Why?

With an effort he dragged himself upright. *"Do svidanya, tovarishch."* Hurt and bleeding, he turned and limped away.

XXXIX

By the time Cole Yeager and the rest regrouped
and entered the town, rising wind was hurling scattered drops of rain and the town was full of animals.
They were everywhere—geese sauntering along a
boardwalk, a nimble goat testing a porch swing,
buffalo munching contentedly in someone's garden,
sheep flocking in a public street, a sandhill crane on
a weather vane, stray chickens followed by a duck,
glimpses of antelope, and cattle everywhere. They
thronged around the mill, tasted the flowers in
dooryards, wandered along streets and through gar-
dens, and made themselves generally ubiquitous.

People ran here and there, trying to get out of
their way. Horses whinnied and bolted, doors
slammed and voices shouted.

"I don't know what this is," Parson said. "They
weren't havin' this when I was here."

"Doesn't matter," Cole said.

"You want to look for that sodbuster first?"

"Later. Let's get to the bank. The time's right."
Turning off Elm, walking their horses, they edged
around skittish cattle waiting in line at Bunker's Mill
and hesitated as a screaming woman with a broom

chased a goat out of a millinery shop. A buffalo calf entered behind her. The riders passed and the bank lay just ahead, a solid brick structure on a street corner. People thronging upstairs windows on both sides of the street ignored them, preferring the antics of their neighbors and the invading livestock.

"Two men with the horses," Cole ordered. "One at the front door, one at the back. Block 'em. Parson, you and me go in."

Parson nodded, then stood high in his stirrups. Coming along the boardwalk, a half block ahead, a tall young man carrying something of sticks and plaid was running interference for a pretty young woman, slapping and jostling at cattle to clear their path. For a moment his way was blocked by a stubborn Hereford that stood its ground, head low and threatening. He shouted at it, stepping between it and the girl. It shook its head, pawed at the boardwalk, then was distracted by a man coming out of a store. It turned, bellowed, and followed the man back into the store. The girl was making notes on a pad of paper.

"I see him," Parson said. "That's your sodbuster."

Cole studied them, watching them approach. His hand went to his gun, but he hesitated. "Bank first," he decided. "We need the money." They drew rein and lined the horses at the hitch rail. Parson dipped his head, letting his hat brim hide his face. The banker, Tienert, had come around the corner and was gawking at the livestock in the street. A buffalo trotted by and the banker turned and scurried through the door.

"That banker knows me," Parson said.

"Let's go," Cole rasped.

Distantly, a bellowing voice rose above the noise of the street. "No cows allowed uptown! Somebody's

445

breakin' the Law!" Somewhere else, glad trumpeting responded.

They paused at the bank door to cover their faces. Then, leaving the Farley at the door, they entered with drawn guns.

They had passed the bulk of the milling cattle and Howard took Penelope's arm to lead her around a pair of officious geese that established a beachhead in front of Baker's Saddlery. He noticed that there was a mule inside. "I never saw anything like this," he told her.

"What?"

"I said," he shouted, "I never saw anything like this!"

"Neither did I. Where do you suppose they came from? Oh, look! Deer!"

"What did your mother say?"

"What?"

"What did your . . . mind the pig, Penelope; why is it wearing a badge? . . . what did your mother say? About me, I mean!"

"She wants to meet you! She's at home, getting settled in! We'll go there as soon as you finish at the bank! Ooops! What is that thing?"

"Sandhill crane! Ignore it! It's just being quarrelsome!"

"I hope these animals don't get into our garden! Mrs. Haskell would have a fit! Howard, I really am worried about those men shooting at you out there! Are you sure they went away?"

"I haven't seen them since! Did I tell you about the elephant?"

"The what?"

"Elephant! That's what made Crowbait run away!

I need to find him! But I wanted to talk to you first! Watch your step here! Cattle leave an awful mess! You see, before I meet your mother, I wanted to settle something between us!"

"What?"

"I said, I want to . . . oh, you mean what do I want to settle?" They stepped up on the bank walk. A hard-eyed man stood directly in front of the door, his arms folded. "Excuse us," Howard said.

The man stood his ground. "Go away. Bank's closed."

"What?"

"I said go away! The bank is closed!"

"No, it's all right!" Penelope told him. "This is my uncle's bank! Excuse me!" She stepped forward. The man stiff-armed her and she staggered back, gasping. Howard caught her. Then he glared at the man, shifted his pipes from his right hand to his left, sidestepped, and launched a roundhouse swing that looped up from behind his knee to take the man full in the face. The man rebounded off the bank door and fell flat, face down.

"Don't you ever do that again!" Howard explained to him.

He turned to Penelope. "Are you all right?"

She nodded. "That man is no gentleman!"

"That kind of behavior should never be tolerated!" he agreed. "But what I was saying—"

"About settling something between us!"

"Yes!" He shoved the unconscious lout aside and opened the outer door. "This is hardly the time to ask, Penelope, but before I meet your mother, I need to know!"

"What is it, Howard?"

He opened the inner door, escorted her through, turned, and closed it. "Will you marry me?" he

447

shouted.

Everyone in the bank — those behind the counters with their hands in the air, W.D. Tienert crouched at his safe, the customers ranked hands-up against the wall, the two masked men with drawn guns — seemed frozen in place by the question.

The door opened again and Wednesday Warren hurried in. "Mr. Sills! I'm glad I — hot damn!" His eyes took in the scene, his reflexes took charge, and he drew and fired. The knot on Parson's bandana exploded and the cloth fell away.

"You!" Howard gasped. He flung Penelope aside and went for his gun.

"It's him!" W. D. Tienert shouted. "He's the —!"

Cole Yeager's pale eyes blazed with fury. He pivoted, leveling his gun at Howard Sills. A man by the wall dropped to a crouch and hauled out a revolver. "Engine killer!" he snarled. His first shot scored Yeager across the back and the outlaw's bullet splintered the door above Howard's head. People hollered and scattered. The chief clerk dived under his counter and came up with a gun. Parson swiveled, wild-eyed, trying to place a shot. Someone tackled him and he went down. Howard snapped a shot at the man who had fired at him, but the man had ducked aside, turning. The bullet missed him by an inch and traveled the length of the bank to punch a neat hole dead center in the back door, which was just opening.

"Howard!" Penelope scuttled away from the fallen Parson, dodging as he swung his pistol at her. Howard tensed and fired. Floorboards between the man's legs erupted. The man howled, rolled, and doubled, losing his gun. The back door swung open and a man fell in, face-down.

Someone bumped Howard and he dropped his

gun. Wednesday was firing, the railroad man was firing, the clerk was firing, and Cole Yeager dodged and danced, then turned and ran. "Hell!" he shouted. "These people are crazy!" Wednesday shot his hat from his head as he went out the door.

Wild-eyed, Parson scrambled to his feet, ducked and ran . . . to double over the startled muzzle of an incoming Hereford. He fell back, the steer stepping over him. It looked down, snorting, as he tried to crawl between its hind legs. Its kick somersaulted him into the street. In the distance the outlaw Cole Yeager was running all out, pursued by a pounding buffalo. Just outside the door geese pecked at the ears of an unconscious Farley.

Inside, Penelope's lavender eyes were huge. "Howard, they're getting away! Use your pipes!"

Puzzled, he shrugged, flung the drones across his shoulder, filled his bag with two fast puffs, and slapped the plaid goose. The loudest song he knew was "The Campbells Are Coming," and the bank building bulged to its blast.

Outside, cattle lowed and pranced, antelope fled, Leonard and the elephant trumpeted somewhere in imperfect harmony, and birds took wing.

A few bars were enough. Fine dust was falling from the plaster ceiling, and most of the people in the bank were scuttling for cover.

"I don't know what good that did," Howard told Penelope.

"Well," she said, shrugging, "it couldn't hurt."

"I started to tell you." Wednesday Warren put his gun away. "I saw your horse and wagon headin' uptown."

"That was Cole Yeager," the railroad man announced.

"No, it was Crowbait, with Mr. Sill's wagon."

"Yes, Howard," Penelope said. "Of course I'll marry you."

"You . . . you will? You really will?"

"Of course, silly. Come here."

He took her in his arms and they kissed across protesting pipes. The drones complained and he pulled her closer, oblivious.

"Wow," Wednesday Warren muttered.

Then windows rattled, plaster cracked, and the world seemed to shift its stance. Pictures fell from the walls. People lost their balance and clung to counters for support. A blast like the clap of doom rocked and roared through the town. The floor pitched, creaked, and resettled. Through the open door drifted the song of mixed animals run amock.

Wednesday stared wide-eyed at the lovers. "Wow," he breathed.

In the fortified office behind Lester's House of Leisure they had worked Bert Thompson over thoroughly. They had taken turns, and now he lay silent, bleeding on the plank floor.

"Is he dead?" Iron Jack asked, pig eyes bright with pleasure.

Packer crouched to study the printer. "Not quite, Boss. You want to finish him?"

"I haven't made up my mind. Who else was out there?"

"That little jaybird. The Russian. You want him too?"

"He doesn't matter. You said you took this thing away from him, Cutter?" He pointed at the iron egg sitting beside his desk.

"Yeah." Ben Cutter stood aside, somewhat pale. He had seen beatings before, but the way they had worked Bert Thompson over was special. "Yeah, the Russian. He had it. I don't know what it is, but he didn't give it up easy."

"You suppose this is what they came after then?" Iron Jack eyed the egg. "Maybe it's valuable." He turned back to Packer. "Those people down there, how'd they take my message?"

"Like they was gonna drop their teeth, Boss. They haven't got any help comin' in. I could tell that."

"You think they've got anything up their sleeves?"

Packer shook his head, grinning. "Not a thing. I don't know what they thought they was gonna do about you, but they ain't done it. I guess the only one that was the least bit feisty was that woman mayor, but what can she do?"

Iron Jack frowned. "Probably nothing. If they're convinced I've already sent for some shooters, my guess is they'll just fold their hands and toss in their cards."

Cutter frowned. "You mean you *haven't* sent for shooters?"

"Don't be such a damn fool." Iron Jack glowered at him. "You know how much even three or four of them will cost me? Why should I pay that kind of wages when all I have to do is just rake in the pot?"

There was a clattering beyond the door. Packer opened it and peered out.

"What is it?" Iron Jack asked.

"Horse and wagon," Packer closed the door. "No driver. Somebody's let it run loose."

Iron Jack was looking at Bert Thompson again. "I think I'll hedge my bet," he decided. "Give those people an example to think about. Cutter." He turned to the ex-marshal. "I'm going to let you earn your keep."

"I always—"

"Shut up. Did you ever hang a man?"

"No." The pale of his face whitened more. "No, I can't say I ever have."

"No time like the present to learn," Iron Jack said. "I want you to take this—" he waved casually at the body on the floor, "—this damn drunk, and I want you to hang him, right out in front of City Hall. Dump him in that wagon out there, haul him downtown, and stretch his neck. And I want him right in front of City Hall, where everybody can see. You understand?"

"But, Iron Jack." Cutter swallowed hard. "I don't think . . . I mean, you can't just . . ."

"Yes, I can," Iron Jack rumbled. "That's the whole point. I can. What's the matter, Cutter? Haven't you got stomach enough for the job?" The threat behind the voice was hard and lethal. "Do I need to get somebody else?"

"No, Iron Jack." Ben Cutter lowered his head. "I can do it. I will. Can I have some help?"

Iron Jack looked around at his assembled toughs. He nodded. "Go along with him, Cooley. Take a gun and back up the marshal while he does his duty. Maybe you can even hold his hand for him." He swung around. "Cutter, you do this right or the next hangin' is going to be yours."

With a nod, Cooley stood and picked up the limp form of Bert Thompson. "Get the door, Cutter."

When the door opened, the wind brought spatters of rain and a chorus of distant sounds. Cutter stepped out, followed by Cooley carrying Bert Thompson. A dapple horse and green spring wagon stood outside. Cooley dumped Thompson into the bed and climbed aboard. Cutter stepped to the seat and took the reins. He turned the rig and they headed away.

In the doorway Packer listened to the growing clamor. "Boys are gettin' an early start this evenin'," he allowed. "Sound like a bunch of damn cattle."

Iron Jack scowled. "They always do. Shut the door." He pulled out a deck of cards, shuffled, and fanned them. "All we got to do now is wait," he told them.

Some of them pulled chairs around the desk. Hemp was starting to doze on the davenport in the corner. Packer looked for a place to sit, then squatted atop the iron egg.

"What are you doin', Packer?" One of them grinned. "You think you can make that thing hatch?"

Iron Jack fanned the cards again, shuffled once more, and cut the deck, then handed it to the bruiser on his left.

"Deal," he said.

Vladimir Nicolayevich Malenkov had made a slight miscalculation in his device. The wax-sealed timing fuse, a complex contrivance vaguely similar to a candle burning from inside out, depended for its combustion on a pair of coils of tubing mounted in the fusing trap. But the draw of the tiny flame in its wax container was less than he had estimated. The miscalculation was enough to add eleven minutes to the time it took for the flame to reach and melt the last layer of wax between itself and the packed blasting powder.

Iron Jack's tough was dealing fourth cards face down when that occurred.

XL

The blast that rocked Jubilation, Kansas, the evening of October 17, 1887, was visible as far away as Pleasant Valley and its echoes were heard from Bad Basin to Buffalo Hole.

Two miles beyond the Kansas border, in the Cherokee Outlet, Robert E. Lee Grant reined in his mount to stare in awe at the climbing fireball in the distance. "I knew it," he told the other Warbonnet hands riding with him. "I just knew some day them boys from H-Four was going to go too far."

In the Pleasant Valley Hotel, where they were waiting for the hay-wagon stage to take them to Jubilation for the Chautauqua, the famed Mercer Twins of Minneapolis, Minnesota, stared from their upstairs window at the sudden, distant glow arising south of the Cimarron Valley. Then they looked at each other. "Do you suppose they've started without us?"

At Bad-Basin, Ambrose was in the house and did not see the fireball. But a few minutes later he heard the concussion of it and went to the door to look out. Pericles darted in and went looking for a hiding place in the loft. Ambrose closed the door and went to the pantry to put on his butler suit, in case company was coming.

Some minutes after that, the shock reached Lazy K, where Conquistador snorted, pawed the ground, and promptly went on the prod, clearing three pastures of Kinley brothers, hired hands, and stock before he calmed down.

On the north rim of the Cimarron Valley Justin Case, on a borrowed horse, had just topped out and was starting across the valley, hoping to meet the new mayor of Jubilation and begin negotiations between her and the saloon owners, for a fee. The fireball rising across the valley brought his horse to a stop, and the blast, when it came, gave it ideas of its own as to where it wanted to go. Justin Case walked home that night, wondering with each step where he had gone wrong.

The primary effects of the explosion were in the immediate vicinity of Lester's House of Leisure, one of seven buildings which no longer existed even in theory. Where they had been was now a crater approximately 300 feet across. Beyond its perimeter Juniper Sloan's slat barn was kindling, four saloons and a two-story cathouse lay collapsed at improbable angles, and Will Slayton's prize windmill hung from its sagging stem, its supports blown away. The uptown warehouse was a shambles of twisted timbers and broken legs. Still further away Whistle Loomis and three customers picked themselves up in a bare lot and wondered where the Whistle Stop Cafe had gone. Pardee's Palace tilted crazily, Milo Shane's card parlor had a flung outhouse halfway through its street window and someone inside was cursing in two languages. There was a hay wagon on Winslow Kline's roof, and the roof of Johnny Dyson's Happy House next door was mostly in the street. In Potter's Field the walking wounded were awake and wandering about, several of them sober.

Windows, mirrors, and glassware were shattered at Patman's and Richardson's. At Max Bigelow's place an H-Four waddie crawled out from under the faro table, found his hat, brushed himself off, and stepped up to the bar. "I'll have another one just like that last one," he said. "And keep 'em comin'."

The blast cost Rajah his chicken and changed his mind about turnips. Halfway up the uptown road, approaching the switchback, he was effectively shielded from the shock, but the sleeping red rooster on his head went flying, end over end, to collide in mid-air with a swooping sandhill crane. An instant later both birds were whisked away, snorting and cawing, their claws sunk deep in the wool of a southbound buffalo. Rajah trumpeted, turned around, and proceeded sedately down the hill, his bulk effectively blocking the stampede that overtook him from the bluff. Cattle and other things spilled off the road and down the slope, arrowing toward the second stampede that had erupted downtown. The two herds joined at the base of the bluff and turned south, heading out the wagon track toward the fork that would join the Higgins-Wentworth Trail at Bugle Rock.

Mary worked her way to the point of the slowing, loping herd just about the time Pistol Pete Olive and his men came up on the drags. "God don't want these cows to go to Dodge!" Pistol Pete shouted, the wind in his face. "God wants these cows to go home! So let's take 'em home, for God's sake!"

In downtown Jubilation the explosion rattled windows and shook buildings. Cornelia Hanks, just arrived home from the Jubilation Research Center and thinking about packing, clung to her bedroom door as the house lurched beneath her feet. "What in heaven's name—" she breathed. Then, steadied, she ran to open a freshly cracked window. Instant sunrise was just fading in the dusk atop Jubilation Bluff. She ran downstairs, grabbed her shawl, and arrived at her front door just as Vladimir limped up onto her porch. There was blood on his face and in his beard, and he clutched his side as he moved. *"Vidite."* He pointed a shaking finger toward the bluff, and she saw tears in his eyes. "Bert Tomsahn *mertvyi. Bomba."*

She didn't understand . . . yet she did. Bert Thompson . . . *mertvyi.* Dead? The blood drained from her face and she sagged against the doorframe. Bert Thompson . . . Bert . . . Vladimir had been clinging to the porch rail. Now his legs wobbled and he sat down, panting. After a moment she went and knelt beside him, fighting back the sobs that struggled in her throat. He needed help. He was hurt.

The sounds of animals had diminished, but now there were other sounds to replace them in the dusk. People were in the streets. The town was shaking itself out, coming to its senses and she noticed again . . . dimly . . . that sense of oneness that came in disaster or danger. They met and mingled in the streets, and from the mingling went out in systematic groups to learn what had happened and decide what to do about it.

A group of men, some afoot and some asaddle, hurried along her street and stopped at the gate. One dismounted and came in.

"You all right, Mayor?" Nat Kinley asked. "What's this . . . Bloody Mare? What happened?"

"I don't know," she said. "I think he's just bruised, but this cut on his head . . . can someone help him?"

"Let's get him over to Emma's," Nat said. "What ever it was, there may be others. Prosper's on h way out to Doc Marcy's place, and Twist has starte for Pleasant Valley to get help. Did you see wher that explosion was?"

"I saw. Up there. Nat, do you know where Be went?"

"No, ma'am. I ain't seen him. Penelope's all right though. She's over at the bank with Howard. Some body tried to rob the bank, but they're all right.

"Rob the bank? But those animals . . . then tha explosion . . ."

He shook his head. "We'll sort it out. Right now we're gettin' some boys together to go uptown. The may need help up there."

From the darkened bluff came the muted sounds floating against the wind. Men's voices. And now there were glows up there. Random flames danced Buildings were burning. Nat stood for a moment then removed his hat. "It's like devastatin' a shrine, he said. "Like the end of an era."

"We all have work to do, Nat." She stood an took a deep breath. "We had better get to it."

It was nearly dawn when Howard Sills and Na Kinley showed up at City Hall. Their clothes wer grimy and soot-stained, their faces gray with fatigue

Cornelia had assembled the City Council an volunteers the previous evening and they had worke through the night, compiling reports, directing as sistance, fighting fires, restoring order in Jubilation

Howard and Nat came in with the gray of morn ing behind them, and stood for a moment watchin the work going on. Then Howard saw the Mayo bent over lists on the conference table, and nudge

Nat. They went to her, hats in hands.

"Can you come outside for a minute, Mayor?" Nat asked gravely.

She looked from one to the other, and dread crept up her spine. In the street a bull voice roared, "Stand aside! Make way for the Law! Law comin' through!" A moment later the door crashed open and Leonard squeezed through. He was carrying a struggling, kicking man, upside down. "This man broke the Law!" he roared. "Somebody tell me where to put him!"

Nat stepped to him and leaned to peer at the flushed, inverted face of the prisoner. "Well, I'll be," he muttered. He straightened. "Would you all look at this? Do you know who this is that Leonard's got? This here is that outlaw, Cole Yeager, in the flesh. Look!"

People gathered to look, while Leonard stood patiently, holding his prisoner with one arm around his middle.

Nat shook his head in admiration. "How'd you catch him, Leonard? What did he do?"

"This man broke the Law!" Leonard roared. "He tried to shoot that Pig! That Pig is the Law! Where do you want him?"

"The pokey's still standin'," Nat told Cornelia.

"Some of you men go with him," she ordered. "Make sure he gets locked up tight."

Again, getting through the door was a difficult procedure for Cole Yeager, but Leonard managed. "Make way for the Law!" he roared, outside. "Law's comin' through!"

"We need you outside for a minute, Mayor," Nat reminded Cornelia. She followed them out. Howard's wagon stood in front, an exhausted Crowbait head-down in the traces. Nat led her to the bed and pulled back a tarp.

"Howard found him in the wagon," he said. "Ju
like this. We wanted to know what to do with him

Bert Thompson was a mass of scars and bruise
Dried blood crusted him. He looked as though I
had been trampled. But as she stared, one of his ey
opened and he licked his lips feebly.

"But soft!" he whispered. "What light throug
yonder window breaks?" A wink performed wil
only one openable eye is difficult, but he manage
it, a sardonic twinkle in his eye. "It is the east, an
Juliet is the sun."

The sobs that she had fought through the nigl
overtook her now, and her shoulders quaked whi
moisture filled her eyes. But only for a momen
That was no way for the mayor of Jubilation 1
behave. She drew herself up, squared her shoulder
and wiped her eyes. She looked at him and shoo
her head sadly. "O Romeo, Romeo! Wherefore a
thou Romeo?"

"You had best take him back to my house," sl
told Howard Sills. "I'll be there directly, with th
doctor. Oh, and please put him in the good bec
He's done nothing but complain about the othe
one."

EPILOGUE

"Things ain't ever exactly the same as things was
efore, ever again," Nat Kinley philosophised.
That's the main thing about things."

"That's a fact, Nat." Will Ambler nodded sagely.
Like I always say, 'How it is ain't how it was nor
nything like it will be.' I say that."

They lounged outside Ambler's shop door, watch-
g the sun rise over what remained of uptown
ubilation and wondering what the Golden Rule had
or breakfast. There was a fresh hint of frost in the
right air.

"Who'd have thought last spring that we'd all be
xin' to get stinkin' rich off Howard's turnips? Just
es to show what a committee can come up with."

"Yeah."

"You know what Harry Patman was talkin' about
hile we was tryin' to put his fire out? He was
gurin' that him and Richardson and some of the
thers might pool their resources and build a race-
ack up there. Lot of money in racetracks, I hear."

"I don't know how the women around here would
ke to that."

"I don't imagine they intend to ask 'em about it.

Anybody hear anything about Ben Cutter?"

"Not much. Just that his horse an' gear are gon an' Ding Cox says his Sunday clothes is missi from City Hall. But Ben'll get by. There's always place for a man like that."

"Yeah. That's a fact."

People passed them on the street, going abo their morning business. A lot of the men we hollow-eyed from lack of sleep, but the town w beginning to bustle. Merchants swept their walk wagons rolled with goods to sell, and tl ladies were out in force to get their marketing do before the Chautauqua arrivals descended and g the pick of the produce.

"Things sure have a way of gettin' back to norma don't they?" Nat allowed.

At a hail from across the street they shaded the eyes to look. Prosper O'Neil was running towa them, dodging buckboards and surreys.

He hauled up, panting. "You fellows better con help us," he said. "We got real problems."

Nat squinted at him. "What now?"

"Well, it's Sweeny. That damn pig has foun hisself an elephant someplace, an' showed it whe the squish is at, an' now they're both out the gettin' drunker than a couple of judges."